In this exciting s
to the doge, as neighboring Padua launches an undeclared war. Mistrustful of diplomats and spies, the doge dispatches Nico on a secret mission to the court of King Louis of Hungary to gauge the king's resolve to aid Padua.

The doge also drafts Donato Venturi, the greatest swordsman in Venice, nicknamed Black Hercules, as Nico's adviser and bodyguard. It's love at first sight for Nico, but he knows nothing about Donato, the son of a Venetian noble and a princess of Mali. Assuming Donato is straight, Nico guards his feelings until an unlikely encounter at the Prior of Brotherly Love proves otherwise

The pair steal moments together, but the war changes everything. Cutthroat political struggles with his own nobles keeps the doge busy in Venice as Nico again confronts the carnage of battle, testing his cunning. This brings him face-to-face with his nemeses, Ruggiero and Marcantonio Gradenigo, forcing an unplanned rescue of his soulmate, Alex.

When the war goes disastrously for Venice, the fate of the Serene Republic hangs on the will of the doge and the skills of Nico and Donato. Desperate to defeat Padua and drive out the Hungarian invaders, they risk everything in a final gambit to checkmate in three. In love as in war, winning and losing aren't what they seem.

THE MAN WITH

SAPPHIRE EYES

Larry Mellman

A NineStar Press Publication
www.ninestarpress.com

The Man With Sapphire Eyes

© 2023 Larry Mellman
Cover Art © 2023 Jaycee DeLorenzo
Edited by Elizabetta McKay

ISBN: 978-1-64890-656-5

First Edition, May, 2023

Also available in eBook, ISBN: 978-1-64890-655-8

CONTENT WARNING
This book contains sexually explicit content, which may only be suitable for mature readers. Depictions of incest, death of a main character, kidnapping, discussion of the off-page rape of a minor, gore, graphic violence/wartime atrocities, betrayal.

To Elaine Mellman Struhl

1937-2022

My big sister forever

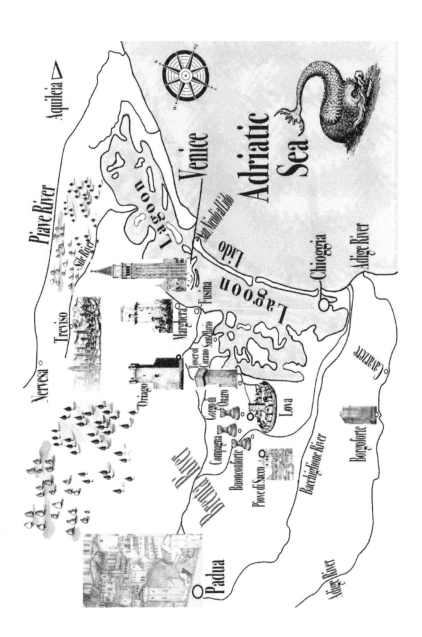

Chapter One

Donato Venturi

I'M SAFE AS long as I'm rowing. No enemy has ever successfully breached the mercurial lagoon surrounding Venice on all sides. For three glorious miles I row free, my stroke easy and automatic. I spent my youth on the lagoon until, at fourteen years and nine months of age, I was randomly selected ballot boy against my will and inclination. Taken from my mother, from my friends, from my home, and installed in the palace with the doge as my boss, my rowing time turned into riding and Latin lessons. I still ache at times for an oar in my hands and a breeze riffling my long black hair.

Midway between the Doge's Palace and Marghera, one of our ports on terrafirma, with the sun in my eyes and the scent of the lagoon in my nose, I savor a moment of sweet peace before embarking on my new mission. Our neighbor and enemy, Lord Francesco Carrara of Padua, regularly burns our farms and plunders our mainland towns. Our amorphous shoreline teems with crooks, assassins, and spies. I don't wear a sword because I wouldn't know how to use one, but my crossbow is at hand, and my dagger hangs at my waist with a special kiss of poison along its razor-sharp edge. I'm rowing to meet a man I've never seen in a place I have never been. Serenissimo assured me I needn't worry, that I would know him straight off, and I trust any man stamped with the doge's imprimatur. He rides from Treviso fortress, ours, to meet me at the inn by the tower of Marghera at Vespers.

I tether my boat in the shadow of the three-story brick watchtower, the lower course of obvious Roman origin. The Romans never ventured onto the marshy islands of the lagoon, confining themselves to solid ground. I stash my crossbow and quiver in my boat, expecting no danger at the inn, only a new friend.

Fishermen's huts clustered at the base of the tower enclose a crude square deserted in the late afternoon. The tower looms overhead, a rook on a chessboard spreading from Carrara Castle in Padua to St. Mark's Square. At the back of the square, outside the inn, three men—desperados, mercenaries, or thugs—watch me approach with an unhealthy interest. None of them looks likely to be Donato Venturi. I place my hand on my dagger to show them I mean business. The doge's ring glints on my finger. Those who respect the power of the doge see the ring as a talisman; those who don't see only a large chunk of gold. One more step and I clearly pick out the splayed red carts, the *carros* of the Carrara, on their blood- and mud-spattered tunics.

"Aw, ain't he pretty?"

"You heard about those Venetian butt boys. Better than women, they say."

As I unsheathe my dagger, three longswords lunge at me, their wielders laughing at the notion that a dagger could protect me from them. I stumble backward, catch myself, stand as tall as possible, and hold up the doge's ring. "Arms down in the name of His Exalted Serenity, the Doge of Venice."

"Exalted Fucking Asshole, that one. Old Contarini got no weenie."

I raise my dagger, knowing something they don't know. They snigger and slash, making their steel blades sing. I cannot possibly nick all three with my blade before they cut my hands off, so I retreat. One of them slip-slides into my space, swinging. The point of his blade slices my doublet, stinging my skin. I swipe with my dagger, desperate to break his skin and deliver the poison kiss, but he flips his sword, grips the blade with his gauntlets, and swings it, braining me with the pommel. I fly backward to general laughter, rolling away as the disrespectful thugs advance to skewer me for the fun of it.

They don't notice until their heads turn, following mine, and by then it's too late. A whirlwind of dust whips toward the square delivering an armed soldier on a lathered white destrier showering foam. He swoops in and circles the Paduans, freeing me to sheathe my dagger and scramble to the boat for my crossbow, but before I can, he disarms all three in a shower of blood. He doesn't kill them, but he may as well have.

He jumps off his destrier, which stands still as a statue behind him, grips my hand in his gauntlet, and yanks me to my feet.

"Are you hurt?"

"Only my pride."

"What did they want?"

"We never got that far."

As the wounded Paduans crawl away, he laughs heartily, slaps me on the back, and says, "Well met, Niccolò Saltano. I am Donato Venturi."

He lifts off his helmet and shakes his head, smacking his right ear with the butt of his palm. I lack words to describe his sudden impact. Even his shadow has tangible presence. But more astonishing are his brown skin and blue eyes. His beauty shatters every canon of classical aesthetics and redefines them. His square face is made up of rounded planes showcasing Arab eyes, a Venetian nose, and plush lips wreathed in moustaches and goatee. No matter how fierce his brows or severe the crop of his black curls, his smile strikes me speechless. He covers my blush and stammer with easy conversation. "I've heard a lot about you from Serenissimo. He brags about you like the son he never had."

"I wouldn't take his word on me. His fondness inclines to dotage."

"And also from General Giustinian, who credits you with our smashing victory at Trieste."

"And yet I know nothing of you but your name."

"Accompany me inside," he says, "and we can remedy

that."

We cross the square to the inn, and he opens the heavy door with one finger, linking his arm in mine to escort me inside.

Men can be attractive in many ways, but Donato Venturi is *sui generis*. Serenissimo neglected to tell me about the color of his skin, like a larch oar oiled by countless palms and buffed to a rich and complex brown, or that a Roman artist crafting an African Hercules might have sculpted him in mahogany. He exudes confidence in an unselfconscious way. Astolfo, lord of Castle Moccò, my previous lodestar for manly beauty, stood well over six feet tall with red-gold curls cascading down his back—a fallen angel or radiant demon. Donato, no taller than I but immensely broader—a bull to my deer—registers as monumental.

Inside the low windowless inn where daylight never penetrates, stubby candles gutter and smoke. The innkeeper stands aside, and we seek a corner far from prying ears. Donato raises two fingers to the innkeeper and blinds him with a smile, suggesting that they know each other. He brings two glasses, a flagon of wine, and a plate of gristly pork scraps. We say nothing until he retreats, and then I raise my glass.

"Greetings and gratitude."

Donato skates over my gratitude. "I rarely encounter a Paduan whose bite is as fierce as his bark. Three of them amount to half an Austrian brute, as you well know."

"No need to be modest, Donato. Serenissimo advised me that you're the greatest swordsman in Venice."

He raises his glass. "To the hero of Trieste from

Venice's premier swordsman. I'm honored to finally meet you."

"Although Serenissimo holds you in the highest regard, he told me nothing about you."

"I am captain of cavalry at Treviso under General Giustinian. Before that, I was an arsenal guard. I apprenticed at the arsenal at the age of eight. They worked me like a dog and treated me worse, but as bad as it got, it was never worse than home."

"How is that?"

"I see our beloved doge has truly told you nothing."

"Not even the color of your skin."

"Aha. Appearances to the contrary, I am a Venetian noble, born in 1343 and raised at Palazzo Venturi until I ran away."

"Ten years my senior. I turn eighteen on the seventeenth of April."

"My father is Jacopo Venturi, of the ancient and venerable house of Venturi, now the dregs of the nobility, although we are all supposedly equal. Living in the Doge's Palace must have taught you all about that. My family was so poor that our rooms were dark for want of candles, and we often didn't eat, but my father never failed to cast his vote in the Great Council."

"What about your mother?"

"She died when I was eight. She was a princess of Mali, kidnapped by a slave trader and sold to my father because, like all Venetian nobles, he wanted to marry a princess. He couldn't afford a European, so he bought an African. He paraded her in silks on Sundays and feasts and treated her like a slave the rest of the time. She was beautiful and loving and kind and did not deserve such a fate. As soon as we burned her corpse, I began planning my escape, and I told no one at the arsenal I bear a noble name. They assumed I was an escaped slave or some such, but after the great plague killed half our men, beggars couldn't be choosers. I worked harder and longer than anyone else until I caught the eye of Orsino Bellarosa, a lord of the arsenal, who liked what he saw. He took me under his wing, directed my training, and advanced me into the arsenal guard at the age of fifteen."

"I know Orsino Bellarosa. He is a brave Venetian, deeply loyal to the doge."

"Like all the arsenal guard. Many years ago, Orsino introduced me to his old friend Andrea Contarini, before he was elected doge, and ever since, our Serenissimo has kept a close but distant eye on me."

"You've known him longer than I have."

"But not in the same way. You see him every day and know his thoughts. Since the election, I see him rarely. But enough about me. What orders do you bring?"

Once again, Donato's eyes linger on mine, concealing something urgent, never wavering until I am forced to blink and turn to business to cover my blush.

"First, a small caveat," I say. "I remember everything perfectly and can recite it to you forward and backward, which I will spare you."

"You are a gentleman and a scholar."

I take a breath and summon Serenissimo's presence. "The Turks have crossed the Maritsa River into Serbia, and no one doubts they're headed for Hungary. The Genoese are killing one another so wantonly that they had to beg Lord Visconti of Milan to keep a lid on them, a mistake they will regret to the end of their days. Lord Carrara of Padua is waging an undeclared war on our towns and farms on terrafirma, a war he can't declare until King Louis of Hungary sends the troops he promised. All of this is well known to you."

Donato busts out laughing. "I'm sorry," he says, wiping tears from his eyes, "but your impersonation is perfect in tone and gesture. He may as well be here. Forgive me. Go on."

"I asked Serenissimo how likely King Louis of Hungary is to aid Padua. He said it would be mad for Louis to send troops to Carrara with the Turk advancing on him, but Louis listens only to God, and there's no telling what He might say. The question is—how far will King Louis go to own the Adriatic, given that he can't build ships, doesn't have a navy, and has neither oarsmen, sailors, nor admirals? More importantly, does he understand that Venice cannot and will not lose to him again, at any cost? We will never submit to a Hungarian yoke, and Louis hates losing as much as he hates us. If he suspects he can't win, he will overturn the board and go home. We need to know what is most likely. Thus, I am sending you to his royal palace at Visegrád."

Donato chuckles. "*You* meaning you or me?"

"Both. I asked him, 'Wouldn't you be better served using trained spies?' And he replied, 'What sort of idiot would trust a paid spy? I know I can trust you. Look and listen. Read the signs without being obvious. I want details. Get as close as you can but not so close as to endanger yourself. Talk to our people there. Find

Giacomo da Murano and use my name. He is an old friend who has grown rich selling glass to Louis's court. Heed what he says and listen to the common folk. Ask direct questions whenever you can get away with it from anyone whose word rings true.'

"I told him I wasn't convinced I was the right man for the job, and he said, 'That's why I'm sending Donato Venturi with you.'

"I asked, 'Who is Donato Venturi, and why have I never heard of him before?' Serenissimo said it was because we live in two different worlds, the palace and the arsenal. One is a place of selfish struggles for wealth and advantage; the other is a place of selfless labor for the good of the Republic, where skill and character outweigh wealth and pedigree. He said I couldn't ask for a better companion on this mission than Donato Venturi."

"High praise from our beloved Serenissimo," Donato says. "We are both honored by his confidence."

"Yes, we are."

"And your memory is remarkable."

"I never wished for it; it's how I am. No matter what I do, I can't forget."

"That must be torture for sure. There's much I'm glad to forget."

"Serenissimo relies on the accuracy of my memory. He says I am a diary no one else can read."

"Do you know how much so-called wise men charge for memory training in Rialto? Anyone who wants to manage a convoy or enter a joint venture or run an abacus or cheat at cards pays through the nose to learn what you do effortlessly. Serenissimo understands the value of a good asset."

"I never considered myself an asset."

"Ah, you most definitely are, or you wouldn't be here with me."

"What makes you an asset?"

"Does loyalty count?"

"Loyalty's not a skill. It's a quality of soul."

"Then it must be my charm." He reaches for a candle, holds it near my face, and stares still more deeply into my eyes. "Your eyes are bluer than mine."

For an instant, he seems as lost in my eyes as I am in his, which I doubt possible.

"I have my father's eyes," I say. "Who donated your sapphires?"

"My mother. You also have the same slight overbite as your father. On him, it's menacing, but on you, it's...something else."

"Did you know my father?"

"Know him? No. But I saw him in action, on Crete, during the rebellion he led. Serenissimo confided that Marcantonio Gradenigo is your father. What a maniac, living for mayhem. If he didn't have a battle, he'd incite a bloody brawl."

"Do you know he's not dead and walks the streets disguised as a monk? He calls himself Brother Bernardo of the Hermits?"

"I hear the same rumors as everyone else."

"It's not a rumor."

"We'll save that for later. I must return to Treviso tonight. When do we leave for Hungary?"

Chapter Two

The Secret Mission

HALFWAY HOME, I hear alarm bells summoning the nobles to an emergency session. By the time I reach the palace wharf, a thousand grim-faced nobles in black velvet robes fill the Great Council chamber, newly enlarged to accommodate them. Palace guards toss out the snoops, imposters, and spies before bolting the doors shut. I sit in Serenissimo's shadow on the dais, his careworn golden robe dappled with dancing rainbows. His six councilors, the Ten, and Marino Vendramin, now head of the Forty, surround him. Sunlight bouncing off the jade water of St. Mark's Basin through the new glass windows spangles us all with jewels, as well as the newly completed mural on the wall behind us, the Coronation of the Virgin by Guariento of Padua.

Marino Vendramin, youngest of the doge's councilors when I was chosen ballot boy, my first minder, convenes the session. Not even Caesar could be heard over the din of nobles arguing, gossiping, and commiserating. Marino nods to the captain of the guards, and they beat their shields with the pommels of their swords until the nobles pipe down.

"Gentlemen of Venice. Fellow nobles..." Marino raises his hands inclusively and waits for silence. "We have been informed on the highest authority that Lord Francesco Carrara of Padua, our best enemy, yesterday received a promise from King Louis the Great of Hungary—five thousand Hungarian troops to aid Padua against us as soon as Lord Carrara successfully provokes us into attacking. King Louis avers that law and conscience forbid him to aid an aggressor, but if we attack Padua first, his hands are freed. We are not prepared for a war on land and must raise the money to pay for it. We must decide whether to defeat Padua in the field before the Hungarians arrive, or bide our time and prepare adequately, despite the Paduan raids, pillaging, and terrorizing of our mainland villages and towns, baiting us to attack."

The floodgates holding back a fratricidal war within the Great Council burst open in a torrent of scabrous debate. Bruno Badoer of the Ten epitomizes the pro-war sentiment among the men hungriest for more territory on terrafirma—for rivers and plains with vast fields, and orchards, all of which our watery situation prevents. Short and round, a red-faced barrel covered in white fur with a white fringe around his ears like a frosted laurel wreath, Badoer always favors war.

"I warned you," he roars. "Nip that jackal in the bud, I said, and none of you listened. Now we have to rip the whole family out root and branch before he seizes our throne and throws us the scraps from his table."

Lorenzo Morosini, third wealthiest merchant in Venice, remains only a senator. Scion of an ancient house joined by marriage to the throne of Hungary, much to his chagrin, he has never been elected to the Doge's Council, the Forty, or the Ten. Thus, he speaks not from the dais, but from the floor.

"Gentlemen, how many times have we heard this same foul wind blowing from Sir Badoer's mouth? It's nothing but bellicose posturing. We are not knights, and this is not a crusade. It is a border dispute with a neighbor. Did not our own Lord instruct us to love our neighbors as we love ourselves? Francesco Carrara is only a man. He is rational. We can negotiate a solution without waging a war we cannot afford with an army we do not possess, and which we must assuredly lose as soon as Hungary enters the field."

"Blow it out your ass, Morosini." Bruno Badoer swats him away like a fat horsefly. "Is your name Carrara now?"

Boisterous laughter and angry shouts volley over the insult. Federico Cornaro, the sugar king and currently one of the Ten, addresses the dispute.

"We have no cause to question Senator Morosini's motives or loyalties, gentlemen. We all know what fighting a land war means. Our fleet, the mightiest on the seas, heroically protecting us from the Genoese, pirates, and infidels, cannot fight on land. Instead of attacking the enemy on land with an army, we need only block the rivers and canals from the Adriatic to the marketplaces of Padua, Vicenza, Verona, Milan, and Austria. See how they like it without salt and pepper. See how long their people will stand for it before rioting. Negotiate, we must. The alternative is unthinkable."

The debate rages back and forth roughly along those lines until the vote is taken, and I count the ballots. The party of diplomacy narrowly but solidly triumphs over the aggrieved warriors.

For now.

Immediately following the vote, Serenissimo suggests he and I pray in the Evangelist's crypt while pandemonium swirls through St. Mark's Square, the everyday folk reenacting the battle just fought in the great chamber. When we closed the Great Council almost two centuries ago, the popular assembly—the voice of the commoners—lost its historic role as decision maker. Now, the commoners can only jeer or cheer what the Great Council of nobles decides. We may be a Republic in form, but one operated by a closed caste of a thousand nobles.

In the sanctity and solitude of the Evangelist's crypt, deep under the high altar of St. Mark's, we pray briefly. Then Serenissimo speaks.

"What do you make of these idiots?"

"We were lucky in Trieste," I say. "We'd better stop Carrara before it's too late."

He shakes his head wearily. "No one on earth hates war more than I do. I also know that sooner or later, as sure as night follows day, we will be forced to defend ourselves against the jackals salivating around us. I don't want war, yet here we are, between Scylla and Charybdis. We must go to war." His head slumps. His shoulders slump. His spirit slumps.

"What if King Louis is playing Carrara for a fool and has no intention of wasting men and money on a loser?"

"Leave for Visegrád at first light. I'll send word to Donato. Find out what the madmen have in mind."

I'm too agitated to sleep. Instead of tossing in bed, I sneak out of the palace as I did when I was fourteen, heading to the same place, the apothecary shop on Santa Margherita Square. I shinny up the ancient vine that seems to hold the building together. Abdul, my oldest and best friend, stands on the makeshift loft outside his window studying the positions of the planets and stars with his astrolabe.

"Do you believe that the stars determine our destiny?" I ask.

My voice doesn't startle him. "Why do you ask?"

"King Louis of Hungary does."

"I believe *determine* is too strong a word. Influence, perhaps. If everything is interconnected in ways seen and unseen, which I do believe, then by what reasoning would human beings be set apart from the dance of celestial bodies? But that's not what you've come here to talk about, is it?"

"No. Have you heard anything from Alex?"

"No. But that's not why you came either." He carefully sets his astrolabe in its case and gives me his full attention. "Tell me, brother, what creases your brow?"

"We are being forced to go to war. I'm leaving at first

light for Visegrád on the Danube to gather intelligence for Serenissimo."

"Visegrád is widely regarded as a highly cultured and civilized court, more French than Magyar."

"What do I need on such a journey?"

"Are you going alone?"

"My companion is the greatest swordsman in Venice."

"Just you and one other?"

"Serenissimo says that's enough."

"Our Exalted Serenity is no fool. We must take him at his word. It's a journey of what? A fortnight each way?"

"More or less."

"Have you met your companion?"

"I have."

"Is he trustworthy?"

"Serenissimo swears to it."

Abdul goes into his closet, opens a cabinet, and runs his fingers over vials and jars, humming a tune I have often heard him play on his oud.

"Definitely this." He takes the now familiar bottle of poison I use to season the blade of my dagger when I'm heading into danger. He also pulls out a fat packet of kindling tissue that never fails to light, and a fresh flintstone. "You never know when you will need a hasty and reliable flame, but you assuredly will." He strokes his chin, looking at these items, doing a mysterious calculation in his head, then spins and plucks two small vials from the top shelf. "Be careful with these," he says. "This one makes you sleepy, and this one banishes sleep. Don't confuse them."

He clearly marks them in Latin for me and stuffs everything in a small goatskin packet.

"Farewell, brother," he says. "Return safe."

Chapter Three

The Storks of Aquileia

DONATO AWAITS ME in a skiff with two oarlocks and plenty of room for gear. We row to retrieve our horses from the stable at Castel Vecchio, the fort guarding the entrance to the lagoon and flanking the church of San Nicolò al Lido, where the saint's bones are buried.

"We stole those bones from the church at Bari," I say. "They're still mad."

"Fuck them. They stole them from their proper tomb in Myra. I imagine they're still mad in Myra, just like they're still mad in Alexandria that we stole St. Mark's bones five hundred years ago. The world has good reason to call us thieves."

"Better thieves than tyrants." I admire Donato's ease

with an oar, his arms and thighs. "You have a very long and even stroke."

"I rowed before I ever mounted a horse."

"Same here. But when I became ballot boy, Serenissimo said an oar and a crossbow were well and good for an urchin from St. Nick's, but I would never amount to anything unless I could read, write, and ride a horse, none of which I could do. Admiral Pisani taught me to ride."

"Impressive teacher." A certain awe tinges Donato's voice. "Pisani is a brilliant tactician," he says, "treated badly by our nobles for all the wrong reasons."

"He's a great man." I cherish Pisani deep in my heart, both as a great Venetian and as an attractive and accomplished man I'm flattered to call my friend.

I stand astern, Donato at the prow, and we lapse into a synchronized rhythm, leaning into our stroke, pushing our oars through the water. We lift and rotate them in the air behind us, swinging them around and plunging them into the water again, stroke and lift, over and again, our arms in fluid motion. Our weight shifts as our legs flex and release, rhythmically and effortlessly. To those of us raised on the lagoon, rowing together is a conversation, a physical exchange of information about ourselves that eludes words. I learn Donato is aggressive but considerate, decisive, never tentative, and settles easily into a shared task with another, something much harder for me to do.

We dock at Castel Vecchio, secure the boat, retrieve our horses, and ride to a fat-bellied cog moored on the Adriatic side of the narrow barrier island we call Lido. After strapping our horses in slings below deck, the captain takes his place at the rudder while Donato and I stand amidships. The wind favors us, billowing our sails, pushing us east and north. The bell towers of Venice soon disappear, and the Alps loom ever closer.

"I trust you prepared our itinerary," Donato says.

"I did. From Aquileia we take Via Gemina over the Julian Alps to Emona, Celeia, Savaria, thence to the Danube and Pone Navata, which the Hungarians call Visegrád."

"Why do you use the Roman names?"

"That's what my sources call them."

"Sources, of course. And you can recite them all, forward and backward..." A bit of a jab delivered sweetly. "Did you know Seneca was like you?"

For a crazy instant, I worry what he might know about me, about Seneca, and where this is leading. Danger lurks in attraction to a man who doesn't share the same inclination. "In what way?"

"As a student, he was easily bored, so he ordered his classmates to read two thousand names aloud, and then he astonished them by reciting them back. Another time, his schoolmates recited lines from two hundred poems, and he recited them in reverse order."

"Where did you learn Latin?"

He laughs so hard that I blush. "That's not my point. My point is that you are not alone with this gift, or curse, or what-have-you—your unnatural memory. But no. Of course I don't read Latin. My school was the arsenal. That bit about Seneca was passed to me by an unknown hand I suspect belongs to Our Exalted Serenity, judging from the illegible scribble."

The morning sun glazes the Adriatic with a golden sheen, stirring the world from sleep, but Donato's expression takes a more somber turn.

"These roads we're taking," he says, "they may have been imperial Roman highways, but they are cracked and broken and infested with cutthroats, pirates, and thieves. Without an armed escort, no traveler is safe."

"Serenissimo has faith in us."

"So he does," Donato says. "But I worry that you don't know how to wield a sword."

"It's your job to teach me."

He starts to say something hasty, thinks better of it, and pauses before resuming. "Everyone agrees you're the best bowman in Venice—"

"I was. I fear counting too many ballots has dulled my eye."

"How long did it take you to master the crossbow?"

"My mother gave it to me when I was eight. She said it belonged to my dead father, and I vowed to be worthy of him, believing he was a heroic bowman-of-the-quarter-deck murdered by pirates. Lies my mother made up out of whole cloth. I began winning contests when I was twelve after my friend Abdul trained me in the Mamluk style. I would say it took four years of daily practice to master of the crossbow."

"It takes equally long to master the sword, even with me as your teacher, and no villain lying in ambush will wait to spring until you're cocked and loaded."

"You're worried I'm putting you in danger?"

Steel flashes from his scabbard, blade twisting, gripped in his right hand, his left hand on the pommel.

The point thrusts straight at my Adam's apple until it stops, perfectly still, an inch short, all before I can blink.

"I'm not worried about me," Donato says. "I'm worried about you."

The captain takes uneasy notice of Donato's swordwork and watches us with a worried eye, inching closer. To starboard, the blue Adriatic undulates like silk in the wind, and to port, islands intermingle with lagoons and river deltas and forests stretching toward the shore from the snow-capped mountains above.

"We must be very cautious in Aquileia," I say.

"We must be very cautious everywhere."

Donato seems to view me as a Latin-spouting little brother, educated but unworldly.

"*Especially* in Aquileia," I say. "The Patriarch of Aquileia supports Padua and Hungary against us."

"He's a good German. His reach extends all the way to Laibach. That's *Emona* to you. You do realize he no longer actually lives in Aquileia, right? He packed up and moved the palace, the markets, the money, everything but the buildings and a few spies, to Udine, leaving a handful of people and a once great city gone to the dogs."

"It's not as bad as all that," says the captain, now close enough to join the conversation. "There are at least a hundred of us left."

"No insult intended," Donato says. "But you know what I mean."

"Sad to say, I do. Once upon a time, Aquileia was second only to Rome. We were the center of trade across the Alps before Attila wrecked us. Cocky son of a bitch. He thought he'd take the city in a day, but our walls showed

Roman resolve. He couldn't breach them and couldn't advance on Rome until he did. So he laid siege, and when his Huns ran out of grub and forage and patience, they started talking mutiny."

"And then, wondrous to tell," Donato says, "Attila saw storks fly out of the tower with their young on their backs. He believed the storks foresaw impending disaster and assaulted the tower. It collapsed, he breached the walls, and Aquileia fell."

"Those weren't their young'uns on their backs," the captain says. "Those were their parents. Like Aeneas fleeing Troy with his father Anchises on his back."

"You've read the *Aeneid*?" I can't hide my disbelief.

"I don't read nothing," the captain says. "Those were the stories my grandfather told me when we fished on the lagoon. According to him, after Troy burned down, Aeneas wandered forever and a day until he ended up here and founded Aquileia. The old man knew all those stories and all about signs and portents. The more he drank, the more he knew."

"My boss," I say, "a man of great learning and experience, also believes in signs and portents. He sees them everywhere. He says the trick is to read them correctly. Do you think Attila believed the storks saw the future?"

"In my humble opinion," Donato says, unbidden, "Aquileia was under siege. The people were starving, leaving no crumbs for storks. Attila read their flight as a sign of starvation and a signal to attack."

"The thing is," the captain says, "the storks always leave the same day every year, year in and year out, from time immemorial, regular as the bells at the monastery of

St. Mary. Now Attila, being a newcomer like yourselves, had no way of knowing that. Maybe it wasn't the storks that caught his eye but the cracks in the tower where they nested. Maybe he figured that as sure the sun rises, a tower with such cracks would buckle under his war machines and lay the town open like meat on butcher's slab."

"All things are possible under the sun," Donato says, and for no reason, but to my immense gratification, he puts his arm around me as we watch the approaching islands and far-off shore. Beyond the island port of Grado, we enter a small lagoon lined with fishermen's huts, little more than reed lean-tos. Snowy egrets and black cormorants with orange bills lurk amid the tall reeds and water lilies, awaiting the fish-laden tide. The bell tower announces that we have reached Aquileia.

My faithful Delfín, released from her sling, happily dances on solid ground, stamping and nickering. She wants to run, and she's not easily restrained.

Donato arches his eyebrows. "Spirited palfrey," he says, his words carrying the faintest whiff of condescension. His Mercury, bigger, pure white, stands perfectly still, nostrils quivering slightly, alert and collected.

As we lash our gear to our steeds, the captain scratches his head. "That sack's pretty full." He nods toward my leather-wrapped crossbow and the sword poking out of my satchel. "Where you headed?"

"We are making a delivery to the monks of Saint Mary's," Donato says.

The captain laughs. "Good luck finding monks there. It's all sisters now. Been that way for a hundred years."

"Of course. I meant sisters." Donato shakes his head

sheepishly.

"We're bringing ink and vellum for their scriptorium," I say. As soon as the captain turns away, I lean into Donato. "Bad mistake."

"Stupid. From now on, I'll keep my mouth shut and let you do the talking."

Chapter Four

Grappling

A RUTTED STONE road of Roman handiwork leads to St. Mary's. Our horses pick their way gingerly through the mud and scree, their pace painfully slow.

"Truthfully," Donato says, "what's life like in the palace?"

"Complicated and dangerous."

"That much I know, but for you?"

I'm uncertain what I can say with Donato, but Serenissimo stands behind him, so I speak freely. "Take last month, for example, when the emperor of Byzantium came to beg for aid."

"I hear he's a piece of work. Had a nasty showdown with King Louis not long ago, bad blood going back to when Louis shunned the Crusade against Alexandria in 1365."

"My friend Abdul, the apothecary's slave, was kidnapped during that fiasco."

"Louis didn't go because God or his astrologer apparently told him his interests would be better served converting his Orthodox Christian neighbors in Bulgaria to the Roman church. As soon as Louis's army won the field, legions of Franciscan missionaries marched in to baptize the heretics."

"Before John V, not a single emperor of Byzantium had ever stepped outside the imperial palace to meet an inferior, and he groveled at Louis's feet, begging aid against the Turks."

"That's what desperation does to man," Donato says. "Free will is a bit of an oxymoron. Most men do what they must to survive."

"It only got worse. After Louis threw him out on his ear, he went to Rome and kissed the pope's foot, begging for a Crusade against the Turk. The pope promised the Crusade if John V converted, not only personally, but his entire people from the Greek Church to the Church of Rome. John V agreed, but six months later, the pope died, and his successor canceled the Crusade against which John V had just wagered his eyes, his freedom, and his throne. That's when he came begging to Venice. It was truly pathetic. He demanded galleys and men to fight the Turks. Marino Vendramin reminded him he owed us sixty-seven thousand ducats since his mother pawned their crown jewels to secure his throne when he was eight. But here's the thing. Serenissimo, two moves ahead, had tasked me to learn Greek between the time the emperor kissed the pope's foot and arrived at our palace. John V confronted the Doge's Council like a cornered fox, full of accusations, threats, recriminations, hysterics, really, which we endured until he called us sinners guilty of usury at which point Marino reminded him of the difference between usuary and simple interest. The emperor said, 'Simple to you, maybe, compounded by my humiliation.'"

"Sounds pretty ballsy to me."

"Considering he's had a knife in his back since the age of eight and that generations of good Christian princes have killed more Byzantines than the infidel, he has every reason to trust no one and to hate us like the plague. Yes, it took big balls to kiss the pope's foot, knowing the risk, but he's vain, arrogant, and blind, a complete failure."

"How did it end up?" Donato asked.

"Serenissimo offered to cancel the old debt in exchange for sovereignty over the island of Tenedos."

"His own jewels for his island. Good move."

"And not just any island, but the island guarding the trade route from east to west. If we don't control it, Genoa will.

"That night, I was one of the oarsmen who rowed the emperor back to the palace we locked him up in until he repaid the debt. He spoke freely with his head minister, assuming I didn't know Greek. He said his great-great-grandfather played a similar game with another doge, at another time, like every emperor in between. He said, 'Here we stand, heir to the greatest empire the world has ever seen, raised high by our heavenly father above all kings, and our treasury is empty. We command nothing. We grovel on our knees before merchants.' His minister said, 'Others may care about God, or justice, or right, but Venice cares only about money. Give them Tenedos, and let them fight to the death with Genoa,' which I duly reported back to Serenissimo. That's life in the palace. A barrel of laughs. How's life outside the palace?"

"A barrel of laughs. I spend most of my time outside our fair city. I make sure embassies return safely and traitors end up dead."

Our horses' hooves clatter across the wooden bridge over a stream, announcing our arrival at Saint Mary's. Brick walls encircle barnlike buildings built around a cloister. The bell tower beside the gate casts a shadow like a sundial. We dismount and wait for the Judas door in the gate to slide open. A wary eye greets us.

"Greetings," I say. "We are two travelers seeking refuge for the night."

The Judas door slides shut, and the gate opens.

"Peace be with you, and welcome, weary traveler." An ancient portress mumbles the well-worn formula. She resembles a tanned and wrinkled scarecrow in a coarse tunic the color of her skin. As we step inside, she barely looks at me. Her eyes, narrowed to hostile slits, focus on Donato.

"You." She points to Donato. "Stable your horses." She points to me. "You come inside. The slave can stay in the stable."

"He's not a slave. He's my companion. You owe him the same courtesy as me."

Donato tugs at my sleeve. "I'm fine in the stable." The

obsequiousness of his smile cues me to acquiesce. He dutifully leads our horses to the stable, and I follow the portress inside, where the abbess awaits. The monastery seems a dim vestige of former glory, as shabby and scrubbed as the abbess in her woolen habit worn thin by washing and mending. Her skin barely stretches over the prominent cheekbones of her noble skull. Her bony finger points the way. Her green eyes are wary, but she welcomes me with a serene smile.

"Thank you for your hospitality," I say.

"We cannot refuse," she says. "You speak like a Venetian."

Betrayed by my tongue. I must be more careful.

"I am, Mother."

"Your bearing bespeaks noble blood."

"Oh no," I say. "I am only a common scribe."

She looks unconvinced. "Your manners are too good," she says. "I know whereof I speak. I, too, was born to a noble house, though you wouldn't think so to look at me."

"It is clearly written in your face," I say. "My companion is also of noble birth."

"What companion?"

"He's in the stable with the horses. Your portress wouldn't allow him inside."

"Fetch him immediately."

Doubt clouds her eyes when she sees Donato, who bows reverently.

"Greetings, Mother Abbess. I am Donato Venturi."

"I knew Venturis as a child," she says. "You don't look like any of them."

"My father Jacopo Venturi married a princess of Mali."

"Ah, yes, I remember," she says with a distant spark in her eyes. She shows us to adjacent cells. "We dine anon. You may join us in the refectory."

As we eat, a sister, invisible behind her habit, reads psalms. The other sisters avert their eyes from us. After the meal, the sisters return to work and prayer. The abbess strolls with us in the cloister garden of medicinal herbs and flowers, a profusion of abundance amid spare poverty.

Donato speaks with his usual ease. "May I ask how you found your vocation?"

"It found me," the abbess says. "I was the second daughter in a family that could only afford one dowry, so I accepted my vocation gratefully. May I ask where you are headed?"

"We are seeking a countryman in Emona," I say. "On the Sava River."

"I know Emona well, but we call it Laibach. Have you been there before?"

"We have not. We plan to follow the Roman road."

"My family had estates there before the current Patriarch sacked the town." She cannot hide her chagrin. "Allow me to pass along a word of warning. The mountain passes are filled with German mercenaries with no war to fight and highwaymen who prey on merchants with fat purses."

"Our purses are pitifully thin," Donato says. "Nothing for them in there."

"Alas, they don't know that until it's too late," she

says. "A word to the wise..."

"Gratefully received and duly noted."

Donato bows as she takes her leave. In the remains of the day, we walk to the stable to humor Delfín and Mercury.

"Not good news," I say. "German mercenaries—"

"Serenissimo didn't send me to protect you from nymphs and naiads. You are his eyes and ears, and I am your bodyguard."

"He also charged you with training me in swordsmanship," I say. "When do we begin?"

"Now is as good a time as any."

"My sword is in my cell."

"You won't need it."

He strips off his sword, his tunic, and dagger. Scars embroider his thickly muscled torso. He faces me, his arms at his sides, and I can scarcely do anything but gape at his body, an anatomy lesson in perfected physique.

"Attack me," he says.

"You're unarmed."

"Try to kill me with your dagger."

"I can't use my dagger."

"Why do you carry it if you can't use it?"

"The blade is dusted with poison prepared by my friend Abdul, a ninth-generation apothecary from Alexandria. One cut from this dagger will drop an ox in its tracks."

"Have no fear. Your blade will never reach me."

His oversized self-confidence flushes me with sheer annoyance.

"What does this have to do with swordplay?" I ask.

He darts in, slaps my cheek, darts back in a flash, goading me. "You're blushing, ballot boy."

Anger overwhelms caution. A slight nick will put him to sleep for several hours before waking up to profound embarrassment. I unsheathe the dagger, feint to my left, and swipe toward his exposed thigh when a lightning bolt paralyzes my arm. The dagger drops from my hand. Donato has hooked his elbow around my neck and twists my body while kicking my leg out from under me, and topples me, laying me gently on my spine, smiling all the while.

"Grappling," he says. "Grappling comes before the sword, before the dagger, to teach you timing, coordination, and balance. You can't properly wield a sword until you master grappling. Once you do, we can add the dagger and finally the sword. Those are the steps to mastery if you wish to excel."

He extends a hand, pulls me to my feet, and patiently shows me the proper stance, how to center my hips and carry my shoulders, how to strike a blow and parry a blow, how to unbalance my opponent and toss him to the ground in one smooth movement. In these slow-motion dances, Donato is in complete control, sometimes too complete, too close, too enticing, his hands lingering on my hips and shoulders. He instructs me to twist him and slowly sweep his leg out from under him so that he falls back, and I collapse on top of him. He squeezes his arms around me, flips me under, and rolls on top. His weight pressing against me makes my head swim, intoxicated with the heat of his body and the scent of his flesh.

"That's all there is to it," he says. He jumps to his feet and wipes his wet skin with dry hay. I have no idea how much Serenissimo told him about me. I can't fathom what he knows or intuits. What may be a flirtatious wink of his eye may not be, and I wonder what he would do if I kissed him, but I don't.

Chapter Five

Claustra Alpium Iuliarum

WE AWAKE AT Lauds and depart before first light. The sisters don't break fast until Prime, the first hour of daylight, but we need all the daylight possible to reach our destination by nightfall. The kitchener gives us two loaves of bread, a fat sausage to split between us, and, at my request, a pouch of dried apples for Delfín.

In order to stick to our schedule and arrive in Emona tomorrow, we must reach the Roman fort of Ad Pirum tonight. The long journey to the Danube weighs as heavily on my mind as Serenissimo's gold cloak upon his shoulders, taking a fortnight under optimum conditions. The merchant logs I consulted in the chancery archive detail the terrain. Neither Donato nor I are willing to change horses along the way although it would have made our travel faster. We need our loyal steeds, as much a part of our armament, our readiness, and our strength, as my crossbow and Donato's sword. We can only go as fast as the four of us can travel together. Serenissimo left these matters entirely in our hands, knowing well that we both perform best when left to our own devices.

Beyond St. Mary's, the road tilts upward into the Alps. Donato asks what comes next.

"This is Via Gemina, named for the legion that built it for Augustus Caesar in year 14 of Our Lord. Emperor Diocletian added walls, towers, and forts, creating the Claustra Alpium Iuliarum a couple lifetimes later."

"How could I forget?" He winks at me, and his lips frame an indulgent smile. I fear he finds me arid and didactic. "Go on, please," he says.

"The Claustra Alpium Iuliarum is a defensive system of high walls with tall towers eyesight distance apart to fortify the imperial border."

"That's a lot of brick and mortar for a legion of soldiers to lay."

I've piqued his interest and press my advantage. "This was called the Illyrian Gate, and armies and merchants alike seeking a land route to Europe from Asia must pass through. Where we're going now, Ad Pirum, was the linchpin of the entire system commanding the most strategic pass. End of story."

"You forgot to add that it's now a pile of rubble razed by the armies it was designed to repel. Rome in a nutshell, right? Amazing builders, drunk on pride and power, and all their engineering genius couldn't keep their world from collapsing around them."

"Your turn," I say with a smile. "Take our minds off the Via Gemina with stories of your own."

"I'd love to, but I'm a lousy storyteller. I forget the punchlines to my own jokes. My mother, on the other hand, was a gifted storyteller. She knew hundreds of tales and vowed to tell me all of them. Unfortunately, she died before she could complete the mission."

"Tales about what?"

"Her life in Africa. About my grandfather, mostly."

"The king of Mali?"

Donato busts out laughing. "My grandfather was a mendicant monk from Nubia, king of nowhere. He plied the Muslim empire from India to the Pillars of Hercules. When he showed up at the royal court of Mali, they laughed at his jokes, marveled at his fabulous tales, and feasted him royally, and he managed to impregnate one of the king's wives. The wife never confessed, the king never suspected, and my mother was raised as a royal princess. Grandfather always found some excuse to revisit Mali and entertain his charming daughter with new tales of the wondrous things he had seen, and my mother remembered every word he ever spoke. Although she lacked your natural gift, she devised schemes to catalog and store his tales in a library she built in her heart.

"Eventually, a squabble broke out between the king's jealous wives, my mother's secret was revealed, and the king sold her into slavery. She tried teaching me to build a library in my own heart to store his tales, but I'm not the architect she was. She insisted the tales would remind me who I am and my place in this world. Unfortunately, our time together was cut short by her death, or murder, depending on who you ask."

As I open my mouth, Donato closes it gently with his right index finger. "Not now. When I know you better."

The road, now dug into the mountainside, narrows and rises at a steep pitch while the chasm to our right falls ever more steeply. We ride single file, close enough to talk, with time on our hands because the horses can't go any faster.

"Tell me more about your grandfather," I say.

"He was born where the Nile River splits in two. One flows north to Alexandria and the other, which we call River Gambia, flows west to the Sea of Darkness beyond the Pillars of Hercules. The River Gambia passes through the great nations of dark-skinned peoples, and Grandfather traveled it from end to end many times. The Arab conquerors built palaces decorated with tiles and gemstones and windows of colored glass hundreds of years ago."

"Was your mother an infidel?"

"She was born in a remote village that kept the old ways. My mother told me the paladins of the Great Caliph burned all books and artifacts of their native beliefs lest they breed discontent with the law of Allah."

"Whenever the Romans conquered a territory, they destroyed the books, documents, and letters of the natives to erase all memory of their history. Do you hold any faith?"

"Only in myself." Donato's smile is sheepish and alluring. "I have seen too much of Christians and Muslims alike to believe what either believes. I trust that if there is a God, he will make himself known to me. Until then, I do what I deem right and proper. Do you accept the faith you were born into?"

"I did until I saw a man whose only crime was loving another man burned at the stake. I will accept no faith that preaches love and practices hate."

"Nor should any man, brother Niccolò. Unfortunately, that leaves neither of us with a prayer to get us through this monstrous pass."

The more I hear how he thinks and what is important to him, the more I hope that his glances, his winks and smiles, and the warmth he exudes are signs that his affection for me is deeper than the camaraderie of the road. We fall silent, too weary to talk, and soon dismount to relieve our equally weary horses of our weight. We walk the final distance. The ruins of Ad Pirum appear as a distant bell rings Vespers. We water our horses at a stream, and Donato inhales deeply through his nostrils.

"My favorite perfume," he says.

"Pine? Not one of my favorites."

"Larch," Donato says. "Distinct and invigorating. It reminds me of the arsenal. To me, it's the most beautiful smell in the world, especially after a day spent over boiling pitch."

He retrieves the bread and sausage given us by the sisters. "It's not much," he says, "but it's ours." Our horses nibble grass by the icy stream. Bread and sausage in hand, we study the outer gate of the ruined fortress. Donato stoops over barely legible Roman lettering carved in the fallen keystone.

"What does it say?" he asks.

I decipher the characters as much with my fingertips as my eyes. "This fort was built in Roman year 833, counting from Rome's founding 753 years before Christ, so this fort was built in the year 80 of Our Lord."

Donato sits on a stone bench in the shadow of the once-lofty tower, chewing bread and waving the sausage until he takes a bite. He is about to pass it to me when he stops, motionless, his eyes closed.

"Are you blessing the sausage?"

He doesn't smile. He nods toward the trees and gestures to his ear. I shrug, hearing nothing. "That," he whispers, looking at me expectantly. "Get the horses behind the tower."

"I don't hear anything."

"A boar got a whiff of this fucking sausage and wants it. Keep the horses quiet."

Donato leaps to the edge of the clearing, hurling the sausage as far as he can. Head cocked, eyes closed, he listens for the beast. I pull Delfín and Mercury behind the tower and grab my bow. I cock and load as I scoot forward until I'm midway between the tower and Donato. Brute ugly, its back bristled, tusks bared, the boar tramples through the bracken toward the sausage, one eye on Donato.

Donato backs away, senses me behind him, and barks at me, "What the hell are you doing?"

"Saving your life."

"Throw me your dagger and get back."

I lob my dagger at his feet. The boar, weighing at least three times Donato, plunges forward, grizzled and fearless. It inhales the sausage and follows the scent toward

Donato's fingers and lips. Four rows of tusks gleam white, the lowers sharpened like razors by the uppers. As the boar reaches the clearing, Donato backs up to the brick wall, waiting for the boar to charge. If he dodges successfully, the boar's fearsome snout and iron jaw will smash into a reasonably solid Roman brick wall. At the very least, it will slow the beast down. If Donato doesn't get clear, the boar will gore him to shreds. He stoops and sweeps my dagger from the ground in one smooth motion. He can lunge, parry, and veer securely to either side, forward or back, brandishing the poison kiss. As the boar charges, Donato bounces from side to side to distract it, which makes it easier for him to dodge the tusks but more difficult for me, from the branches above, to get a clean shot at the boar's heart through the base of its neck.

The boar lunges, tusks first. Donato dodges, but instead of smashing into the wall, the boar twists, rolls over in the dirt, and scrambles upright, pawing at the ground.

"Get out of the way," I shout. "I've got this."

Donato, holding my dagger in front of him with both hands, looks up and sees me hanging from a low branch as a furious cloud of dust gains traction. Donato lures the boar in my direction, grabs a branch, and flips up into the tree behind me. The boar rumbles directly below. The bolt tears through the thick armor of muscle and fat. A fountain of blood means I hit my mark. The force of the bolt topples the boar. Not knowing it is already dead, it thrashes, its hooves and tusks slashing the air, struggling in vain to gain its feet. It rears up, tusks swiveling toward the tree as death blinds its terrible eyes.

Chapter Six

The Itinerant Friar

WE LASH THE boar to Mercury and look for a place to sleep. Mold has blackened Ad Pirum's stonework, and I am disappointed to find no stoic columns with Augustan capitals, no lofty vaults, no carved arches, only rubble. The outer wall has been vandalized for its materials, and the insides spill across the central square. Nine towers, their crowns long toppled, mark the corners and guard the long-vanished gates. Wrecked piecemeal over time, the barracks, officer's quarters, workshops, stables, and granary offer no shelter against the cold Alpine night. A small fire burns in the bare skeleton of a great hall. As we walk our horses toward it, a brown-robed mendicant appears out of the shadows and waves at us.

"Hail, travelers." His voice, creaky with age, still rings with good humor. He eyes us to ascertain what weapons we carry before smiling and beckoning us forward. "Welcome to this godforsaken refuge. Come warm yourselves by my fire."

"Don't mind if I do," Donato says. "But first, we must put this mighty heap somewhere safe from man or beast."

We unlash the boar, stow it in what remains of a stone sarcophagus, and huddle by the friar's fire, chafing off the night chill. Our stomachs grumble so loudly he cups his ear with gnarly fingers, looks afar, and winks.

"That's a mighty thunder."

"That mad beast ate our supper and would have eaten us had the fickle queen of destiny not had other plans."

"Takes more than good fortune to survive such a beast. What you call fortune I call the beneficence of Our Great Lord God, who smiled upon you this night. I fear you'll need a bigger fire than mine and a few hours' time to roast that hulking brute."

"We hope to trade it for board in Laibach and stave off starvation with fine mountain trout from the stream."

"I wouldn't know about fish, never eat the slimy things, nor anything else with eyes. You are welcome to share my meager gruel to quiet those barking stomachs of yours."

"These mountain fish are sweet and clean," Donato says. "We'll try our luck before we empty your larder."

Beside the stream, Donato cuts thin branches from a larch covered with baby cones, then shaves and sharpens them to fine points with his dagger before handing me one. I look at the water, but the moonlight glinting off the surface obscures what lies below. We hunker down where the stream widens into a pool. High clouds obscure the moonlight as Donato peers into a ringlet of stones, slowly raises his spear, swiftly thrusts, and pulls out a fat trout wriggling to free itself. He yanks it from the spear and shoves it into his pack. Soon he has another, and another, and notices me watching him intently.

"These are mine," he says. "If you want some, you'd better get busy."

When our packs are full, we cook the trout over the friar's fire. As he eats his gruel, he watches us stuffing our mouths with mountain trout.

"Where might you be traveling?" he asks.

"We're headed for Savaria," Donato says.

"That's a long journey. Been there many times. I imagine you'll be spending next night at Laibach."

"God help me if we're only in Laibach by tomorrow night."

"What's your hurry?"

Donato jerks his thumb at me. "He's impatient to meet his bride." He winks to the friar, who nods knowingly.

"Spring it is, and the sap is rising," the friar says, setting his bowl aside. "No stemming that tide. Those slimy creatures you're stuffing yourself with look almost eatable."

"Delicious," Donato says. "Are you sure you won't partake?"

"Well," the friar says, "since you put it like that."

Donato pulls a trout off the spit and plops it in the friar's bowl. Deftly wielding a tiny dagger, the friar expertly bones the trout, cuts it to pieces, and eats them from the point of the blade.

"One good turn deserves another," he says. From the pack beside his old and sleeping donkey, the friar grabs a flagon, pulls the stopper, and offers it to us. Donato raises it to his lips, guzzles, then hands me the monastery beer, yeasty and sweet.

"Watch your steps beyond Laibach," the friar says. "The hills are rotten with all manner of unsavory vermin. Most folk travel in packs, not that it does them much good."

"So we've heard." Donato hands back the friar's ale. "Do you know it for a fact? Or is it tavern gossip?"

"A long time has passed since I took the road north from here, but I can't imagine it got any better."

"Emona," I say, "I mean, Laibach marked the border between Rome and the Pannonia province now called Hungary."

"There's a bunch of ignorant bullies for you," the friar says. "Huns and Magyars. They'd kill you as soon as spit and take what's yours for their own. 'If you don't take it, you don't have it.' That's their motto. May the good Lord judge them mercifully."

"We are girt with the blessed armor of our faith," Donato says.

"And that sword poking out of your cloak. It's bigger than a satyr's cock. No man carries a sword like that who don't know how to use it."

"I've had occasion to use it from time to time," Donato says.

"*Domine vobiscum*," the friar says. "The ruffians

never bother me because I got nothing worth anything to them. Even my ass is worthless. She no longer carries me. Half the time, I carry her. A useless beast."

"Why do you keep her?"

"In truth, she carries my flagon and gruel and a few precious bones—holy relics with healing powers that otherwise I would have to carry on my aching back."

"Holy relics should be worth a highwayman's while."

"Highwaymen don't believe in God, or miracles, or saints and don't see any use in old bones. Even if they did steal them, who would buy a bit of bone from anyone but a humble friar returning from pilgrimage with the proper words to say over them?"

"Might you know of a safe inn where we can eat a respectable meal, take a proper shit, and catch forty winks?"

"The monks have already sung their nocturnes. You'd be better off sleeping here and break your fast in town once the sun rises. Me, I'm heading in the opposite direction. No Magyars for me. Between here and Trieste, I know every village with a humble church, a stingy bishop, and a bawdy housewife with plenty of hay in the barn and a spare penny for a knuckle from the little toe of St. Agnes of Todi. I don't know much about inns, but I do recall from days gone by a certain inn down Laibach way."

"Does this inn have a name?"

"It may have been called the Gray Goose."

As soon as the friar excuses himself, Donato puts his arm around my shoulder and whispers in my ear, "It's time to grapple."

"Seriously? I can barely move."

"This world's no place for weaklings. The moon is

bright. Let's go."

Dark trees encircle a space that may have had a sacred purpose in times gone by but now offers a perfect arena for intimate combat. The moon sheds a spare light, and low branches screen us from prying eyes. We strip down to nothing but the linen binding our loins.

Donato stands three feet from me, the moonlight silvering his torso, relaxed, alert, and powerful. I assume the stance, that being easy; my memory tells my muscles exactly what to do. My problem is my erection triggered by Donato stripped to his loincloth. He, too, has paused, studying me with eyes as hungry as mine, crystal clear for the first time.

"Come at me," he says. "Hard. Take me down. I don't care how."

I hesitate. He slaps me hard and leaps back, leaving my ears ringing, challenging me to lunge arms first. But before I can grab his shoulders, he sweeps me aside with his leg, wraps his arms around my body, and lays me at his feet. He leans forward, dry and calm, a sweet smirk on his lips close enough to kiss me.

"That was stupid. What were you thinking?"

"Clearly I wasn't," I say.

"The first rule, control your mind. Lose focus, lose the battle. Think. How did you get down there?"

I close my eyes and visualize what happened too quickly to register in real life. "You slammed my chest with your palms to annihilate my breath and balance, grabbed my arm, swept your left foot under me, and pushed, laying me on the ground."

"Exactly, while you were waiting for Athena to spring

forth and lay me low because you read too many Greek books. Never charge blindly. Plan. Now do it again."

"Why must I always attack?"

"Because that's how you learn. If I attacked, you'd be where you are now, every time, faster than you can say *pontifex maximus*. Very boring. You wouldn't learn anything. Attack me with purpose; make me worry that you might actually hurt me."

I can't do what he probably expects me to do lest I end up flat on my back in a flash, and I lack the skills to do what he does. But I can surprise him, and surprise is all. Donato has a thousand eyes and nothing escapes him. I can give nothing away, neither my fear nor my intent, while he grins at me with laughing eyes.

"Come on," he says. "We don't have all night. I swear I am not invincible. No mortal is invincible. You can do anything if you want it enough."

I want to see Donato staring at me with earnest, startled eyes, saying, "Damn, I didn't think you could do that."

I lunge wide—which he isn't expecting—swivel behind him, hook my arm around his neck, and yank him backward over my leg. Surprised for an instant, he grabs my foot, bringing me down on top of him, arms squeezing me. He flips me under him—my turn to be shocked, feeling his cock, rock hard, pressing against me, while I was terrified he would see mine.

He leaps to his feet, looking away, trying to act as if nothing had happened. He says, "We had better get some sleep now. Long day tomorrow."

He watches to see if I'll contradict him, and I don't because I'm afraid it's all a terrible misunderstanding. We spread our blankets, lie side by side, and stare at the stars. The chilly mountain silence dissipates the heat of the moment.

"We've been lucky so far," I say. "No brigands or thieves. Just a generous monk who wanted nothing."

"Never trust the man who wants nothing."

"I can't imagine being you," I say.

"Why's that?"

"Everyone looks at you differently. They don't see a great swordsman of the Republic. They see a dark-skinned African and turn frightened and contemptuous."

"True, they see my complexion first, but next they see my physique which, in combination, induces fear that works in my favor. They're more afraid of me than I am of them. That makes them wary and gains me the high ground."

"But everyone we've encountered has treated me kindly and you like a slave."

"We're no longer in Venice, crowded with people from everywhere, slaves, freemen, princesses, pirates, mendicants, kings. There, nobody looks twice at me. Here, I may be the first Black man they've ever seen. As long as they fear me, I'll take the advantage. Sweet dreams, ballot boy. We have a long journey ahead of us."

I close my eyes, sensing the weight of his body beside me, and drift into a reverie in which Donato cradles me in his arms, crushes me against his chest, and as he starts kissing me, I feel the sharp point of a blade press against my throat. I hear scuffling. I open my eyes. At the periphery, I see two men fighting with Donato. It's no dream.

Clumsy and stupid, they think we are too. With a thug

hanging from each of his arms, Donato yanks them off-balance, cracks their skulls together, and drops them as two more appear. Seeing his bloody accomplices crumpled at Donato's feet, the thug holding his sword to my throat forgets me and watches Donato face off against his cohorts. Sword high to strike, Donato spots the blade at my throat and shouts something I can't understand.

Swinging his sword in a wide arc, Donato clears a path to me. As his attackers leap out of his measure, he shouts something else. One of them barks back. Donato laughs and spits a reply. In his element now, he acts with absolute certainty, unafraid, genuinely savoring their fear and confusion. He's the inevitable victor, and they know it.

The thug pinning me sees the glitter of gold under my shirt and grabs the chain around my neck to eye the doge's gold ring and the dolphin with the ruby eyes. He shouts something to the others, dragging me toward them. A roar, Donato lunges, hacking one down and leaping back before the other can raise a hand, so fast and sharp they have no time to react. In the noisy confusion, I twist powerfully, breaking the hold of the thug dragging me. I jump him, and he falls, rolls free, and whips out his dagger. He springs, aiming for my heart.

Chapter Seven

The Inn at Emona

DONATO LEAPS FORWARD and slashes him. The thug drops his dagger and retreats, screaming, cradling his bloody arm. Turning back to the others, his sword pointed straight like the lethal prow of a war galley, Donato menaces them, and they shout back. Slowly, slowly, Donato lowers his sword, and they lower theirs. Donato laughs, and then they all laugh, except for my inept assailant, rocking back and forth on the ground, cradling his arm, whimpering. Donato turns danger into hilarity, and the brigands reluctantly shake hands with him, nod at me, and razzing their wounded comrade for being a baby, they shuffle toward our camp where the boar lies trussed in a marble bed.

"That's what they wanted all along," Donato says. "Let them have it."

"What else did you say?"

"I asked them if a couple gold trinkets were worth dying for, and they appreciated the clarity of my thinking."

"You saved my life."

"That makes us equal. Yesterday, you saved mine."

The brigands can't untie my nautical knots, so I oblige and together we wrestle the boar on one of their nags.

Returning to the dwindling fire, I notice our erstwhile companion, the mendicant friar, has vanished, along with his ass and his holy bones. "Where do you suppose the friar is?"

"Long gone. I suspect he was one of them." Donato shakes his arms wearily. "Fuck him," he says, grimy with sweat and blood. "I don't know about you, but I need to wash those vermin off me. What did he call that inn?"

"The Gray Goose."

In old Emona, the Roman bones of the town have been sutured together with a mixture of dried clay, straw, cow dung, and lamb grease, plastered over with torch-charred lime. Over the tavern door, a carved stone goose takes flight, the work of a Roman soldier. Thick soot defines the underside of the broad, outstretched wings and serpentine beak, transforming an ordinary greylag into a fierce raptor. Once a Roman bathhouse, the ramshackle tavern and its adjacent stable leak the only light to be seen on the deserted street. The stable gate squawks, and a figure emerges from the inn.

"Who have we here?" a woman barks loudly, not

worried about waking up her neighbors because she has none.

Donato throws back his cloak and hood, exposing his brown skin and blue eyes, and greets her with a bright smile. "Two weary travelers with two weary steeds."

If she is frightened, she doesn't show it. She stands short and round, her face wide with a gap-toothed smile, her eyes blaze with intelligence, or cunning, or both. "How long might you be staying?"

"We must leave by midday to reach Celeia."

"Ain't leaving yourself much time unless you plan to fly like the old gray goose."

"My friend here is off to meet his bride. We will fly if we must."

She sizes up the sword hanging on Donato's thigh. "I hope you know how to use that thing."

"I do," Donato says. "In fact, I've already had cause to use it traveling your fine roads."

"Then what are you waiting for? Come inside."

The guttering candles smell like pork chops. Overhead, birds flutter from rafter to rafter of the peaked ceiling. Our hostess steers us toward a trestle in front of the fire. "How might you gentlemen break your fast?"

"With roast goose, if you please."

She ripples with laughter. "Goose is for the abbot. An omelet is all I have for you."

"Make it plentiful. I could eat a horse."

She shoves a loaf of bread our way and pours us some ale. It may be weak, but she pours generously. "You must be Venetians," she says.

"What gave us away?"

She raises one eyebrow. "Where do I start?"

Donato speaks to her in a dialect I don't recognize, but I can guess what she's saying as she's so much like the baker's wife in St. Nick's parish where I grew up, with her pawnbroker eyes and cashbox for a heart.

"I don't understand a word she's saying," I tell Donato. "Why do you?"

"It's the same Low German the mercenaries in Treviso and Bassano speak."

"Do you really think the friar is a highwayman?"

Donato ruffles my hair indulgently, reducing me to an innocent younger brother.

"Is the pope French?"

"I'm really stupid, aren't I?"

"No. You just haven't figured out how to use the things you know."

The hostess brings our omelet, easily a dozen eggs, with more bread and ale.

"We should get off this highway," Donato says.

"It's the only road to Savaria that I know."

"There must be others."

While eating, I leaf through the volumes of maps stored in my memory.

"Look at it this way," Donato says. "We are in Tartarus, where no man rules and no law prevails. We're better off in the realm of Louis the Great, where a ruthless army scares the highwaymen shitless."

After eating, we tend our horses and nap in the hay. We depart by a narrow path that skirts the town walls and continues through a forest. We travel more slowly, but we encounter no one else. The road twists across rivers, hills, and dales. The scant path only permits a leisurely gait for Delfín and Mercury, and time weighs heavy. Our horses stay close together. Since saving each other's lives, an invisible force draws us closer—an amalgam of awe, gratitude, and, on my part, desire. Perhaps on Donato's part, too, although I have yet to put it to the test. I feel emboldened to ask Donato a question that has buzzed in my brain like a hornet.

"What makes you think your mother was murdered?"

"I don't think. I know."

"Who murdered her?"

He smiles sadly. "I don't think this is a conversation we should have right now. It's painful from every angle."

"Worse than war?"

"Like that, possibly worse, lodged in your brain and you can't get it out. Ever. Certainly not you, who never forgets. Sometimes it's best to let sleeping dogs lie."

"I don't want you to suffer such pain in the telling."

"I wasn't talking about me. Not knowing is often better than living with what you can neither fix nor alter."

"Your mother has nothing to do with me."

He hesitates, falls back, advances, and speaks. "Your father killed her."

A bombard bursts behind my eyes.

Donato reaches over and squeezes the back of my neck. "Now do you see what I mean?"

"I know he's a killer, but why would he kill your mother?"

"She was innocent and young and beautiful, and he was consumed by lust. He raped her repeatedly, and my father allowed it. When he tired of her, he cut her throat.

A quirk of raging appetite."

"Did you see it?"

"No. But she wasn't quite as dead as he thought she was. I found her. She told me. My father spread the lie that she died of plague."

"Why would he do that?"

"So his own throat would not be slit, and mine into the bargain. No soul in Venice doubts your father is capable of anything."

Stunned, eyes down, sorry that I asked, I ride cloaked in a silence Donato respectfully does not interrupt. For mile after mile, we see neither house nor church nor farm. Soon, we intersect the Roman road we previously avoided. Weary and hungry, I trail behind Donato, watching the passing trees and listening to birds hidden in their branches as night floods the road in darkness.

"We have to rest," Donato says. "Here's as good a place as we're likely to find."

On the edge of a meadow, behind a crumbling wall of ill-fitting stones, we build a fire. Donato listens intently for signs of something to eat, eventually discovering meadow rabbits. We are as grateful for them as for manna from heaven. While the rabbits roast over the fire, we find a pool of moonlight in which to grapple and spar.

"You learn fast," he says. "Forget the dagger. Get your sword."

"But you said—"

"I know what I said, but we lack the luxury of time."

Positioning my body with his hands, he adjusts my stance and shows me how to grip the hilt and wield the sword with one hand or two. He says nothing, speaking only with his hands, adjusting my fingers, wrists, and shoulders. He then focuses on my knees, my neck, my hips, and feet. I begin to feel the sought-for balance in the weight of my sword, how to raise it, how to control its path, to mark its behavior throughout the various strikes, which I repeat until my arms ache.

"Not bad," he says, his arm around my shoulders once we have finished. "You look like you know what you're doing, which is half the battle. I am comforted by your appearance. Next, you must learn combat, but for now, we eat and sleep. We are alive, safe, and behind schedule."

As we prepare to sleep, Donato says, "I wanted to say something about last night..."

He rarely hesitates. Does he feel the need to say something about his hard-on when we grappled, to make an excuse or a confession?

Finally, he leans forward until I think he might kiss me and says, "Get closer. It's cold. We can keep each other warm."

Nestled into my back, he embraces me. His breath grazes the back of my neck like a down feather. I can scarcely breathe, praying that he'll kiss me and terrified he might, collapsing the distance between us into an intimacy I'm afraid I can't navigate. Paralyzed by indecision, I fear the moment will pass if I don't seize it, but I panic at doing so. To all appearances, he wants what I want, but how can I be sure he's not simply snuggling for warmth?

A nearby rustling sits us both up. We turn toward the sound as a cluster of fireflies moves toward us, lanterns crossing the meadow. A convocation of monks emerges from the dark. Their torches illuminate gentle smiles and porridge-colored cowls glittering with dew. They carry baskets laden with cuttings, no weapons in sight. They approach and kneel in a circle around us, not threatening us but offering palpable goodwill.

"Greetings, brothers," their spokesman says. "I hope we haven't alarmed you."

"Far from it," Donato says. "But you have aroused my curiosity as to who you are and what you're doing here so far from village and cloister."

"We were gathering valerian before the morning birds and bees disturb our work. And we saw you sleeping so sweetly behind the meadow wall. It's dangerous so near the main road. Desperate souls lurk in the shadows. Allow us to take you to our priory, where you may sleep or eat as you wish. We are behind that stand of birch and offer you respite from the woes of this world."

Chapter Eight

The Priory of Brotherly Love

THE HAND-HEWN STONES of the hidden priory fit exactly, without mortar. Precision cutting and the will of nature hold these walls firmly in place. Reeds strewn on the floor, mixed with lavender, rosemary, and thyme, fill the interior with a delicate sweetness. The monks disappear in pairs as our Virgil guides us to a nook of fire-warmed stone. The cloister lies outside an open door.

"If you'd be so kind as to wait here, I will fetch Brother Ivo."

We warm ourselves by the fire under the icon of a saint with a beatific smile staring at a simple wooden cross hanging above the cloister door. Donato shakes his head, baffled, but unruffled.

"Where do you suppose we are?"

"In a dream, I think."

"Yours or mine?" He stretches mightily and shoots his glance my way, catching me admiring him. "And what of our horses?"

"As safe and comfortable as we are, I assume."

"That begs the question where we are…"

"We'll know soon enough."

Donato steps into the cloister. "The shadows tell me Prime rang long ago, but not a single bell has sounded."

Brothers in simple white robes file into the cloister and begin working in the gardens, silent, organized, and disciplined. Their smiles suggest their discipline is a blessing, not a curse. Our Virgil chats with one of them, then disappears, while the other approaches us with a confident stride, smiling with his lips and eyes.

"Welcome, brothers, to our humble priory." His voice caresses. "Weapons are unnecessary within these walls."

I clutch the dagger at my waist. "I'm sorry. I forgot I was wearing it." I unfasten it and hand it to Donato, who deposits it with his sword beside the hearth.

"My deepest apologies," Donato says. "We had no idea we would end up here."

"That goes without saying. I am Brother Ivo, abbot of our Priory of Brotherly Love."

"We humbly thank you for your hospitality. What of our horses?"

"In the stable being curried and fed."

"Again, gracious thanks. I am Donato Venturi, Venetian."

"*Nigra sum, sed formosa*," Ivo says. *I am black, but*

comely. Ivo gently kisses each of Donato's hands.

"My companion," Donato says, "is Niccolò Saltano, a public scribe. We are bound for Visegrád and cannot linger."

Ivo bows deeply and kisses my hands. "We can't allow you to leave without breakfast. Eat with us, and let us get to know one another. Hospitality extended is nothing if not accepted."

Starving, I see no reason to refuse Ivo's offer of food. "We will travel faster for being refreshed."

Donato slaps my back. "My thought precisely."

"Wash and refresh yourselves; then follow your noses to the refectory."

He leaves us to ourselves in a vacant cell. An ewer of water stands on a simple table flanking a plump bed of hay and down that tests my resolve to resist. Bright coals glow in a brazier. Donato strips down to his loincloth, splashes himself with water, and dries with a towel hanging beside the table. When he's done, I follow suit, hoping the shock of cold water will wake me from this dream. Instead, the warm water only soothes me.

The monks gather in the refectory without the benefit of bells, as if summoned by a bee's buzz. Ivo waits for us in the cloister and leads us to the refectory.

"Why have you no bells?" Donato asks.

"We have no wish to draw attention to ourselves. Our deepest desire is to be left in peace, offering our hospitality to those whom God provides."

"Your hospitality truly is a blessing."

"Dear brothers, your company is the blessing."

The youngest among them stands behind a lectern

reading a passage from the *Book of Samuel*, relating the love between David and Jonathan, Saul's son. When he finishes, Ivo addresses his flock.

"Brothers, the love that radiates from God's heart to our own, which warms us and informs us and makes our work a pleasure and our pleasure a devotion, graces us with visitors. Though they come as strangers, may they leave as brothers."

"Pray tell us, Brother Ivo," Donato says, "something about your order, concealed from the world and thus from our knowledge."

"Father Aelred of Rievaulx founded our order two centuries ago. Father Aelred traveled widely to spread his message of spiritual love. His brothers and disciples built priories like ours wherever they might thrive and prosper, always far from the eye of pope and emperor alike. Each priory strives toward the fullest realization of spiritual love between brothers. Thus, we conceal ourselves from the ignorance and suspicion of those benighted by the Church of Rome. Conversely, men such as yourselves are gifts from the divine."

"How could you tell we posed no danger, armed as we were and potentially hostile?"

"The same way you recognized us as messengers of light. Looking at you is like looking into a mirror. I see only grace and beauty."

"And what does my appearance tell you?" I ask.

Ivo gazes into my eyes. "Your soul is thirsty, and we are the cup, but you don't yet know what fills us to the brim, so you hesitate to drink. As soon as you sip, your unease will turn to love, like water to wine."

"Can you enlighten us," Donato says, "as to the nature of this spiritual love between brothers?"

Ivo addresses Donato like a tutor. "Friendship is better than loneliness, is it not?"

"Undoubtedly," Donato replies like an apt pupil.

"Scripture tells us to pity anyone who falls and has no one to help them."

"So it was spoken."

"Scripture also tells us that 'if two lie down together, they will keep warm. But how can one keep warm alone?' Is that not so, brother Niccolò?"

"I am confused. Are you speaking of love or friendship between men?"

"The word *amicitia*, friendship, derives from *amor*, love. Of friends does not Solomon say, 'Let him kiss me with the kiss of his mouth.'"

Donato's thigh presses against mine.

Rent by fear and exaltation, I blurt out, "Isn't that sodomy?"

"There is no such thing as sodomy." Ivo speaks with the quiet fury of truth. "Sodomy is the perverse nightmare of a mad bishop. Sodom was a place that flouted the divine law of hospitality, a sin we need not worry about. The friends lucky enough to share spiritual love are soulmates, two spirits becoming one, concealing nothing from each other, fearing nothing, withholding nothing, and denying nothing. Do you think such friendship could be sinful, Niccolò?"

Ivo speaks a truth I never imagined hearing from an abbot.

"No love is sinful, Brother Ivo, if it is truly love and

not merely lust." I glance at Donato and see no disagreement, which further encourages me body and soul. What I most fear and most desire draws closer.

Donato plays the devil's advocate on my behalf and still remains charming. "How can you know if a friendship is truly spiritual and not lust in sheep's clothing?"

"A spiritual friend," Ivo replies, "is loyal, always putting your interests before his own. He does not seek to enrich himself from your closeness, is discreet about your private life, protects you from gossip, and defends you from lies while patiently supporting you, criticizing with neither anger nor malice, guided solely by concern and affection. Fidelity is the mark of true spiritual brotherhood."

Donato and I have each put the other's interest before our own. We saved each other's life with no thought for personal safety. We have not lied, as far as I know, nor dissembled much. The only thing I conceal from Donato is my desire.

"Now, let us eat," Ivo says, and the delectable food eclipses our conversation.

When we have eaten our fill, I say to Donato, "We must go. Much depends upon our haste."

"Haste makes waste," Ivo says. "Please, before you leave, let me reveal the healing waters of our sacred grotto."

Caught between duty and desire, I defer to Donato who says, "What's another hour? Well-rested and refreshed, we can easily make up what time we lose."

Ivo leads us from the refectory, down steps cut into the underlying stone that lead to the narrow crypt sculpted from bedrock and adorned with fantastic images. The artist had to be mad to work here in what must have been sheer torture on cramped scaffolding, by torchlight, assaulted by splinters, spiders, cramps, and paint in the eye. Like a flagellant, he had to embrace the pain for his art.

"Brother Isaac was fleeing the Black Death," Ivo says, "mistakenly thinking he would be safer here. He painted little during his short life, so we are blessed with his work, created when those who were not dying wandered mad in the streets, unable to tell the living from the dead."

Pictures cover the walls and barrel vault of the crypt. Ivo pauses at the pool of gently steaming water in the apse. He passes his torch over a marble plaque that is not marble but painted like marble, looking more real than real. Latin capitals etched into the illusory stone spell ME-MENTO MORI.

Ivo hands the torch to Donato. "Do you know the meaning of the inscription?"

"Something on the order of *carpe diem*, if I'm not mistaken."

"'Remember, you, too, must die.' The words whispered by the lowest slave into the imperator's ear during his moment of triumph."

Donato slowly passes his torch around the crypt. On the left, three coffins stand under blossoming orange trees at the base of a hillside covered with pomegranate shrubs laden with fruit. A rock defile opens onto wizened monks unfurling a scroll upon which is written *Quia pulvis es, et in pulverem reverteris*. "Dust thou art; to dust shalt thou return." The open coffins reveal first a queen, beautiful still, her splendid robe and jewels glittering with color but her skin ashen in death. A serpent slithers over her rounded belly. In the second coffin, rot has devoured her face, and nightmare jackals eat her eyes. A monster, part fish, part dog, gnaws her right leg. In the final coffin, only her skeleton remains, infested with spiders and snakes.

Facing the coffins on the opposite wall, a royal hunting party in brilliant array, who had the moment before been laughing and flirting, young and carefree, stare with horror into the coffins. Even their richly caparisoned palfreys and springing greyhounds hang appalled in midair. A hooded falcon on the queen's arm spreads its black wings, threatening to engulf them. Riveted by their inevitable end, they cannot turn away.

In the vaults above, a mountain of tangled corpses towers over everything. Popes with tiaras askew and upside-down kings tangle with lepers, cripples, beggars, whores, and earnest townsmen with grotesque grins, tumbling into the abyss. The Grim Reaper rides a darkening storm on a skeletal black destrier, her black robes flying open to reveal her fleshless skeleton. Her hair streams a mass of angry, venomous snakes into the firmament behind her. Under her paralyzing gaze, everything blossoms with worms, corruption, and putrescence.

"*Vanitas vanitatum, omnia vanitas*," Ivo whispers across the crypt.

The murals, so lifelike, appear to move when I turn away and freeze when I turn back. The horses' eyes quiver with panic. The greyhounds, mid-leap, recoil from the demons gorging on the dead queen's toes.

Ivo points to the crowned figure amid the hunting

party. "That is King Louis the Great," he says. "Painted in his youth and as like him as a mirror."

Short, with thick lips and heavy jowls, a voracious appetite excites his eyes, appetite writ large across his features, but not for sustenance. He is not fat. Appetite for blood, for death, for power.

"And this," Ivo says, "is our miraculous pool, fed from hidden springs, which is to the body what prayer is to the soul. I shall leave you alone now and invite you to wash away the fatigue of travel. Think of it as holy water in the highest sense. *Asperges me hyssop, et mundabor; lavabis me, et super nivem dealbabor.*"

Cleanse me with hyssop, and I will be whiter than snow.

Donato gazes around us, his eyes wide with wonder. Ivo's voice trails after him like a line of chant.

"*Tempus fugit*, dear brothers. Make the most of it."

Like sleepers slowly waking, we strip at the edge of the pool as the pungent vapor scintillates our noses. Donato stands before me, the fulfillment of my profoundest desires, manly, brave, loyal, kind, and beguiling. I cannot imagine wanting a man more. When his eyes finally rest on my erection, he places my hand around his own.

"This is what you want, right?"

"From the first moment."

"Why wait so long to let me know?"

"I was afraid."

"Afraid of what?"

"That you wouldn't want me. I was waiting for a sign."

"And I, from you."

We sink into the pool, kissing, his erection overflowing my hand.

"What do you want me to do?" I can barely speak the words.

"Whatever you want."

"But what do you want?"

"I'm doing it."

We enter *terra incognita*. A flood of excitement collides head-on with a tidal wave of desire, plunging us over the precipice, heady and exquisite, until a mad jolt of pain pierces the ecstasy so intensely that I scream.

Donato looks stricken. "Did I hurt you?"

Are those tears in his eyes?

"No. Yes. Don't look so sad."

"Should I stop?"

"No. Make this moment last forever."

He lifts me into his measure, intent on annihilating the last barriers between us—flesh, denial, fear, separation—until my knowing and seeing and feeling merge in the nameless rapture of union.

"Oh, God!" Donato bellows; his body shudders. He grips my hair with both hands, pulling my face into his chest. "I love you, ballot boy."

Chapter Nine

Legio XV Apollinaris

AT DUSK, WE camp beside the Arrabo River. Tomorrow, we officially cross the border into Hungary and will soon reach Savaria, the erstwhile capital of Roman Pannonia. At Savaria, we turn northeast on a Roman military road crossing the great Pannonian plain to the Danube. In three more days, we will reach the royal palace at Visegrád.

Dense branches of alder, ash, and willow canopy the banks of a meandering stream. We camp under the branches of tall willows weeping purple catkins in the water. We snatch lazy brown trout with our hands. Donato cleans and guts them while I whittle a skewer and tend the fire. When we ride, we rarely talk, unable to keep our pace and carry on a conversation at the same time. We opt for speed. At night, we speak freely.

"I wouldn't mind something besides fish," I say.

"Stop whining. Tomorrow, we dine on quail and partridge. The woods are infested with them. We will eat better than a French king."

"What does the French king eat?"

"Swans and peacocks covered with gold leaf. Pigs stuffed with crabs. I heard they bake pastries with live birds inside. When the pastry breaks open, the birds fly out, and the ladies unleash their hawks on them."

"King Louis is French-born after all, from the House of Anjou. His great-great-grandfather was King Louis VIII's second son."

"Lousy luck. Seconds don't count."

"When the first son was crowned king of France, the pope gave him the crown of Sicily and Naples, half of Italy, as consolation. The dowager queen of Hungary, Louis's mother, is a Polish princess of the blood."

"Old Louis isn't Hungarian at all—"

"He's half French, half Polish, and half Hungarian."

"A mongrel, like me."

"Here's the grisly bit—Louis's little brother Andrew was married off to Joanna of Naples when he was seven, to consolidate Hungary, Poland, and southern Italy under one crown. Petrarch called Joanna and Andrew two lambs led to slaughter, but Serenissimo says Joanna is a tiger, not a lamb. She conspired to murder Andrew when he was seventeen."

"What happened to her?" Donato asked.

"She was safe as long as the pope was on her side, but

after Andrew was strangled and hung out the window by a rope tied to his willy, the pope had second thoughts."

"And your source for that information?"

"The diaries in Petrarch's library. He gave his books to the Republic. We keep them in a corner of St. Mark's. Over two hundred titles."

"And you've memorized them all."

Donato still smirks when he says things like that, but it no longer concerns me. He teases me from affection and admiration, not jealousy and scorn.

"More than anything in the world," I say, "King Louis wants revenge against Joanna. He conquered Naples twice but couldn't hold on to it. He considers Naples and Sicily his, stolen by an assassin whore, no offense to whores."

"Had I known that, I would have turned this assignment down."

"Have you ever turned down one of Serenissimo's assignments?"

"How can I refuse him? And speaking of the old man, it's time for your training. With any luck, you'll be able to wield a sword properly by the time we get back to Venice."

*

AT VESPERS THE following day, the seventeenth of April, my eighteenth birthday, we sight Savaria. On Saturdays, the town bustles with a weekly fair, bringing buyers and sellers from far and near. I pause to look at the stump of a Roman milestone along the road.

"According to this," I say, "we are six hundred

seventy-three miles from Rome."

"But whose miles?"

"Roman miles. Five thousand feet, based on Agrippa's foot."

We reach an abbey atop a knoll less than a mile outside the Roman wall around the old town. A round castle crowns the city's highest point.

"That's a singularly charmless castle," Donato says.

"The archbishop of Salzburg built it over the old Roman baths."

"What was he doing here?"

"He ran the region until the Arpads ousted him, and then the Mongols ousted them and leveled everything."

"We should stop at the abbey briefly and avoid the town altogether, as much as I know you would prefer to sift through the ruins of your Roman ancestors. Trust me. Louis has legions of spies and assassins at his command. I'd rather he didn't know we're here until we want him to. If we want him to."

"I yield," I said. "You are much better schooled at this game than I."

"Which game is that?"

"Life outside the Doge's Palace."

We both pause a long moment to admire the carved apostles in pillared niches between the twin towers of the abbey church of St. George.

"Now that's an impressive pile for the Hungarian hinterlands," Donato says. "But this is no Priory of Brotherly Love, so watch your tongue. No intimacy until we're safely back on the open road. I will humbly ask the abbot the quickest way around the town."

The abbey's Judas gate slides open, revealing a hazel eye embedded in wrinkles under a bushy white eyebrow.

"We are strangers traveling to Buda," Donato says. "We beg your hospitality. I am Donato, an oarsman, accompanying Master Niccolò, mapmaker and scribe."

"Welcome, travelers, in the name of Christ our Lord, who said, 'I was a stranger, and you welcomed me.'"

His eyes flicker mistrustfully over Donato's complexion while granting us entry. He shows us to our cells and leaves us to our own devices. After an intense grappling session in a remote orchard, we take up daggers and swords, followed by a cooling dip in the stream before joining the monks in the refectory.

Red-ochre designs cover the chalky white walls like the borders of illuminated manuscript pages. A monk much younger than I, with a brush of thick blond hair below his tonsure, reads at the lectern, looking as though he'd rather be herding sheep.

"...*qui dormierit cum masculo coitu femineo uterque operati sunt nefas morte moriantur sit sanguis eorum super eos.*" Flushed and uncomfortable, he recites the Latin clumsily.

"What's he reading?" Donato asks between mouthfuls of savory lamb stew with carrots and peas from the kitchen garden.

"Leviticus. If a man has sex with a man as with a woman, both of them have committed an abomination. Put them to death; their blood is on their own heads."

"A warning to this little flock."

The abbot strains to hear us. Donato lifts his bowl, begging for more, and we eat seconds and thirds, to the kitchener's dismay.

"A meal fit for a king," Donato says.

The abbot replies, "All our guests are kings. We are humble servants of the Lord."

"Kindly tell me, if you will, the quickest way around the town. We wish to avoid the market crowds."

The abbot directs us to a narrow donkey trail cutting a wide circle around the walls of Savaria and ending at the birth parish of St. Martin of Tours. Behind St. Martin's, we take an oxcart trail running northeast over the hills and meadows of the Pannonian plain. We camp in a secluded dale cloistered with trees and share the food the monks handed us as we left.

A stream ripples through the trees, and the air throbs with the heat of dusk. We grapple until we are dazed and covered with sweat. Donato embraces me, we kiss, we kiss again, making love as if for the first time ever, starving, then sated, then spent. We lie in a pile like wet laundry waiting to be hung on the line. Donato raises his head, staring past me with a quizzical expression, and I turn to see what he sees: remnants of a Roman sarcophagus. I crawl closer to examine the inscription in the stone.

"Can you make it out?" Donato asks.

"There's not much left."

I trace the characters with my finger. CLAVDIVS Ti—. "The rest is broken off," I say. "The reign of Claudius Tiberius. This must have been a necropolis."

We scratch through the roots and stones, finding shards of statuary and fragments of tile, unearthing bones beneath the debris. Donato kneels beside me.

"What are you looking for?"

"Whatever I find."

He digs near me and unearths another skeleton. Plucking something from a shattered finger bone, he scrapes the dirt off and shows me the silver ring with an insignia shaped like a crossbow, arms spread wide, and a star-shaped stud on the tail and a string of stars along the body.

"It's Cygnus," I say. "The brightest constellation in the summer sky."

Donato turns the ring over to reveal an inscription on the reverse. "What does it say?" he asks.

"Legio XV Apollinaris. The fifteenth legion, called Apollinaris. The man wearing this ring dug these roads and built forts until he retired, six hundred seventy-seven miles from Rome." I close Donato's fingers around the ring. "It's a treasure worthy of you." I kiss his closed fist, which he opens to proffer the ring to me.

"Take it," he says.

"It's yours."

He tries to put it on. "It doesn't fit," he says. "It's not mine."

The ring slips easily on my left index finger.

"See. It's yours."

"A birthday gift," I say.

"More than that. A symbol of our bond."

He holds my hand in his, his other hand around the back of my neck, pulls me toward him and cradles my head on his shoulder.

"Love is an elusive boon," he says. "Men lie about it every day, poets have sung about it since the beginning of time, and only a few ever truly know it. From what I've seen, most men are like dogs, sniffing at everything, fucking whatever they can, moving on without a second thought, or doing without and jacking off. But swans, like Cygnus here, mate for life. Did you know that? In the great lottery of love, Fortune favors them with the perfect match the first time out. Humans should only be so lucky. Even the Priory of Brotherly Love screens out the false to protect the true. Yet against all odds, swans get right the first time what humans fuck up over and over. But what Brother Ivo said touched me deeply. I believe you and I share something precious, a matching pair of souls, worth having under any circumstances. Let this ring bind us in an unbreakable circle wrought by destiny."

I must give him something in return. I can't give the doge's gold ring, which seals an equally solemn pact of loyalty and devotion. Instead, I hand him the gold dolphin with ruby eyes on the chain around my neck. "I can only accept the ring and all it means if you take this as a mutual seal on our bond."

Chapter Ten

Constantine's Motto

THREE SQUARE TOWERS mark the hilltop citadel guarding Visegrád. Once the mightiest Roman fortress on the Danube, the citadel crowns Castle Hill, a granite tor jutting a thousand feet above a bend in the broad river. A wall links the citadel to a lower fortress with massive square donjon and towers. A brick and stone barbican squats beneath the lower fortress, where royal guards man gates across the main road, alert for contraband and spies.

Our ferry lands us inside the gate for an extra ducat. We debark beside the royal palace flanking the riverbank. Silk standards bear two coats of arms, that of King Louis's father, Charles Robert, broad red-and-white stripes on the left—all that remains of the vanished Arpad dynasty—and the gold fleur-de-lis of the House of Anjou against a field of azure on the right. Louis's arms are quartered, the Arpad stripes and Angevin fleurs-de-lis in the upper left quadrant, the eagle of Poland on the upper right, the crowned bears of Dalmatia in the lower right, and in the lower left, a triple mountain with a royal crown on its peak encircling the double cross of Hungary.

A prosperous town sprawls along the riverbank between the royal palace and the citadel. Near the town gate, a merchant galley drops anchor amid a flotilla of rafts ferrying merchandise and travelers. The royal guard wear white surcoats emblazoned with Louis's coat of arms over their mail. The buildings along the main street remind me of the palaces of Rialto, their ground floors displaying merchandise, with luxurious living quarters on the floors above. Windows in the limestone-white walls offer glimpses of splendid fabrics, exotic spices, and carved wooden furniture, proclaiming prosperity. We dismount and join the jostling crowd near the gate. Merchants and travelers mingle with local vendors hawking fruit, fish, and ale. An old merchant stumbles against us, apologizes, looks again, and speaks in an alpine dialect Donato can parse.

"He asked where we're from. I told him we hail from Padua. He said, 'Poor you,' and switched to our tongue, more or less."

"Why you come from so far of home?" the merchant asks.

"We are going to the monastery of St. Margaret," I say, the name springing to mind from a map deep in my brain tied variously to *Margaret, daughter of Bela IV, Arpad dynasty, nun, island monastery, Buda.* Donato and I wear the coarse robes of lay brothers over our clothes to conceal our weapons, but the hilt of Donato's sword pokes through the threadbare burlap.

"Highwaymen you be, or lawyers?" the old man asks, his eyes twinkling. "No friar wears such sword, but highwaymen and lawyers won't be caught dead without one."

He laughs uproariously, and we join him.

"If we were either," Donato says, "we wouldn't be so poor and hungry. How is it that you speak our tongue?"

"I fought with good King Louis in your foul swamps, boy. I learn all your tricks and manners." He winks at Donato and nudges me with his elbow.

"We are looking for a countryman resident here. Giacomo da Murano."

"A rich friend for two friars," the merchant says. "There"—he points toward the river—"you find Giacomo da Murano, caught between the Hungarians and the Germans. Like your home."

The glassware displayed in front of the open door bears the distinctive enamelwork of Venetian glassblowers. When we tell Giacomo da Murano we are compatriots, he plies us for news, and we obligingly prime the pump with merchant gossip from the Rialto. Once inside his establishment, I flash the doge's ring.

"Your old friend, Andrea Contarini, now doge of Venice, sends his greetings."

Giacomo crosses himself, saying, "Ten thousand blessings upon his head."

I continue. "His Exalted Serenity is mistrustful of

official embassies that traffic in lies and gossip, and of spies who cannot be trusted. He sent us because he knows he can trust us. We are his eyes and ears, gauging the intentions of good King Louis. Incognito, of course."

Giacomo nods at Donato, murmuring, "As far as that is possible. Don't see too many like you north of the Alps."

Donato says, "Surely there's more than one dark-skinned man in Hungary."

"One might imagine so, but that's of no moment. Have you an audience with the king?"

"Not unless we announce ourselves as the doge's men, which defeats our purpose. Serenissimo believes that the soul of a king is revealed in the lives of his people."

Giacomo chooses his words carefully. "Only God knows what fills Louis the Great's soul, but Venice has good reason to fear him. He subscribes to Constantine's motto—one God, one church, one empire, one emperor. As long as it's him. You must be weary and hungry. Let me ply you with good Venetian food while I collect my thoughts."

We sit in a small dining room overlooking the bend in the Danube. Giacomo confers with his cook, who immediately brings in delectable tidbits while she prepares a Venetian-style meal for which we are unspeakably grateful.

She serves us steaming polenta and mushrooms with fat chunks of crispy pork and apples.

Giacomo says, "You asked about the king. All you really need to know is that he was born with a crown on his head. He is superior to you in every way. His extreme piety is well known. He never misses a prayer. Unlike the

English kings, he is highly educated and speaks many languages, including our own. He possesses a magnificent library and maintains a school of astrologers who advise him at all times. He makes no move unless the stars are favorable. He lives for two things only—war and the hunt."

Donato wipes his mouth on his napkin. "Is he good at either?"

"I am a poor judge of both," Giacomo says, "finding them equally distasteful. I can only say that whatever King Louis lacks in brilliance, he makes up for in boldness, often misguided."

"And what does he admire in men?"

"In a word, audacity. During his war against Venice, Louis often snuck away from his royal camp at Treviso to the banks of the Sile River to read dispatches and ponder his next moves. A Trevisan tradesman, Giuliano Baldichino, saw Louis alone beside the river and conceived the addlepated notion of abducting him and delivering him—dead or alive—to the Ten for a reward of twelve thousand ducats and the governorship of Castelfranco. When the Ten summoned Baldichino, he refused to reveal his failproof plan until they paid him, lest they steal his idea. They took him for an idiot and a charlatan and threw him out.

"After the war, victorious Louis heard of Baldichino's offer and appealed to the doge to send him to Visegrád for an audience, no harm intended. Baldichino was given a private audience with the king. 'Are you the man who promised to deliver me to the Ten for twelve thousand ducats, dead or alive?' Baldichino prostrated himself before the king. 'It was I, Your Majesty, may the Lord above forgive me.' To which the king replied, 'Tell me, what was your plan?' And Baldichino said, 'To hide among the rushes along the riverbank, and when I was certain you were alone, I'd throw my rope around your neck and drag you to the opposite bank. And if you made too big a stink, I'd have strangled you.' King Louis laughed at Baldichino's idiotic simplicity and shouted, 'Bravo, I applaud you. I wish my men were as audacious.'"

"To your knowledge," I ask, "has Genoa been courting the king?"

"Secret embassies don't wear signs," Giacomo says. "But I hear from one who has cause to know that Lord Visconti of Milan, who presently runs Genoa, is no friend of King Louis."

"True enough," Donato says. "But given how great a liar and coward Lord Carrara is, would Louis stake his throne on him? I mean, given what war costs and given Carrara's infamous treachery, can Louis afford it?"

"If my dear friend, the doge of Venice, wants to spend a single ducat, he must beg the Senate and the Ten for it. And if they say no, he goes without or risks his head in the spending of it. Nobody can say no to Louis, especially now that his mother is locked away in a monastery. He does exactly what he pleases."

"Would he risk something certain to fail?"

"He would never see it that way. The greater the risk, the more invincible he feels. After all, God placed the crown on Louis's head. He can do no wrong. When he fails, as in Naples, twice, he denies, retreats, and waits until the stars align properly."

"He's that kind of man, is he?" Donato rubs his thighs.

"He's that kind of *king.* Nobody elects him, and it is a mortal sin to depose him. Unfortunately for him, he's not as smart as he thinks he is, and he believes in himself the way he believes in God, without limit and without question. The only thing you can rely on is that as soon as his armor's off, he'll be hunting."

"He's hunting right now, is he?" I ask.

"Behind the citadel, in the forest by the river, where none dare trespass upon his solitude," Giacomo says. "It's a wonder there's a hart or hare left."

After lingering over exceptional sweets served with delectable wine, we thank Giacomo for his hospitality and insight and set out for the royal forest.

Rounding the bend where the Danube turns sharply southward, we traverse hills thickly forested with tall beeches veiled in a thin, vaporous mist, sweet and wet, turning the sunbeams penetrating the dense canopy the color of spring olives. Giacomo directed us to stay on the trail until it intersects a small stream, then follow the stream to where the Danube splits around the island the Romans called Ulcisia Castra.

Quaking aspen hide the island's cloistered inner bank from sight. But for the purling stream and the coursing of the river, silence reigns. Here, we are told, Louis tarries alone, apart from vassals, courtiers, and guards, steeped in solitude, thought, and prayer.

Knowing he's nearby, I am still shocked to see him.

"The king..." I stammer. Donato nods.

"How do we approach him?"

"We don't," Donato says. "We are foreigners, trespassers, either poachers or spies. The longsword at my side and the crossbow on your back make us as much prey as any beast. Watch and listen for now."

While King Louis wanders alone, lost in thought beside the stream, his entourage relaxes in an uphill clearing, dressed in luxurious silk surcoats and tunics of pink-and-turquoise brocade, golden threads glinting in the sun. Exotic feathers decorate their striped bonnets and tall, wide-brimmed hats. The manes of their palfreys have been curled and plaited with ribbons. The royal stallions gleam with bright gold.

"They don't seem particularly concerned about the king," I say.

"They don't dare disturb his privacy."

"How do you address a king?"

"That depends on whether his sword is drawn."

"Dare we approach?"

"On our knees if we want to keep our heads attached to our necks."

"But Giacomo said he admires audacity—"

Donato stops in his tracks and dismounts without making a sound, signaling the end of our conversation. He listens and watches as I tie Delfín and Mercury to a tree.

Chapter Eleven

A Chance Encounter

SIX HUNDRED POUNDS of great brown bear emerges nose first from a thicket and shuffles into the clearing, rooting in the ground, clumsy and clownish. The hungry giant prowls for reptiles, rodents, insects, anything. It dislodges a thirty-pound stone with its paws, sticks its nose into the hollow, and eats whatever crawls underneath. Lumbering to an uprooted tree at the water's edge, the bear tugs with both paws but cannot dislodge the tree. A single swipe of its massive forepaw with claws like scythes would rip a man open.

As the bear opens its cavernous mouth to sink its teeth into the log, two cubs tumble out of the thicket and scamper toward the king, who watches from across the stream, mouth agape with surprise and excitement. The great mother wheels to chase them as they head in Louis's direction. Upright, she stands seven feet tall. Her angry bark rends the silence, frightening all but her cubs, who continue their uphill run with her in pursuit, heading directly for the king.

"Fortune favors us," Donato says.

I pull my monk's robe over my head and rip my crossbow off my back. Cocking and loading while Donato draws his sword, I cannot suppress a prayer to St. Nicholas and the Virgin that springs unbidden from the depths of my childhood. Donato presses his back against a tree, unseen, as I step into the open. Louis sees me at the same instant as the bear. Both face me. The bear rears to her full height, raking the air with her claws as I aim where her heart should be.

My bolt slamming into her hurls her backward. Blood spouts from her chest. She thuds down on all fours, lurching toward me. Even death cannot stop her. She fairly gallops, spouting blood, claws raking the space between us. I calculate her apparent speed and distance, and there isn't enough time to reload.

"Run," Donato shouts as he leaps directly into the bear's path, sword raised over his head. Gripping the hilt with both hands, he plunges it through her as she collides with him.

King Louis gapes in mute fascination, his curiosity obviously more forceful than a normal man's fear, riveted by the bear defying death with frenzied persistence. Fatally wounded by my bolt, she fights on, swatting Donato's sword, locking it between her fangs, and shaking her head in blind rage. She wrenches it from Donato's grip, blood pouring from her mouth. She roars, and the sword falls to the ground. Donato stands helpless, his sword out of reach. Her foreclaws rake his shoulder. Blowing bloody foam from her mouth, her fangs scarlet, she spins, staggers backward, hits the ground with a final groan, then utter silence as her cubs playfully disappear in the bracken, not yet aware of their loss.

The king's hunting party runs downhill, shouting. By the time his guards encircle him, the bear is dead. They surround us instead. Disbelief roots Donato to the spot, and I am too stunned to move.

Louis I, king of Hungary and Poland and lord of Dalmatia, claps loudly, shouting, *"Bravo! Forza! Magnifique!"* as if watching a gladiatorial battle.

I throw my arms around Donato, laughing because we both eluded death and triumphed. The king is thrilled. He is ours.

At a single gesture from Louis, the guards back away from us as he examines the dead bear. He gestures for us to approach. Eyes down, heads bowed, we advance slowly, uncertain not only what to say but which language to use.

I bow deeply as I have often seen foreign ambassadors do before the doge, and knowing the king speaks Latin, I say, *"Salvete, regiis maiestas."*

He tilts his head and nods toward Donato. "Your slave?"

"No, Great Majesty. He is my equal in life and master in arms."

"And you?" Louis asks.

"A traveler far from home," I say.

"Time for that later," Louis says. "You saved my life. I am delighted and grateful."

He smiles, his lips not entirely free of condescension. I suppose he can't help himself, being so lofty and us so base, but he also can't entirely suppress his excited admiration. Shorter than I imagined, he cuts a fine figure. His moustaches curl up around a beaky nose Serenissimo calls French. His neatly trimmed beard blends into dark, frizzy hair exploding around his head. His lips, full and pendulous, fill me with repugnance. He speaks with precision and supreme authority. Looking us up and down, his amused smile never wavering, he surveys Donato's tattered tunic, his bleeding shoulder, and me in bloodied breeches.

"Exemplary bowmanship," Louis says, searching my eyes before turning to Donato. "And masterful swordsmanship."

"He says you're a masterful swordsman," I say to Donato.

He replies, "Not masterful enough."

Louis chuckles, making clear that he understands our native tongue.

Donato bows toward me. "Master bowman takes the laurel wreath today."

"Rock steady under fire," Louis says. "Perfect aim. I could use more men like you."

"We are humbled by your compliments, Your Majesty." Donato bows again, never raising his eyes to the king.

"Your crossbow," Louis says, hand extended.

I approach, bow deeply once again, and hand it to

him. He hefts it, sights, tugs the string, and examines the mother-of-pearl inlay.

"Spanish," he says. "The Saracen artistry is obvious. A superior piece of work. Whose arms are these?" He traces the pearl inlay of the Gradenigo dolphins with his finger.

I can't lie. He knows from our accents we are Venetian. It now becomes our task to convince him that although we *are* Venetian, we are discontented, in search of a better deal from life.

"My father left it to me," I say. "He was bowman of the quarterdeck on a great galley. Genoese pirates killed him shortly after I was born."

"You are noble?"

"Half noble, sire. And half common."

Louis points to Donato. "And what about him?"

"He is noble and royal," I reply. "His father is a noble Venetian, his mother a royal princess of Mali."

Louis lips curl in distaste. "He's an infidel?"

"He is Venetian and Christian, baptized in the true church."

"What brings you to us?"

"The hope of worldly advancement," I say. "Venice has little to offer men such as ourselves. Too many poor nobles sucking the teats of the Republic. Men who will do anything for crumbs." I quickly translate the exchange for Donato.

"I have observed this," Louis says. "Disgraceful."

"We seek a broader field, Great Majesty, more suited to our talents."

The courtiers draw close, looking down their noses at

us, annoyed at their sovereign's frank interest in two half-naked strangers, one strapping and dark skinned, streaked with blood, and the other pale and robust, scarcely more than a boy.

Louis fires off another question.

"He wants to know how we came here," I tell Donato.

"May I speak my own tongue?" Donato points to our horses tethered in the trees. "We rode from Aquileia."

"Accompany us to our palace," Louis says, adopting our tongue. "I will show you my gratitude."

A courtier steps forward, Donato's age, sweaty and peevish in a sumptuous fur-trimmed cloak, his moustache a poor imitation of the king's.

"Permit me, sire." He bows low, sweeping the ground with the feather in his cap. "You don't know these men. They could be spies or assassins." He speaks French, thinking we don't understand, but his meaning is obvious as much from his expression and tone as the words he uses.

"I know everything I need to know." Louis speaks so we can understand him. "If these men wanted to kill me, they could have let the bear do it for them, keeping their own hands clean. But no. They killed the bear. Not me." His voice reeks of sarcasm.

Stung, the courtier bows low and backs away. The hunting party mounts up. Preceded by the guards and the carcass of the bear, we ride to the royal palace.

In no time flat, Donato and I settle into marble tubs filled with steaming water. If I close my eyes, sleep will sink me. A lush Eden limns the walls, Adam and Eve before the apple. Bright-eyed beasts peer between the painted foliage. Pages assist us to bathe and dry, then dress us in leggings of English wool, shirts of Egyptian cotton, and knee-length peacock-blue tunics embroidered with gold fleur-de-lis. I have never seen Donato dressed so regally. The rich fabric and fine leggings flatter him. Wearing velvet slippers instead of our dirty boots, we are led into the royal chambers, passing through a reception hall to the king's private dining room. We detect no sign of Louis's queen. No bishops join us, neither ambassadors nor interpreters, courtiers nor councilors. I can't wait to tease Serenissimo with Louis's delectable solitude, for our doge has none. He can't even open his own mail without a councilor reading over his shoulder.

Louis's table groans under a vast array of delicacies, and our gold-filigreed Murano goblets sparkle with a pale wine that tastes like summer flowers. Louis waves everyone away. The guards stand outside the door.

"Almost magical, your appearance." Louis uses our tongue with a slight sneer. "Anyone might have known where I was likely to be. I cannot assume our meeting was accidental, but no one could have foreseen the bear. Nor could I have foreseen your strength and courage. My astrologer needs to study the aspects of our meeting."

He gestures, and a venerable ancient of Syrian provenance steps in from the anteroom.

"Tell him," Louis says, "the location, date, and hour of your birth."

"Venice," Donato says. "On the eleventh hour of the eleventh of May in the year 1343."

"Venice," I say, "on the seventeenth day of April in the year 1353."

"At what hour?"

"My mother says shortly after the midday bell, but she often makes up what she doesn't know."

The astrologer nods and silently departs with the scribe who recorded our answers.

Upon their departure Donato says, "May I speak freely, Your Majesty?"

"That's why you're here."

"We did know where Your Majesty was to be found."

"From whom was this discovered?"

"Ask anyone on the street," Donato says. "A vendor near the gate knew as much."

Louis seems surprised, showing himself out of touch with his people.

"What did you hope to gain from me?" Louis asks.

"Whatever Your Majesty wishes to bestow," Donato says. "Your beneficence is proclaimed far and wide. We are unhappy with the course our Republic has charted and our place in it, but only a fool jumps ship without first looking for sharks. We have heard much praise for the opportunities Your Majesty provides men of bravery and character. Alas, what men say and the truth aren't always congruent." Donato raises his glass to Louis. "To truth."

Louis expects us to be awed, so we lavish him with awe. As soon as we finish eating, he rises and invites us into his private study, indicating where we should sit before taking his gilded chair. Larger than ours, taller than ours, more ornate than ours, though not quite a throne, it proclaims his loftier position in relation to God and all creation.

On his left sits a table loaded with documents, charts,

maps, ink and quill, and the royal seal, which makes any-thing true. On his right, an ornately carved lectern with ivory inlays holds an open Gospel, opulently illuminated. His well-used armor stands behind him, and weapons hang on the wall. Maps cover the opposite wall—maps I desperately want to see, but Louis has seated us with our backs to them. We face axes, longswords, lances, bows, maces, body armor emblazoned with the royal coat of arms, and the august majesty of the king himself, his vel-vet tunic brocaded with gold fleur-de-lis under an ermine-trimmed robe thrown loosely around his shoulders. His gold buttons look like ducats, bearing Louis's likeness in-stead of the doge of Venice. He wears a golden circlet of fleur-de-lis for a crown, his hair bursting from beneath it.

Beaming at us intently, more inquisitor than host, Louis wields absolute power of life and death over every-thing in his realm, including us. His whim is law. We must never allow him to suspect our motives. I should not allow Donato to do all the talking lest I appear weak in the king's eyes, but I must defer to Donato's superior ability to fab-ricate a credible misrepresentation on the spot, one we won't trip over on our next move. Either Louis has met his match, or Donato has.

Louis abruptly dismisses us with a peremptory "You must be tired. You will be awakened for Lauds with us."

Guards lead us to a chamber with two narrow beds on opposite sides of the room.

Donato kisses me quickly and instantly pulls back, barring me from his bed. "It's too dangerous," he says. "The walls have eyes."

Sleep comes easily to a brain taxed to its limits. I

escape from the anxiety of our situation into a confused concatenation of dreams. I have no idea how long I've slept when my eyes open. Accustomed to Donato's snoring, the silence startles me. He is not in his bed. He must have left stealthily so as not to wake me, but any foul play would have awakened me, without doubt. I have vowed to trust him, and so I close my eyes and recite a favorite entry from Book II of Marcus Aurelius, over and over, until the repetition and exhaustion lull me to sleep.

Chapter Twelve

Lauds

TWO GUARDS WAKE us at first light to join Louis in the royal chapel. Sixteen days have elapsed since we left Venice; we have reached our goal, but our mission is not complete until we have the audience Louis has promised us. Despite the king's demonstrations of piety and goodwill, we cannot trust him, nor can we assume he trusts us. Should he choose to trust us, we need an exit strategy that won't arouse his suspicion. Being lowly pawns on his board, the king could sacrifice us with less qualms and more enthusiasm than a twelve-point stag.

Situated between the king's and queen's apartments, the royal chapel dome displays a triumphant Christ soaring above ranks of angels and concentric rings of the saved. Skeletons lead a dance of death across the arches below. A dozen courtiers sit on carved wooden benches facing four monks in simple robes and a priest in a red chasuble brocaded with crosses and fleurs-de-lis. All heads turn as the guards open the door from the king's chambers, and Louis ascends a throne in front of the altar, emphasizing his loftiness relative to our insignificance. His green silk mantle is embroidered in gold, trimmed with ermine, and tasseled with ranks of black tails. He has promoted himself, ermine traditionally being reserved for emperors and popes. Aquamarines, emeralds, and diamonds stud his mantle's gold clasp. Unlike my doge, Louis doesn't have to pay for his own clothes. He wears a king's ransom to walk sixty feet from his bed to his chapel to express his glory, which is God's glory, refracted through his glittering presence. He reminds us of what he is, lest we forget.

"Deus repulisti nos, et destruxisti nos: iratus es, et misertus es nobis."

The monk's voices blend into a single sweet sound. The sixtieth psalm. I close my eyes. The beauty of the chant encourages me to believe in God, not their God who hates me, and even if He doesn't hate me, His priests do. They would happily light my pyre in His name, which is a far greater sin than mine if all love partakes in God's infinite love as Brother Ivo affirmed. While the monks chant, I silently recite my own prayer.

"Great God of all creation, in which every one of us partakes, every woman and every man, every beast of the forest, every flower, every tide, the moon and stars, each lynx and marten, boar and bear, every honeybee and the clover they suck, every wren and egret and owl, each sunset a lullaby and each sunrise a hymn of praise and gratitude. I am grateful for this life filled with opportunity and danger, for the trust of my doge, the privileges granted me by lottery, for the sorrows that remind me of failure and loss, for the endless possibilities in your creation, and for Donato, who answers the call of my heart and soul, making me a better man, amen."

Psalm 50 follows, with a long "Alleluia." Then blessings, praises, and a lesson from *Chronicles*—King Saul's fall, King David's rise—recited by a fresh-faced boy, followed by a hymn and canticle. An Our Father closes Lauds. The monks and the priest, eyes down, silent and humble, file out of the chapel. The nobles approach King Louis, but he waves them off, and they watch suspiciously as he gestures for Donato and me to follow him. Walking into the king's study, I scan the maps on the wall and the two parchments spread on the large table underneath them. Louis does not know they are now sealed in memory.

"I am David to my father's Saul," Louis says. "God didn't require my father to fall on his sword, of course. Disease took him before his time, but that is also a judgment. He knew that I would surpass him, and that curdled him."

"We just heard how David was the greater sinner," I say, "burdened with remorse."

"Ah, yes, but a king's sins are different." Louis's eyebrows rise, and he tilts his face upward. "Only God can judge a king."

"Doesn't the pope mediate between a king and God?"

"Popes are elected by cardinals," Louis says. "Kings are born." He sounds like an impatient schoolmaster. He pauses, then softens his tone. "God smote Saul for his sins but elevated David above all others despite his."

"I beg your indulgence, Great Majesty," Donato says, "but surely we are not here to debate King David's sins."

Louis smiles as if relieved to divert the conversation. "Patience, warrior. Patience." Louis spreads his hands out on the desk, notices where my eyes have been lingering, and brushes the astrological charts aside, suspicion frosting his expression. No matter. I have already seen them and they are mine even though I don't know beans about their significance.

"Let us be frank," Louis says, with the unspoken caveat that "frank" means something different to a king than to two young foreign petitioners, one Black, one white, no matter how agile and superior in arms nor how they managed to inveigle their way into the king's privacy, audacious, but hat in hand.

"Your Republic is tottering," Louis says. "Your doge is senile, and your nobles are chained like oxen in a mill, turning in circles, each envious of the next despite being yoked to the same stone."

"Precisely, Great Majesty." Donato's face hardens with sad anger. "We were all ruthlessly betrayed by the closing of the Great Council."

"No noble of royal blood would accept such tyranny." The king purses his lips as if he smells something putrid. "As for your so-called nobles, they are nothing but a pack of merchants and pirates aping the outward grandeur of royalty. The few in their midst whose blood and history are noble have no hope of assuming their rightful station."

I suspect he has Lorenzo Morosini in mind, but it is true that the closing of the Great Council did lock the people out of their government and create the self-perpetuating despotism of a thousand nobles in a hundred committees with precious few of them holding real power by virtue of their vast fortunes and ancient names. Louis is not right, but he is not wrong. Regardless, we are obliged to agree, and he must believe us.

Donato shakes his head sadly. "Who can fathom a state run by committees?"

"No need to imagine it," Louis says. "I went, I fought, I conquered."

"To your everlasting glory, Sovereign Majesty, you recaptured the title of Lord of Dalmatia from the doge. You have seen how many Venetian nobles are low and servile, nursing the dregs of an ancient fortune, milking the Republic for their miserable salaries to keep their illustrious houses from crumbling, like mine." Donato's voice darkens, his lips curl slightly, his squint pained. "After the plague, we nearly died of hunger. More than a mill, Great Majesty, the Serene Republic reminds me of a cruel device that distracts by its complexity, glittering and spinning but going nowhere, its sole purpose to stay the same."

If I did not know differently, I would think Donato believes the complaint he opines, that of Bajamonte Tiepolo, the noble rebel; of Marino Faliero, the renegade doge beheaded for his treason; of my half-brother, Ruggiero Gradenigo; and of our father, Marcantonio Gradenigo—Brother Bernardo of the Hermits—who hate the doge and the other nobles of the Republic almost as much as they hate me.

"You asked what brought us here," Donato says, "and we said that Venice no longer offers us a promising future. Can you?"

"You cut straight to the quick." Louis brightens at the audacity. "But you are putting the cart before the horse. Besides excellent swordsmanship, what can you offer me?"

"Our lives, Great Majesty," Donato says. "Unfailing loyalty with commensurate rewards. We fear neither danger nor death. We only fear being deprived of our rightful spoils of victory."

"You risked your lives to save me from a bear," Louis says, "but that is child's play compared to Bernabò Visconti or Sultan Murad the Magnificent or Joanna of Naples, the bitch from Hell."

Joanna still eats away at Louis. He wants Naples and Sicily and everything in between, all of Italy.

"I treasure my life, sire," I say, "and all that it may bring, but if Your Majesty knew me you would understand that I fear no obstacle, least of all death."

"You must be certain of God's final judgment," Louis says.

"I'm certain of me."

"We are prepared to prove ourselves beyond doubt," Donato says. "In any capacity."

"Do you yield to my power over you, God-given and absolute?"

Donato kneels and kisses the hem of Louis's robe. "Yes, my sovereign liege."

Louis turns to me, and I follow Donato's lead.

Kneeling, I kiss Louis's jeweled hem, but unlike Donato, I am tongue-tied. Louis believes Donato has swallowed the bait but seems uncertain about me. Looking, unblinking, into my eyes, he says, "Don't resist. Swear your fealty. At your young age, the great pleasures and triumphs of life lie before you. Would you rather end up in a pile of dead soldiers, or bind your destiny to mine with title and fief?"

"I swear my fealty freely given and absolute, Great Majesty."

"Now," Donato says, "what does Your Majesty wish from us in return?"

"That you return to Venice immediately," Louis says. "The farcical standoff between Venice and Padua must end. I need to know who among your nobles will die for your doge and who will welcome the troops I am sending for Lord Carrara's victory, which will free Venice from the tyranny of the Council of Ten. Recruit the Judases in your midst willing to undermine the Republic, organize and discipline them like busy little termites so that when my armies reach the lagoon, the Republic will fall like a house of straw. Can you do that?"

"Whatever you wish, Sovereign Liege, but surely you have spies aplenty for that. All you need do is summon the poet Petrarch and ask him. He has the ear of every lord in Italy, a loose tongue, and never turns down a free meal."

That makes Louis laugh. "Vain fool," he says, "scurrying from Avignon to Rome to Milan to Padua and back again, peddling gossip and sad little love songs. As a poet he is *sans pareil*, of course, but as a diplomat, he is either incredibly stupid or criminally cynical. As far as spies go, how can a king trust the loyalty of any man who sells himself to the highest bidder?"

"But you trust us?"

"We shall see," Louis says. "We judge results, not promises."

"We can do all that you have asked, my liege," Donato says, "and more, willingly, gratefully even, at risk of death. But it will be costly."

"I dispose freely what your doge can never grant, land of your own and serfs without number, even titles if you deserve them. Your rewards will be tantamount to your service."

"What use have I of serfs?" Donato plays the jester. "They spend all summer storing up food for winter and all winter trying to survive until summer."

"When your estate lies fallow, you'll sing a different tune. Until then..." Louis takes two fat leather pouches from his desk, hands one to Donato and one to me. "This is enough gold to get you home and keep you solvent for a time."

"You intend for us to leave today?"

"You're of no use to me here. Unfortunately, many of my nobles, like your pathetic merchants, stew in vain jealousies. For your safety, I am sending an armed guard to escort you to our border. Beyond the border, spies seeing you with my men could prove more lethal than any highwayman you might chance to meet on the road."

"You insult us, Majesty." Donato looks superbly offended. "No escort is necessary. We got here alone; we shall return alone."

Donato presses forcefully because we don't want an escort. We need time alone before returning to the hazards of palace life.

Louis seems to think he's doing us a favor. "When you came, you were not sworn vassals," he says. "I am now obliged to protect you as you are bound to protect me."

Our further resistance can only arouse suspicion.

Chapter Thirteen

Morituri te salutamus

KONRAD COMMANDS THE company of soldiers escorting us to the border. He pays them out of his own pocket with money paid him by King Louis. His armor-lined surcoat covers a knee-length hauberk of chain mail. Round armor plates protect his shoulders, elbows, and knees and shiny steel greaves cover his calves and shins. Finely articulated armor on his gloves fastens to leather underneath. He holds his lance in his right hand, its weight borne by the bucket attached to his stirrup. The winged helmet covering his head has no visor; he sees through a thin horizontal slit. The sun shines bright and hot, and I can't fathom how Konrad sits so erect over so many long miles wearing eighty pounds of silver, lead, and steel.

Two men-at-arms clad in mail hauberks under leather armor flank Konrad. Their kettle helmets and longswords, common gear, and their unimposing steeds, render Konrad more magnificent, his black destrier caparisoned in silks. Donato and I ride between the men-at-arms with eight infantry behind us, swords at their sides and only coarse tunics over their mail. Legs bare, heads bare, barely eighteen, they mock the fearsome image of the Magyar warrior.

Donato says, "There are Magyars and Magyars; some are masters of the sword, lance, and saddle; others belong behind a plow. These country boys were lured into service with promises of endless ale, whores, and loot."

We can't be certain if any of them understand our tongue, forcing us to speak quietly, yet not so quietly as to appear secretive and attract suspicion.

"Do you recognize Konrad's armorial bearings?" Donato asks.

Thick black crosses quarter the escutcheon on his surcoat and shield, with thinner gold crosses potent etched upon them. In the center, a black eagle spreads its fierce beak and blood-red talons.

"The Roman Imperial Eagle was lofty and severe," I say. "This one looks maniacal."

"It's the emblem of the Teutonic Knights. A few of them owe fealty to Charles IV as Holy Roman Emperor; the rest would murder him for a glass of ale. They claim territory from the Caucasus to the North Sea. The country folk call them the German Order and quake in their boots at the sight of them. But Konrad may not be a true knight at all, maybe his father or uncle was. Those boys command a high price from any king rich enough to pay them and idiot enough to trust them."

"Maybe we should consider ourselves lucky. We're well protected."

"Or perhaps," Donato says, even more quietly, "Louis has something else in mind. What if he noticed you eying the maps and astrological charts? What if he knows more about us than we think? Fortune staged our entrance, we put on a good show, we aroused his curiosity, but only a child would imagine we gained his trust. He asked the exact date, hour, and location of our birth. Our charts have been cast, and we have no idea what his astrologers are telling him. Suppose he wants us dead?"

"Are you serious?"

"Rule out nothing," Donato says. "Don't say anything you'll regret. Keep your eyes and ears open, never drop your guard, keep sword and dagger near at hand. When we stop, you might want to reload your dagger with poison, and perhaps your bolts."

"I have very little left. I peppered the boar with it before we handed it off to those lowlifes. They should still be sleeping."

"Use what you have wisely. It's Louis's game now, and Louis's rules."

Donato's finality ensures that I am not sidetracked by my incessant doubts, stumbling into a tangle of conflicting "ifs" and "buts." I hold my tongue, and Donato bursts into laughter as if I'd said the funniest thing he's ever heard. He punches me in the shoulder playfully, leaning close. "I'm almost certain someone saw me kiss you."

"We were alone. It was so quick..."

"Idiotic. I could kick myself. As I did it, I knew I shouldn't, but I was momentarily overwhelmed by love for you."

I could hardly fault him for that.

Donato listens intently to the Magyars lagging behind us.

"Do you understand them?"

"They speak some sort of Low German dialect. They may not be Magyars at all, but alpine half-breeds."

"What are they saying?"

"How much they hate Konrad and his men-at-arms."

We proceed slowly, owing to the weight of Konrad's armor.

"What are they laughing about now?"

Donato signals for silence and continues listening until they lapse into a dogged and silent march behind us.

"As far as I can tell," Donato says, "Konrad told King Louis he wouldn't murder anyone else until Louis pays him for the ones he's done. It appears Louis only pays debts when it suits him, and in this case, it didn't. These guys were laughing at the idea of Konrad taking the king to court for unpaid murders. Apparently, when Konrad demanded payment for his last kills, Louis offered him double or nothing to slit our throats. These boys said Louis thinks Konrad is a barrel of piss pretending to be ale. That's what the hilarity was about."

"They plan to murder us?"

"Not until we're far enough from Visegrád that the blood doesn't splash on Louis."

"How far is that?"

"Sunset, I imagine."

At the end of the day's march, we set up camp. The Magyars put up a tent for Konrad and the men-at-arms, then unfurl their bedrolls beside it, always keeping an eye on us. Although they never crack a smile around Konrad, as soon as he retires to his tent, they fall to horsing around, no different from country boys anywhere.

Donato yanks me roughly toward a circle of dead pines in full view of everyone. "They can see us, but they can't hear us," he says. "We're going to argue, and then we're going to fight. Fight like your life depends on it because it does." His voice sounds louder and angrier. "They'll let us fight because they want to know how dangerous we are, and if one of us ends up dead, that's less work for them. Now strike."

"They'll see I don't know what I'm doing."

"Shut up. You're smarter than all of them, and that counts as much as strength. Focus on me. Win at my expense."

"What if I hurt you?"

"Then I deserved it."

He slaps me, hard, across the face, to grab the Magyars' attention. "You little shit, try that again and I'll shove this sword up your ass."

The Magyars turn, edging close as Donato eases back. His unblinking eyes lock on mine, the veins in his neck bulging like the ropes restraining sails in a mad sirocco. His anger frightens even me, who knows it to be false. His sword points toward my heart. I mirror him until our swords almost touch, searching his eyes for his intentions. I remember his words: *Action is faster than reaction.*

I feint, strike, our swords clash. He forces mine to the

ground. I manage to free it, gripping the hilt with both hands as he slides out of measure. I inch forward, and my lessons fly out the window. Sweat, anger, and frustration pour from my scalp and pores. Donato strikes, slamming my blade aside, tripping me. I fall on my knee, yelping in pain. The Magyars cheer Donato. Three seconds have passed.

A second skirmish lasts almost six seconds until he catches my sword in his crossbar and flips it from my hands. More cheers from the Magyars.

"You look pathetic," he snarls under his breath. "Do something scary."

He lunges, and I hop aside, grabbing my sword. I swing my blade against his with a shivering crash, driving his point to the ground. He didn't give me that. I caught him in a rare off-guard instant. He falls back and lunges again. I twist as his sword smashes mine and hop back. We circle. Strike. Parry. I manage to smash his blade aside so that his middle is exposed and slam the sole of my boot into his belly, a grappling move he definitely doesn't expect. He falls, rolls, and springs up. He leaps forward, slams my sword to the ground, and whacks the side of my head with his pommel.

When my eyes open, Donato thrusts his hand toward me. He yanks me to my feet, smiling, scarcely panting, winking at me as the six Magyars scoff and turn back to their dice.

"Grab your crossbow," Donato says. "Now."

He saunters casually toward the camp, his sword sheathed, as I sidle by our gear and lift my crossbow from my sack. The front flap of Konrad's tent opens like an awning, and the Magyars gossip with the men-at-arms, paying little attention to us. With a glance over his shoulder, Donato checks that I'm cocked and loaded.

"I've got the Magyars," he says. "Take out the men-at-arms. Leave Konrad for me."

He spins to his left, points in the opposite direction, shouts "over there," and runs. The Magyars take off after him. The men-at-arms burst out of the tent, laughing at the Magyars chasing Donato. Amid the distraction, I circle to my right. One of the men-at-arms, hands on his hips, watches Donato and the Magyars. I cock my bow, waiting for the perfect moment I know with absolute certainty will come. The second man-at-arms eases behind his partner to see what he sees, and I fire. My bolt penetrates both as Konrad bursts out of his tent in a confused rage.

The Magyars circling Donato turn slowly and lunge witlessly, trampling one another's measure, hasty and heedless. Donato dispatches them two by two, a death machine. I'm riveted to Donato when Konrad snatches his lance and shield and points the lance at me. Leaving the Magyars in a bloody pile, Donato races toward us. Konrad hurls his lance, and Donato chops it in two before it pierces him. Konrad drops his shield and draws his sword. Startled from his leisure and not fully suited up, the Teuton wears no helmet and only a mail hauberk.

Taking advantage of Konrad's distraction, I cock my bow, but they clash before I'm loaded, and I can't fire because they are moving too fast. Steel upon steel shivers the air. In a single movement, Donato breaks Konrad's arm over the hilt of his sword and throws him into the tent, which topples on top of him. The Magyars' bodies litter the camp, the men-at-arms are not dead, but useless, and by the time Konrad rips his way out of the tent, we are mounted, our steeds racing through the forest to freedom.

Chapter Fourteen

The Border Stones

DONATO AND I enjoy eight glorious nights alone under the stars before reaching Venice. We don't dawdle, but we don't race, uncertain what the future may bring and distracted by love. No sooner do we arrive than Serenissimo immediately dispatches Donato to Treviso as captain of cavalry under General Giustinian. I beg to be sent with him to train bowmen, but Serenissimo silences me with a glance. "I have something else for you," he says. "But first, what's the most important thing you learned in Visegrád?"

I hand him the maps and charts I reconstructed on the way home. They clearly demonstrate King Louis's imperial ambitions.

"The New Rome," Serenissimo says. "A madman's dream and a sane man's nightmare. How much support does he have?"

"All he needs. The barons of Hungary and Poland, his nephew Stephen, Voivode of Transylvania, and, some say, the dukes of Austria."

"Reliably unreliable, old Austria," Serenissimo says. "Never count them in or out." Lost in thought for a moment, he closes his eyes and covers my hand with his.

"The jackal Francesco Carrara builds forts on our border while his irregulars burn our towns and sabotage our waterways. And we can't lift a finger to stop him, thanks to King Louis and the pope."

Serenissimo pauses to listen for telltale traces of anyone spying, even though he speaks so softly that no one could possibly hear us. Like the nobles in the arcades, he masks his lips with his fingers so no one can read them. "You must verify the security of the abbey at Sant'Ilario and my farm near Gambarere. Above all, document the location of the border stones and what the hell is going on at Oriago."

"Why waste time. It's obvious what he's up to..."

"I need proof for the Holy Father and the princes of Italy."

"Isn't my time better spent helping Donato forge a credible land army?"

"Others can do that. You must do this."

I know better than to argue.

*

DRESSED AS A boatman, rowing a small skiff, I set out when the sky has barely begun to blanch and light fog veils the lagoon. Neither my tatty jerkin with baggy leggings nor the small skiff I'm rowing will raise unwanted interest among the thieves, spies, and river patrols. The sun shows above the eastern horizon as I approach Fusina, our port at the mouth of the Brenta River, now fogged in. Oriago lies five miles upriver, but Serenissimo's indigestion over the security of the abbey of Sant'Ilario requires a southerly detour into the tangled eaves of the lagoon, a phantasmagoric landscape of marshes and bogs continually reshaped by storms, floods, and tides. The detour lengthens my journey by a day, which Serenissimo well knows, providing me the opportunity to check on Alex at the monastery of Poor Clares near Padua.

Serenissimo forbade me to take my crossbow because being apprehended with it in Paduan territory could land me in chains, but he allows Ruggiero's dagger which threatens nothing more serious than a slap on the wrist. I carefully wrapped my mapmaking tools in my quiver, and Serenissimo entrusted me with the crude parchment drawn as part of the contentious treaty of 1358 demarcating our border.

A light in the monastery tower on the tiny island of St. George in the Seaweed guides me toward Fusina at the mouth of the Brenta. The port still sleeps, the docks cluttered with boats waiting for the sun to disperse the fog. I cautiously skirt the shore, bearing south toward the channel to Sant'Ilario, one of several such channels dug to divert the Brenta's flood waters into the lagoon. By the second morning bell, the stone tower of Sant'Ilario looms above me. Low, undistinguished buildings surround the tower, built in the year 819 by Benedictine monks at the behest of a doge who understood its strategic location between Rialto and Padua. The adjacent salt pans, extensive shallows where lagoon water evaporates to salt, which can be raked and sold, encroach on the abbey. As soon as I show the abbot the doge's ring, the monks answer all my questions and permit me to map their territory. They deny any threats to their safety and integrity from Lord Carrara. Venetians, they hate Lord Carrara and respect the doge. They have no reason to lie. As soon as I leave, I hang Serenissimo's ring on the chain around my neck and tuck it into my jerkin. From this point forward, it can only harm me.

From Sant'Ilario, the drainage canal—only navigable to boats as small as mine—angles west and north to the Brenta, crossing the contentious border zone, the area of greatest danger, toward Oriago Castle. I row slowly enough to memorize the details of the landscape, and as I near the confluence of the canal with the Brenta, Nones—the midafternoon bells—ring from the church towers. Boats clutter the river, some with oars, some with sails, some pulled on ropes by horses or donkeys or desperate men, vessels laden with barrels and bales and crates, and some, no doubt, with contraband salt. Patrol boats as thick as flies on seaweed troll for smugglers, taking no notice of me because I bear no cargo. The pouch Serenissimo gave me weighs heavy on my waist. He stuffed it with gold ducats and made me take it. He thinks it's comforting, but carrying gold in a world full of desperate men feels like a target painted on my back.

According to the treaty map, the border stones stand less than 300 yards east of the bridge crossing the Brenta near Oriago. At the apex of a sharp turn before the river cuts straight toward Oriago, I notice the contested markers two miles early and wonder what difference those two miles make. The unmistakable markers show the arms of the Carraras, the *carro*, a cart with four splayed wheels joined by a yoke, on the side facing Venice. The side facing Padua bears the lion of St. Mark, his paw on the Gospel, his eye unblinking.

I tie up my boat and take out my tools to draw the new location of the markers on my map. As soon as the ink dries, I row slowly toward the twin towers of Oriago Castle. Four hundred yards shy of the bridge crossing the Brenta, I creep along the bank until I find the holes where the markers once stood. After hiding my boat among the reeds, I set out on foot toward newly constructed houses north and east of the bridge. Farther on, I see the riverbank rife with freshly painted docks and palisades. The embankment overlooking the river has been shored up by new palisades and teems with the crowds, carts, and stalls of an illegal open market where Venetian taxes and duties are flouted and all profit accrues to Padua.

While I make a mental inventory of the merchandise and prices, a young man on the dock hustling a ride from itinerant merchants catches my eye. He's powerfully built, with a well-worn sword at his side, twenty years old, I imagine, no more. Thick chestnut curls, pulled back behind his shoulders, tumble down his back. His quilted black tunic, unfastened at the neck, reveals his throat and chest. Perhaps an inch under six feet tall, his body commands my admiration against my will. I turn away as shame burns from my insides out that so soon after swearing love and fidelity to Donato, I could be so easily waylaid by another man, not half his equal but differently attractive, cocky and aloof. Certainly, Donato would frankly admire another handsome fellow and laugh at my guilt over an involuntary boner, but that doesn't remove the sting that lust, real and spontaneous, flourishes beyond reason. The fellow must have noticed my eye because he nods, takes me in with a glance, and dis-appears among the boatmen crowding the dock.

I run back to my boat and sweat out my guilt, rowing along the channel and angling toward the doge's farm. I remember his vineyard and the profile of the land exactly. Here I rode, a fishmonger's apprentice who could neither read nor write nor ride a horse, seated behind Admiral Pisani on his steed, my arms tight around him, terrified. I was part of the delegation of nobles presenting a recluse farmer with a crown he did not want but could not refuse, making him my doge and master, and both of us servants of the Republic.

Stands of cypress screen the house from the river. Two men doze beside the gate. One lounges in the sun, his legs splayed in front of him, his back against the gatepost, tunic open to the sun. The other sprawls in the shade opposite him, his back toward me.

I greet them loudly, and startled, they grab their swords.

"Who the hell are you?"

"A messenger from His Exalted Serenity."

They disbelieve me because my clothes are shabby.

As soon as I fish out my ring and show it to them, they straighten up double-time.

"This way, sir."

They have turned the house into the kind of mess men make in the absence of women. Gear and garbage cover the oak table in the middle of the great room.

"Where is everyone?" I ask.

"Working the vines. To what do we owe the honor of your visit, sir?"

"I'm mapping the border for His Exalted Serenity."

They look at each other and then back with dull incomprehension. "We have maps."

I spread mine on the table. "Show me the border stones."

One of them points to where it should be.

"Funny," I say. "I was just there, and the marker wasn't."

"Where was it?"

I point the new location. "Two miles closer to the lagoon, placing illegal fortifications and a duty-free market inside Padua."

They look dumbfounded. They may be truly ignorant, or else they have been paid to forget. The Ten will decide if they're traitors or just stupid.

"We don't know anything about that," says the taller of the two, obviously in charge, behaving like the typical third son of a poor noble house, believing he deserves the best of everything because his grandfather sat on the Great Council but currently owning nothing more than the lint in his pocket. I imagine he has the morals of a guttersnipe and would sell his grandmother for a plate of beans.

I roll my map and slip it back into my quiver. "I've had no food since last night. Do you have anything fit to eat?"

"Nothing suitable to a man such as yourself. We wouldn't touch it if we didn't have to. The tavern upriver is your best bet, on the island. You can't miss it. Drink ale, the wine is swill, and the eels will rot your guts."

I shove off and row until the Brenta River splits around a small islet east of Mira covered with cherry trees. I tie-up at the dock, walk to the inn, drink beer, and wolf down a basket of bread and olives while the host grills my eels.

"Where are you headed?" he asks.

"Do you know the Convent of Poor Clares?"

"In Arcella, where the blessed St. Anthony died."

"Do they allow visitors?"

He shrugs and throws up his hands. "Life's too short to visit a house of poor virgins."

"I have my reasons."

He hands me my eel, which looks and smells delicious.

"I imagine a lot of people pass through here."

"Ha. Do I look rich to you?"

"Certainly there's a lot of soldiers along the Brenta..."

"I don't see anything, son. Don't see, don't hear, don't talk."

I'm Venetian, and he has nothing further to say to me.

"Do you, by chance, know of any construction nearby?" I ask. "I'm damn good with tools and in need of a job."

"No jobs in Venice?"

"Can't find work there for love or money."

Venice's pain makes him smile. "If I was you, I'd get moving. It's a long way to Arcella."

Behind me, a figure lingers in the doorway. Turning, I recognize him from the dock at Oriago. A trace of a smile plays on his lips. As I acknowledge him, his smile grows bolder. The host treats him like a stranger. I pay the host, who otherwise does his best to ignore me. The stranger follows me to the dock.

"Your boat?"

"It is."

"Nice," he says. "I see two oars. I can row. I'm headed to Padua."

He rests his right hand on his sword pommel and shifts his weight so the muscles flex under his leggings. Men like us aren't allowed to show our desire openly, but I am beginning to understand the unspoken language through which attraction is communicated. He clearly wants me very much to want him. Under other circumstances, I would very much want him, but my love of Donato and the urgency of my mission eclipse his legs and shoulders.

"I'm sorry," I say. "Another time."

"Don't you like what you see?"

He opens his jerkin revealing the curly hair on his handsome chest. His jaw is square, covered with stubble down to his Adam's apple. The dance of his deep black eyes promises excitement.

"Sorry," I say, "truly, but I must be on my way."

"You think you're too good for me?"

"No, I'm in a hurry."

"So am I."

He grabs me and pulls me to him, triggering Donato's lesson number three. I thrust my arm under his and yank him around while sweeping his leg out from under him. He scrambles backward and draws his sword.

"You'd best back off," I say, "or you'll be sorry."

He smirks, making my ears burn with rage, and lunges, but instead of striking me, he snatches the map from my pouch. I grab for it only to meet the point of his sword. He eyes the map.

"What's this for?"

"It's my hobby."

Nobody can see us, and we're too far from the tavern for anyone to hear. As I reach for my dagger, he slams the pommel of his sword into my chest, knocking the wind out of me. I fall, the world spinning. He plants his foot on my chest.

"Sorry about that," he says. "Just so you know who's boss."

"That's unnecessary," I say. A credible diversion. Anything to get the map back to the doge without having to kill anyone. "I'll give you whatever you want."

I fumble for my pouch and pour gold ducats in the dirt. He grins at the sight of them. Then he notices the gold ring around my neck.

"Hand that over too."

With the map and ring for proof, Old Carrara can scream to the pope that we're spying and scheming. Half of Europe will attack us.

Sword dangling, the thug rocks back and forth. "Who

are you drawing this map for?"

"Who wants to know?"

He's had plenty of chances to kill me and take what he wants, but he hasn't.

"Exactly how many men have you killed?" I ask.

"More than you."

"I've killed hundreds, maybe thousands."

"Fuck off."

"Is anything you see here really worth dying for?"

He grips his sword to still the trembling of his hands. My calm voice convinces him I speak true. In a flash, I grab his wrist, twisting. His sword drops before his bones crack.

Eyes stung by sweat, he squints involuntarily as I knee him in the stomach. He gags, curls up, and rolls until I swoop and slash his thigh with my dagger. Startled by the searing bite of the blade, he grabs his leg, his eyes bulging.

"What did you do..." The words stop as the poison deadens him. Then his jaw locks. Making incoherent noises, he topples backward, whacking his skull against a cherry tree. His eyes roll back in his head. I untether my boat and row as fast as I can to Arcella. His eyes won't open for at least an hour, and he'll spend another hour or two trying to shake the paralysis from his limbs. I know because Abdul and I experimented on each other. I scoop up my ducats and set out for Arcella.

Chapter Fifteen

Holy Sanctuary

THE MOON, AN orange globe, swells up over the hills, and Compline rings from tower to tower. I row upon a ribbon of silver between shadowy banks. The river offers neither the mighty terrors of the sea nor the treacherous shallows of the lagoon, and the hours pass uneventfully. I row until I can row no more. What I am doing is wrong. I shouldn't be here at all. I completed my assignment, and I am placing myself in mortal danger for nothing. I should be back at the palace. I picture Serenissimo pacing nervously, but I cannot return yet.

Before Donato, Alex defended me from my demons, and I defended her. I swore an oath to free her from the prison whose bars were her father and whose chains were her mother. They intended to imprison her in a gaudy palace, married to a monster she abhors, Ruggiero Gradenigo, my half-brother. Alex tried to end her life once and told me that at the bottom of that downward-spiraling abyss, she found the courage to escape, to fight for a life of her choosing, free from her parents. That dream keeps her going. I saw her last, nearing the Convent of Poor Clares in Arcella, an hour's walk from the north gate of Padua, where she need only beg for holy sanctuary to be safe under a sacred roof until the danger of her father and mine has passed.

The Piovego Canal linking the Brenta River to Padua runs arrow-straight for six miles. I reach the city before the midmorning bell and enter the moat surrounding the city walls. I tether my boat below the millwheels, creaking and groaning in the current beside the bridge built by Caesar's legions.

The road from the city splits in two. A farmer, his ox-cart piled high with fodder, points me in the direction of Arcella. A cluster of cottages appears beyond a meadow, olive orchards, vines. Traveling farther on, a convent rises beside a simple stone church the color of dust with fruit trees hanging over the cloister wall.

A sister stands outside the cloister gate scattering breadcrumbs to a flock of squabbling chickens. "Just like children," she says, "afraid someone is going to get theirs no matter how many times I tell them there's enough for all." Her black veil flutters in her breath, revealing a face hollowed by devotional fasting. She looks directly into my eyes, reads my soul, and seeing no danger, smiles.

"St. Francis preached to the birds," she says. "He

loved all living creatures, from high to low." She cocks her head, squinting slightly. "Have you business here?"

"I have a message for an unfortunate soul seeking sanctuary here."

"Surely you know I am bound by my vows to say nothing of anyone here. I can't even tell you that no one has taken holy sanctuary here in half a year."

"I understand your vow to protect and shelter. I'm not asking to see her. I only ask that you deliver a message and return with an answer."

"I can't very well deliver a message to someone who isn't here, can I?"

"You're absolutely certain she's not here?"

"I am the portress. I know everyone going in and out."

"But I accompanied her myself, four months ago. She carried two sacks."

The portress shakes her head. "Never happened."

"She was dressed as a boy to travel safely."

The sister shakes her head with even more conviction. "No," she says. "You are mistaken."

"I beg you, in the name of the Blessed Virgin, let her know her brother is here."

"Stay where you are," the portress says. She disappears into the cloister.

The abbess returns with the portress. "I will not lie," the abbess says. "Four months ago, a stranger stood where you are standing and rang the bell. Portress was fasting, and I answered myself. The young man asked me where a pilgrim such as himself, being of great spiritual longing, could find refuge in return for labor and devotion. I was impressed by his sincerity and moved by his plea. I told him he would certainly be welcome at the Church of the Hermits in Padua."

My stomach shrinks and fear roils my blood. "Which hermits?"

"The monks of St. Augustine at the church of Giacomo and Filippo. Near the old arena of Padua, by the palace of the Scrovegni."

I bolt before she finishes closing the gate, running as fast as I can, stopping for nothing. Mama used to bolt with no warning and for no apparent reason. Her eyes wild with terror, she would drop everything and run with me in her arms or on her back. As soon as I learned to row, she would make me ferry her to the farthest reaches of the lagoon. I would wrestle the clogged marshes with my oar as she stood on the prow, shaking her fist at heaven.

Now I, Niccolò Saltano, ballot boy to the doge of Venice, hero of Trieste, beloved of Donato Venturi, hurtle down a country road as blind and driven as my desperate mother, running for the same reason. My father. Marcantonio Gradenigo.

I squint against the midday sun, paying no heed to the travelers cursing me and scratching their heads in my wake. I veer around oxcarts, squeeze between wagons, and when sheep block the road, I run wide through grass and bogs, as fast as I can.

As a child, I never knew my father. I only knew the lies Mama told, that his stuck-up noble family forbade him to marry a commoner, that he shipped out Beyond-the-Sea and was killed by pirates, making me a bastard and my mother a whore. That's the story retold in our parish and which I discovered was a fabric of lies.

Mama loved to tell me how handsome he was and that he loved her even more than the Madonna. She said he was bowman of the quarterdeck on a merchant galley and died a hero. A shipmate returned the crossbow that made him famous, bequeathed to me with his dying breath and which I carry still. But she lied. She always lied. She lied to make things better and ended up making them worse. I can't be angry anymore. Lying is how she keeps her own monsters at bay. Running, so madly desperate, I appreciate how she ran and what she feared.

Alex, for whom I would die as readily as for Donato, made a grievous mistake forgoing the sanctuary of the Clares. She now faces mortal danger, or worse yet, has already met it. I fear I am too late. I run and run, my lungs burning from the inside out. I become the road. Alex beckons at the end. She does not yet know the danger lurking at the hermitage. As brutal, ruthless, and immeasurably rich as her own father may be, he would hesitate to kill her. My father won't. He will kill her or sell her into slavery or marry her himself, whichever suits his needs. Officially dead, the man who raped my mother when she was ten, Marcantonio Gradenigo, now wears a humble friar's robe and calls himself Brother Bernardo of the Hermits, a roving mendicant living on alms. But he never begs.

Serenissimo put a price on Brother Bernardo's head for high treason and spies watch for him constantly, but he outsmarts them at every turn. Now, church jurisdiction protects him, and Serenissimo can't touch him.

I run past the mills and over the bridge flying red *carros* from the towers. I force myself to slow, to stop, to bend over, hands on my knees, to catch my breath and throw up instead. I rinse my mouth at a well crowded with laughing girls filling their buckets who remind me of the girls in my own parish, St. Nicholas of the Beggars, the butt of Venice. The sun beats down. Drenched in sweat, smelling like a pigsty, my head throbbing, I take off my jerkin, dunk my head in the fountain, splash my armpits, and sit in the sun to dry.

Trumpets sound tantaras to startle and awe the little people, clearing the street for the important ones. I duck behind a kiosk until the armored horsemen pass. Then I put my jerkin back on and, head down, enter the city. For a coin, a beggar gives me directions to the hermitage, and I find it beside the ruined arena stripped of its marble to build the palace of the richest usurer in Padua. Crabapple blossoms cover the ground like snow where ravenous lions once clawed sand soaked with gladiator blood.

The hermit's church resembles a grain warehouse on a Venetian dock, a brick rectangle some fifty feet wide and three times as long. Pilasters and arches decorate the square brick tower, topped with mullioned windows. The stone plaque above the portal reads, *Adore the Lord in this holy place*. The heavy doors groan loudly as I open them. Bright shafts of sunlight pour down from high windows, alternating with stripes of thick shadow. Master craftsmen wove the ceiling trusses into shallow baskets of carved larch.

Far-off voices within the chancel move closer, and I duck into a side chapel where I can hear them, but they can't see me. Opposite me stands St. Augustine, founder of the black-robed order, freshly painted by a master in the pay of a rich sinner. The saint bids farewell to his heartbroken mother. She weeps and prays for his safety. I know the scene too well, but now I understand why Mama wept. My father hangs over us like a sword of Damocles.

Two men exit the choir and cross the nave, both wearing black robes. The first, shorter and rounder, stops in his tracks and glowers at the other who towers over him. "I am abbot of this order," he says. "You cannot intimidate me."

The tall one laughs. His height alone should have alerted me, but when he turns with a withering sneer, his profile hits me like a fist. My father. Marcantonio Gradenigo. Brother Bernardo of the Hermits.

"It's not intimidation to point out the simple truth," Brother Bernardo says.

The fringe of white hair under the abbot's tonsure looks like a rabbit's belly, but there is nothing comical in his stance. Without raising his voice, he ups the intensity of his words. "I am abbot general of this district," he says. "You obey me, not the other way around."

"I don't dispute that you are my superior in the order." Brother Bernardo makes it sound like an insult.

His glare never wavering, the abbot says, "Against my rule, the rule of this order, you roam disastrously and create havoc wherever you go."

"I'm an itinerant friar. What should I do? Stay here and preach to the choir? That, my all-powerful abbot, is not my calling."

"The bishops of Padua, Treviso, Chioggia, and Venice would love to interrogate you about your calling."

"Alas, those bishops have no jurisdiction over me. That honor is yours alone."

"Insofar as you are a friar of the order of St. Augustine, that is true. But insofar as you are a renegade from monastic rule, it's not true."

"Dear Abbot, you ordained me."

"We all make mistakes. Praise God, I can also excommunicate you. Let the civil courts decide what to do with you."

Brother Bernardo raises his hand to strike, catches himself, and quickly lowers it. "I wouldn't if I were you. Not if you value your life."

The abbot looks as if he had seen Medusa. He pauses, breathes, steps away. "Do what you must. I refuse to sacrifice my immortal soul on the altar of your depravity. My joy lies in my resurrection. You can go to hell. Now leave this sacred place and never return."

Brother Bernardo masters himself with visible difficulty, summoning a calm but hostile voice. "As you wish." He exits through the side door as the bells toll and the friars march downstairs, single file, to the choir for the holy office, arranging themselves by voice. I scan their faces.

Alex obviously passed her month as a postulate. She looks the same, but different. Her expression, posture, and mannerisms are a young man's. Beneath her tonsure and blond fringe, her eyes, her lips, the line of her eyebrows—a mark of boundless curiosity—are pure Alex, Alessandra Barbanegra, my sweet companion and soul sister. Singing elbow to elbow with far less enchanting boys, she looks safe and serene. Brother Bernardo has been excommunicated and expelled. I pray for her continued safety until I can engineer her escape from Padua.

Chapter Sixteen

The Undeclared War

"STOP!"

Serenissimo's voice echoes through the crypt, where he always speaks in whispers.

"I can't abandon Alex." I'm fighting back tears, trying to excuse my tardy return. I expected Serenissimo would be annoyed. I had no idea he would be apoplectic. "Alex and I swore to protect each other," I say. "Would make me a traitor to my vow?"

"I said *stop*." His icy stare banishes all traces of my friend from his face. "There are things you must never say, which I cannot hear under any circumstances. Things I don't need to know. Things I can't know. If you are going to willfully put yourself in that sort of danger, you must assume all the risk. No one else can be implicated. The penalty, remember, is death."

"My death? Or hers?"

"Mine. For the last time—her father's will is sovereign under the law. No one can interfere."

Serenissimo can harden his heart the way Donato hardens affection when we spar, fighting ferociously, willing to wound me to teach me the lesson.

"I can't walk away, sire. It's too important."

"More important than your oath to me? Than the fate of the Republic? If you intend to remain by my side, you must forgo petty personal concerns. The Republic must always come first. Always. I command you to step out of your little shoes and into my big ones."

Duty compels me to yield. "Yes, Exalted Serenity."

"It's cruel, and it's unfair, I know..." Sadness seeps into his voice. "I warned you of that when you swore the oath that made you the man you are today. Like it or not, duty rules."

I love Serenissimo as much as Donato, although far differently. Turning my back on one means turning my back on the other. That cannot be. I comply, accepting that aiding Alex must remain a secret from Serenissimo at all costs.

"Did you read the documents I gave you?" he asks.

"Yes, sire, instead of sleeping after a treacherous journey home."

"A small price for a big mistake." He assaults me with his eyebrows and adjusts his gold robe for high dignity. "We are not a bakery cranking out loaves here. We're making history, which never sleeps."

In the Senate chamber, sixty senators, the Doge's Council, and the Ten seat themselves on the dais facing the assembled foreign ambassadors. Serenissimo grimaces on his stool, too low and too uncomfortable for a man his height. One squire carries the stool, another carries the gold cushion used in the ducal processions, accompanying Serenissimo wherever he goes. He can't leave the palace—even to cross the square—without a full complement of trumpeters, drummers, canons, ambassadors, senators, and grooms. Squires carry the stool, the pillow, and the gold umbrella he walks beneath, a privilege reserved for emperors and kings, conferred on Doge Sebastiano Ziani two centuries ago by Pope Alexander III.

Embassies from Padua, Hungary, Florence, and Pisa sit scowling at us. The bishop of Como occupies the place of honor on Serenissimo's right. On Serenissimo's left, Lodovico Forzatè, Lord Francesco Carrara's uncle, wears the silver spurs of knights palatine, vassals of the Holy Roman Emperor Charles IV, intended to intimidate us and keep the pope on edge. The bishop of Como looks frail, but his eyes blaze more fiercely than Forzatè's armor. At this meeting, he wields the highest spiritual authority when he speaks.

"*Contritionem praecedit superbia et ante ruinam exaltatur spiritus,*" he begins. Pride precedes destruction; a proud spirit precedes a fall.

"We must never yield to pride," the bishop admonishes, "nor can we squabble among ourselves. Our common enemy, the infidel, threatens our Christian lands. We, here, one and all, must join arms and hearts as brothers and not war amongst ourselves."

We have all heard the appeal before. Destroy the infidel and recapture the Holy Land—the pope's answer to everything. It elicits little more than impatient grumbling from all except Lodovico Forzatè, who bows his head like a humble altar boy and servant of the church.

"Thank you, Monseigneur, for your wisdom and blessing." Serenissimo reins in his sharp tongue admirably and smiles at the bishop.

Pantaleone Barbo, our talented diplomat, scion of an ancient and wealthy noble house, speaks for Venice. "Your sentiments are holy, esteemed bishop." He bows his head and pauses dramatically before continuing. "But our enemies' are not, nor do their actions bespeak a sincere desire for peace." He directly addresses Forzatè. "Ungrateful Padua, do you not remember that we freed you twice from the hands of tyrants and placed the Carraras upon your throne? Yet you have invited Hungarian armies to threaten Venice once again and built forts to attack us on land stolen from us. Can you possibly imagine no one sees what you are up to?"

Forzatè, weighed down by armor, creaks to his feet, his face red, his hand clenching the pommel of his sword. "We see the pot calling the kettle black."

Barbo fixes his gaze on the bishop of Como. "We see an undeclared war against us."

The Florentine ambassador speaks out. "Are you saying that Lord Carrara has no right to protect his people from your aggression?"

Barbo faces the Florentine with steely resolve. "It is well known that Lord Carrara diverted the Musone River to flood us and dammed canals to deprive us of the lumber to build ships and lay foundations for our homes and churches. Nor is it any secret that he is expanding the salt pans at Chioggia and Sant'Ilario in violation of our legal monopoly."

Forzatè pounds the arm of his chair with his fist. "A river flooded. Marshes dried to salt pans. Francesco Carrara cannot be held to account for blind acts of nature."

The Hungarian ambassador, a hawkish cousin of King Louis, seizes the floor. He speaks our tongue awkwardly, making him difficult to understand, but his intent is unmistakable. He bows deeply to the bishop of Como. "We are thankful for this opportunity to address the unfortunate squabble between our Italian brothers." Lean and athletic, he radiates the invincible self-assurance of the heir to an ancient title and noble blood. Unlike the Paduans, he exudes tact and gravitas. He puts one hand on Forzatè's shoulder, reaches for Pantaleone Barbo with the other, and brings the two men together.

Beaming approval, the bishop of Como says, "We are all Christians after all. It is time to act like it."

"If I may?" Hungary glances at the bishop, who nods agreement. "I would like to propose a remedy."

The bishop nods enthusiastically and checks Serenissimo, who gestures for the Hungarian ambassador to continue. Unlike black-robed Venice, or Padua suited up for battle, Hungary's robe scintillates with emeralds and pearls, the royal arms emblazoned on his fur-lined cape. Thin-faced, with thick sideburns and long, drooping moustaches, he bows deeply to the doge.

"Exalted Serenity, Sir Barbo, Lord Forzatè, noble gentlemen of Venice. Not so very long ago, my king won a war with the Republic of Venice which returned all Dalmatia to Hungarian rule. In return, we renounced all interest in your terrafirma and relinquished Treviso."

"I helped negotiate the treaty," Serenissimo says. "You were... What? Twelve?"

Hungary blushes. "Fourteen, Exalted Serenity. My sovereign, Louis, king of Hungary and Poland and lord of Dalmatia, wishes me to express how grateful he would be to all parties concerned if you immediately cease hostilities and declare a truce to allow men of good faith to settle their grievances. We all gain when peace among us frees us to vanquish the infidel."

He's talking complete crap. There's nothing Padua, Venice, Pisa, Verona, or Milan want less than a crusade, which would only overtax treasuries and wreak havoc on Mediterranean trade. Their animus is against one other. They want solutions in Italy.

"How long a truce are you proposing?" Serenissimo asks.

Hungary bows and smiles. "One year."

Serenissimo scowls, the Senate groans, the Paduans whisper anxiously. No one approves, each for his own reason.

Hungary addresses the Paduans. "How long a truce can Lord Carrara promise?"

Forzatè steps forward. "Six months, more or less..." His indecisiveness reveals that only Lord Carrara can make the decision for Padua.

The Hungarian ambassador turns to Serenissimo. "And Venice?"

"One month." Serenissimo speaks with rocky resolve.

"Only one month?" Hungary, looking deeply wounded, turns back to the Paduans.

Forzatè deflects, tentatively asking, "What would the pope and King Louis prefer?" His master, Francesco Carrara, has no wish to disappoint either.

"King Louis would prefer a long enough period to hold thorough and sincere negotiations," Hungary says.

"The church wants peace in Italy sooner rather than later," the bishop of Como says.

Serenissimo and Pantaleone Barbo draw close to exchange whispers before Serenissimo replies to the bishop. "Two months is the most we can offer." Addressing the Senate surrounding him, Serenissimo says, "Can we agree on a two-month truce?"

The majority of black-robed senators agree. No vote is required. We all need the truce to prepare for war.

"What says Padua?" the bishop of Como asks.

"We must consult Lord Carrara," Forzatè says.

"While you're at it," Pantaleone Barbo says, "tell him we will only accept a truce if he demonstrates the sincerity of his intent by tearing down the illegal city and market he has built near Oriago and the new fortifications at San Boldo, which are acts of aggression against our Republic and expressly forbidden by treaty. We also require that he reimburse us for the destruction he has wrought on our territory on terrafirma."

Forzatè sneers at Barbo. "You can ask for the moon; that doesn't mean you'll get it."

"Nobody cherishes peace more than we," Barbo replies, "but we cannot abide broken treaties."

"I beg one further condition," Serenissimo says. "A

Venetian must present our terms to Lord Carrara."

Senator Lorenzo Morosini speaks out. "Is that really necessary, Exalted Serenity? The bishop is witness to our terms."

"The bishop is not Venetian."

Morosini clears his throat. "Do you have someone in mind?"

Our Venetians all wear the same black velvet cloaks, unornamented. Any deviation is a telltale. Morosini, Lord Carrara's staunchest apologist in the Senate, wears a jeweled medallion around his neck bearing the arms of the house of Morosini. It entwines the Hungarian Cross, added when his great-grandmother, daughter of a doge, married the king of Hungary and gave birth to Andrew III, the last Arpad king before Louis's father overthrew them. Morosini toadies to foreign dukes, princes, and kings, while treating our doge like a hired hand.

"You shall speak for us," Serenissimo tells Morosini.

The proud Morosini pales at being asked to deliver our harshest terms yet to the tyrant whose favor he curries and whose wrath he fears.

"I am honored," Morosini says, "but ill-equipped for such a mission."

"Use your skills as a trader," Serenissimo says.

Chapter Seventeen

A Night in Treviso

"NONE OF OUR nobles would dare object to sending Morosini," Serenissimo says as soon as we retire to the Evangelist's crypt. "They're all too busy thanking God I didn't send them. Now watch the pope come down on Carrara's side. We must immediately refortify terrafirma, from Treviso to Bassano."

"Can we do that under a truce?"

"There is no truce yet. Not until Carrara agrees to our terms. It's time we tell Verona to put their money where their mouth is and let us recruit men in their countryside. Meanwhile, Carlo Zeno is negotiating in the east for all the Turkish bowmen he can buy, but we have no guarantee when they'll arrive. That's why we offered Raniero di

Guaschi a sack of gold to lead our land army."

"We hired a mercenary as captain general?"

"It must have been while you were away. Barbo proposed it to the Ten, and I reluctantly agreed. We must do something before it's too late. Now go, immediately."

"Where to, sire?"

"Treviso, of course. Tell General Giustinian everything I just said. Tell him to batten the hatches until Raniero arrives."

An hour later, a favoring wind fills the sail of my flat-bottomed barge. Delfín nickers and stamps at her restraints, but I ply her with apples to calm her. From the dock at Fusina, I ride north, Delfín racing happily, glad to be back on solid ground. The fortress of Treviso stands in the center of a fertile plain sluiced by rivers descending from the Alps to the lagoon. The war may be undeclared, but the Paduans raiding the Trevisan countryside make this journey treacherous. I do not fear the enemy; I'm drunk on the prospect of seeing Donato. On any day, at any hour, I would do anything to meet with him.

The river Sile circles Treviso fortress like a moat. At the drawbridge, I shout to the guards.

"I come for General Giustinian, from His Exalted Serenity."

As soon as the drawbridge touches ground, Delfín's hooves clatter across. A guard jumps in front of me and grabs Delfín's reins. I flash the doge's ring, and he runs into the fortress as I dismount and lead Delfín to a watering trough. Giustinian soon sprints toward me and hugs me with both arms. A groom leads Delfín to the stable, and I follow Giustinian to his quarters.

"Is Donato nearby? Serenissimo wants him to hear the news I bring."

Giustinian sends an orderly to fetch Donato and proffers me bread and cheese. "You must be starving," he says. "Eat. Our food's not great since the town is shut up tight as an oyster, but it's better than nothing."

I push the food away. "I'm not hungry." I only want to see Donato.

"Eat," he says, pushing the food back toward me. "Then talk."

I'm stuffing my mouth with food when Donato runs in and laughs to see me.

"Hail, brother Niccolò." He grips my shoulders in his massive hands, kneading them while I eat. Giustinian insists I wash the food down with ale. Donato sits across the table, playing with my crusts as Giustinian paces behind us. I wipe my mouth and clear my throat to speak.

"Serenissimo asked me to inform you that the Ten has agreed to hire Raniero di Guaschi as captain general of our land army."

Giustinian's eyes dart from me to Donato. He signals for his orderly to step outside and shuts the door behind him. Before Giustinian can open his mouth, Donato shouts.

"Raniero of Siena? That bullshit braggart who goes to the highest bidder?"

"Pipe down," Giustinian orders.

Donato shakes his head. "This cannot end well."

"Is that all of your news?" Giustinian asks me.

"We are entering into a two-month truce with Padua. Serenissimo wants the forts from here to Bassano strengthened before the Hungarians arrive."

"It may already be too late for that," Giustinian says. "We captured three Paduan raiders, and Donato interrogated them. Tell Nico what they said."

Donato smirks as if telling a dirty joke. "The first one sang the loudest, and the others agreed with anything he said. According to him, one thousand five hundred Hungarian cavalry with four thousand foot soldiers are set to cross the Alps, descending through Feltre to the Piave River on their way here. Louis covets our Treviso and intends to recapture it before launching an attack on our islands."

"So the war has started," I say.

"It's just a rumor," Giustinian says. "No one actually saw anything."

"You'd best believe Carrara is on his knees this very moment," Donato says, "praying we don't attack before the Hungarians arrive."

"Carrara must know he can't trust Louis," I say, "and vice versa."

"Nobody trusts anyone," Giustinian says. "That's the problem." He shakes his head and taps a log smoldering in the grate with the toe of his boot.

I jump up. "I must alert Serenissimo." Striding toward the door, I note Donato's dismay, turn back, and turn away again, torn yet again between duty and desire, blushing as Giustinian laughs at my indecision.

"You needn't be so alarmed at the word of an enemy scoundrel. The Republic won't fall if you rest before returning. In fact, that's an order. Donato, show Nico to bed and don't leave until he's snoring."

"Yes, sir." He throws his arm around my shoulder and steers me into the corridor, and through a door. We traverse another corridor to another door, where he lights a lantern.

"Is this where I sleep?"

"Patience, my love."

Holding the lantern aloft, he illuminates the stairs to a subterranean tunnel, dark, straight, and damp. Outside the halo of Donato's lantern, the tunnel goes black. Deep inside, Donato covers my face with kisses.

"Finally, you're here," he says. "I was going crazy." More kisses, bear hugs, and backslapping follow. He pulls me toward a stout oaken door at the tunnel's end, secured with three hefty crossbars, which he opens one by one. He pulls a key from a hidden cleft in the brickwork, unlocks the door, opens it, and drops the key in his pocket. Chunks of Roman marble form steep stairs to the top, where Donato lifts the heavy trapdoor. He hangs the lantern inside and closes the trapdoor behind us.

The fortress towers cast long shadows across our path, and the domes and bell towers of the sleeping town emerge from the trees. To our left, cottages and orchards lie in the lee of a great cathedral with a spindly bell tower, to our right, deserted nighttime streets, not a lamp in sight. We cross a stream splitting around a small island with an abandoned mill. The waterwheel creaks as it turns in the current. Drifts of white blossoms fallen like snow scent the air with sweet spice. Donato opens the millhouse door and lights a candle. Branches growing through cracks in the walls have transformed the loft into a leafy bower. He hoists himself up to the loft and pulls me after him.

"What do you think of our little palace?"

"It's like a dream."

"A dream come true. You're all I think about, all I dream about. Just you. I knew you would come. I willed you here." He strips off his tunic, drops it on the hay, and then his shirt. For an instant, I fear waking up in my empty room.

Donato looks confused. "What are you waiting for? Strip, damn it, before I rip your clothes off." He watches me undress in the moonlight streaming through the disintegrating roof. Hands on his hips, his eyes drunk, a leer on his lips, he makes me forget the world.

"You're all mine now." He pulls me down into the pungent hay and crouches over me, his fingers locking in mine. I can see myself reflected in his eyes. He starts licking me like a mad dog, smelling and tasting me, raking me with hungry fingers. His tears run down my neck. I close my eyes, blinded by so much joy. We spin out toward the stars, and we tumble in the void, screaming, laughing, crying, exploding, and collapsing, too exhausted to move.

When the church bells ring, Donato's arms tighten around me to keep me abed.

"Lauds," I say, struggling free of his embrace. "I must go."

"That's only Matins. Lauds is hours away. The nightingale is still singing."

"That is the lark, the harbinger of dawn."

He silences me with kisses. "You have no idea how much I love you."

"As much as I love you."

"Not so," Donato says.

"Why do you say that?"

"Because it's true. I long for the day you love me as much as I love you, and no longer withhold anything."

"I love you beyond measure, beyond words."

He pins me to the hay. "Do you?"

"Of course I do."

"Yet you hold back. I feel it."

"This is all new to me," I say. "It takes time to learn the moves and make them my own, like grappling, or swordplay. I need practice."

"I'll give you all the practice you want so that one day, you'll surprise me and let loose."

Our bodies tangle again. We dally until the bells at St. Nicholas ring Prime.

"That *was* Lauds, you idiot." I pummel him until he restrains my wrists. "I should be halfway to Rialto by now."

"Hey, look at all the practice you got."

I hurl his boots at him, and he ducks, scooping up my clothes and hurling down them to the millhouse floor.

"Go, you mad fool," he shouts. "Warn Serenissimo the hairy, hungry Hungarians are coming to eat our brains right out of our skulls."

Chapter Eighteen

The Truce

NOT LONG AFTER I return to the palace, Serenissimo knocks on my door. He summons me to the meeting of a private council in a secret chamber prior to the doge's morning Mass, to hear Lorenzo Morosini report on Lord Carrara's response to our demands. The doge twists the fat gold buttons on his robe, rubbing his thumb on the symbols of his office, a sure sign he's uneasy. This group of the most powerful men in Venice meets in a windowless chamber, low-ceilinged and stifling. Old men in thick velvet cluster by the light of fat candles creating more heat than light. Sweat drips down their foreheads.

Morosini twiddles his jeweled medallion and worries his lower lip with his teeth, his face rigid, his eyes manic.

No one questions my presence any longer; they have become accustomed to me and know my memory is an infallible record.

"What did Lord Carrara say?" Serenissimo asks.

"He said no, Exalted Serenity."

"No to what exactly?"

"To everything."

"Who else was there?"

"The usual pack, including Ugo Scrovegni, the mayor of Belluno."

"There's a dirty sack of money if ever there was one."

"All Carrara's men are singing the same hymn," Morosini says.

Serenissimo crosses himself as he speaks. "Scrovegni is thick as thieves with the leaders of the pope's party. At least the Holy Father wasn't there."

"His legate was, Exalted Serenity."

Serenissimo's expression sours. "The half-wit from Como again?"

"No, Exalted Serenity. Uguccione da Thiene."

"Ah. Uguccione..." The doge's eyebrows go all the way up. "The pope is serious."

"I should also add," Morosini says, "that unofficially, I heard Pisa is offering to support Padua against us."

"Did Uguccione listen to our demands?"

"He did, Exalted Serenity."

"Did he say anything about them?"

"He demands proof. They all do, and we have nothing to offer."

Serenissimo pulls my map from the folds of his robe, opens it, and hands it to Morosini. "You call this map meticulously drawn by Nico here nothing?"

"A scrap drawn by a ballot boy untrained in mapmaking."

"Your memory is short this morning. This ballot boy is the hero of Trieste. He risked his life many times over to save yours. He stood toe to toe with Duke Leopold of Austria, was tortured, and did not flinch, because he is faithful, loyal, and true to the Republic."

"That doesn't mean he can draw a map." Morosini conceals his sneer behind jeweled fingers.

"I defy anyone in this room to show me a more accurately drawn map." Serenissimo snatches the map back. "Your *misunderstood* friend Francesco Carrara spits in our faces. He eats our salt revenue and contrives to smash us. Any fool can see he must be stopped."

"I only said that Lord Carrara has grievances, Exalted Serenity."

"Name one."

"We are bound by the treaty of 1358 to never attack Padua."

"And we haven't. Yet."

"That's not what he says, Exalted Serenity." Morosini massages the bridge of his nose with his fingertips. "We closed the palisades, cutting him off from the lagoon, which is tantamount to an act of war."

"An act of war? It's an act of self-defense, like his forts."

"While I was in Padua," Morosini says, "Lord Carrara received a letter from King Louis in which Louis opines about this unfortunate situation, urging him to stand tall against us, and promises an army to support him if he is attacked."

"That's not entirely good for Carrara," Pantaleone Barbo says. "Louis's promised troops are still premised on our attacking first."

Not allowed to speak, only to listen, I tug at Serenissimo's sleeve. He glances at me, irate. I lean into him and whisper in his ear. "A Paduan prisoner told Giustinian that Hungarian troops are preparing to cross the Alps." Serenissimo's eyes register the weight of the words, and he turns away.

"Enough of this bullshit," shouts Bruno Badoer at his fiercest. "Attack now and cut Carrara down to size before those Huns get a chance to fight again on our soil."

Morosini's gold rings betray the trembling of his bony fingers. He can't risk touting Carrara in front of these men, nor can he fail to appeal on Carrara's behalf lest the vindictive lord of Padua take revenge. He twists his gold medallion, carefully framing his next words. "Lord Carrara reminded all present that he was forced to sign an unjust treaty in 1358, criminally subjugating his sovereignty to ours. He feels betrayed and prays we listen to reason and act fairly before going to war. That—"

"Enough," Serenissimo says. "What about this proposed truce?"

"They await us in the Senate," Morosini says. "Let them speak for themselves."

Hundreds of nobles throng the palace corridors, gossiping and arguing nervously, while throngs of anguished commoners ape them outside. The palace guard and half the arsenal stand sentinel over the palace and its wharf. Everyone, from the richest merchant to the poorest beggar, waits to hear if we are at war.

The Paduan delegation awaits us in the Senate chamber. Uguccione da Thiene, the papal legate, wearing a red silk cope worked with gold thread and jewels, sits in the place of honor on Serenissimo's right.

"We greet you all with great honor and humility," Serenissimo says, "but we cannot negotiate with a treaty-breaker. If you cannot meet our demands, you have wasted your time."

With a clank of armor Lodovico Forzatè stands. "My Lord Francesco Carrara has asked me to inform you that the town and market at Oriago have been razed to the ground, the vineyards and orchards uprooted, and San Boldo tower reduced to its former state of ruin."

Serenissimo, blindsided, blinks in disbelief, glancing at me for verification. I can only shrug. The damage must have been done after my visit. Carrara has cleared the way for a truce while the Hungarians cross the Alps.

"See for yourself," Forzatè says.

"We shall," Serenissimo says. "We certainly shall."

"We took these measures," Forzatè says, "as a pledge of good faith toward a truce between our two states, as our Holy Father, Pope Gregory XI, so fervently urges, that we might achieve a permanent and lasting peace."

We have been outmaneuvered.

"All in good time," Serenissimo says. "All in good time."

Lorenzo Morosini, watching through lowered eyelids, looks a little too satisfied and not the least surprised.

"With such generous compliance on Lord Carrara's behalf," Uguccione says, "I believe the roadblock to negotiations has been removed. Gentlemen, please, make your arrangements."

Serenissimo hates an ambush. After the meeting and the feast celebrating the truce, the ambassadors depart, and Serenissimo invites me to pray.

"Damn it," he says after his *paternoster*. "I hate war."

"I fought only one war," I say. "A small one at that, but the stench of death still haunts my sleep."

"War eats the soul," Serenissimo says. "From the greatest warriors, Alexander, Caesar, Attila, all the way down to pipsqueaks like Carrara and his liege lord, the French king of Hungary, they are obsessed with conquest, and like it or not, we have been thrown into the ring with them. What use to recognize the stupidity of war if you're not smart enough to stop it? We must fight, or they will smash us like ants. I can't allow that to happen."

"At least it's a war worth fighting."

"Like all wars. For the winner, absolutely. For the loser, never. Enough. To business. That man is a weasel."

"Morosini or Carrara?"

"Both. We harbor a viper in our midst."

"Can't the Ten charge Morosini with treason?"

"He's too rich for that. Even if we caught him red-handed—which, right now, we can't—the other nobles, including the ones who hate him most, would rise to his defense and proclaim him a saint."

"I hear that anyone with a purse can hire an assassin in Padua."

"That would only make Morosini a martyr for the enemy to emblazon on their banners when they cry out for vengeance. That's not how it's done."

"Then how is it done?"

"We discredit what Morosini stands for, reveal him as a contemptible traitor, embarrass him enough that the other nobles will fear to be spoken of in the same breath. Taint his cause to cut off his balls. You must return to Treviso and tell General Giustinian to put his house in order immediately because he will be negotiating with the enemy for two months."

*

THIS TIME, FOUR men-at-arms escort me to Treviso. We debark at Mestre, taking the Terraglio, a road to Treviso blazed by shepherds leading their flocks to the high-mountain pastures since Roman times. Farms reclaimed from marshes by earnest monks three hundred years ago line the road, their rich produce traveling to markets up-river and down. The smoke from burning farms occludes the verdant fields and marshy dales of the Trevisan countryside. My guards are on constant lookout for hostile raiding parties, pausing only to let our horses drink and catch their breath. We reach the fortress shy of midday.

Donato's eyes flare when he sees me, but he stands fast, girded by the sergeants he is dressing down for sloppy discipline.

"Now get your sorry asses out of here," he says. "Find the enemy and drag them back from the tails of your horses."

The sergeants waste no time escaping his wrath. Once the door closes behind them and we are alone, Donato embraces me.

"Not now," I say. "Where's General Giustinian?"

"Somewhere between here and Bassano." He buries his lips in my hair.

"Donato, listen to me. This is important."

"Nothing is more important than your being here. I didn't dare hope to see you again so soon." He keeps squeezing me, and I keep struggling free.

"Serenissimo sent me to bring General Giustinian to Venice. How soon will he be back?"

Donato shrugs. "He didn't say."

"We have to fetch him."

"What's so urgent?"

"He's our lead negotiator with Padua during the truce. Serenissimo needs time with him."

Donato's smile loses its luster. "That's fine," he says.

"What's bothering you?"

"You. I worry about you."

"I'm safe in the palace. You said so yourself."

"You're here, aren't you? Serenissimo will send you other places. We are at war, our lives constantly threatened. Did you bring your sword? Have you been doing what I ordered?"

"Not every day, but whenever I can."

"That's changing as of right now. Follow me and bring your sword."

"Wait, Donato...this instant?"

Derailed by urgency, Donato draws me in his wake. I am disappointed whenever Donato the soldier triumphs over Donato the lover, and intimacy flies out the window. He takes me to a deserted courtyard and works me hard. Fighting fiercely, he challenges me and often terrifies me as we spar, displaying what his adversaries see. All the while, he shouts, "There! There! There! There!" at each of my mistakes, for what feels like hours without a moment's respite until I collapse, unable to lift my sword any longer.

Donato stares at the floor between us. Even he breathes heavily after pushing me further than I thought I could go. The anger and urgency ebb from his face as he regains his breath. He speaks softly, methodically, a sympathetic teacher rather than an angry captain. "You have the moves," he says. "Perfect, I'd say."

"I see them forward and backward and from all points of the compass."

"No doubt," he says. A "but" hangs in the air. "You are strong in that regard, mentally, but you lack strength and stamina. You're sweating like a slave loading cotton on the docks of Alexandria in August. You tire too easily, and fatigue leads to defeat. All your fine movements aren't worth shit without the stamina to sustain them."

"Sorry to disappoint you." I trace patterns on the floor with the tip of my sword.

He imitates my posture. "Don't sulk."

"I'm not sulking."

"Yes, you are. I told you; your moves are great. You just need to beef up those arms and thighs to sustain you in battle. You need to train like a Roman legionnaire."

"Run twenty miles a day with a forty-pound pack on my back?"

"Exactly. And when they could do that between Lauds and Sext, they had to do it in half the time. Every day. When they sparred, their weapons were weighted, twice as heavy as their regulation sword, shield, and spear.

When you practice, you must use weighted weapons and do exercises with heavy objects to build your endurance."

"Girolamo da Burano, Giustinian's lead oar at Trieste and the fittest old man I know, grabs a branch or beam above him and pulls himself up until his chin tops the beam, then lowers himself and does it again. He says he can do that one hundred times."

"Being able to lift your own weight can get you out of more jams than you might imagine. You are hereby ordered to strengthen your arms and thighs and back and shoulders. Your years of rowing laid a good foundation, but you lack the endurance to last a day's battle. Swear to me. Every day."

"Yes, master."

"You jest, but it's the difference between life and death on the battlefield. Strength alone won't always win the day, and you are annoyingly smart, which can also win the day. But your body, make it strong. Make it indomitable."

"The next time you see me, you won't recognize me. I swear."

He jumps up as if we had been loafing for hours and sweeps me into his arms. Donato the lover finally eclipses Donato the soldier.

"We can't chase after Giustinian until first light," he says. "Got any ideas?"

Chapter Nineteen

Borgoforte

DESPITE THE RUMORS, no Hungarians cross the Alps. An early winter descends, and everything hangs fire as all sides take advantage of the snow-bound mountain passes and frozen rivers to prepare their spring offensives. Venice, agonizingly poised at the brink of war, resembles a dry hayrick where idiots play with matches. A blur of secret trysts with Donato, military training, and frustrating attempts to wrestle the fractious nobles into a semblance of cohesion occupy our time, chasing our tails as days turn into weeks.

Finally, on my nineteenth birthday, April 17, 1372, I depart with our negotiators for Carrara's castle at Borgoforte in three boats, leaving at dawn. Donato and I accompany Giustinian and Lorenzo Morosini. A fair wind propels us up the Adige River, making our oarsmen tense at having little to do but scour the shores for danger.

"I don't understand why we agreed to this ambush," Donato says. "It's a witless no-win risk. We may well be walking into a trap."

"Because we are statesmen like Lord Carrara, not hooligans," Morosini says. He moves as far from us as he can, pretending not to listen.

"The next meeting will be in our territory," Giustinian says. "In Chioggia."

"If there is a next one." Donato refuses to be placated.

"There will be, and another one after that," Giustinian says. "We're waiting on Raniero's army, and Carrara is waiting for the Hungarians."

"We should smash Padua now," Donato says. "Before the bloody Hungarians cross the Nervesa."

"Attack now and turn all Italy against us?" It feels good needling Donato for impatience now that the shoe is on the other foot.

"Raniero brings winners and killers," Giustinian says. "At least we'll have a fighting chance."

"Something else I don't understand," Donato says. "Why does Serenissimo trust a hired hand with no stake in the game to lead our army?"

"He doesn't," I say. "His council does."

"We need a Venetian general," Donato says. "One who fights to win or die, not to rape and loot."

Giustinian scratches his chin. "I can only think of two or three Venetians up to the task."

"Yes," Donato says, "and they're from the wrong

families, or on the outs, or gave a senator horns, or have a jealous rival on the Ten. Like Pisani, never convicted but never forgiven. Pisani's only mistake was to make the men who fight under him love him. Being popular with the people isn't a noble quality, is it, Sir Morosini?"

Morosini ignores Donato and stares into the water. At Cavarzere, the last Venetian garrison on the Adige before Paduan territory begins, the river makes a sharp turn, and we lose the wind. The oarsmen row the wide, smooth river, reshaped by centuries of merchants and armies into an aquatic highway through low green fields and reed-choked marshes. The sun stipples the landscape through the clouds, the herds grazing in the meadows, the bell towers of the country churches, the fields and orchards, and the occasional village barely big enough to have a name.

Borgoforte Castle sits on the bank of the river in the *bassa Padovana*, lower Padua county. The Adige flows down from the Alps, splits Verona in two, crosses Vicenza, and continues eastward south of Padua proper until debouching in the lagoon south of Chioggia. Control of the Adige makes a war between Venice and Padua a matter of desperate interest to the Della Scala family, Lords of Verona.

"Carrara did this," Giustinian says as we dock at Borgoforte. "He transformed a family castle into a stone fortress with a twenty-seven-foot tower to intimidate us."

Morosini separates himself from our group as soon as we debark and mingles with the delegates from the other two boats. Borgoforte Castle, its pale freckled stone crenellated with battlements and a three-story brick tower, commands the river in both directions and stands sentinel over castle and dock.

"Carrara has armed men hiding in every corner," Donato says. "Count on it. Out of sight, itching to shed Venetian blood."

"They can't afford to harm a flea with the pope's legate watching," Giustinian says.

Donato is unconvinced. "I put nothing past them."

Giustinian's jaw tightens with impatience. I studied him during the war in Trieste and know his telltales. Donato's cynicism irritates him. "What would they gain?" Giustinian asks. "In front of an audience of princes and bishops, Carrara's minions will act as civil as you please to appear reasonable while courting the support of the pope and King Louis."

"I hope you're right about this diplomatic dumb show." Donato shakes his head sadly.

"It's our opening," I say. "We restate our conditions, Padua publicly refuses, and the war begins."

The great hall of Borgoforte Castle rises two stories, dark and plain, crisscrossed with thick unpainted oak beams which form the skeleton of an upside-down ship's keel ceiling. Carrara lavished no splendor here, fashioning a military fortress, not a princely residence, filled with ugly chairs and tables, time-darkened and unadorned. He also wasted no money on candles, lighting the hall with rushlights and torches. Capable of accommodating an entire garrison of soldiers, the empty hall echoes as coldly as a deserted cathedral in winter. Armored guards, their surcoats emblazed with red *carros*, block the entrance. They demand our swords.

"Hands off, soldier." Donato starts to draw his sword, but Giustinian stays his arm.

"This is a diplomatic mission," Giustinian says, "not a war party."

I unbuckle my sword and hand it to the guard, who can't see the dagger under my tunic. In the center of the great hall, two long tables face each other, ten feet apart. A dais stands at the head of the tables, a spectator's gallery for the lords of Verona and Ferrara, the ambassadors of Pisa and Florence, the mayor of Feltre, the Hungarian ambassador, and Uguccione da Thiene, the papal legate with a retinue of bishops basking in the splendor of his authority. Under their eyes, Padua indeed stages everything with strict formality. This opening session—with opposing armies of warriors and diplomats—must hammer out the rules with subsequent meetings attended only by the ten negotiators, five ours and five theirs.

"Uguccione looks like a courtesan's jewel box," Donato murmurs.

Six tassels dangle from Uguccione's hat, indicating his status as papal chamberlain. His red velvet cope, embroidered with enough jewels to ransom a princess, speaks volumes, but his most potent symbol of power hangs around his shoulders. The plain white pallium, embroidered with black crosses, signifies that the pope himself delegated his authority.

"Uguccione is a great asset to the pope," Giustinian says. "He's a good mediator between Verona, Vicenza, and Padua and is intimate with their families and their ways. We have nothing to fear from him, at least not yet. His connection to the Carraras is long-standing, but he hitched his wagon to the pope."

"Making the question, whither the pope?"

"That's always the question," Donato says. "Straight to hell if we're lucky. Thus far, he has been quite content to coddle Francesco Carrara."

Lodovico Forzatè again leads Carrara's negotiators. He places his helmet, sculpted with a rampaging boar in gilded silver, alongside his armored gauntlets on the table in front of him.

"He's wearing his sword." Donato's fists clench with outrage.

"He's a knight palatine of the Holy Roman Empire, for Christ's sake," Giustinian snaps. "It's ceremonial."

"So is mine," says Donato, "but in my ceremony, he's the one who dies."

Forzatè, armored from his skull to his ankles, wears more red *carros* than the walls of Padua. His white beard and steely gray eyes mark a man who has always held power in his hands and expects lesser men to yield. The rest of his delegation, an undistinguished lot, wear satin or velvet robes embroidered in silver and gold. The Venetians, as always, wear somber black robes and caps, except for Giustinian, clad in his military uniform. Morosini hides behind our other delegates, not front and forward as usual, anxiously twiddling his medallion.

Uguccione raises his hands for silence and stands up from his crude oak throne.

"I wish only to remind you proud rulers of our fair lands that our hours race swiftly toward life's end, and as our great poet Petrarch reminds us, death is always only one breath away. Yes, you still breathe, but be mindful of the inevitable reckoning when, stripped of your worldly trappings, you stand naked before Almighty God. I beg you, unfurl your brows, lay aside all hatred and scorn, and end your civil strife and slaughter. Our Gracious Lord and Savior offers you an opportunity to cleanse your souls with deeds of generosity and acts of grace. Seek your place among the blessed, not among the fallen. Let sweet civil concord and heaven-blessed peace guide you. Those are the prayers of our Holy Father, the Vicar of Christ, Pope Gregory XI, to those assembled here."

No prince presides to point and say, "You. Begin." Giustinian stares across the table at his Paduan counterpart. They stand at the same time and assume the same military posture, the only difference being Forzatè's forty pounds of armor and great sword. They speak at the exact same instant and, hearing each other, stop, bow, then gesture for the other to speak. By virtue of being a knight palatine, Forzatè takes precedence, but Venice presents the conditions for these negotiations to proceed.

Once more, they speak at the same time, and this time, Giustinian keeps talking until Forzatè sinks into his chair, the weight of his armor taking its toll on aged knees and hips.

"Thank you, great lords and gentlemen," Giustinian says. "I am no orator, so I will stick to the message I carry from His Exalted Serenity, Andrea Contarini, sixtieth doge of Venice, and the nobles who elected him. We demand, as prerequisite to a lasting peace, that Lord Carrara repair the damage he has inflicted upon our property and reimburse us for the revenues denied us at the free market he built upon our land."

Forzatè listens tensely, fingering the armored gauntlets on the table in front of him.

"Furthermore," Giustinian continues, "Padua must restore our treaty borders and cease all salt production, buying salt only from Venetian vendors."

Silence ensues, so complete I can hear a boatman whistling on the river. Forzatè, as red as the *carros* on his surcoat, the veins in his forehead pulsating, rises as Giustinian sits.

"Your imputations are lies, and your demands are ridiculous."

Giustinian replies, loud and clear, "Our demands are the result of your crimes. They are factual and must be redressed for peace to prevail. Do you deny before these men of honor and station that you fraudulently moved the border stones two miles into our territory?"

"Of course I deny it. How dare you slander our integrity."

Giustinian unfurls my map. A guard passes it from Giustinian to Forzatè. Clutching the map, Forzatè's hand moves in and out, his old eyes straining to focus. The map, small and densely plotted, is deadly accurate.

"You call this a map? I can't make out a damn thing."

"Let Scrovegni look for you," Giustinian says. "At least he can see."

Forzatè hands the map to the man on his right, who examines it closely. Giustinian jumps over his table, trespassing the neutral zone to lean over theirs.

"This dotted line represents where the stones were originally placed per our treaty of 1358. The dashed line represents where they stand now. You illegally annexed our land."

Forzatè booms over the cacophony rising from the dais. "Who made this map?"

"I did, sir." I stand. I'm wearing my one and only uniform. The doge is generous in matters he deems important, not so much on the little things. He thinks my uniform is stupid and prefers me in military garb, ready for action. In a room coded with symbols of station, my uniform denotes the lowest rank.

Forzatè rumbles like a small temblor. "Who are you?"

"I am Niccolò Saltano, ballot boy to His Exalted Serenity, the Doge of Venice."

"You can shove those little gold balls up your ass, boy. What do you know about making maps?"

"A master from our arsenal taught me." A convenient lie, but I gain nothing from the truth at this point.

Forzatè glares at Uguccione da Thiene and the others on the dais, his face twisted in utter contempt. "This map is worthless." He holds it with two fingers as if it reeked of dog shit.

Giustinian snatches it back and hands it to Uguccione, who examines it carefully, saying, "This looks very accomplished to me. Why should I doubt its accuracy?"

"The man who made it is reason enough," Forzatè says.

"It is entirely accurate, sir," I say. "I used the latest techniques. I made maps of Trieste, Muggia, and Moccò during our war with Austria, and they were used extensively to plan our victory. General Giustinian can attest to the accuracy of their detail."

Uguccione smiles like a kind uncle. "I would not be

inclined to quibble with the hero of Trieste." His response changes the temperature of the room.

The politics have become too complex for Forzatè to navigate. He lumbers and fumes, but he can't tongue-lash the papal legate. The message Uguccione sends the rulers of northern Italy makes clear the pope's favor remains in play. Forzatè's mail clinks as he lumbers toward Uguccione like the brown bear, blood in his eyes, and snatches the map from his hand. Giustinian grabs Forzatè's wrist to prevent him from damaging the map, and Forzatè yanks his hand back, clinging to it.

"I will present this to Lord Carrara," he says. "Our experts will determine its accuracy."

Without thinking, I leap over the table and stand beside Giustinian. "I made that map," I say. "It stays with me."

"Fine. I'll take you too." Forzatè grabs my arm and points at Morosini. "Him too."

Giustinian steps between us, breaks Forzatè's grip, and pushes me behind Donato, who has no sword but can easily kill men with his bare hands. In an instant of blind rage, Forzatè draws his ceremonial sword and swings it high. The spectators on the dais gasp. Forzatè slashes at Giustinian, misses, stumbles, drops the sword, and falls to one knee as if suddenly aware he has forfeited the high ground and sullied his cause. He fumbles for his sword and shouts to the armed soldiers pouring from the shadows into the great hall. Once again, Donato called it right; they hid everywhere.

Forzatè faces the dais. "Gentlemen, I apologize for this outrage, but you heard us insulted in our own house, called liars with no more evidence than a boy's map, a servant to the doge. This stinks to heaven."

Fear flickers in Uguccione's eyes, but his blank expression never changes. "Peace," Uguccione pleads. "Peace, lords of Italy. Peace."

"There's no peace with liars who will say anything to advance their tyranny." Forzatè turns to his captains. "Take him and him," he says, pointing at me and Morosini. "Let the rest of them go to hell."

Uguccione rises from his chair. "They are negotiators, not prisoners. Where are you taking them?"

"To argue their case before Lord Carrara," Forzatè says.

Uguccione pauses, gauging the mood of the room. "That's probably a good idea," he says. "As long as no one gets hurt. The Holy Father forbids bloodshed."

Padua has been warned.

"I'm offended you give credence to our enemy and impute such intentions to my Lord Carrara," Forzatè says. "We want to get to the bottom of this, that's all. As soon as we finish with these men, we will return them to Venice with bells on."

It takes six men to subdue Donato, fighting to hold on to me.

"If you take them," Giustinian shouts, "you must take me."

Forzatè looks him up and down like a week-old piece of meat.

"We don't need you. These two will do."

Donato spins free and pulls Forzatè's sword from its sheath. "Take us or go straight to hell right now."

Chapter Twenty

In the Jackal's Den

UGUCCIONE ACCOMPANIES US to Carrara's royal palace, so we travel at an agonizingly slow pace. No one is in a hurry but me, Giustinian, and Donato. Morosini would rather the journey never end, so greatly does he fear Francesco Carrara. His past attempts to defend the lord of Padua were ineffective, laughable really, and to that extent, he let Carrara down. To pass the time, Giustinian recounts how Carrara double-crossed Louis of Hungary during the siege of Treviso the last time they fought together.

"Your version of history is slanderous," Morosini says. He acts offended by Giustinian's bias. "Carrara would not be lord of Padua if he weren't good at what he does."

"Don't be ridiculous. We placed him on his throne," Giustinian says. "Had he proved loyal, we would still support him. Instead, he goes for our jugular, leaving us no choice but to disarm him."

"He's not the madman you paint." Morosini shows little faith in his own words. "He is a rational statesman."

"Then why are you scared shitless?" Donato asks.

Morosini shakes his head mournfully. "Because in this world, nothing can be taken for granted."

Towers, a forest of them cinched tight by the three-ply city walls, cast long shadows as the sun declines. Carrara built the outer walls, twenty feet high and ten wide. Ezzelino the Tyrant built the middle walls, and Romans built the inner walls. A squadron of cavalry escorts us down the main road, platted by Roman military engineers.

The Palace of Law looms over the sprawling markets surrounding the city center. The clock in the tower, still a novelty, shows the passing hours. Through portentous gates, we enter an orchard surrounded by the graceful loggias of the women's palace, thick with perfumed wisteria and jasmine. We continue into a complex of kitchens, barns, stables, and barracks behind stout walls garrisoning Carrara's personal army. Any beggar can approach our ducal palace and admire its splendor. Here, only insiders dare approach.

We dismount, and soldiers escort us upstairs, no longer as diplomats but as hostages, tightly girded with armored guards. In the gilded antechamber, the guards encircle us until we are called into the Hall of Illustrious

Men. Half the size of our Great Council chamber, the hall is frescoed with scenes from the lives of great Romans.

On the wall behind the dais where Carrara sits, a triumphant Caesar vanquishes Pompey at the Battle of Pharsalus, his army smaller than the legion of soldiers in plain view. The lord of Padua wants us to understand his strength in arms. His son Novello stands behind his father, their profiles identical save the deep lines etched in the elder's face. Age wise, Francesco Carrara could be Serenissimo's son and Novello, not yet fourteen, his grandson. Novello already possesses his father's hungry eyes, leaving nothing boyish about him. I feel sorry for him. I know what it's like to have a monster for a father, mine gratefully absent from the better part of my life. At least I was not raised by him.

Knights usher Uguccione to the seat on Carrara's right. His uncle Forzatè sits on his left. Morosini cowers behind Giustinian and Donato, his jaw clenched, his eyes darting, his hands trembling as we are presented to our host. Carrara savors Morosini's fear and speaks only to Giustinian, a calculated insult.

"It is an unexpected pleasure to see an old comrade-in-arms," Carrara says. He thrusts his words like a sword into Morosini's heart while smiling pleasantly at Giustinian. "General Giustinian and I fought together in the league against Bologna," Carrara explains to Uguccione, who still wears white silk gloves trimmed with gold lace and velvet slippers trimmed with pearls.

"That was the only war in which we fought on the same side," Giustinian says, "hopefully not the last."

"The Lord works in mysterious ways," Carrara replies

with a smile.

Giustinian bows respectfully to the man on Forzatè's left. "Greetings, Simone." He addresses Donato and me loudly enough for everyone in the hall to hear. "Simone Lovo, as fine a warrior as God ever created, and captain general of Padua."

Another piece in the game. We bow. I know him by reputation as the kind of general we sorely lack. While Carrara doesn't have a seaman we'd allow to mend our sails, nor an admiral save those he can buy, he boasts sly and audacious generals. The lord of Padua exudes a manic charm, clearly an enthusiastic player in games of life and death. Like Louis of Hungary, he craves circumstances that make ordinary mortals shudder, and when the thrill drains from the moment, he loses interest and grows impatient.

"General Giustinian," Carrara says, "would you be so kind as to share your message from His Exalted Serenity?"

"At Borgoforte we laid out the charges the doge and Senate of Venice have made against you, of which you are well aware, my lord. We showed all in attendance this newly drawn map which confirms our claims regarding the disputed border."

"The charges are old. The map is new. Let me see it."

I hand the map to Lord Carrara. He looks at me with withering contempt and snatches the map from my hand, glances at it, flashes an amused grin, and drops it on the table.

"Why should we believe you drew this map accurately and not to suit your purpose?"

"I mapped what is there, not what people say is there.

For example, the exact location of the border stones as opposed to their original location."

"If those stones were moved, and I'm not saying they were, it was without my knowledge," Carrara says. "A man can't be everywhere at once."

"Does that mean," Giustinian asks, "that you also know nothing personally about the fort recently built at Lova?"

"Show me where the treaty of 1358 stipulates that I, lord of Padua, am barred from protecting my interests and those of my people."

"And you deny illegally selling salt below our price without paying the duties?"

"We have panned salt for generations."

"At Chioggia and Sant'Ilario, which belong to us by treaty?"

"You know as well as I that treaty was extorted from us and violates our sovereignty."

"But you signed it."

"Your greed, then as now, is extortionate," says Carrara.

With tempers rising, Uguccione raises a hand to defuse the confrontation. "My lords, generals, Christians, brethren—please, peace, I pray."

Giustinian kneels before Uguccione, crosses himself, and kisses the jeweled hem of his robe. "I am sorry you are forced to witness such barbarism."

"Not as sorry as I am," Uguccione says, giving Giustinian no quarter.

Carrara's restless fingers worry the map to death as he addresses Giustinian. "Tell His Exalted Serenity that

Lova is ours. Sant'Ilario is rightfully ours. Everything from here to the lagoon, including the salt pans, is ours! As for this map…" He holds it up and shreds it with his jeweled dagger.

The swords in the Hall of Illustrious men, all drawn at once, ring like bells with a single menacing tone. If for nothing else, I am grateful to my demon half-brother for the dagger concealed under my tunic, the only thing of value he ever gave me, his mercy-maker, crusted with Abdul's poison, twice fatal.

Carrara drops the tatters of my map at his feet and sticks his dagger in the table, never taking his eyes from Giustinian, whose fingers, hard as marble, dig into my shoulder, holding me fast as I shatter the silence.

"You can destroy the map, my lord. But I saw with my own eyes where the stones are supposed to be and where they now stand."

"Be careful of those eyes." Carrara's own eyes twinkle. "They would be a terrible thing to lose, blue as the sky." He kicks the scraps of map from the dais, scattering them around me.

"Map or no map," I say, "the stones don't lie."

"The stones?" Carrara's harsh laugh lasts but an instant. "What are stones? Inert matter. They can't wield a sword or fire a bolt. They are nothing."

"They are a measure of your honor," Giustinian says.

"The border was drawn under duress. Tell His Exalted Serenity we shall remove the stones and smash them to pieces. Tell him we control terraferma from the lagoon to Euganean Hills. We control the rivers with forts along their banks. We control commerce between the hinterland and the lagoon. Lumber, grain, silk, pepper. And salt. We control the salt."

The last hits hardest. Whether the seas storm or scarcely raise a wave, whether the pirates plunder or retreat, whether Indian pepper ebbs or flows, salt has been our native trade since the founding of our Republic. Our only natural resource, it didn't make us great, but it always paid our way and always can.

Giustinian loosens his grip on my shoulder. "We will deliver your message to His Exalted Serenity." He nudges me toward the door. Morosini, ignored, hides behind him. Donato covers our backs as we try to exit the Hall of Illustrious Men.

"Not so fast."

At a nod from their lord, Carrara's soldiers close ranks around us, forming a wall with their shields. We can't escape without a fight, and we have no weapons.

Livid, Giustinian rages at Carrara. "We are members of a delegation the Holy Father requested from His Exalted Serenity. Call off your men. We will deliver your message."

"You and your soldier can deliver the message," Carrara says. "The ballot boy and the senator are hostages to your honor."

"Impossible, my lord."

"Don't fret," Carrara says. "You'll get them back. I'm anxious to hear what the ballot boy has to say in greater detail. Your senator stands for his honor and integrity. I certainly have no other use for them." He signals the guards to put up their swords.

Donato leaps onto the dais, grabs Carrara by the jaws,

and turns the tyrant's eyes on me. "Him for me, and I'm the better man."

"I have all the demons I need."

Eight guards pile on Donato.

His eyes dart around the room until he finds me. "I'm sorry," they scream silently.

Morosini grabs Giustinian. "You can't leave me. He'll kill me."

"No," Giustinian says, "he won't, but you may wish he had."

Uguccione staggers to his feet. "Stop this in the name of almighty God."

"Release my captain, esteemed lord, and we will leave, knowing that the word of the Holy Father and his appointed legate ensures their safety. But be certain that if any harm comes to these two, we will raze this palace and sow the ground with salt before we hang your head on a pike at the Roman gate as warning to all tyrants."

At Carrara's nod, the guards stand down and create a narrow aisle for Giustinian and Donato. Then he turns an evil eye on Morosini, but he clearly doesn't give a shit about me. I'm a nuisance caught in the crossfire.

The measured tread of the guards' boots rattles the painted walls as we march from the Hall of Illustrious Men, through the palace, to a loggia overlooking the courtyard of flowering trees. The door at the far end of the loggia leads onto a rampart twenty feet above the street. The rampart, wide enough for carts to trundle back and forth, is girded with battlements and leads to the city wall, enabling Carrara to escape if necessary without using the street below.

The guards throw us in a cart surrounded by a cohort of mounted soldiers. After jostling a quarter mile over rough-hewn stones, we cross a drawbridge to the outer city wall. Morosini shoves his terrified face in mine.

"Do you know where they're taking us?"

"Does it matter?"

Two towers rise up before us, the farther half again as tall as the near, both painted in a checkerboard pattern. The afterglow of sunset turns the red squares the color of blood.

"The tyrant Ezzelino built this tower," Morosini says. "His prison. He starved his enemies to death in a windowless pit."

The river encircles the city like a moat. Judging by the tower's strategic location and the lower course of stonework, Romans built the original. That means there is a way out.

Morosini screams in my ear. "We have to do something, or we're going to die."

I push him away. "Act like a noble for Christ's sake. The guards are laughing at you."

Morosini keeps whining. "If I could only talk to Carrara alone, he will listen to reason."

"There's no reasoning with rabid dogs."

Short of a miracle, I see no honorable way out but combat and death. They stalk us as surely as they stalked the hundred illustrious Romans painted on Carrara's walls, now dancing with the grim reaper. Morosini's cowardly desperation makes me sick. Death terrifies him. He's never been in battle. He doesn't know that death also frees us from the tyranny of fortune and time. Donato understands that and won't fault me, whatever I do.

Morosini can't stop babbling. "You've got Carrara all wrong. I know him. He's not as mad as he pretends. It's all an act, everything you see. He's smarter than you think."

"That makes him more dangerous."

Chapter Twenty-One

A Credible Diversion

CARRARA OUTSMARTED HIMSELF by inviting the papal legate. He wanted legitimacy and ended up with an eyewitness. He will have to answer to the pope for anything that happens to Morosini or me. For a man like Carrara, that only raises the stakes and makes the game more challenging.

In the center of the tall tower, sparsely lit by torches, a hook hangs over a massive trap door in the center of the floor, poised to raise it.

"They open the trap door to throw you in," Morosini says. "It slams shut. You eat each other to keep from starving." His face resembles a gargoyle's. Fear overflows his sails, pushing him in mad circles as prison guards yank us from the cart.

The palace escort leaves, pulling the empty cart behind them. The tower gates slam shut, and prison guards drag us up three flights of stairs. Morosini pleads with them as if they could do anything.

"There's been a mistake. I must speak to Lord Carrara. I am a senator of Venice, ambassador of the doge."

The guards pay him no more mind than a pig squealing on its way to the butcher's block. They throw us into darkness and lock the door behind us. The moon rising past the high window provides our only light.

Morosini keeps shouting. "Let us out of here. This is a mistake. I am a noble of Venice. You must listen to me." He pounds on the door until his hands bleed.

"Save your breath and make yourself useful."

He looks at me blankly, his face dripping sweat and tears. I position him under the window.

"What are you doing?" His eyes widen with incomprehension.

"I'm going to see where we are. Lock your fingers."

"What on earth for?"

"Didn't you ever scale a wall?"

I show him how to lace his fingers under my foot. I walk my palms up the wall, but as I reach for the bars above me, he collapses under my weight. I manage to grab two bars above me, but one of them cracks the masonry, swings loose, and sprays dust into Morosini's eyes. He coughs, crumpled and useless as I dangle by one hand. I get hold of another bar, steady myself against the wall, and hoist myself high enough to gain purchase on the windowsill. Donato nailed it again; being able to lift my body weight comes in handy.

I look down. The river below makes my head spin. Vertigo. Another curse, like my memory, my father, my stepbrother, my heart, my life. I squeeze my eyes shut too late. The darkness spirals inward. I know better. I know what vertigo does to me. I looked down because I'm an idiot.

"Think first, then act."

Abdul's words, repeated over and over during our crossbow lessons. "If you act before you think, you're re-acting to emotions, not to what's going on." He repeated the words every time I did something stupid, the same exact words Donato used.

Sweat soaks my hair and palms. I can't open my eyes. Blindly, I dig my fingers into the crumbling mortar and cautiously lower myself into the cell. I don't open my eyes until my feet hit the floor.

Morosini blinks convulsively, his eyes, red and swollen. His skin green, he shivers with panic. "What did you see?"

"Death."

A thin line of blood drips down his forehead where he pulled some hair out.

"They can't do this." He weeps. "They have to listen to me."

"They have to do what their boss says. If he tells them to flay us and make sausages with our skin, they will. Now shut up so I can think."

Battle taught me that yielding to panic makes everything worse and also taught me how to control it the way I control Delfín, who terrified me until I learned to master her. Panic loses wars. None is so brave, Caesar said, that the unexpected won't make him shit his pants. I close my eyes, breathe, and deconstruct this room in my mind, viewing it from every angle. It measures twelve feet by eighteen. The door, the only way in and out, can only be opened from the outside. The pile of straw we're supposed to sleep on reeks of piss. That's all there is, no table, no chair, not even a hole to shit in, just a cracked masonry jar in the corner beside the door.

Morosini matches my height and weight, give or take an inch and a few pounds. The guards never looked at our faces. His robe, the worse for wear, is more valuable to them than the man wearing it. My uniform, torn and filthy, contrasts starkly with Morosini's velvet, rendering me worthless. They do this all the time and don't give a fart about prisoners, only how much money their clothing can fetch on the street. They assayed our clothes, not our faces. My pouch still contains my compass, my flint, and the kindling tissue Abdul pressed into my hand, saying I could never be too prepared. Hidden in my tunic, Ruggiero's dagger still smacks of poison.

Morosini smiles weakly at me, like I'm his best friend in the world. He has no choice. I'm the hero of Trieste, and he needs me to save him.

"What do we do now?" He pulls out more strands of hair.

"Sleep."

"Who could possibly sleep?"

"A soldier. When death isn't at your throat, you sleep so you can fight if you're lucky enough to wake up."

I pace the floor like a pendulum. Morosini watches

me, a frightened cat. Soon, the moon will pass behind us and plunge the cell into blackness. No one has checked on us yet, meaning no one likely will until morning. Distant voices echo up the empty stairwell. They're eating, drinking, and rolling dice for anything from pennies to the wide world.

I piss in the cracked jug, then run my fingers along the thick doorframe. The Judas gate opens from the outside so they can look in. The door, secured with a crossbeam outside, opens with a key. We're locked in an empty storeroom, not a proper cell. That means there are others on this floor. If I'm lucky, there's even an armory.

Morosini whimpers, "Where are you? I can't see a thing."

"There's nothing to see."

If he shuts his mouth long enough, exhaustion will overwhelm him, and he will fall asleep. I sit on the floor opposite and wait.

As soon as his breathing lulls into shallow regularity, I slip off my tunic and boots and place them within easy reach. I find Abdul's twin packets of powder, the one to bring sleep and the other to banish it. I can't see them, but I remember exactly how I placed them. I slip the poison in my linen, ease off my leggings, rip one leg into strips, and tie them around my thighs. I unsheathe my dagger and lay it gingerly on my tunic. Sprawled on his back, Morosini wakes as soon as I slide beside him.

"What are you doing?"

"Helping you relax."

I massage his shoulders as Abdul taught me. As soon as the tension in his neck releases and he drowses, I pepper my palm with sleeping powder and bury his face in it. He goes limp without a struggle. My nose touches his cheek. I watch his eyes roll back in his head. His mouth opens, and his lips move, but he only drools, his head flopping. He's gone. I strip off his robe. He pissed his linens and tights, so I leave them on him and squeeze him into my tunic. He has breasts like a girl. I truss him and gag him with the strips tied around my thighs, and lay him face to the wall.

His robe hides my shoddy slippers. His velvet cap covers my eyes and half my face. I fasten his silver belt around my waist, tie on my pouch, and hang my dagger from it. Abdul's gifts come in as handy as he knew they would. I wrap hay with the flammable tissue, stuff it under the door, and strike the flint with the pommel of my dagger. The tissue bursts into flame and the hay creates more smoke than fire.

The guards carelessly left the Judas gate unlocked. I push it open and fan the smoke into the corridor, praying that someone notices before I go up in flames. Voices soon echo from the floor below:

"What the hell is that?"

"Smells like fire upstairs."

The second voice sounds more annoyed than alarmed.

"Go find out."

"You go."

"You're closer."

Laughter. Scuffling, perhaps shoving, then feet climb the stairs.

"Jesus Christ. What's going on in there?"

Another voice from below.

"Say what?"

The crossbar grates against the door. The key clanks in the lock. I hide behind the door with the piss jar in my hand. The jailer coughs from the smoke and stamps the flames with his feet. Thrusting his torch farther in, he sees Morosini's body.

"Hey! You over there. Are you dead or just stupid?"

As he advances, I break the piss pot over his head. He drops to the floor like dirty laundry. I dose him with sleeping powder and take his keys. Voices echoing from below reassure that the rest remain unconcerned downstairs. I grab the jailer's torch from the floor and bar the door behind me making certain to lock the Judas gate. Inching onto the landing, I count three other doors on this floor, arranged around the tower, open from roof to pit. The first door doesn't need a key; the room is empty. A second room contains ranks and files of barrels and jugs and sacks stacked haphazardly, leaving no room to move let alone store weapons.

A voice shouts from downstairs. "Ho! Fabrizio. Lost?"

"In your mother's cunt," I shout as gruffly as possible. Laughter echoes downstairs.

As I try to open the last door, the jailer's keys jangle too loudly. They all look alike. I notch the key I start with and work my way through as fast as I can. As ever, the last key opens the lock. I push the door open and thrust the torch inside.

Pikes. Halberds. Swords. Crossbows. Racks of them. I size them up quickly, grab two, cock and load them. I stuff bolts into a quiver and sling it over my shoulder.

Leaving the torch inside, I shut the door behind me. At the bottom of the stairs, a long rectangle of light bisects the landing with nobody in it.

"Go see what happened to that dumb cluck."

"Just be glad he ain't here. He's a fucking pain in the nuts."

Laughter.

"Nah. Go get him. I'm the one to answer for his pimply ass."

I press my back against the wall adjacent to the stairs, my crossbow raised, waiting.

Footsteps, heavy and irregular, maybe drunk, grow close. The guard emerges slowly, headfirst, then stomach, chest, and legs. I can't shoot until he clears the stairs lest he be thrown back down. I can't risk one stumble or scream. Death must be certain, swift, and silent.

Coming off the last stair, he fumbles for the torch that isn't there.

"What the hell..."

He looks straight at me without seeing me. My bolt pierces his chest. He gapes in shock and grabs the bolt to yank it out, which only makes him swoon. I've seen so many wounds like that. He'll probably live to lie about it. He slides down the wall to the floor, and I cock and reload the crossbow. Downstairs, the others are listening to a particular loudmouth, laughing and calling him out.

I hear them, but I can't see them. The familiar voice doing all the talking echoes from inside a cell. I ease down the stairs, a crossbow in each hand. On the last stair, I inch forward until I can see four men crowded in the light spilling from the open cell. One guard leans against the wall, another rolls dice on the floor, and another leans against the doorframe, laughing and egging the prisoner on.

"I swear on my father's honor, my mother was a princess of Byzantium. Her brother was crowned emperor at the age of eight."

The prisoner triggers uproarious laughter among the jailers but curdles my blood.

"If you're so fucking royal, what the hell are you doing here?"

"Highway robbery. They were Venetians, and I needed the money. Where's the harm in that?"

"But you're a Venetian..."

"A Venetian? Not only a Venetian. My great-grandfather was doge. I may be doge one day. Then won't you be sorry."

The jailers laugh their asses off.

The voice belongs to Ruggiero Gradenigo, my half-brother, my nemesis, supposedly dead after the Battle of Trieste, but not really. Later banished from Venice for trying to kill me while robbing me, he appears to have run afoul of the law in Padua as well. Ruggiero's mother was indeed a Byzantine princess, married off by her uncles at the age of ten to the noble Marcantonio Gradenigo, our father. The Byzantines, always on the lookout for influential Venetian nobles to keep in their pockets as pawns, considered him a good catch. They wed in Constantinople; he forced her to Venice, and locked her in his palace. She was plain, and his interest in females stopped as soon as they grew pubic hair. As soon as her brother was overthrown in a palace coup, she died mysteriously. Ruggiero claims she was murdered, like Donato's mother, by our father.

I single-handedly doomed our father's big plans for Ruggiero by helping Alex escape to sanctuary. Without her famous dowry, their plans became smoke and mirrors. I ruined Ruggiero's life. Worse than that, our father switched horses, reasoning that since I became the hero of Trieste, I would be a better prince than Ruggiero after their coup. He never bothered to ask me and remains absolutely convinced he will eventually turn me to his side. Since he abandoned Ruggiero, my mad half-brother lives only to kill me and win his father back. His dagger hangs from my waist with a surprise on its cutting edge.

Ruggiero harangues the jailers. "When Lord Francesco Carrara realizes who I am and what I can do for him, I'll be out of here before you can blink. I'll be your boss, and when I am, I'll crucify you in front of the Palace of Justice, every pig-screwing, shit-brained one of you, like Caesar did to the pirates who laughed at him."

That gives them a big laugh. I was the one who told Ruggiero the story.

"Laugh now, weep later," Ruggiero says. "Who wants to roll for the rest of your wine?"

With two crossbows, I can hit two of them—three if I'm lucky—until I have to reload. Not good enough. I prop the crossbows against the wall. I have a better plan.

Inside my pouch, in the third packet, I find the final dose of Abdul's poison. I break the wax seal and open it very, very carefully. Death turns on a slip of the finger. The veins of the parchment are pressed into the powder inside. A little makes a man stumble and fall, almost instantly paralyzed for hours. More kills him.

The powder crusts the dagger's blade like fine honey crystals. If I so much as break their skin, they will turn to stone. If I stab them, they will die. I can't sheath the dagger without losing too much of the poison, so I clamp the jeweled pommel in my armpit, the blade sticking out behind me. Gathering Morosini's robe around my ankles, I descend the stairs with the cocky assurance of a man who owns the world, like all Venetian nobles, even if they're so poor they peddle gossip for pocket change.

Stepping into the light, I startle them. Deceived by my robe, they take me for Morosini, a Venetian senator in expensive velvet.

"Everything that reprobate told you is a lie." I even sneer like a noble. Morosini is an easy target. I sound just like him, whiny and superior. Morosini's robe declares my importance, but they also know that no matter how important I am in Venice, here, I'm not as important as I think I am.

I approach slowly so they don't suspect I'm up to anything, keeping my eyes on Ruggiero, waiting for him to recognize me.

"Who dares call me a liar?"

"Lorenzo Morosini."

"Then who am I, according to you?"

"The lowest Gradenigo rat everyone thought dead."

Ruggiero blinks. Flinches. "You're not Lorenzo Morosini."

I turn to the guards. "Gentlemen, who am I?"

"How the hell should we know?" the guard says. "Ask Fabrizio."

Ruggiero fights to break out of his cell, but the guards

tackle him. He roars and tears at their hands. As they wrestle him to the ground, I slide closer. I nick three of them so lightly they don't notice, their hands full with Ruggiero, growling and kicking.

One of the guards falls to the floor. His mouth foams. Ruggiero watches, fascinated. The second one howls, grabs his throat, and collapses facedown on the cold stone, blood dribbling from his nose. Before the third guard can do anything, his eyes snap wide open, and his jaw clenches tight, shutting his mouth. His legs buckle, and he collapses, grabbing at me until his arms lock. Unable to scream, he gurgles like a dying chicken.

"They've been poisoned," I tell Ruggiero. I menace him with the dagger until he recognizes the jeweled pommel. This time I must kill him, not because I hate him, but because I know he's capable of anything. He wouldn't just hunt and kill Alex. Nothing that simple. He will torture her because he knows how much anguish that will inflict on me.

The last guard standing, the one I couldn't cut, tries shoving Ruggiero back into his cell. Ruggiero shakes him off like a dog and lunges at me. I raise the dagger high to slash, but the guard whacks my hand. The dagger clatters on the floor, and Ruggiero dives for it, but the guard blindsides him.

Chapter Twenty-Two

A Leap of Fate

AS THE GUARD grapples with Ruggiero, I snatch the dagger from the floor, shove it back into its sheath, and run. Using the jailer's last key, I open the oak door to the outside. Wind whips through the ramparts. I strip off Morosini's robe lest it turn into my shroud underwater, and hurl it over. The wind tumbles it down until it snags on a tree. With my leather pouch tucked under my family jewels, I tighten my drawers and jump onto the parapet.

I shut my eyes and hurl myself off in blind terror. Pulling my knees to my chest, I lock my arms around them and tumble head over heel into the rushing void. My back slams against water that shatters like ice, dirty, thick, and cold. I open my eyes and can't tell up from down. The water swirls with garbage. My body doesn't belong to me; the current owns it. Muffled thunder batters my ears. The void exhorts me to release my earthly burdens and yield to oblivion.

My jaw smacks against mud, and I taste the riverbed. I know which way is up. I dig my toes into the muck, push up, desperation propelling me to the surface before my lungs burst. The shock of air fills me with clarity. I'm alive. I'm free. I have obligations.

I float facedown like a dead man to the opposite bank. As my panic ebbs, pain energizes me. I don't know the time. I can't remember the last bell I heard. I try to look up, but the sky still spins madly. I'm winded and light-headed. Once the sky stands still, the stars shift into focus, then the moon, poised between the horns of the bull. First light is two hours away. In the darkness, no one can see me amid the reeds, but soon they will. I touch every part of my body to make sure I'm whole. Behind me, twenty guards clamor on the rampart; another ten with torches comb the bank along the base of the tower. A captain leans over the wall, shouting down.

"Find him yet?"

"Just the robe."

"He probably stuck to the bottom."

"The moon is pulling a heavy tide, and the current is strong. He could be clogging a mill halfway to Saint Anthony's by now."

"The old man will eat your balls raw for breakfast if you don't show him the body."

Upstream, a boat bobs against the bank. The current here runs away from the prison, toward the hermitage. I crawl through the reeds spitting mud and slime. The boat, twelve feet of rotting wood, is worthless except to haul my ass away. From the nearest house, about thirty feet back, dark and quiet, a dog barks as I grab onto the boat. Once. Twice. Loud. Three times. Louder. Someone shouts, "Shut your goddamn mouth, you mangy cur." A loud thud. The dog yelps and scampers.

I ease the boat into the river. As soon as she floats free, I hoist myself in and lie flat on the bottom so no one can see me. I inventory my pouch, toss the sodden packet of poison, open the packet that banishes sleep, and lick the inside on the chance enough remains to get me through the day. I fumble for my dagger, still in its sheath but certainly washed clean by the river. Leaning to starboard, I drift on the current, pushing off with the oar whenever I get stuck. Where the river angles north, well out of view of the tower, I stand and row. My body aches, but functions. I see no people, only shades hiding from sight, more frightened of me than I am of them. When the bell tower of the hermitage hoves into view, I tether the boat to the bank and hide my dagger under a stone. I stumble through a field of melons toward the cloister gate as the rising sun turns the ruins of the Roman arena pink. The bells ring Prime.

The beggars in Padua must be a very scurvy-looking lot because no one looks twice at me. I ring the bell and press my face against the Judas gate. It slides open, revealing tired brown eyes, milky and sad.

"I beg you, worthy brother, grant me sanctuary."

"Welcome, pilgrim." He cannot refuse, and even if he could, the bruises on my body scream for pity. The door swings open.

I step inside and, with bowed head, strip off the sorry remnants of my undergarments and stand naked before him. "I come like blessed St. Francis, having nothing, wanting nothing but sanctuary."

"We follow the rule of St. Augustine, but you're welcome here. Come inside before you catch your death like that. I am Brother Giuliano." His voice trails behind his coarse black robe. "First, you must wash. I'll get you something to wear."

I scrub the river bottom off my skin in a tub of water. Brother Giuliano returns with a coarse black robe and sandals. We go to the refectory as the friars file in. From the back, heads bowed, they all look alike. I scan their postures for Alex. It's time to get her out of Padua.

"Please," Brother Giuliano says, "share our humble meal."

Two rows of tables with benches fill the refectory, high and vaulted, the walls and ceiling covered with pictures from the life of St. Augustine. The friars carry their bowls from a serving table set crosswise at the head of the room, where two priors silently ladle porridge under a painting of manna falling from heaven. Everyone eats. No one speaks.

I pause at the serving table, able to see everyone on both sides of the room, aided by the fact that they are all looking at me. A fat prior raises his ladle and waits for Brother Giuliano's nod before serving me.

Alex sits at the far table near the cloister door.

At meal's end, I ask the brother next to me, "Who is that fellow fourth from the door? I think I know him..."

"Brother Ambrogio." He tries not to move his lips and checks to see if anyone sees him speak.

"What does Brother Ambrogio do here?"

"Shhhh. We can't speak."

"Where does he work?"

He scribbles on the table with his finger.

I whisper, "Scriptorium," and he nods.

After the meal, Brother Giuliano escorts me into the cloister.

"Might I see the scriptorium?" I ask.

"Is that where your inclinations lie?"

"Were I lucky enough to be a brother, that would be my calling."

"We are known more for our bookkeeping skills. We copy the ledgers of all the important bankers and merchants. The numbers must be copied correctly. Mistakes are very expensive."

Now that I'm clean and clothed and smiling like I'm interested, Brother Giuliano likes me much better.

"Our door is always open to men of faith with pure hearts."

"I fear my heart is not as pure as my faith."

"Few are," he says. "We all have crosses to bear."

In the scriptorium, the brothers wordlessly clean and arrange their knives and cut fresh nibs while a monitor fills their inkpots and hands out the day's ledgers to be copied, marked where to start and where to finish by day's end. I can't fathom how Alex endures it. She works alone in a niche with a narrow window, copying columns of numbers from a ship's log into a proper ledger.

"This is Ambrogio," Brother Giuliano whispers. He

nudges me closer to her work. "In the short time he's been here, he has become our fastest and most accurate scribe. He has talent; the others only have discipline."

I watch Alex, the boy I met on the beach before I knew he was a girl, now fully grown. Beautiful Alessandra has become fair Brother Ambrogio. Nothing dulls her luster. If I didn't know she was female, I'd assume she was a beautiful boy without question.

"I wish we could talk," I say. "I have a million questions about the work."

Alex questions Brother Giuliano with her eyes. He cogitates before speaking.

"It's highly irregular," he says. "We're not supposed to speak among ourselves, let alone to outsiders."

Just then, the porter comes looking for Brother Giuliano. Distracted, Brother Giuliano halts before leaving us and admonishes Alex. "Talk to him in the cloister for a minute or two, no more."

He leaves Alex and me sitting on a secluded bench under an olive tree.

"What happened to you?" She touches my bruises gingerly, on the verge of tears.

"It's a long story we don't have time for. I'm fine. We have to get you out of here."

"Maybe there is a God after all." She clutches my hand and steadies her breath. "Yes, we have to get the hell out here. The abbot who took me in was murdered. I heard rumors that Lord Carrara is appointing Brother Bernardo the new abbot."

"He can't. Brother Bernardo is a criminal, under ban in Venice, with warrants for his arrest."

"But he can. He has. So long as he lives under the rule, he is only subject to his abbot, and he will be his own abbot."

"Serenissimo won't tolerate it. But that's not all. Promise not to jump, or curse, or do something stupid. Don't do anything at all. Just listen."

She nods, squinting, her nostrils flaring.

"Ruggiero is alive."

The color drains from her face. She tenses, and I fear she'll snap like an overdrawn bowstring. Her eyelids twitch. She whispers through clenched teeth. "You swore he was dead."

"The Gradenigos have a way of dying without dying."

"You're certain?"

"Right now, he's locked in Carrara's tower, but I'd wager not for long."

She breathes erratically, squirming. "What were you doing in Carrara's tower?"

"Carrara kidnapped us from Borgoforte, but honestly, we don't have time now. How do we get out with no one knowing?"

Her eyes race in their sockets. She cracks her knuckles and pulls on her forelock like in the old days, thinking hard.

"I have a boat nearby," I say. "It's a piece of shit, but it will get us out of here. If we make it to Serenissimo's farm, we're safe."

"Where are you planning on taking me?"

"To Venice."

Again, her jaw clenches. The bowstring tightens to snapping. Her lips barely move. "Are you nuts? My father still searches high and low for me."

"You only need to be there long enough to get you out safely. There's no other way."

"Don't say that." She cracks a knuckle so hard I'm afraid she'll snap her finger off. "You want me to go back to the lion's den."

"You are in the lion's den. This may sound crazy to you, but Venice is the safest place to be, hidden in plain sight. Abdul will make sure."

She shakes her head in mute refusal.

"A hundred thousand people live in Venice. Your father sees a hundred people on an average day. A hundred more if he goes to his counting house. He rarely sees anyone else."

"He's got a private army searching for me."

"They're here, or in Ferrara, or Ravenna, or Ancona. They've given up on Venice."

Her eyes drift as if she catches a glimpse of something that could possibly lead her out of this terrible darkness. "I can do sums now. I can keep ledgers. I'm no swaggering swordsman, but I'm a damn convincing boy. I can sign on as a ship's clerk Beyond-the-Sea."

I shake my head, and she looks appalled. "Not yet," I say. "We're going to war. None of our merchant convoys will sail. Every man will be fighting Padua and Hungary."

"I can go to Ancona. Merchants there will travel anyway."

"First, we have to get out of here."

Chapter Twenty-Three

Beata of the Woods

BETWEEN THE FINAL night service and Matins, the hour before dawn, the monastery sleeps and silence reigns. Throbbing pain and the lingering effect of Abdul's waking powder vanquish my exhaustion to hold sleep at bay. While I lie motionless, my mind races, scanning maps and exploring escape routes. I keep one eye fixed on the high window opposite my cot. As soon as Cygnus hangs over the monastery tower, I tiptoe to meet Alex at the kitchen gate leading to the river. Alex digs up her belongings, which she buried before presenting herself to the abbot and surrendering her worldly possessions.

We stumble across the tangled vines to the dock only to find my boat gone, stolen or swept away by the current.

But my dagger is still where I stashed it. We cross a dangerously neglected Roman bridge to an east-running cart trail and follow it until it veers south, forcing us to set out across the hills and marshes with only the rapidly fading stars to guide us. At dawn, monstrous thunderheads flood the sky, plunging us into utter darkness. We pause until our eyes adjust and run for cover as hail explodes, bloodying our hands and cheeks before we reach the shelter of a haystack veiled in diamonds. We huddle together the way we did when Alex's father raged uncontrollably or my mother temporarily lost her mind. Shivering and hungry, I know I shouldn't, but I speak anyway.

"You'd be safe if you had stayed with the Poor Clares like you were supposed to."

"Nobody is safe anywhere. You should know that better than anyone."

"You know what I mean. What were you thinking?"

"With the Clares, I would spin and weave and sew. Women's work. With luck, I could illuminate a psalm. But the abbess thought I was a boy and directed me to the hermitage, where I would copy ledgers, logs, and account books—things I need to know to survive Beyond-the-Sea. Which would you have chosen?"

"That's not the point. We will find you a safe escape from Venice. We promised. But you should have stayed with the Clares until we do."

"But I didn't. Now look what I know."

"Look where that got us."

"Stop it. I'm better prepared, and here we are, free together."

"You're free. I'm still a prisoner of the palace, and

what's worse, I'm starving."

"I could eat an ox. Let's go."

The hail begins melting as the morning sun grows warm. We set out almost due east across the convoluted landscape toward Venice, over hills, fording streams, slogging through marshes. I offer to take Alex's sack, but she insists on carrying it until we grow so exhausted we drop, heads throbbing, muscles aching, and stomachs growling.

"Look," Alex says. "Above those trees."

A thin plume of smoke curls above a cluster of bare persimmon trees. We creep toward a fire burning beyond the trees. The flames dance, but nothing else moves. We edge closer until Alex grabs my arm to stop me, nodding toward a shadowy figure silently watching us.

Tangled red hair like skeins of uncombed wool hides the face of a spectral woman thin as an arrow, a trick of light and shadow, her eyes ablaze with refined fire. More fantastical than malign, she approaches slowly.

"Don't be frightened," she says. "I am Beata of the woods. I live within."

Alex advances to meet her. "Is this your grove?"

"Oh, no. This grove was old long before the Lord planted me here."

She wears the threadbare habit of a recluse, a female hermit. With neither monastery nor convent to anchor them, the church frowns on solitary recluses. Occasionally, they burn one for witchcraft. Whatever she is, Alex and I must eat. Circumstance throws us on her mercy.

"We are humble friars on our way to Sant'Ilario," I say. "We lost our way in the storm."

"You look half dead. When did you eat last?"

"Two days ago."

She takes us by the hand and tiptoes through the trees to a shelter of bark and reeds blending into the landscape.

"I only have gruel and water to offer. And these, of course..."

She proffers a basket of wrinkled red persimmons, skins split and oozing sweet sticky pulp. As we devour the persimmons and gruel, Beata murmurs softly. "I was born near the village of Sambruson forty-seven years ago, and I've been a recluse since the Great Death. Some call me a saint; some call me a witch. Some call me mad, and some come to witness my visions."

Alex listens quietly, open and unsuspecting, unlike me, with my perpetual skepticism. I see only how deeply we are in trouble while Alex sees a fascinating opportunity and endless possibilities. She needs to pull her head out of the stars like I need to get mine out of my ass.

Alex draws closer to Beata. "When did you start having visions?"

"When I was six, I fell down shaking in every limb. My family feared I was possessed. When the fit passed, I wept out of fear of another one, and when it came, I writhed on the ground and foamed at the mouth. I almost bit my tongue off. When it ended, I felt like I had been beaten to death by clubs. I could scarcely breathe. My parents took me to the Sisters of Sant'Ambrogio and begged them to save me. They fed and sheltered me until I had my first ecstasy when I was ten, banishing all my agony. With eyes wide open, I saw legions of burning angels fill the sky like a great sunflower. In the golden center, an unimaginably beautiful face radiated love and forgiveness. Our Lord's mother, the Blessed Queen of Heaven, beckoned me. She slipped a golden ring on my finger, filling me with bliss, and told me my cup would overflow with divine ecstasy.'"

"Does it?"

"It does, now and again. After the first vision, I begged to live in solitude, but they said I was too young. So I lived with seven sisters, a life of penitence, fasting, and prayer, all of us bound by the mystical golden ring. My sisters all died in the Great Death along with my family, leaving me an orphan and a recluse, alone at last with my God."

When Beata's eyes close, I nudge Alex's foot and make crazy eyes. Alex shakes her head, her brows knit, and her eyes implore me to be merciful and kind, which is like asking a lion to eat figs. Alex listens raptly, but I can't. My nerves tingle with danger signals urging my body to flee.

"What do you see in your visions now?" Alex asks.

"God overflows me," Beata says with a weary sigh. "I see everything. What do you want to know?"

Alex's lips and hands start to tremble. She shakes her head. "I don't know..."

"I can't give you an answer until you do."

Sated on persimmons and gruel, we fall to silence until Beata opens the flap of her hut.

"Come," she says. She mounts the torch on a tripod of striplings. The interior walls weep where a plume of steam curls up from inside the earth through a crack in the floor. Beata stands over the crack breathing the vapors. "Ask me now while I can still hear you."

Uneasy, I press my hood over my nose and mouth so I don't breathe the vapors. Standing near Beata, Alex breathes deeply.

"Come on, Alex," I say. "We must go now."

She shakes her head. "Nothing bad is going to happen. Sit down. We'll be on our way soon enough."

Beata hands Alex a twig as thick as her index finger and twice as long. "If I fall, there will be no prophesy. Wedge that in my mouth so I don't bite off my tongue. If I remain standing, listen carefully. Now your question, quickly."

"Don't, Alex. Let's go."

"Your question," Beata shouts. "Now!"

"Will I ever live as I choose?"

Beata twists, screams, and grabs her stomach.

"Alex, look what you've done. Take it back."

Alex ignores me, watching Beata's eyes roll back into her head, eyelids pulsating, fingers trembling as if a demon were throttling her. Her head whips around like a Medusa with snakes for hair. She stumbles but catches herself and doesn't fall. Her ashen face twists, her tongue thick and leaden.

"I...cannot...answer." Beata groans like a birthing mother.

"Why not?"

"He won't let me." She points to me.

Alex takes my hands, pleading. "Why won't you let her?"

"I'm not stopping her, but I don't believe her."

"How can you doubt her?"

I know there's no end to it if I don't agree, and I can never refuse Alex anything. "Answer her, Beata."

A wraith of vapor beads Beata with iridescent pearls. Her hands flutter like startled birds. She opens her eyes. "There! See? There. And there. Angels of heaven with lightning spears."

Beata spins like a top running down, fluttering her arms as if the air around her were on fire. "Lightning from the north lights the horizon ablaze. Demons with burning spears flood the land. Hear the roar of their wings. So many wings. Warriors robed in blood and sun massing for battle."

She stops, overwhelmed by something we cannot see. Covering her ears with her hands, she crouches low. "No. Stop. Please. You're breaking my ears."

She rocks back and forth, hands pressed to her head, eyes darting everywhere, mouth agape as her anguish crests and breaks like a wave. Gazing outward to nowhere, she stands tall and raises her palms to shield her from an invisible splendor, her eyes brimming with ecstasy. Her form, no longer old and wretched, radiates grace and supple power. She smiles radiantly.

"The future is no mystery to me," Beata says in a different voice altogether. "Knowledge is the cross I bear. Do you dare know the truth? If not, be gone quickly, for vision is rising from the earth and descending from the pinnacle of heaven."

"Speak, Beata," Alex says.

"Daughter of Saturn, beware wily Venus trining Neptune, stinging with a toxin more dangerous than Cupid's dart, igniting a raging flame of war devouring the sails of a thousand battling ships lashed together to prevent their flight. Your sun rises in the eastern shore; you flourish among enemies, far from treacherous countrymen. As the celestial orb rises westward, bringing you what you most desire, it also sets, vanishing into darkness where your enemies conspire and danger dogs your days. Knowing what you never knew before, before you die you will extinguish an even greater fire."

Beata whirls about, fastening her eyes on me. "Beware the second conflagration, when enemies encircle you, and their armies outnumber you. Only love can sustain you. You alone bring glory."

She sags, weary to death, onto her stool. "What love gives, fortune takes. What fortune takes, love restores..." She sinks back into shadow. "Waste no more time. Go now and do what must be done."

Chapter Twenty-Four

War

SERENISSIMO, GAUNT AND shaken, shatters protocol and clasps me to his chest. He sprinkles me with tears and kisses me gently on the forehead. "Thank our ever-beneficent Lord in heaven on high for your safety," he says. "Since that maniac kidnapped you, I've been kicking myself in the ass for stupidly thrusting you in harm's way."

"You couldn't have imagined such an outrage, Exalted Serenity. No one could have. What about Donato? And General Giustinian?"

"They're both safe in Treviso by the grace of our loving God."

"Do they know I'm back?"

"I dispatched a messenger as soon as I found out."

He quickly composes himself and herds me into his study where Marino waits impatiently. "Now tell me everything," Serenissimo says. "And I mean, everything."

I hit the highlights up to and including our imprisonment in Padua and my escape, only leaving out my detour to rescue Alex, now safely in Abdul's care.

"You look like you were run over by rampaging bulls," Serenissimo says, angry and pained at my suffering.

"I jumped forty feet from the parapet of Ezzelino's tower into the river, and I didn't go in headfirst."

"A few bruises, no broken bones..." He crosses himself. "The price of heroism."

"What did Carrara do to Morosini?"

"Nothing."

"He didn't torture him?"

"No, but he certainly rattled his cage. Your escape expedited Morosini's return. Carrara was shitting himself that he'd have to answer to the pope for your untimely death, so he tossed the other hot potato back in our laps. Morosini recovers at home, though much the worse for wear. They say he looks like a ghost."

"Speaking of the devil," Marino says, "he awaits us along with the rest of our nobles."

We proceed to the Great Council chamber, where I do what I always do for important votes: Keep the nobles honest and tally the results. Of the nobles, 956 show up, with 37 no-shows, duly noted, to be accounted for later.

Giustinian delivers the official account of the outrage in Padua, igniting a shouting match between the warriors and diplomats of the Great Council. Pantaleone Barbo stands to quiet the noise and addresses the nobles.

"A great many speeches have been given here of late," Barbo says. "Speeches concerning the crimes Lord Francesco Carrara commits daily in his undeclared war and how we should respond. We are Venetian nobles, schooled in the art of government and the practice of diplomacy. So tell me, gentlemen, how is it that even if we had set out to fail, we could not have befouled ourselves so completely? Carrara's murderers rampage freely on terrafirma because we egregiously neglect our duty. I say to every noble in this room without exception, if you want to end the terror of Francesco Carrara, fill your empty words with noble deeds. We must secure our territory and defend our people, our homes, our sacred churches, our family tables."

"And our salt," a second-tier senator shouts, his family major salt dealers. The ensuing laughter breaks the tension of Barbo's withering condemnation.

"Here's something worse than stealing our salt," Barbo says. "Secrets vital to our survival are being passed by one of our own, a noble of Venice, to Francesco Carrara."

Barbo triggers a tumult of accusations and denials and continues shouting over the discordant voices. "We know this, yet it goes on." Guilt and recrimination subdue the tumult. "The greatest patriots in this room once before warred against the unholy alliance of Francesco Carrara and the king of Hungary, with whom we have agreed to a so-called truce, myself included, yielding to the self-interest of our neighbors and the pope. We now, one and all, understand that Francesco Carrara will commit any atrocity, and we are complicit unless we stop him. If he destroys us, we have only ourselves to blame. We pay religious attention to our galleys, inspect them, repair them, test them, make them ready for anything the sea might throw at them. We don't debate; we *do*. We must handle Carrara with the same resolve. Yet here we are again, hiding behind diplomacy to avoid our duty. The time has come to shoulder up to our responsibilities or be destroyed."

Lorenzo Morosini, a ruin of a man in a splendid velvet robe, rises unsteadily, treading the knife's edge of suspicion and terror. Whatever Lord Carrara may have told him remains between Morosini and God, but from the looks of things, it was nothing good. With important nobles already suspecting him of treason, he can't afford to hand the Ten more rope to hang him with, nor does he want Lord Carrara to send an assassin after him.

"How are we to pay for a land war?" he asks, a comment worthy of a weak senator, not to the point, not hostile toward the enemy.

"The way we always do," Bruno Badoer snarls. The nobles laugh because they know exactly what *the way we always do* means: every man, woman, and child, noble and common, squeezed for money and work like grapes in a press to gain nothing but ravaged territory, smoking ruins, and mountains of bodies.

Morosini sinks into ignominy. "The Great Death of 1348 took half our people. We have scarcely recovered the manpower we lost. We lack experienced land soldiers. Our ability to feed and defend ourselves depends on trade which war entirely disrupts."

Bruno Badoer shakes his formidable fist at Morosini

and shouts to the back benches. "Don't let the merchants scare you. They only care about their fortunes. Any noble with the Republic at heart knows we must alert Louis the Great that he'll have no more victories at our expense. We're Venetians. We do what we must. Whatever it costs, it's a small price to pay for ridding ourselves of Francesco Carrara."

Huge shouts and cheers greet him, and if he weren't so fat, he'd be carried on his allies' shoulders. War vanquishes the appeasers. Hating war as he does, Serenissimo still sides with his erstwhile adversaries to stop the enemy at all costs. Forbidden by his oath to openly advocate for war, he bites his tongue, beaming silent approbation at the warriors.

Morosini answers Badoer with a question. "Are you suggesting we hire a mercenary army?"

"The best money can buy."

"Have you forgotten the desperate warning of our poet laureate Francesco Petrarch that we must abjure hiring foreign mercenaries at the risk of losing our souls?"

"He should stick to his verses and leave war to the generals." Cheers erupt again around Badoer. "Our lovesick little poet bellies up to every tyrant in Italy, praising them to their faces and ridiculing them behind their backs. Fuck Petrarch."

"The question is not whether Petrarch is as good a statesman as poet," Morosini says, "but whether we empty our treasury to buy an undependable army to go to war against a more powerful enemy, a war which we are bound to lose at the risk of our immortal souls. You are overreaching, sir. We cannot win against the combined armies of Padua, Hungary, and Austria."

"That's why we're hiring mercenaries. We could march every Venetian from fourteen to eighty onto the field of battle, round up every farmer and shepherd and oarsman, and end up with nothing but a gang of green boys and old geezers with pitchforks for lances. We need soldiers who win battles."

"For how much?" Morosini drops the question like a gauntlet.

"One hundred thousand ducats."

"For how long?"

"For the three months it will take to decimate Carrara."

"Has this already been discussed?"

"Discussed and decided."

"Without putting it to a vote in the Great Council?"

"If you have a problem, take it up with the Ten."

Precisely what Morosini doesn't dare to do.

We proceed with the vote. The draped ballot box has been loaded with gold ballots on one side and silver ballots on the other, accessed by a single opening. Each noble selects in secret and deposits his ballot in the hidden urn. When they have all voted, I count the ballots. Yes votes have 689 against 262 noes. We are at war. The Great Council erupts in turmoil, and their agitation spreads onto the square, quickened by the blare of trumpets, the beating of drums, and the clanging of bells.

"Before you disappear again," Serenissimo says, "we must pray for a favorable outcome."

Kneeling in the silence of the Evangelist's crypt, Serenissimo says, "War makes strange bedfellows. Bruno

Badoer, a pain-in-the-ass blowhard at the best of times, is the man you want beside you at war. Lorenzo Morosini, a genius at making money and manipulating foreign markets, a cornerstone of our maritime dominance, invaluable in peace, is our enemy at war. I only know we dare not lose."

"We won't because we can't."

"Never forget; tomorrow we repay what we spent today. It's not our money, and it's not limitless. If we don't win quickly, it will be our downfall."

"I agree wholeheartedly—" Knowing how angry he can become, but unable to put it off any longer, I need to tell him about Brother Bernardo, but he cuts me off.

"No more," he says. "These old bones are too weary to listen to another word. I need to lie abed and count sheep. You should, too, lest palace life wear you down to a useless stub before your time. Go. Unwind. Do whatever you do to make the world go away."

Fiercely true to my vow to Donato, whenever a window of opportunity opens, no matter how tired or preoccupied I find myself, I exercise in the palace courtyard. Perpetually littered with piles of bricks and pieces of marble and lumber from the endless rebuilding, the yard provides all the tools I need. I strengthen my arms with a brick in each hand, raising and lowering them twenty times, then two bricks in each hand, and lastly three, roped together so I can grip them. When my arms rebel, I set the bricks aside. In the stonemasons' corner, I rope a marble capital of some forty pounds to my back and climb from the courtyard to the top portico, 107 stairs each way. So weary I could cry, wounded and frustrated, I barely make it to the top before my legs give out. Usually, I go up and down twice before collapsing on the bottom stair and crawl to bed, consoling myself all the way that my sword feels lighter by half and I can wield it twice as long.

A guard emerges from the shadows of the portico where he has been watching me with some curiosity. "If you want to really make yourself cry," he says, "do this a hundred times." He drops to the ground, poised on his toes and his palms, lowers his chest to the ground, pushes himself up with his arms, and then repeats it a dozen times before collapsing. "The Romans called it Constantine's Lever. The legions had to do a hundred before breakfast. Guaranteed to fuck you up."

"Next time," I say. "I'm done for tonight."

I sit on the edge of my bed, limbs aching and leaden, my mind still tied in knots that repel sleep. The painting on the wall opposite my bed, the work of one of Guariento's students with a daringly realistic approach to the human body, depicts a magnificent sailor pulling a great galley from the lagoon, a votive offering to the Virgin. Her radiance gilds his exquisitely articulated body, and he arouses me, not for the first time. I fumble with my trousers and take myself in hand and drink in the sweetness of his down-turning eyes and the magnificence of his form. I know this indulgence will unravel my knots and yield, the solitary pleasure feeling so blessed I cannot stop.

"So that's what you do when I'm away."

With the shock of a bombard, Donato leaps into the room from my high window and lands beside me, having scaled St. Mark's and tiptoed through the domes to reach me undetected. He ogles the painted sailor critically. "You might at least paint him brown. I wouldn't mind so much."

Caught in flagrante, I flush with shame and have no reply.

"Don't mind me," Donato says. "Carry on. I merely came to find out what the fuck happened in Ezzelino's tower and how you managed to escape."

"Ruggiero was also in Carrara's prison, probably not for long."

"Did he see you?"

"He tried to kill me. I had to jump into the river from the tower to escape."

"I'd love to hear the details, but that can wait. I interrupted you..."

"Fuck you, Donato. I didn't know you were coming..." I sputter against the futility of any excuse.

"Had I been in your shoes, I would have known," he says, "and here I am, at your disposal, unless you prefer him..."

I fall on my knees and cover his legs with kisses, stripping off his gear and throwing it aside. He grabs me under the shoulders, lifts me to my feet, and undresses me, paying careful attention to my bruises, softly kissing them before lifting me gently onto the bed.

"I'm afraid I'll hurt you," he says.

"I look a lot worse than I feel. Do your best and see if I flinch."

Soon our sweat glistens as we tangle. Donato proceeds with extreme caution until I wrestle him under me and ride him, a magnificently shiny stallion, rising and falling, galloping through a landscape of ecstatic sensations, wave after wave, until our tide ebbs, leaving us satiated and inert.

"I love you so much," I say.

"I'm beginning to believe you."

Idly stroking Donato's back, I say, "It must be hard for you, alone in such close quarters with so many men. I've seen them. I might even call some of them irresistible."

"No one compares with you."

"*Love flows toward absent lovers*. Sextus Propertius. *Elegies*, Book 2. *Semper in absentes felicior aestus amantes*. But imagine if we weren't forced to live apart. In Ezzelino's tower, the thought of never seeing you again was worse than plunging forty feet into a very dirty river. In an instant, I saw an entire lifetime lived together like the monks of Brotherly Love, bound by vows and never apart, free to love each other endlessly."

"Men like us are never free of this world," Donato says. "We weren't minted to be humble friars. Our destiny is to protect others so they can live their ordinary lives free of tyranny. It's what we're good at. It's who we are. We have to be content with a few happy hours in a safe harbor."

"And that's all we'll ever have?"

"It's all anyone ever has, but most of them don't realize it. For better or worse, we are called to a higher purpose beyond counting our daily profit, fucking our wives, and beating our dogs and children. When Carrara and Hungary attack Venice, could you turn your back and hide in my arms in some sweetly scented cell? No, my love. You will rush to her defense and die if necessary to save what is good in the world. That is our honor and our doom."

"I will never lose you, Donato. I will grapple Death for you."

He ruffles my hair. "That's why I love you so. You're quite mad, you know."

When sunlight stripes the wall, Donato rubs the unshaven stubble on his chin, polishes my buckler with his shirt, and gazes at his reflection. He enjoys looking at himself, practicing his smile, lowering his eyelids, and turning his profile. I avoid mirrors.

"How can you shave without looking?" he asks. "Does your radiance blind you?"

"Remarks about my appearance always sound like lies. Marino does it all the time."

"Marino is quite smitten with you, my love."

"Don't be stupid. What I'm saying is that I don't see whatever they see. I see imperfections, big nose, crude lips, unruly teeth."

"Ah, I understand. You're totally fucking blind."

I twist the ring he placed on my finger in the necropolis of Savaria. "Serenissimo asked me about this ring. I told him everything except what it means."

"Don't you trust him?"

"In all things but one. He can fuss like a nursemaid, worrying about the wrong things. He knows about Astolfo. Everything. But he made it clear he doesn't want to know any more details, only that I'm happy."

Donato pulls me back onto the bed and wraps himself around me. "Do you know what you are?" He twirls a lock of my hair around his finger.

"Besides being me?"

"Besides being whatever it is you think you are. You don't know your own best quality. It's not that you're heartbreakingly beautiful—because you are. Or too smart by half, or challenging, where you break all records. None of those. You are beguiling. It's the only word. And that's why, every time I see you, I forgive everything to kiss you."

He squeezes me tight against his body, his chin resting on my head. "What do you know of the Battle of Tours?"

"Nothing."

"It's one of the most important battles ever fought. Had it not been for Charles Martel, king of the Franks, the Moslems would have overrun all of western Europe. They rode north from their capital in Andalusia, across the Pyrenees, and savaged their way through Aquitaine on their way to Tours, where the line was drawn. At a certain distance from its base, an army exceeds the limits of its supply line and lives off the land, burning everything behind them so no else can have it. Caesar did it. Attila did it. We still do it.

"As they approached Tours, the Moslem supply wagons were crammed with loot. While looting and burning, they never considered the possibility of retreat. After all, they were the invincible army of Allah, and they outnumbered Martel three to one. The Moslem cavalry was peerless, the best horses and the best men wielding deadly razor swords and deadly accurate bows. Their general, Abdul Rahman, scoffed at Martel's armed phalanx, which Martel had drilled to Roman-style discipline. While the overconfident Moslems were busy sacking Tours Cathedral, Martel seized the high ground for his phalanx and concealed his meagre cavalry in the trees. Abdul Rahman charged, and the phalanx repelled them in a grueling daylong battle. The same outcome was repeated each day for a week. On the last day, Martel secretly dispatched his cavalry behind the enemy lines to set fire to their supply train while they battled the phalanx. When the Moslems saw the smoke, half of them bolted to save their booty. The rest were slaughtered. Abdul Rahman died that day, and his army scattered."

"That's great, but what I want to know is, after the war, how can we be together?"

"The war is never over. Peace is nothing but a breather between clashes. Can you remember a time when there wasn't a war?"

"No, but I'm only nineteen."

"I'm twenty-nine, and we've always been at war or preparing for another. Serenissimo is seventy-four, and I'm sure he'll tell you the same thing. Ask the dead, and they won't disagree. You and I must find ways to be together for as long as we can. When we're apart, we savor those memories until we're together again."

The bells ring Lauds, and Donato bolts from my bed, throws on his gear, and leaps for the window ledge. Hanging by his fingers, he turns back.

"Remember two things from the Battle of Tours—always stake the high ground and never exceed your supply lines."

Chapter Twenty-Five

A Love Letter

WE SMELL IT before we see it.

Watchmen atop St. Mark's Tower see the fire at Santi Apostoli first, across the Grand Canal from the Rialto markets. The Lord of the Night dispatches runners who report Marino Faliero's abandoned palace up in flames. Neighborhood captains activate bucket brigades to fight the fire. Peacekeepers manage the churning crowds. Venetians fear fire above all things except plague. The restless anxiety fueled by impending war can easily whip any fear into a rampage until the arms of the Republic put it down. Standing next to me on the palace roof without his golden robe, Serenissimo faces the fire as a citizen, not as doge. He would be on a bucket brigade, but his oath forbids it.

"Do you suppose it's a sign?" he asks. "The old tyrant's palace going up in flames..."

"I've never been good at interpreting signs, sire. That is your gift."

"You think I'm an old fool who believes in ghosts, but I have lived long enough to accept that signs exist even if I don't always interpret them properly."

"I hardly think you're a fool. I just lack your talent for recognizing signs. Gifts are not distributed equally. Sometimes they even go to the wrong people. My father is cunning beyond all measure, and we all wish he wasn't."

"I know this fire is a sign," Serenissimo says, "because it follows closely upon a disturbing dream."

"What was the dream?"

"Marino Faliero visited me, clutching his severed head in his right hand. 'Remember,' he said, 'I was a member of the Ten at the age of thirty-eight, a successful politician and a victorious general. I married a doge's daughter, and when we took Treviso, I was the first governor. Following that, I was governor of Padua twice, knighted by the Holy Roman Emperor along with Francesco Carrara and Lodovico Forzatè. I wore my silver spurs when I fought King Louis of Hungary. We lost Dalmatia; we kept Treviso, and booted Louis out of terrafirma. But I needn't remind you; you were there...'

"I asked why he had come. 'To release you from guilt,' he said. 'I forgive you for condemning me to death. I plotted to murder our nobles and rule as a tyrant. I was discovered and judged by the men I tried to murder. I confessed my guilt and accepted my death sentence. Had my conspiracy succeeded, not one of my judges would have lived to condemn me. To the victor go the spoils.'

"He brandished his severed head, the mouth doing the talking. 'This is the result of failure, not of being wrong. No matter how just his cause, the loser is always wrong. I lost, I confessed, I was beheaded. My name lives in infamy, my face covered with a black shroud for all time. Now it's your turn. Win, old friend, or share my infamy.' As he disappeared, he whispered, '*Memento mori.*' You, too, must die."

Marino Vendramin has been nervously nearby, waiting for Serenissimo to finish. He gives me our secret sign, meaning he wants a private word with me. The lords of the night return with a new report to Serenissimo, and I take my leave.

"Greetings, hero of Trieste," Marino says. His avuncular smile hangs off his mouth like a frown.

"I'm just a guttersnipe from St. Nicholas of the Beggars."

"Such sublime modesty, still. I heard the terrible news about Ruggiero Gradenigo."

"That he's in Padua?"

"That he is a traitor."

"A casualty of war," I say, alluding to my father, not Trieste.

"Aren't we all?" Marino takes me literally.

"You've never been in battle, Marino."

"Surely you jest. Every day in the palace is a battle. But combat in the field? Never."

"Then you can't imagine it. If you had been, you'd never forget."

"Alas, war has turned even my beautiful bright-eyed boy into a cynic."

"Let's just say it opened my eyes."

Marino looks genuinely sad. "I'm sorry to hear that. Carefree boyhood is so fleeting."

"I was never carefree."

"No, you were not."

He looks around as he speaks. When no other eyes are upon us, he whispers in my ear, covering his mouth with his hand. "Take this." He slips a letter from his sleeve into my hand so deftly no one could possibly notice. "I don't know who it's from," he says, "or what's in it. I never gave it to you. Don't read it where anyone else can see it, and destroy it immediately."

"Another love note from Ruggiero?"

"Worse, I fear..." He shakes his head as he descends from the palace roof.

I examine the wax seal. Unbroken. Points for Marino unless he found a way to break and reseal it. No mark appears on the paper aside from the intact seal, which I study until its mark reveals itself. Three dolphins. My stomach turns. The erstwhile emblem of the doomed house of Gradenigo, now broken into antagonistic factions. Tearing it open, I stare at the handwriting before I grasp the words.

> *Please don't be frightened. I have wronged you, much to my regret. Speak with me this once. You are my son. Find me upstairs Thursday next at Vespers at the Mermaid Tavern. I await you. Your repentant father, Marcantonio Gradenigo.*

I race to warn my mother and Alex that Brother Bernardo is in Venice to menace us. I run to St. Nick's the way Mama used to run, arriving sweaty and winded, beating on her door, startling her.

"Nico. I never know where you are these days."

"I'm here to warn you."

Upon my return from Trieste, I confronted her with the truth of my father, the nexus of all her lies. She refuses to accept he's alive because she desperately needs him to be dead. Instead, she shot the messenger, turning cold, distant, and distrustful of me ever since.

We argue, as usual, and she refuses to listen.

"Sometimes," I say, "what you don't know *will* hurt you." I feel helpless to tear away the web of lies she spins to shield herself from an unacceptable truth. And I have never been able to shake her conviction that the Virgin miraculously protects her. She responds as if I said nothing.

"Why don't you wear your beautiful uniform anymore? You look so handsome in it."

"I saw both Ruggiero and my father in Padua, with my own eyes."

She shakes her head wordlessly. She knows when it comes to the Gradenigos, anything is possible. "Ruggiero." She spits out the open window. "He's nothing to me."

"We are in danger."

"He wouldn't dare show himself in Venice."

"Listen to me. Please, stay somewhere else. Hide until the war is over."

"Giasone can protect me."

I don't trust Giasone, her feckless husband, who

married her for the money she'd get when I was selected ballot boy. "I'm worried about you, Mama. This war is flushing the rats from all the gutters."

"War? Boh. That's nothing but a rumor."

"As of this morning, it's fact."

"What if it is? Giasone says war is good; it means more work building galleys."

"It's not that kind of war. We won't need galleys. It's a land war, the kind we can't win."

Her mask slips. She may be crazy, but she's smart. She grasps the gravity of what I am saying. "I must pray to the Virgin," she says, turning to her handmade altar and falling to her knees before the Virgin. Since the Virgin saw fit to make me ballot boy, Mama's belief in their special bond waxes stronger than ever.

War is too big, too impersonal for her to parse. She thinks only of herself. Her gestures, the way she twists and untwists her curls around her fingers, unaware she's doing it, her eyes focusing in the middle distance, her mouth pouting, the mouth of a beautiful woman abused by life— she fashions herself thus, donning a veil of indifference concealing her flirtatious smile. The parish still regards her as beautiful but pathetic, and she guards that not a single soul knows what really goes on inside her head. Only the Virgin knows, and I pity her the task of transforming the world, miracle by miracle, to my mother's measure.

"My father sent me a letter." I hold it out to her.

"You read it," she says. "My eyes are tired."

She still has not learned to read. I recite the note from memory, and she raises her hands in supplication.

"Promise me you won't go, my beautiful, beloved boy." Her icy reserve shatters, and she becomes the mother who loves me too much.

"I must go."

"Please, please, my darling son." Her reserve dissolves in a mother's desperate tears, like St. Augustine's mother painted on the hermitage wall. She covers my hands with kisses. "In the name of our Lord and Savior Jesus Christ and of his Holy Mother, the Blessed Queen of Heaven, I beg you do not go."

"Look at me, Mama." She raises her eyes, and I show her my ring. "I dare Marcantonio Gradenigo to harm me. I'm no longer a know-nothing snot-nosed bastard from St. Nick's. If he touches a hair on my head, the doge will dog him down and kill him slowly. He knows that."

"That doesn't stop men like him," she says.

"Men change."

Her laugh could turn sweet wine to vinegar. "Maybe men get better. Monsters only get worse."

Knowing she has lost, she dries her tears and goes to the chest beside her bed, where she keeps her valuables and secrets. She hands me a psalter from under a mirror, a candlestick, a painted Virgin torn from the sail of a boat, and the pouch of gold coins she receives each month from the state treasury as compensation for robbing her of her son, all so familiar I stopped noticing them years ago.

"Take this from your mother, who loves you, and use it."

I take it and turn to leave.

"Not so fast." She tugs me back. "Open it first." She hands me a tiny key for the lock embedded in the leather coverboard. I turn the key, hear a tiny click, and the coverboard springs open. In a hole cut into the pages, a mercy-maker lies in a vellum coffin, a blade of the hardest steel, thin as a garment pin hammered flat, with a palm-sized pommel to push it in deep.

"This was to protect me from men like him." She presses a fingernail between two of my ribs. "Right there. Stick it between the bones. He'll drop dead before you can say *Hail Mary*."

Chapter Twenty-Six

Hail and Farewell

ALEX PACES ABDUL'S rooms above the apothecary shop. The apothecary bought Abdul at the Rialto slave market because the slave trader bragged he came from nine generations of Alexandrian druggists. The apothecary assumed the slave trader was exaggerating, bargained hard, but still paid a lot. He soon realized the extent of Abdul's genius and began treating him very well, short of setting him free. He promises to do that when Abdul pays back what he cost him. For reasons known only to himself, Abdul is in no hurry.

"Calm yourself," Abdul says.

Alex cuts him with a glance. "Don't you understand? I can't stand being here another instant."

"When the monks ring Sext, we'll leave," I say. "You can't show up at Cavarzere before the pilgrims arrive from Padua. You just have to wait."

She kicks the leather pilgrim's sack stuffed with her gear. "I can't wait to be free of my father. Free of my mother. Free of Ruggiero Gradenigo and his evil father. Free of this slavery."

"I am a slave," Abdul says. "You are free."

"I am a slave until I am free of Venice."

"And you're almost there," I say.

Abdul takes her hands and looks lovingly into her eyes. "How many times must I reassure you? The path is clear. Your superior intelligence can solve any problems that arise along the way. You need only follow the steps we have laid out. Have you packed everything you need?"

She kicks the pile of gear next to the leather sack: a capacious, coarse pilgrim's robe; a floppy-brimmed pilgrim's hat; a veil to conceal her face as necessary.

"Open the sack," Abdul says.

Alex complies, and Abdul inventories the contents, the source of many arguments between them until they stripped the sack to bare essentials: a dagger, various packets of Abdul's poisons and powders, a letter of introduction to his cousins in Alexandria, a *kamal* to practice celestial navigation, and a book whose pages are thin wafers of pressed ground seeds and nuts that will stave off starvation and provide nutrition. Alex and Abdul sewed fifty gold ducats inside the coarse robe to cover her fare to Alexandria and beyond. If she carries her pack properly, no one will notice the hidden crossbow and quiver.

"Perfect," Abdul says, closing the pack. "Only one

more thing..." He ducks into his closet.

Alex flashes me a weary smile. "Where is Donato tonight?"

"Treviso, trying to turn sheep-fucking farm boys into soldiers."

"A labor worthy of Hercules."

Abdul pops back in with three osier cages, a pigeon in each, small, smaller, and smallest. "We didn't want the journey to be too easy for you," he says, "so you must take these. I made the cages especially for these birds, and if they remain inside, they will eat crumbs, seeds, the occasional worm. Talk to them when you can, stroke their heads, and treat them kindly. They are noble creatures. Release them from smallest to largest. The older are less bothered by the cage. Once released, they will fly back to me, no matter where or how far you go. You may wrap a short message around the leg, like so. Release this one when you arrive in Ancona, that one when you are safe in Alexandria, and the last when you reach Constantinople. We will know you are alive and well. Tell the other pilgrims you're bringing the birds to the Holy Father for his blessing. No Christian will quibble with that."

As I examine one of the cages, Abdul notices my silver Roman ring. "This is new."

"Donato gave it to me."

Abdul examines it carefully. "Cygnus," he says. "The celestial swan."

"Swans mate for life. They represent fidelity."

"Among other things." Abdul strokes his chin, his eyes half-closed. "Orpheus arose as a swan after the bacchantes slaughtered him, representing rebirth. The legendary phoenix may well have been a swan, or vice versa. In India, *hamsa*, the divine birds, are swans who accompany the Sun God. They represent strength and virility, whereas others believe the firmament is a heavenly lake where the clouds are female spirits who bathe daily in the form of swans."

Even Alex comes out of her sulk. "Zeus, the king of Heaven, assumed the shape of a swan to rape Leda."

"Don't blame the swan," I say. "It was overpowered by an indomitable force."

"Right. Lust."

"One might call Cygnus neither masculine nor feminine," Abdul says, "but a fusion of the two. Wear your ring well, my friend."

The instant the bells ring Sext, we set out across the lagoon. A favoring wind saves us from strenuous rowing. I raise the sail and hold steady, south and east, through the deep channel to the port of Chioggia at the southern end of the lagoon.

"It's easy enough with the wind behind us," I say to Abdul, "but if the wind prevails, we'll be heading into it all the way back. Prepare yourself."

"You seem to forget that I know more about sails than you know about rowing. My home, Alexandria, like our fair Venice, has more boats than horses or camels."

"What kind of boats did you sail?" Alex asks.

"My father owned an ancient type of boat, broad in the beam, shallow draft, much like this but with two triangular sails and eight oars. The year before my kidnapping, Father took us down the Nile to Giza. We moored on the river and hiked past the Great Sphinx, half-buried in sand, to the base of the Great Pyramid, which is taller than the bell tower of St. Mark's by half. The shiny white limestone cladding was later stripped off to build walls for the palaces of Cairo. Only the apex still gleams white like the top of an Alp in summer.

"I was quite young but seeing the great pyramid gave me my first inkling of what being mortal means and how little our mightiest efforts matter in the vastness of eternity. One day, the splendid monuments of our Serene Republic will be reduced to remnants of their present glory. My father said such is the fate of all human endeavor. Only God is timeless and eternal, and we mortals amount to little more than fireflies on a summer night twinkling and disappearing in an instant."

Sudden turbulence catches us off guard, nearly pushing our sail into the lagoon before we can drop it and take up oars. We bear as close to shore as possible and can barely keep our boat off the shoals until the turbulence passes.

Abdul's story troubles me. "If our lives are no more significant than fireflies on a summer night, why do anything?"

"Because it's our nature to do things. Our destinies unfold on the weft of ideas and the warp of action, bringing us as close to understanding as possible, or, in the case of others, distancing them as far from true understanding as their greed and stupidity predicate."

Alex protests. "It's simply not true that everything is forgotten. The pyramids still stand, even if stripped and exposed to the desert winds. The church of St. Mark will stand for all time. Not all our achievements are lost to the future."

Abdul shades his eyes with his hand and stares beyond the horizon. "That depends on how far into the future you look," he says. "We pathetic mortals can't see very far, so we think our monuments eternal. If we could see farther, every trace of what we build disappears into new worlds we can't begin to imagine."

"I'm sorry," I say, "but that's a very sorry way to look at life."

"Not at all, dear friend. Everything we do influences the future. Even if all memory of us is lost, we have contributed."

At the port of Chioggia, we pass into the Adriatic, rowing past the mouth of the Brenta River to the mouth of the Adige and upriver to our fort at Cavarzere, seated strategically on a plateau overlooking a sharp bend in the river. The original Roman *castrum* was leveled, another built, that leveled, and another, and another. The location not only commands the river in both directions, but the stone embankment, reinforced over a thousand years, protects the promontory from eroding in spring floods, high tides, and the endless flow of the river.

The quay, a stone and earth apron at the base of the embankment, teems, carnival-like, with tents and booths in preparation for the arrival of the pilgrims from Padua on their way to Ancona. The savory smoke of roast pork hangs over the city like a fog, making us even hungrier. We watch the procession of chanting pilgrims enter the city to the accompaniment of the fort's drums and trumpets. Alex blends right in with the identically dressed pilgrims.

"Don't forget the pigeons," Abdul says.

Alex can't speak. Forcing back her tears, she squeezes Abdul, her first and best teacher in the ways of the world, and then she squeezes me, her soulmate, unwilling to let me go. She whispers in my ear, "Don't do anything stupid, or I swear I will kill you when we meet again. And, please, please be kind to Donato. Love him well."

"Stay safe..." I can say no more.

As Alex departs on the greatest adventure of her life, I cannot but envy the road that lies before her. She rightly reminds me I have Donato now, and to cherish him. In the space of an Alleluia, Alex is swallowed by the procession. I need to tell her a thousand things, but it is too late, she is gone, and no matter what I say or don't say, she's on her own, navigating her own course. My heart aches with sadness even as it pounds with jealous excitement.

"Tonight, the moon is full, and sky will be clear," Abdul says. "If we rest and take nourishment, we can be home before Cygnus shows her tail."

"I could eat an ox," I say, trying to conceal the ache in my heart, bereft of the peculiar love that Alex and I share.

Abdul puts his arm around me, pressing his forehead against mine. "Alex will be fine. We trained her, after all. She is primed, determined, and above all, desperate, which will keep the wind in her sails."

I hear someone calling me, and out of the crowd, my old friend Matteo emerges, recognizing me despite my monk's robe.

"Nico!" He crushes me in a bear hug, slaps my back with his palms, and kisses my face, laughing. "How long has it been since I last saw you?"

"One year, ten months, twenty-seven days."

Matteo turns to Abdul. "Only this fine scholar could answer so precisely and be correct."

"And how do you know he's correct?" Abdul winks, and Matteo blushes.

"Because I, too, can count." Matteo embraces me again. "What brings you to this shithole?"

"A bit of reconnoitering."

"Serenissimo is checking up on us, hey?"

"On everything. What are you doing here?"

Matteo and I met in the palace stables when we were both lads of fourteen, he a groom and me, the new ballot boy. After Marino Vendramin—who didn't count because he was my minder and tutor—Matteo was my first friend in the palace. We shared our thoughts, our dreams, and our bodies. I was able to explore, and Matteo was able to revel in our pleasures, free of shame, with no fear of burning. He told me that he loved me and was angry when I said I loved him as a friend, only as a friend. After the war in Trieste, Serenissimo promoted Matteo to the post of equerry at Castel Vecchio, our fortress at San Nicolò di Lido, which guards the entrance to the lagoon nearest Rialto. When I visited him at Castel Vecchio, we galloped across the grassy dunes of Lido like we had as boys, riding to beat the wind and making love in secluded coves.

"You must be Abdul." Matteo squeezes Abdul's hand. "I've heard so much about you. I have long wished to thank you for all I learned from you, courtesy of our mutual friend."

Abdul bows. "Anyone dear to Nico is dear to me."

Matteo slaps his head. "Madonna! I almost forgot. I

wanted to tell you and couldn't figure out how without, you know..." Matteo leans into my ear. "It's about *him*..."

"Ruggiero?" I ask.

"No. Worse. Brother Bernardo of the Hermits. I saw him."

"So did I."

Matteo's eyes widen with horror. "Did he see you?"

"Fortunately, not. Did he see you?"

"He doesn't know me from Adam. But you..."

"I saw him in Padua, at the hermitage, for only a moment. Where did you see him?"

"In Chioggia. We were sent to flex some muscle of the Republic around town. The word was that these scurvy types from Padua were looking like they might be up to no good. They spooked the mayor. We watched a tavern and a whorehouse, checked their comings and goings to see if bad things happened. I saw Brother Bernardo while we were checking the bridge near the monastery of St. Domenico."

"When was this, exactly?"

"We were there on a Thursday and Friday, so it must have been eight nights ago."

"Was he coming or going?"

"He was definitely coming."

"Did he leave?"

Matteo shakes his head. "We checked out the bridge and the walls for signs of mischief, but we saw no damage, and having no reason to stay, we reported it to the mayor and left."

"Did you mention it to anyone else?"

"Only to my captain."

"Are you certain it was Brother Bernardo?"

"One look at those eyes was all I needed. Same color as yours, but cold as a dead man's dick. And his nose. Same as Ruggiero. It was him as sure as I'm me and you're you."

"What did you tell the mayor?"

"I included Brother Bernardo among the suspicious characters we sighted. I am sorry I have no more to tell, but I knew you'd want to know—"

"We must leave now," Abdul says. "If we wish to make it home tonight."

Matteo hugs me again. "How I wish we could have fun like the old days."

I free myself from his arms and show him my silver ring. I have no qualms sharing secrets with Matteo; he has more than once risked his life to save mine. "That's from my lover, Donato Venturi. Do you know him?"

"There's not a soldier in Venice who doesn't. I should have known you'd fall for him. Have you seen him?" Matteo asks Abdul.

"I'm sorry to say I haven't had the pleasure."

"He's my height but half again as broad. Monster shoulders and arms. Behind his back, they call him Black Hercules. I never thought Nico would fall for a man like that."

"Are you jealous?" I ask.

"Shit yes," Matteo says. "Is it true his cock is bigger than a salami?"

"In the first place, it's none of your business. In the second place, it's bigger."

"Fuck you." Matteo punches me in the arm, laughing,

and embraces me, again whispering in my ear, "I miss you more than you know, old friend. Until we meet again."

Chapter Twenty-Seven

Rendezvous at the Mermaid Tavern

GUFFO, THE ONE-HANDED beggar from St. Nick's parish, sits on the corner of the palace beneath the sculpture of Adam, Eve, and the serpent, his legs spread wide on the ground. The stump of his right arm rests on his cap, open for alms.

"Greetings, Guffo. Tell me, does it chasten you to sit beneath the fall of man?"

He glances up at the sculpture. "I never did understand that part of the story."

"Mama says we had to fall so we could be saved."

"She is as simple as she is beautiful. Would it not have been far easier if the Lord, in his infinite beneficence, skipped the torment and simply opened the gates of heaven?"

"Mama says you can't truly appreciate salvation if you haven't suffered sufficiently."

"Point well taken," Guffo says, "but one I can do without." He taps the psalter in my hand. "What have you got there?"

"Mama's psalter." I hand it to him, and he fingers the lock.

"This better not be what I think it is," he says

"Since civilians can no longer carry arms, I carry this for protection."

"Certainly, things have gotten bad. No weapons. In Venice? We'll all be dead soon. But seriously, if some lamebrain peacekeeper looks inside, I don't care who you are, ballot boy or not, he will twist your nuts till your dick falls off. And you will sing whatever song he wants to hear."

"I have a high tolerance for pain, and the peacekeepers are busy watching for fires."

"God, I hate fires." He shakes his head. "Seriously bad for business." He overturns his empty cap. "Right up there with naval defeats. Now decapitations, hangings, burnings—those swell the coffers. Can't get enough of 'em."

"What can you tell me about the Mermaid Tavern? I am meeting someone there."

"Fine friends you've got."

"I didn't say it was a friend."

"Good. Because the Mermaid is the filthiest whorehouse in Venice."

"*Praemonitus, praemunitus.*"

"Come again?"

"Forewarned is forearmed."

"Right. Don't catch the clap."

I approach San Cassiano from Rialto Bridge, through the market filled with vegetables, fruits, and spices. I make my way through the stalls of fish and meat, around kiosks of silks and woolens and cottons from Persia, England, and Egypt. Continuing beyond the wharf, where until recently slaves were sold, I reach the disreputable square where the Mermaid stands.

Crooked wooden houses are wedged between a palace and a parish church, ramshackle hovels all. The low tavern faces the church. Women gossip around the wellhead, their homelife spilling into the street. One of them screams as a man crashes backward through the tavern door into the square and smashes against the wellhead. He shakes his head, pats himself, and staggers upright until another screaming man jumps him, and they try to kill each other with their bare hands. Two bystanders struggle to separate them and can't, while more brawlers strike more blows, nobody knowing why, the free-for-all spreading. I duck into a doorway to avoid the riot as bells summon peacekeepers who arrive in time to save the tavern from being trashed and burned.

When everyone moves indoors, the square grows silent. No one goes in or out of the Mermaid. The open shutters upstairs reveal nothing but shabby drapes and a bored-looking whore hanging her breasts out the window to drum up business. The shutters at ground level, locked tight, permit no glimpse inside.

The broken door hangs open. Bells ring the hour of my appointment. Inside the Mermaid, two men argue in the shadows.

"Fuck him," one says. "Before he fucks us."

"We can't kill him."

"Why not?"

"Are you stupid or what? He's one of *them*."

"Fuck that. It's him or me. I don't take his shit sitting down."

"You won't be sitting down. You'll be flat on your back under a blanket of mud."

He notices me lurking in the doorway. "Hey, you nosy prick. Fuck off before you wish you had."

"I'm meeting someone here."

"Oh yeah, who? Him or me? Because that's all there is."

"A man upstairs."

The one looks at the other. "You hear that? A man upstairs." He looks back at me. "There ain't no man upstairs. So fuck off before I smash your pretty face."

Clutching the psalter, I retreat toward the door. "Can I look upstairs for myself?"

He stands up, ugly angry after a bad day and ready to take it out on me. "No. You can haul your ass out of here before I shove that book up your ass."

"You can try," I say. "But you'll be sorry."

I stand to my full height, emphasizing my heftier physique. I have known many such cowards who bark worse than they bite. The big mouth leaps to attack me. I drop the psalter, catch him under the arm, and break him over my knee. He falls, moaning, and his companion backs away. I pick up the psalter and head upstairs.

The whore hanging her breasts out the window

covers them modestly with her hands. "Don't hurt me," she says. "I've got nothing to do with it."

"Nothing to do with what?"

"Whatever you were fighting about."

"Don't worry. I have nothing to do with it either. I seek a gentleman who asked me to meet him here."

"I wouldn't know about that either. Been no gentlemen in here for years, just drunkards and dullards like the two downstairs."

"So no one has been here?"

"I've been looking out my window since midday, imagining someone like you would come along instead of the usual deadbeats."

"It's possible he couldn't make it, but that would be odd. He's my father."

She squints slightly in disbelief and tilts her head, weighing probabilities. Her tight smile suggests fear, not amusement. My father has that effect on people.

"Oh..." she says. "I might know who you mean. He was called away. Suddenly. Another gentleman came to fetch him."

"Can you tell me what the other gentleman looked like?"

"No, I cannot, as I didn't see him. I heard him come up the stairs and leave with the other man, is all. They were in a hurry."

"How long ago did they leave?"

She shrugs and smiles, earnest and hapless. "I couldn't say. I was looking out the window, daydreaming, you might say. Today for sure, but I couldn't tell you when."

It's obvious this well has run dry. Even if she has more to say, she won't. Anyone who knows my father, and many who don't, fear him. I leave the Mermaid, hoping I never have reason to return.

No sooner do I duck into a narrow alley than I sense someone behind me. I speed up, but my follower quickens his pace until his fierce hand grabs me and pushes me into a crawl space too narrow for a fat man to pass. Not tall enough to be my father, he stays hidden under his cloak and hood, twisting my arm behind me and propelling me forward. A leather gauntlet armored with strips of steel muffles my mouth. If I resist, he can break my arm. I can't twist. I can't run. I can't win. I yield, hoping to catch him off-balance.

He kicks open a door and shoves me into a storeroom filled with empty casks, moldy sails, cobwebs, and shadows, the walls thickly crusted with gauzy mold and salt stars. Rats skitter across the floor, angry at being disturbed. Still twisting my arm behind me, he forces me to sit on a barrel. The psalter falls to the floor at my feet. Never relaxing his grip on my arm, he removes his gauntlet from my mouth so I can speak.

"What business had you at the Mermaid?" His voice is as gruff as his grip is fierce.

"I'm in need of a whore," I say.

"You didn't go with any whore."

"I had second thoughts."

"What were you doing there?" He twists my arm harder. "Don't make me hurt you."

"Nothing. A whore. I got scared. It's my first time. What does it matter to you?"

"It matters very much to me."

He releases me slowly. Squeezing my shoulders, he leans forward and presses his forehead into my hair. Donato's breath fills my ear. "I love you, you beautiful idiot."

"What are *you* doing here?"

"Our mutual enemies include certain lowlifes who frequent the Mermaid." He kneels in front of me, raises my chin with his fingers, and smiles. "I worry about you."

"That's why you almost broke my arm?"

"I wanted you to know the stakes in this game." He picks up the psalter. "What's this?"

"Mama gave me her psalter." I unlock it; Donato sees the contents and whistles.

"Very clever," he says, "and quite useless. By the time you get this open, you'd be dead."

"It's better than nothing. Us civilians are no longer allowed to bear arms in public. Why aren't you in Treviso?"

"I'm tracking a lowlife well known to you. A relative of yours, in fact."

"My father?"

"The other Gradenigo traitor, Ruggiero, who is near. Tonight, I seek to cut short his brief career as an enemy agent."

"My father is also here tonight."

Donato drops his smile. He never shows fear but is less accomplished at concealing his concern. "How do you know that?"

"He sent me an invitation to meet him."

"At the Mermaid?"

"But he wasn't there. A whore said he left with

someone a while ago."

Donato smolders, fierce and implacable. "Go back to the palace. Now. Why would you even consider meeting him alone?"

"He's the only one who can answer certain questions."

"And you'd risk your life to riddle a madman? No, my heart, you can't, and you won't. I might as well slit your throat now as let you meet him alone."

"It doesn't matter. He left before I got here. Take me with you."

"Absolutely not. Ruggiero has something up his sleeve, and if I don't stop him, good men may die. I won't let you be one of them. Go back to the palace. Because if you don't, I will break your arm. One crack, and you won't be firing your bow or wielding a sword until Advent when the war is long over. You don't want that, do you?"

He hunkers beside me and stares up into my eyes. "You can't understand now, but soon you will." He gently kisses my hands. "Go back to the palace and forget this madness. If he summoned you here, it's to kill you, and I won't lose you that easily. He killed my mother. He can't have you."

Chapter Twenty-Eight

The Brothers DeLazzaro

AFTER A WEEK of sleepless nights away from Donato, my need to see him grows urgent. Finally, I can depart at sunrise, rowing the deep channel southeast to Chioggia. Serenissimo didn't say why I had to go but was emphatic that I meet Donato in Chioggia at noon under the clock in the town hall tower.

This channel runs parallel to the chain of narrow islands from Jesolo in the north to Chioggia in the south. From the water, they appear as an unbroken line of dunes and villages, rarely more than a mile wide. Three gaps, which we call "mouths," separate them, through which the Adriatic flows in and out of the lagoon. The mouth closest to Venice is at San Nicolò. The next mouth, at Malamocco, separates the lido of San Nicolò from the lido of Pellestrina. Farther south, the third mouth separates Pellestrina from the lido and port of Chioggia. By accident of nature or the will of God, over untold centuries, the rivers coursing from the mountains pushed silt, stone, and seeds into the Adriatic, miraculously depositing a ribbon of pine-covered dunes without which we would have no channels, no islands, no city, only the Adriatic beating upon the mainland shore.

At the port of Chioggia, I exit the lagoon and continue south past vineyards and orchards. Two miles farther, the Brenta River empties into the Adriatic. I row against the Brenta's current until I pass the fort at Brondolo, guarding the canal leading directly to Chioggia. A half mile beyond the fort, the canal splits, the right branch diverted to the fisheries in the shallow lagoon between Chioggia and its *lido*, the left branch forming the commercial sea lane along Chioggia's western flank. All manner of boats crowd the wharves along the quay, and I'm lucky to find a spot at the public dock.

Like Venice—although barely one-third our size—Chioggia was built on a cluster of small islands, with buildings touching shoulder to shoulder. Unlike Venice, the streets of Chioggia do not meander and get lost. They form a grid, like most Roman cities. The street I take runs straight as an arrow from the dock to the cathedral. I have time on my hands, so I count steps, measuring off the cathedral's length, two hundred feet, and breadth, a hundred fifty at the transepts, impressive even by Venetian standards. In a city numbering only a few thousand, the cathedral accommodates most of them. The cathedral and paved piazza trumpet Chioggia's prosperity, the power of salt. Actually a wide avenue, the piazza runs from the city's south gate, beside the cathedral, to the port and salt pans at the north end. The streets intersect the piazza with Roman regularity, reminding me of the raised center walkway of a great galley with oars extending to the right and left at precise intervals. The piazza must have begun as the *cardo*, the main north/south artery of every Roman city, intersecting the *decumanus*, the main east/west artery, at the city's center.

In the center, a massive grain warehouse astride sixty-four granite pillars fronts the piazza. A market occupies the open ground floor, while the grain stays safe and dry in the two upper stories. The town hall flanks the granary, equally imposing, with twin brick towers, square and stern, one with the famous clock from the same maker as Carrara's. The clock hand points to the sixth hour of day and Sext rings from the bell towers, but I see no sign of Donato. Impatient, I climb the wide outside stairs of Istrian marble leading to the main entrance, where guards bar me until I show them the doge's ring. Inside, Donato and two of his cohort are greeting the mayor of Chioggia.

Chosen by the Great Council, the mayor, fat and prosperous, blinks at the oily perspiration running from under his cap into the deep bags around his eyes. His twiddling fingers and darting eyes betray the intense anxiety common to provincial appointees when Venice taps them on the shoulder. Donato looks particularly fierce and splendid in his dress uniform, a red silk tunic emblazoned with the gold lion of St. Mark. He grasps me like a long-lost brother and beats my back with his fists, more diplomacy than sentiment.

"Good to see you," he says.

"Any word of my father?"

Sotto voce: "Not now. This comes first."

Serenissimo ordered Donato there but didn't tell me why. Donato introduces me to the mayor as "my esteemed colleague, the hero of Trieste, and the finest bowman from Grado to Cavarzere, a confidante of the doge."

"Of course, I recognize our ballot boy." The mayor bows deeply and grows sweatier.

"He's only here to observe," Donato says, "at the request of the Ten."

Ten. The most powerful word in Venice. Only the Ten can arrest, interrogate, torture, sentence, and execute whomever they find guilty, up to and including the doge, with lightning speed. Their verdicts cannot be appealed. No court can alter their decisions. The limits of a doge's powers are quickly reached, but not the Ten's, and under their scrutiny, a doge treads as lightly as a traitor.

The color drains from the mayor's face, and he wobbles a bit on his feet. Donato slides a chair under him to prevent him from collapsing in a pile of wet brocade. Smiling brightly, Donato grips the mayor's shoulder in his leather and steel gauntlet.

"Have no fear, esteemed lord mayor," he says. "We are only interested in the brothers DeLazzaro. We heard they are currently in Chioggia, and we need to ask them a few questions. Can you tell me where they lodge?"

The mayor twists his face as if trying hard to remember something, afraid to answer too quickly lest we think he knows more than he does, and equally afraid to answer too hesitantly lest we think he's withholding.

"They are thugs," Donato says, "not noble. Can't risk being seen in Rialto."

The mayor rubs his head. "Tall? Nasty-looking? A few years older than you?"

"I've never seen them."

"One has a gruesome scar across his left cheek?"

"You have seen them?"

"I've heard of them. The innkeepers are required to report weekly, naming all foreigners to our council. I'm told these men sleep all day and whore all night."

"Men with big appetites?"

"Men with money to burn."

"Money like this?"

Donato tosses a coin on the table stamped with the *carro* of Carrara. The mayor nods, and sweat runs down his colorless cheeks.

"Where might I find them?"

"Can you tell me to what purpose?"

The mayor must surely be worried whether he's in hot water for harboring them.

"Nothing that concerns you personally." Donato offers reassurance to prime the pump.

"I understand," the mayor says. "Of course. The Ten…"

"… wait most impatiently."

"It's hard to remember so many faces and names. I seem to recall being told they board at the Spotted Leopard."

At Donato's behest, the mayor orders his men to cordon the island's three main bridges to the mainland, to keep order on the piazza and guard the Spotted Leopard. Donato's men accompany us to the inn, a wood and brick building tucked into a tight corner near the wharves of the Lombardo channel. The innkeeper, Lenten-lean, with eyes sunk deep into his cheeks, notices everything and reveals nothing.

"You are the proprietor?" Donato asks.

"I am. Who might you be?"

"Captain Donato Venturi of Treviso, representing the Ten."

"And what might the Ten want from one such as myself?"

"The brothers DeLazzaro."

The innkeeper wrinkles his brow into a semaphore of ambiguity designed to give nothing away for nothing, shuffles, and shakes his head, not easily intimidated.

"We know they are here," Donato says. "The only question is, which room?"

"I had no mind to lie."

"I wasn't suggesting it. I assure you we indemnify your person and property." Donato pulls a freshly minted ducat stamped with the image of Andrea Contarini from his leather pouch and hands it to the innkeeper with the tacit promise of more. "We are grateful in advance for your cooperation."

The possibility of a significant reward lightens the innkeeper's scowl. "Second landing, far door on the right."

"Please wait in the kitchen." Donato signals one of his men to accompany the innkeeper, posts another at the street door, and another at the door to the thimble-sized inner courtyard bordered by collapsing wooden cottages with thatched roofs bearing scars of a recent fire. The well in the center is not like ours. Our wells collect rainwater; in Chioggia, wells feed from underground springs, a resource which, rich as we are, we entirely lack.

A single stairway ascends to the second floor, a warren of closed doors. The innkeeper wastes no money on lighting. Donato's men guard the dark stairway and landing.

Donato kicks the door open and grabs one DeLazzaro, while the other, halfway out the window, sees the cordon of peacekeepers and soldiers below. As I yank him from the window, I catch a glimpse of a third man vaulting between chimneys, disappearing over the rooftops. I shout to the peacekeepers below, and they beat their shields with their swords, sounding a general alarm.

Donato thrusts the point of his sword at DeLazzaro's heart as I push his brother into a chair.

"He got away," Donato's man shouts from below. "Like to have flown from chimney to chimney."

DeLazzaro doesn't hide his smirk.

Donato leans into his blade. "That amuses you?"

I'm worried the man who escaped is a Gradenigo. "Shouldn't we give chase? It could be my brother or my father."

Donato scoffs at me. "Your father, fly across the chimney tops?"

"The power of pure evil."

"Certainly, but he's gone. They say a bird in the hand is worth two in the bush, and we have these boys to deal with." Donato strokes DeLazzaro's Adam's apple with his blade. "State your name."

"Moncorso DeLazzaro."

"And your brother's name?"

"Leonardo DeLazzaro," Moncorso says.

"Leonardo," Donato says, "you keep your mouth shut while I question your brother. You'll get your turn. Moncorso DeLazzaro, who fled out the window?"

"A worthless piece of shit."

"His name, Moncorso?" Donato leans harder into his sword.

"I don't know his name. I told you, he's a worthless piece of shit."

"We have ways to make you talk."

"He drank with us a couple times, came upstairs for the whores. I don't know his fucking name."

"Why did he run?"

"What coward wouldn't run from you?"

"We know you pass secret documents from our Senate to Francesco Carrara."

"I said I don't know his name."

"That's a lie." Donato's blade breaks Moncorso's flesh.

Moncorso blinks. "How do you know that?"

"It doesn't matter. Tell me the name of the traitor who passes these documents to you and where he gets them."

"I don't know what you're talking about."

"Does the man who escaped bring them from the traitor?"

"Christ, no. I told you, he's a drunk from the bar."

Donato shakes his head sorrowfully. "I was hoping you'd make this easy."

"You're the one's gonna suffer for this. We are Paduan, under the jurisdiction of Lord Carrara. He's the only one who can arrest or judge us. So say the treaties between my lord and yours."

"The same treaties Lord Carrara breaks six times a day and seven on Sunday?"

"I wouldn't know about that."

"But you know who provides the stolen documents and what's in them."

"We can't even read them," Leonardo DeLazzaro shouts in panic. "They're in Latin."

"So you've seen them?"

"I didn't say that." The blood drains from Leonardo's face.

"Then how do you know they're in Latin?"

Moncorso explodes. "So what, we seen 'em. We don't know what they say and don't give a crab's ass. I don't know where they come from. I don't know the asshole's name who brings them. I get paid to pass them on."

Donato winks at me and laughs uproariously. Both brothers flush with vexation. "Have you seen our torture chamber?" he says. "I'll let you in on a little secret. Nobody who has wants to go back, least of all you. The man who escaped, tell me his name and where he gets the documents."

The specter of the torture chamber makes Leonardo DeLazzaro sob. "I swear; we don't know."

"What does he look like?"

Leonardo, too shaken to speak, stares desperately at his brother.

"Tall, dark hair," Moncorso says.

"How tall?"

"A hell of a lot taller than you."

"How much taller?"

"How the fuck should I know? My height."

"Age?"

"Never shows his face. He drops off the package and leaves."

"Give me the documents he brought," Donato says.

"He didn't have none this time. He came to borrow money to keep him out of big trouble he got himself into. I was telling him to fuck off when you broke down the door, and he jumped out the window." Moncorso's fists clench and unclench. He does his best to sound earnest, but what he says does not figure.

"More lies." Donato remains calm, showing no rancor, only certainty. He turns to Leonardo DeLazzaro. "We're after him, not you. He knows our traitor. You don't. Unfortunately, we've got you, not him, and you are only useful if you talk. Give me his name, Leonardo DeLazzaro, before we strap you to the wheel."

"I don't know."

"Do you think I'm joking?" Donato yanks Leonardo's hair until tears stream down his cheeks. Like spring ice, Leonardo cracks under the slightest pressure.

"Ruggiero..."

"Ruggiero what?"

"He never said."

"Describe him to me."

Moncorso shouts, "Shut up, shut up! Just shut the fuck up."

"You shut the fuck up!" Livid and shaking, Leonardo

turns on his brother. "I'm not going to let them smash my nuts to save that asshole."

Moncorso's chin drops to his chest. He knows he has lost. "Gradenigo. Ruggiero Gradenigo. A close friend of Lord Carrara." To Leonardo he says, "Don't even think about what he'll do to us now."

"Have no fear," Donato says, brisk and businesslike. "We'll have him by nightfall. Did he mention any other names?"

Moncorso shakes his head, a beaten man. "He reckoned we were too stupid to care, being good for free drinks and whores, that's all. He said his man in the Senate is rich as fuck; that's all he said. No reason to know anything else."

Chapter Twenty-Nine

La Gobba

"THE BROTHERS DELAZZARO are cheap thugs," I tell Serenissimo. "Hired to fetch and carry for their lord. They have no more loyalty than an English mercenary. They named Ruggiero, but I wouldn't put it past my father to tell them he was Ruggiero. What baffles me is why anyone as smart as my father would risk his neck with losers like that."

"Beggars can't be choosers," Serenissimo says.

His brow furls in a different direction. "Our Brother Bernardo knows where all the skeletons are buried, and that gives him power over too many Venetian nobles who know there's nothing he won't do. He and Carrara are two sides of the same coin. I'm certain Carrara had no trouble extorting secrets from Lorenzo Morosini, but we can't convict Morosini without a signed confession. My hands are tied. Brother Bernardo belongs to God, not Caesar. If I touch him, the pope could excommunicate us—the whole damn Republic, from Grado to Cavarzere—and then our goose is cooked."

"I have a confession to make, sire."

His shoulders sag. "Must you? Now?"

"What I have to say bears directly. After I escaped from the tower, I rescued a certain someone from the hermitage of the church of Saints Filippo and Giacomo. That certain someone heard a rumor that the abbot had been murdered, and Carrara intends to make Brother Bernardo the new abbot."

The impact of revelation eclipses my trespass. Serenissimo growls at the audacity of Lord Carrara.

"Brother Bernardo must vanish," he says. "If only I could doff this golden robe and fight like Visconti of Milan. When the pope excommunicated him, he shredded the Bull of Excommunication with his dagger and made the legate who delivered it eat it, parchment, lead seal, silk strings, everything." Serenissimo crosses himself. "Men like that are beyond reason. Nor can you reason with a pope appointed by God Almighty. If we cross the Holy Father, he will come after us."

Marino Vendramin flies down the stairs to the crypt like a whirlwind. His robe indicates he comes as an ex officio member of the Ten. "Your presence is required, Exalted Serenity," he says. "Someone has denounced our traitor. We are about to interrogate her."

Serenissimo puts his hand on my shoulder, and in the

weariest of weary voices perfected for times such as these, he says, "Tell them I am ailing. Nico will report everything to me, so it doesn't matter if I'm there. Nobody listens to me anyway." He grimaces at Marino, meaning he will brook no opposition. Declining meetings is one of the few prerogatives left him. Marino matches Serenissimo's heavy sigh with a heavier one and pulls me along after him.

He fumbles for his keys, unlocks a hidden door to a secret stairway, and we descend to the deserted hall of the lords of the night. In the scriptorium adjacent to the main hall, clerks and canons transcribe scribbled sheets of paper: charges, testimony, tortures, confessions, verdicts, punishments. The doors of the torture chamber remain open lest anyone forget the penalty for wrong answers. Marino does not chitchat, which is unusual, and walks fast instead of his usual saunter, a sign of extreme agitation. He opens another secret door behind a lattice of carved marble which I always dismissed as a decorative flourish. The lattice conceals a cell the size of a marble confessional, cold and unlit, with only a single stool. Seated on the stool I can see the entire hall with the dais directly opposite me, but no one can see me.

"Hopefully the interrogation won't last forever," Marino says. "That stool can get very hard. I know. The Ten understands what Serenissimo has known all along—you're worth a legion of scribes. But I must warn you that like us, you are sworn to secrecy. If you are indiscreet, you will not outlive it."

"But what exactly—"

Marino, a veteran of my questions, lays his finger

across my lips.

"Say nothing," he whispers. "Hear everything. And pray with our doge afterward." Marino closes and locks the door behind him.

The Ten take their places on the dais. The Lord of the Night follows with the Head of the State Advocates. All aspects of the law are represented. The state advocate's chair flanks the torture chamber. He uses a perfumed napkin to hide its noxious exhalations.

Guards lead a slight figure concealed in a black cloak into the room. The cloak comes off, revealing a bony woman old enough to have survived the great plague and any number of wars. Her hooked nose hangs over thin lips fixed in a tight line. The jagged scars on her cheeks tell sad stories. Her robe stretches tightly over a hump between her shoulders the size of a two-year-old.

Marino speaks for the Ten. The others may be richer, or lead battles victoriously, or twist foreign kings around their ringed fingers, but Marino Vendramin is sly and conducts interrogations while the others sit silently, exchanging discreet hand signals and eyebrow semaphores.

"You are Catteruzza di San Cassiano?" Marino's condescending tone with the old crone seems like a mistake to me.

She looks him straight in the eye. "I am called La Gobba, the humpbacked madam of Rialto." She sounds like a gruff old man, not a spindly scarecrow. Marino steps back, wiping the obsequious smile off his face. From his sleeve he withdraws a document.

"And you wrote this denunciation?"

"I did not. I spoke it to a gentleman of my acquaintance who wrote it for me."

"Tell us his name, please."

"Don't play me for a fool," she says. "You know his name as sure as you know mine, and if you don't, even torture won't pry it from these lips. He did what he was supposed to. This business is between you and me."

"His identity matters in so far as he knows the matter of this denunciation."

"All that paper says is I heard something I shouldn't have."

"Upon its delivery it was suggested that the denunciation concerns the identity of a man of interest to us. I apologize for putting words in your mouth." He slowly refolds the denunciation and slips it back into his sleeve. "Would you be so kind as to tell us what you heard, where, and from whom?" Marino adjusts his tone to the level of her gravitas.

"Four rowdies from Padua took rooms at my house. Gentlemen, to hear them tell it, but they didn't fool me. I've seen too many like them for far too long. They threw a lot of silver on the table for girls and drink, slept half the day, caroused all night, and did it again. Two nights ago, another of them came, but I couldn't see his face for his hood. A lot of shouting went on between them, which I could hear plain as day."

"The fifth man, the hooded man, can you describe him?"

"He was wearing a cloak and hood. I only saw his back."

"How tall was he?"

"A lot taller than you. I didn't see much of him."

"Did any of these miscreants identify the man who passed the stolen documents?"

"What stolen documents?"

Marino's composure slips. La Gobba's question confounds him.

"The secret documents one of our senators is selling to our enemy." Marino's expression says he shouldn't need to tell her this. She narrows her eyes, wary that he is pulling a fast one.

"I know nothing about stolen documents," she says. Marino casts an eye at his cohorts on the dais who glower in angry confusion.

"It appears we have more than one conspiracy on our hands," Marino says to La Gobba.

"I don't like the sound of that," she says. "All I did was listen, and as soon as I heard what they said, I denounced them as quick and as secret as you could want."

"I'm not accusing you of anything," Marino says. "I was merely stating a fact. Please tell us what you heard."

"That they're planning to kill you," she says.

"Who? Me? Marino Vendramin?"

"Not only you. A bunch of you."

Marino pales. "Who besides me?"

"Lorenzo Dandolo, Pantaleone Barbo, Lorenzo Zane."

"The same Lorenzo Zane who wrote this denunciation?"

She ignores the question. "There's more," she says.

"Let me be clear. You are saying that Francesco Carrara paid assassins to enter our city and murder certain of our nobles?"

"If you're on the list," she says, "you're a dead man."

"There's a list?"

"In their pocket. If you're against Lord Carrara, you're on the list."

"Madam, you are risking your life denouncing this plot."

"What's my life compared to all yours, your lordship?"

"Can you name the other nobles they intend to kill?"

"Only those I heard. What I said before, plus Leonardo Cornaro, for one."

Marino staggers slightly. Sweat beads under Bruno Badoer's eyes.

La Gobba stares directly at the dais. "Maurizio Barbarigo, and Bruno Badoer over there..."

Marino sags onto a bench.

"Ain't finished yet," she says.

"Who else?"

"Luigi Molino."

Head of the State Advocates.

"Pietro Bernardo."

One of the doge's councilors.

"Is that all?" Marino appears exhausted.

"All that I heard," she says. "I doubt that's all."

"How were these assassins planning to kill so many of us?"

"Set fire to your houses and slit your throats when you run out. All at once. Before you knew what hit you."

Bruno Badoer's face contorts with blind rage. "Seize the men plotting this atrocity. Draw and quarter them."

Marino returns to La Gobba. "Do you know how

many assassins are involved?"

"A lot," she says. "How many? I don't know."

"But some you know."

She nods gravely. "I know the ones I saw."

"They might be a mere fraction of the cabal," Pantaleone Barbo says.

"These names you reported," Marino asks, "are they the only ones you heard?"

"I told you everything I know."

Pantaleone Barbo addresses La Gobba. "And none of them mentioned anything about the state secrets being passed to Lord Carrara?"

"I told you. I heard nothing about that."

Badoer bangs the table. "Give one hundred gold ducats to the brave woman who saved our lives."

La Gobba glares at him with undisguised contempt. "Is that why you think I came here?" She summons the dignity of the prioress of a mendicant order, grave and unshakable. "I spit on your money. Don't be fooled by my looks. I'm richer than half your nobles, all those who couldn't give me their money fast enough."

Shaken to his core and brutally embarrassed by Badoer, Marino bows deeply to La Gobba. "We know why you did it, and we are grateful beyond measure, madam."

"I'm sure you are, my good lord, though some of you whose necks I'm saving would have me burn in hell for corrupting their worthless sons. They don't know me, but they hate me, which is to say, I'm not saving their necks because I like them, because I don't. But I know what you do for this Republic, and for better or worse, you're the best we got. Thank Jesus, Mary, and Joseph we got no tyrant like old Carrara lording it over us. We have you sirs. So take a good look at yourselves, at the man next to you, at the men you break bread with, because the rest of us depend on you. Hang the killers and the traitors, and keep this Republic safe and free. That's why I came here. I did my job. Now you do yours."

Chapter Thirty

The Baker's Wife

SERENISSIMO FIDGETS, FULMINATING about people's gullibility. A stone dropped in a pond sends out ripples to the far banks, which echo back, crossing themselves in contrary motion. Just so, rumor sweeps through the halls and the porticos of the palace, onto the streets and into the squares, to the farthest margins of the city, and echo back all twisted. Every man, woman, and child fears a mortal danger.

Two nobles in the portico overlooking the basin speak behind their hands. "One man's meat is another man's poison," one says to the other, casting a sidelong glance.

The guards at the palace gate argue amongst themselves without noticing me. One of them says, "Every tyrant is poisoned by distrust."

With fear and real danger afoot in the city, with all trust undermined and all security threatened, the Ten lifts the ban on personal weapons in public places, turning the city into a militia to protect its nobles from the assassins. Fires become treason as rumor gains more dangerous purchase.

I need to check on my mother's safety and state of mind, but the boats jamming the Giudecca Canal make for slow going to St. Nick's. The wharves crackle with uncertainty. Old-timers who would ordinarily wave to me don't, distracted. I dock at the wharf behind St. Nick's Church and walk toward Mama's. Rounding the corner by the bakery, I hear shouting in the square and sprint double-time to check it out.

The entire parish jostles in a tight circle around the well, shouting at one another and at the peacekeepers trying to quell an unrest growing out of hand. Guffo, the one-handed beggar, sits on the deserted steps of the church, his empty cap upturned. I drop in a gold coin, and he smiles.

"You're a good lad still," he says. "None of those cheap bastards from the palace give me gold. Those who can afford it most drop pennies."

"What's going on here?"

"Rumors have poisoned this fine day."

"Rumors of what?"

"Poison."

"What poison?"

"Listen to the baker's wife; she's been ranting on it all day."

The baker's wife has squared off against the captain of the peacekeepers and pummels him with her fists, shouting, "No, I didn't see them with these two eyes, but I know it was them because he who told me don't lie. They're poisoning the wells right under our noses. They're trying to kill us all! And here's you, bothering me instead of catching them. Don't you care if we die? Go catch the killers poisoning our wells."

The peacekeeper stares her down. "Nobody poisoned your well."

"Oh yes, they did. How many of us has to die before you believe me? I've seen those scurvy bastards from Padua lurking around for no good reason."

"Give me the name of someone killed by this poison?"

"Nobody yet. Thanks to me, not you."

As the peacekeeper and the baker's wife wrangle, her hands on her hips, shouting defiantly in his face, and he uses every drop of self-control not to bash her skull with the pommel of his sword, a skinny piebald hound of indeterminate breed, panting and thirsty, nudges the baker's wife, casting woeful eyes at the well.

"Give the hound some water," the peacekeeper says. "That'll settle it."

"Not my Duchess." The baker's wife grabs the hound and shoves it behind her.

Her son and daughter, no more than six or seven, clutch the hound, crying, "Don't hurt our Duchess."

"Better your hound than your young," the peacekeeper tells the baker's wife under the watchful eye of a crowd now silent and transfixed. The peacekeeper hoists a full bucket from the well. It sloshes on the mud at his feet. The children wail behind the baker's wife as she stares down the peacekeeper.

"That miserable beast has seen better days," he says. "We'll know if the well's been poisoned or not if your mangy bitch croaks, which she won't, not from this water anyway."

"Let her drink," terrified parishioners shout, dealing the baker's wife an unexpected blow. "Then we'll know..."

The baker's wife pulls her children off the hound. "If she croaks," she snarls at the peacekeeper, "you're next."

Cowed by the stares of the anxious crowd, the hound slinks toward the bucket, plunges her snout in, and laps loudly. Everyone jumps back, as if a drop of the water might strike them dead. The hound finishes, shakes her head, and scratches herself, pondering what to do next under the stare of the entire parish. She walks a few feet, squats, pisses, shakes herself again. The crowd parts around her as if she could kill with a touch. She runs toward the quay, and the baker's children chase after her. A peacekeeper guarding the wharf turns the hound around, and she runs to her mistress, cowering at her feet, very much alive, gnawing her forepaws.

"She looks fine to me," the peacekeeper says.

The baker's wife watches the hound, both angry and relieved. "Don't be so sure." The hound licks her hands, but she pushes the snout away from her face and wipes her hands on her apron.

"Tell me again who told you about this poison?" the peacekeeper asks.

"One of us," she says, "who saw them by the well at dawn."

"But they didn't poison the well, did they?" The peacekeeper kicks the hound who woofs balefully. "The man who told you he saw someone poison the well, what parish is he from?"

"He is a man of God, I tell you. He came from Archangel Raffaele."

I shout over the crowd. "What was he wearing?"

"What they all wear—a black robe and hood. He warned me they were going to set fires to houses and poison our wells."

"What fires?" The peacekeeper explodes all over again.

She snaps back at him. "You don't know nothing, do you?"

The crowd drowns out the baker's wife and the peacekeeper arguing whether the hound is as right as rain or may yet be dead by sundown, and what fires there may or may not have been. A fistfight breaks out, and more peacekeepers pour into the square to quell the brawlers.

Still watching from the church stairs, Guffo shakes his head. "The stupid fucks will believe what they want. Alive or dead, the hound proves nothing. Like the wise man said, the dose makes the poison."

"But they could poison our wells. I wouldn't put anything past Carrara."

"If they're poisoning the wells, they're doing a lousy job. Nobody's dead yet."

"You've got a point."

"What brings you here anyway?"

"Checking on Mama. I wonder why she's not here. She never misses a brawl."

Guffo's eyes soften at the thought of her, and he scratches his head. "Most likely she's home praying. That's all she does lately, with Giasone at the arsenal day and night."

*

I OPEN THE unlocked door to find the house deserted. A pot hangs on a hook over the fire, onions, garlic, beans, fennel, still simmering, neither in need of water nor burned. The low fire crackles. I check the bed, the chest, the table, looking for a clue where she has gone. Wine soaks the table beside an overturned glass. As I lock the window, I notice dark red squiggles, blood or wine, staining the plaster beside the door. Three squiggles. Three fingers dipped in wine, scratching three undulating lines for someone to see and grasp what only I can fully grasp. The three dolphins of the ancient Gradenigo crest. My father.

I run. Head down, eyes fixed on the ground in front of me, stumbling around corners, darting across courts and squares, small and big, leaping stairs onto bridges and jumping off, tearing through a city losing its wits. An angry mob in front of the apothecary's shop at Santa Margherita wave their fists at Abdul struggling to shutter the shop. I elbow my way toward him and help hold the crowd at bay before we squeeze through the door and bar it behind us.

"They're mad." His eyes are black pools of incomprehension. "I told that crazy woman that antidotes are poison-specific. Which poison have you taken? She flies at me, screaming, 'What poison? Paduan poison, that's what!' I say, 'You must be more specific, madam. Hemlock? Foxglove? Monkshood? Henbane? Arsenic? Give me a name, and I can tell you if I have an antidote.' By then, the mob formed, and that's when you came."

"Do you have an antidote?"

Smiling, Abdul kisses my forehead. "Could you be more specific?"

From Abdul's window, we watch peacekeepers and parish police storm the bridge from San Pantalon and cordon the crowd with their shields. The apothecary, Abdul's owner, cowers behind a rooftop chimney, terrified of the mob.

"Mama is missing," I say.

"For how long?"

"The time it takes wine to dry on stucco. My father kidnapped her, I'm certain."

"How can I help?"

"Brother Bernardo started a riot in St. Nick's Square for cover. He told the baker's wife Paduans poisoned the well. There was a riot in the square when he abducted her. Everyone was there. By the time I got home, she was gone. Somebody must have seen them, but I have to get back to the palace before Serenissimo splits a gut. I beg you, find her for me."

"Of course."

I fight my way back to the palace. Next to the church of San Polo, peacekeepers and lords of the night battle another mob of outraged Venetians storming Carrara's palace, a gift of goodwill given the lord of Padua by the nobles of Venice upon signing the treaty Carrara has pissed on. Madmen throw torches—insurrection in any language—

shouting about the poisoning of the wells, whipping the tumult in the square into a firestorm. The city no longer seethes; it boils over. Rumor has triumphed.

Rialto Bridge sways precariously, jammed to a standstill. People inside scream, frightened and frustrated, unable to move forward or back. They panic as bells sound alarms driving more people toward St. Mark's, noble and common alike, for news, for explanations, for reassurance, for orders. They churn around the Columns of Doom where we routinely hang, behead, and burn men alive.

Arsenal guards and army regulars use pikes, swords, and shields to control the crowd outside the Doge's Palace. Trumpets blare from the balcony of St. Mark's where a herald proclaims there is nothing to fear, the poison is only a rumor, no one has died. The agitated crowd grows bigger. The announcement repeats at the next ringing of bells with even more people in the square, but by now, nobody can hear the herald. Nobody believes him anyway. They believe what they want to believe.

"Do we know if any wells were actually poisoned?" I ask Serenissimo.

"Only with rumor," Serenissimo says. "And my people act like their mothers and sons are dying on their doorsteps, gasping with their last breaths, 'If only old Doge Contarini had been more vigilant.'"

"Nobody could blame you, sire."

"They will, whether it's true or not. It's not about poison. Everyone is desperate for a sign we are not doomed. This sign was for me, as only Carrara can deliver it, laughing at us because we are so beaten and demoralized that rumor is as deadly as poison. Doing nothing is the poison killing us. The only antidote is action. Direct, decisive action. Attack. We can't wait for Raniero or anyone else. Giustinian must attack Carrara; the bullshit stops now."

"That will bring the Hungarians down on us."

"That's why we hired Raniero. We certainly didn't hire him to smash Carrara. Any halfwit can do that."

"Attack where, sire?"

"It doesn't matter as long as we win. Go. Immediately. Tell Giustinian we need a victory before we lose without ever fighting. Help him. Hit Carrara hard with everything we've got where it hurts him most."

"But my mother, sire..."

His brow furls angrily, and he opens his mouth to roar at me.

"My father abducted her."

His mouth closes. He winces, weighing my words. "Do you know that for fact?"

"Yes, I do."

"Leave it to me. We'll find her and hang him. You do your job."

Chapter Thirty-One

Solagna

GIUSTINIAN LOOKS UP from the document in his hand and smiles weakly. "What dire news do you bring this time?"

"It's not dire this time. I bear orders to attack immediately."

"We? Where?"

"Serenissimo says attack Carrara where it will hurt him the most. We need a solid victory to head off a rebellion."

"What rebellion?"

"Angry people from every parish whipped to a frenzy by Carrara's plots and rumors. We need a victory to restore their hope and confidence."

Giustinian rakes his fingers through his hair. "Where does Serenissimo want us to attack?"

"He left that up to you."

"And where's our vaunted captain general?"

"He's on his way with four thousand strong, but he's not here yet. It's our move."

Confident and decisive at sea, on land Giustinian fumbles and overthinks. The obstacles and tactics of land war make him visibly nervous. He unfolds a map, scratches the back of his neck, runs his finger over the forts and towns and rivers, shaking his head slowly. "Spies report Hungary is about to cross the Alps. Possibly through Gorizia to Bassano and then here. Treviso is still the apple of Louis's eye; has been since he lost it twenty years ago. Meanwhile, the Paduan army rampages and re-treats randomly, so we're never sure where they'll strike next..."

A knock on the door and a voice from outside inter-rupts him.

"Captain Venturi, sir." Without waiting for a re-sponse, Donato strides in. He closes the door behind him, slides around the table, and leans over the map. "Are we finally doing something?"

"The doge has ordered an immediate attack on the enemy," Giustinian says.

"At last." Donato rubs his hands together. "Where?"

"Where it will hurt them the most," I say.

"Serenissimo left it to us." Giustinian leans over the table between Donato and me, still poring over the map. "We were just discussing it."

"There's nothing to discuss." Donato plants his finger

between Bassano and Feltre. "Attack there. Solagna."

Giustinian takes Donato's self-assurance for insolence, and it annoys him. "You can't just pull something out of your ass."

"You know Donato better than that, sir."

"If we take Solagna," Donato says, "we breach Carrara's line running from the mountains to the walls of Padua." He sweeps the arc with his finger. "We win control of the route the Hungarians are most likely to take."

Giustinian stares at the map, his brow knit with indecision. "We can't be certain which route the Hungarians will take."

"Only one route makes sense," Donato says. "Our spies reported a garrison of foot soldiers hammering and sawing day and night, building something that resembles a fort at the tower of Solagna. Carrara clearly understands its importance. He also believes we won't strike until Raniero arrives, giving us the priceless advantage of surprise. We can catch them with their pants down, and before they can wipe themselves, we'll capture the fort."

"Carrara's pickets will likely spoil the surprise."

"Not if we march by starlight at double-time," I say. "Like Caesar's legions."

"Don't underestimate our troops, sir." Donato remains controlled but insistent. "I have been drilling them for months. Each man is a match for Achilles."

"When do we leave?" I ask.

"When Cygnus shows her tail," Donato says. "We'll catch them in bed."

Giustinian points an imperious finger at me. "You're not going anywhere. The boss will draw and quarter me if harm comes to you."

I know I cannot change Giustinian's mind, but I'm surprised Donato doesn't second me. He nods at Giustinian, at me, and leaves me to sulk in the courtyard. An infantryman exits the barrack and sees me doing pull-ups from the branch of an oak.

"Where's your uniform?"

"I'm not going."

"Why the fuck not? It's time to pay those bastards back for all the evil they've done."

"Doge's orders."

He backs away. "Can't argue with that."

He's happy. I am not. The cavalry rides out suited up, their horses armored. Foot soldiers pour out of the barracks and assemble in the central square, their chain mail jingling. They carry spears over their shoulders, and longswords hang at their waists. The gold lion of St. Mark emblazons their crimson surcoats. Giustinian leads them in fine plate armor, a crested helmet with a fierce gargoyle visor, and steel gauntlets glinting in the torchlight. Donato rides alongside him, covered from skull to knee in chain mail under hard leather armor.

"It's time to show those cowards what we're made of," Giustinian shouts. "Win or die."

"Win or die!" the troops echo.

Jealous and humiliated, I cannot look Donato in the eye as he rides out. He crosses the lowered drawbridge beside his general, followed by standard bearers, cavalry, infantry with swords, spears, and tall triangular shields slung over their backs, and mounted bowmen. That's where I should be.

They form a line a quarter mile long, and by the time the supply train disappears into the darkness, the first star of Cygnus appears overhead. The rest of the garrison raises the drawbridge, bars the gates, and hits the hay, except for a night patrol watching from the ramparts. Scarcely a soul in the fortress sleeps. We await the light of day and news of the battle. To keep myself occupied, I exercise and hack straw dummies with my weighted sword. Weary of that, I curry Delfín. When day breaks, I drill the remaining bowmen. I don't know what hurts more, that Donato is there or that I'm not.

The morning creeps endlessly. Shortly after the bells ring Terce, a cloud of dust appears on the road from Fusina, the opposite direction from the battle raging at Solagna. We open the gates and lower the drawbridge.

Accompanied by two pages blowing trumpets and four armored riders bearing standards of St. Mark, a herald clatters across the drawbridge. He dismounts in the courtyard and ascends the platform awaiting him. The garrison gathers in the yard around him. He unfurls his scroll and recites.

"His Exalted Serenity, the Doge of Venice and the glorious nobles of the Great Council here make known that Luigi Francesco, senator; Alvise da Molin, state's attorney; his son-in-law Lorenzo Morosini, senator; and Maurizio Barbarigo, of the Council of Forty have been charged with conspiring to sell state secrets to Lord Francesco Carrara of Padua and are to be tried and sentenced forthwith."

The remnants of the garrison pound a funereal beat with the pommels of swords against their shields in grim approval.

"One Francesco Gratario, the leader of the assassins sent by the same Lord Francesco Carrara of Padua to murder all patriotic nobles of Venice who opposed said Lord Carrara, having been apprehended, tried, and sentenced, was taken by barge to Santa Croce, there tied to the tail of a horse, thence dragged through the streets to Rialto, where his right hand was severed and hung around his neck on a rope. From thence, he was dragged to St. Mark's Square, and his charges read to all and sundry. Whereupon, he was beheaded and quartered between the columns, and the quarters were mounted on posts thereby until the following day, when they were staked in the main channels of the lagoon to warn all entering or leaving our city how justice is done."

"Death to the traitors," the men shout.

"What about Brother Bernardo of the Hermits?" I shout.

"He still has a price on his head." The herald rolls up his scroll and prepares to depart for our forts at Asolo and Castelfranco. Serenissimo's bold prosecution of our most notorious traitors needs only to be topped off with a decisive victory.

Shortly after the sixth hour, another plume of dust speeds toward Treviso. We lower the bridge and open the gate. A single rider, his horse lathered white, gallops into the yard.

"Victory is ours," he shouts.

Mad cheering ensues. If only the herald had heard this news, he could have carried it with him. A short while later, more horsemen gallop into the yard, Donato in the lead. He vaults off Mercury, lifts me up, and swings me around.

"We drenched the field with their blood. Solagna is ours."

He heads straight for his quarters to strip off his armor. I help him unbuckle his breastplate and greaves. Bone-tired, his arms heavy, his eyelids half-closed, he nuzzles me.

"You need rest," I say, but he doesn't think so. He grabs me and pulls me onto his bed.

"Don't be stupid, Donato. Somebody could walk in."

"Let them. If they have a problem, they can take it up with me."

He tugs at my clothes, slathering me with kisses.

"Later." I push him away. Even his lips are tired. "Rest."

"Plenty of time for that in the grave." He's about to yank open my tunic when a knock at the door stops him.

"Captain Venturi, General Giustinian orders you to report immediately."

I accompany Donato to the general's office, where Giustinian greets him with a handshake.

"Brilliant plan, brilliantly played," Giustinian says. "Your cunning and bravery will not go unheralded."

They embrace and collapse into chairs, bodies drained, brains on fire. We drink, we toast, we make jokes. All the while, Donato's eyes linger on me. The remainder of our troops straggle in, the wounded tended to in the barracks while the able-bodied sprawl in the courtyard under the leafy oaks, exhausted and battle worn but triumphant.

In the dead of night, an alarm from the tower shatters our repose. We climb the ramparts to watch a cloud of dust swirling toward us from the southwest. In the distance, bright flames flicker across the Trevisan countryside.

"Carrara didn't take long," Giustinian shouts. "Secure the fortress and the town."

Trumpets sound. All who can stand gather in the armory, grabbing spears, javelins, longbows, crossbows, bolts, and arrows.

Carrara's army reaches Treviso, boiling over, hurling everything they've got at the drawbridge and gates, at the walls and towers of our fortress. Arrows whistle overhead; javelins bounce off brick or stick in wood. Flaming bolts fly into the yard as two catapults rumble forward and fling boulders to shatter the oak and masonry protecting us.

No enemy ever properly takes into account the impregnability of Treviso fortress. We repel them with flaming bolts and showers of arrows and streams of boiling oil. They outnumber us, but we have an arsenal at our command, and they have a short supply train barely able to keep up with them. Soon, they flag, stalemated, and pull out of range of our projectiles. In the dark, they light fires. Roving bands of country boys scream curses and threats, jeering, launching flaming bolts and arrows that do little but light up the night. Having thrown everything they have at us, they try annoying us to death. As the nearby monks sing Matins, a chorus of Paduans under our eastern tower serenades us with obscenities about our doge, our Senate, our Ten, our women, and our manhood.

"This way," Donato says. I follow him into the

armory. He heads straight for a well-traveled wooden chest. Using a key on his belt, he unlocks and opens it and shows me the neatly packed glazed earthenware balls the size of small melons. He grabs one in each hand. "What are you waiting for?"

I grab two. "What are they?"

"Quicklime. Too much can blind you, even kill you, so be careful. This way…"

We climb to the parapet and run toward the east tower above the serenading Paduans. Donato, still bleary-eyed and battle-weary, explodes with excitement. He jumps high and hurls a globe at the Paduans. Shattering on impact, it fills the air with a billowy white cloud producing screams of pain and furious curses.

He wraps his arms around me. "They're singing a different tune now."

We race west to a new position.

"Your turn," he says. "I know how you hated not being at Solagna. Here's your chance."

Arrows and bolts whistle around us but don't touch us. I jump and smash the quicklime into the enemies' midst. Donato hurls his second globe. Another smash, the cloud blowing toward the Paduan tents. I leap past Donato and hurl my second into the center of the scattering foot soldiers. Donato cheers, embracing me. Others pour from the armory to harry the retreating Paduans, and Donato pulls me across the yard, where we disappear through a door, and another, to a place we can be neither seen nor heard, mad beasts starving for each other.

Exuberant, he tears off his uniform and tackles me. We grapple, naked and blind, until the tide of our passion quickly ebbs under the weight of exhaustion. Even before my eyes have closed, I drift into oblivion. I see my mother's face, twisted in terror, a knife at her throat like a lamb at the slaughter. I am not there. I cannot reach her. She cannot hear me. I scream.

Donato slaps his hand over my mouth. I pull away, startled awake.

"My father was killing my mother."

He rocks me in his arms. "Don't waste this fugitive hour on nightmares."

"He abducted Mama. He will kill her."

"Why? She's no use to him dead. Her only value lies in the leverage she gives him over you. Dead she's nothing, like all the dead. As long as she lives, she's useful."

"I must find her and kill him."

"We will."

Nothing changes, but I feel better. My love for Donato and my belief in him never fail to fuel my hope and endurance. "I don't know what I'd do without you."

"That's how it is for men like us, always has been, and always will be."

"I want to join the army to be with you."

"You're a mad fool, but you have a point. Join the army. Ride with me."

"Serenissimo refuses to allow it."

"Is it his decision, or yours?"

Chapter Thirty-Two

A Turn of Fortune

"QUICKLIME!"

I fear Serenissimo's eyeballs might burst.

"I had a chance to strike a blow, and I struck."

He erupts like Vesuvius, venting indignation, out-rage, and disappointment. "What in the name of Almighty God and all the saints in heaven got into that fevered pea brain of yours? You could have blinded yourself. Or worse."

"I did my duty, sire, to protect our Republic and our honor."

"Don't bullshit me. You wanted to prove yourself to Donato for reasons I can't begin to fathom, and it was an egregiously stupid thing to do. It's bad enough when I throw you in harm's way, but to throw yourself in the middle of bad business repeatedly is unconscionable. You are essential to us, and yet you persist in doing profoundly stupid things as if you had no more sense than a chamber pot. Smart men learn from their mistakes; only imbeciles make them over and over again."

"You can't keep me out of this war forever."

"Watch me."

"It's a terrible mistake, sire. To my everlasting regret, war is what I do best."

"And you're smart enough to know that in war, one man never makes the difference."

"Caesar charged into the thick of battle and single-handedly turned defeat to victory."

"So you're comparing yourself to Caesar now?"

"No, I am not. I'm saying that the right man in the right place doing the right thing at the right time can make all the difference in the world, like Donato at Solagna."

"Donato was schooled for this, groomed and trained to be a warrior. You were not. We expect it of him, not of you. He has his rules; you have yours."

"I defeated the Austrians at Trieste. You said so yourself."

"I should have kept my mouth shut. Get this through your thick stubborn skull—we have bigger plans for you than getting skewered and roasted for a two-penny prank. What you did was egregiously stupid and selfish. I told you to think big. Instead, you risk your life lobbing quicklime at a gang of Paduan pond scum. It's beneath you. Almost unforgiveable."

I can no longer bear his brutal glower. "A thousand

apologies, Exalted Serenity. I won't do it again."

"That's all you had to say. Now get out of here. I need time to think."

I'm glad to get out but must turn back. "Mama is still missing…"

"We're doing all we can, but Brother Bernardo is sly, and we're not magicians. All your worrying won't help. Do what you can. We'll find her."

*

I COMMANDEER A boat. After docking near Santa Margherita Square, I duck into the alley and scale the ancient vine to Abdul's balcony.

"At last," he says. "I was beginning to give up hope."

"What do you mean?"

"Didn't you see my mark?"

Since my first days in the palace, Abdul has left a chalk mark on the lion column by the palace when he needs to see me.

"I didn't see it. I just got back from Treviso. Have you found Mama?"

"It isn't easy getting anyone to talk. Everyone is so frightened of knowing the wrong thing or talking to the wrong person. I failed miserably until I bumped into Sebo from St. Nick's. He said the lay brothers at La Grazia all joined the army, and the monastery has few monks left and one visitor at the hermitage."

"Of course. What was I thinking? I wasn't thinking; that's the problem. He hid there before. He's protected by sanctuary there." I bolt toward the door, but Abdul restrains me.

"One other thing, impatient one. On a brighter note…" He reaches into his tunic and pulls out a pigeon. "She returned two days ago with this…" He hands me a miniscule bit of parchment, tightly rolled, written in a hand so small that I can scarcely read it, or am I blinded by tears?

Never travel with pilgrims. I have reached Alexandria. Wish me luck.

Alex, alive and free, bounding toward her destiny, elates me for a singular instant before I dash to my boat. How utterly war and Donato distract me. I should have known my father would hide at La Grazia.

I row around Giudecca to the dark monastery, imperceptible but for a thin thread of chant from the chapel. The hermitage, on an isolated spit of rock facing northeast, reveals itself in memory. I could draw the dock, the stone wall, the pilaster, the heavy door bolted shut, and the ledge under the window above the dock where I almost cracked my skull. Once again, I pull myself up to the window and peer down into the bare room lit by a single candle. Brother Bernardo paces back and forth. Mama sits riveted to her chair by his malevolence.

I smash the door with the pommel of my sword. When it flies open, Brother Bernardo sees my sword.

"You've learned new tricks," he says. "But there's no need for that. I don't intend to hurt anyone. I was wondering how long it would take you to find us." He lobs his dagger onto the table and steps back. "I am overjoyed to see my talented son at last. I wish it wasn't so difficult to convince you to meet with me."

"Don't listen to him," Mama screams. "He'll be the death of us all."

"Quiet, woman!" He silences her with a glance. To me, he says, "I was wrong about you. I admit it, openly and humbly. I stupidly placed my bets on the wrong son. I was shortsighted, and believe me, I have paid. Surely you can forgive me."

"Some things are unforgiveable."

"You must think bigger," he says. "Forget for a moment the rules and allegiances drubbed into you by a legion of small-minded bureaucrats. Consider other ways to create a future in which you are not only beautiful and gifted, heads above other men, but powerful enough to shape the destiny of Venice. That's what I offer you."

"Keep it."

"Don't be hasty. You must also consider the position you're placing your poor mother in with your obstinate refusals."

"Satan, get thee behind me." Mama snatches Brother Bernardo's dagger from the table and holds the blade across her throat, pleading with me. "My life is worthless. He saw to that. I'd rather be dead than bait in his trap."

The big bell of St. Mark's shatters the night silence, clanging urgently. Outside the window, Cygnus shows her star-studded neck overhead, meaning we are between Matins and Lauds. Tolling no holy office, the bell summons the Great Council to an emergency session.

Seizing on my distraction, Mama crushes the candle with her palm, plunging us into darkness. I back up to shield her with my body. The bell stops. The echoes subside. Neither of us dares breathe. I no longer hear Brother

Bernardo.

"He's gone," I say to Mama.

"Vanished," she says, "like a demon from hell."

"I can't chase him. The dark conceals him, and the bells summon me."

"Do what you must," she says.

I row her to Santa Margherita and entrust her to Abdul, replacing Alex under his wing. He solemnly vows he won't let her out or anyone else in.

By the time I reach the palace, boats jam the wharf, and horses throng the square. The nobles assemble in the Great Council chamber, all but Serenissimo. As soon as they see me, Pantaleone Barbo, Federico Cornaro, and Jacopo Priuli circle me.

"Serenissimo is praying," Barbo tells me. "He assuredly hears the bells and doesn't come, but we dare not intrude on him."

I enter St. Mark's through Serenissimo's private door, and the faint sound of sorrow leaks from the crypt into the choir. Two monks, ancient and deaf, tend the candles.

Serenissimo doesn't notice me enter the crypt. No gentle weeping, his. He bawls, a big, red-faced, seventy-two-year-old baby. I clear my throat. He looks up, sees me, and stifles his tears. "*Ecce homo,*" he murmurs. "Even doges cry."

"A man who never cries can't be trusted."

He nods and wipes his nose on his golden sleeve. "Faliero, a devil if ever there was one, wept bitter tears in his cell. I heard him. Andrea Dandolo, an angel of the Lord, wept endlessly. I heard him too. Even God Almighty must sometimes weep…"

"Everyone awaits you, sire."

"And I am sick at heart. I opposed a land empire. We rule the sea. Our arsenal is a wonder of the world. Nothing compares. What a fool. We can't rule the seas without securing the coasts and ports, no matter how rich we are."

He fumbles in his sleeve for a linen to blow his nose and drops it on the wet floor of the crypt. "My fingers always did what I wanted; now they refuse to take orders. Growing old is nothing if not an indignity. I fear I'm too old for my job and shudder that the fate of the Republic rests on these weak, unworthy shoulders. Come. We have miracles to perform."

Serenissimo enters the palace, and the procession forms around him. We exit the palace gates and march around the square into St. Mark's. On the balcony above the portal, gold and silver trumpets, trombones, and tubas blare as bright and splendid as the polished armor of the Knights of St. Mark lining the steps. The canons of St. Mark's, a flock of embroidered egrets, chant the Magnificat.

The nobles jostle to catch sight of the man who, until now, was only a reputation. From balconies and porticos around the square, gorgeously arrayed women peer down, the wives and daughters of nobles shielded in silken bowers from the eyes of the rabble thronging the square. The crowd pushes against the procession, and armored guards push them back, clearing a path through the tumultuous excitement fired by so many jewels, so many great men, and especially, by Captain General Raniero di Guaschi of Siena, the new commander of the Venetian army. Following swiftly upon our victory at Solagna,

Raniero's investment as captain general crowns a wave of hope.

The Primate of Venice leads a solemn Mass. Christ ascendant hovers majestically in the golden dome above our heads, where sunlight pours through the windows of the transepts over the gold tiles framing the last scenes of Christ's earthly journey. As Judas kisses Christ, anxious Romans clamor on one side, querulous Jews on the other. The central figures, so beautiful, so human, caught in such an intimate and infamous moment, look more like brothers or lovers than betrayer and the betrayed.

After Mass, Serenissimo ascends the pulpit and calls Raniero forth. The armored general clanks up the porphyry steps to join him.

"In the name of the Great Council and of the people of the most serene Republic, I, Andrea Contarini, sixtieth doge of Venice, herewith confer upon you this baton which represents your authority over our armies. Defend us from our enemies." He hands Raniero the baton and takes hold of a standard. "This standard, the lion of St. Mark and of our Republic, representing our glory and our honor, now rests in your hands. Serve us well and bring us victory."

Trumpets and trombones blare, accompanied by chanting and cheering. The five domes magnify the din, which echoes outward onto the square. The nobles reform the procession, and we march from the church, once again around the square through the delirious horde, and back to the palace.

After the din of bells, trombones and trumpets, the crowd, the drums, and the tread of the procession, the silence in the chamber of the Ten presses upon us, palpable. The leaders assemble to set the rules of engagement for our new commander.

Pantaleone Barbo addresses Raniero. "How familiar are you with our situation?"

"I have heard the story from many different sides, so I use my intelligence to put it together in a way that makes sense to me. Lord Carrara of Padua, a worthless criminal, has convinced King Louis of Hungary, another worthless criminal, to join Padua against you. Yet no Hungarian troops have arrived. You, the rulers of Venice, would like me to lay waste to Padua before they do."

Pantaleone Barbo clears his throat, disarmed by Raniero's bluntness. "Are you aware that Austria has joined them against us?"

"Austria? Bah. Their promises are like Venetian laws, here today, gone tomorrow."

Raniero appalls the merchant princes and thrills the warriors. Serenissimo certainly evinces a willingness to give him the benefit of the doubt, but I can tell by the angle of his eyebrows, the outsides rising and the insides crushing his nose, that he is not entirely convinced Raniero is the man for the job. He cocks his head, both to hear better and to alert me to pay special attention.

He says, "Please lay out your plans for us."

"Solagna was a good choice," Raniero says. "A very good choice. I would have done that myself had we been here. So now, we march on Bassano, destroy it good, then campaign south, destroying their forage, their meat, their farms, all the way to Padua."

"What about the Hungarians?"

Raniero looks around the room. "I don't see Hungarians. Do you? Do your spies? They may never come. Only King Louis's astrologer knows for sure. In the meantime, we crush Padua."

"No siege," Serenissimo says in a tone not to be contradicted. "Unless we say so."

The nobles who consider Raniero's plan reckless raise objections, but Raniero scoops up the support of the majority like so many chits thrown down on a gaming table. Beaming at the general approbation, Raniero addresses the council.

"If I may, gracious lords..." He breaks the cardinal rule of not speaking unless spoken to, which he probably doesn't know is the rule and obviously wouldn't care if he did. The first payment of gold already jingles in his purse, the rest to come in monthly payments, extendible by mutual agreement.

Raniero speaks directly to Serenissimo. "What should I do with Lord Carrara?"

"Defeat him," Serenissimo says.

"After that?"

"Drag him here on his knees to beg our forgiveness, to deliver a very large sum of money, and to meet other conditions to be detailed upon his surrender."

"Pity I don't get to slit his throat."

"You will have to forgo that pleasure until we settle our accounts."

Raniero exits through a secret door, departing for Mestre, where his army waits. Serenissimo and I depart for the Evangelist's crypt.

"Your mother..." He still feels guilty for taking me

from her. "She's...?"

"She's safe in the care of my friend and brother."

"Not good enough. Tell me where to find her, and I will see that she is granted sanctuary at the convent of San Zaccaria. The abbess is as fierce as an Amazon, but just in case, we will post guards night and day until Brother Bernardo swings by his neck between the Columns of Doom."

"Thank you, sire. I worry so..."

"I know you do." He gently squeezes my hand. "Now that that's settled, what did you think of our Raniero?"

"Does it matter? He obviously thinks a lot of himself."

"That's part of his job. We assume he can defeat Hungary, but a Venetian would battle to the death. I'm not so sure about Raniero di Guaschi."

"We must steel the Treviso garrison to protect us if he fails. Exalted Serenity, I have a request."

"You only address me that way when you want something big. What is it this time?"

"I beg you yet again to assign me to Treviso under Captain Venturi for the duration of the war. We can ensure victory even if Raniero fails."

"I thought we settled that."

"I beseech you, Serenissimo."

He pinches my ear, a dunce. "No."

"You sincerely want me to attend meetings and count ballots until the war's end?"

"I didn't say that, did I? But I have your work cut out for you."

"What work?"

"If you'd listen respectfully instead of going off halfcocked, you would already know that we need riverboats to command the waterways from here to Padua. Mark my words, they will determine the outcome of this war. You must advise our shipbuilders. They can build anything you want, and you know those waterways better than anyone. Make sure everything is ready before the Hungarians cross the Nervesa River. Orsino Bellarosa is waiting for you."

Chapter Thirty-Three

Donato's Tale

THE STENCH OF pitch suffuses the arsenal air, mingled with fainter hints of larch, oak, pine, and charcoal from the bonfires burning outside the warehouses. A somnolent silence permeates the wharves and warehouses since two-thirds of the workers joined the army against Carrara and King Louis. Ghostly galleys loom in darkness, waiting to be called back to life. Dante described the arsenal as an inferno, but tonight, in the dancing light of bonfires, purgatory better describes the scene.

My life here consists of nonstop work briefly interrupted by restless sleep. Nothing matters but getting the job done in time and getting it right. Long after the last bell at night, I pore over maps, remembering the width and depth of strategic waterways, making notes to the boat builders on every critical stretch that is too shallow or narrow for easy passage. From these notes, we derive the necessary dimensions for new boats able to manage the challenges while carrying sufficient weight to be worth their salt. The numbers benumb my brain while the answers calculate themselves without my intervention. My hand moves on its own, writing as I slip into a half-alert, half-asleep trance. Staring at a map, the depths I sounded inserting themselves into the calculations, I feel eyes boring into the back of my neck through the half-open door.

Donato stands half in and half out of my quarters.

"I've been watching you almost an hour," he says. "Uncanny. I don't know what goes on in your mind, but your body has nothing to do with it; wherever you are, your hand keeps writing, neatly and precisely, dipping your nib in the ink and never making a blot, your eyes not closed but definitely somewhere else."

"The real maps live in my mind, but it's easy to get lost there, so these papers remind me where I am. How did you find me?"

"Giustinian told me Serenissimo assigned you to the arsenal. The rest was easy."

He removes his cloak and throws it on my bed. A vague gloom weighs on his presence, disconcerting me. He surveys my quarters, hardly more than a hut, really, like my home in St. Nick's before I was pirated to the palace.

"Not quite the Doge's Palace," he says, "but you hate that anyway. You should be very comfortable here."

"Just like home."

"Clearly, you're not joining me at Treviso any time soon."

"I grappled with Serenissimo more than once and lost every bout. You have no idea how hard I tried."

"Yes, I do. I know you."

He goes quiet, as if drifting on a current, eyes unfocused.

"Are you going to tell me what's wrong?" I ask.

"No. It's nothing." He leafs through the documents on my worktable.

"Is it the war? Or Raniero?"

He drops the papers and looks at me, his lips twisted with exasperation.

"Raniero is worse than I feared. He burned and pillaged his way from Bassano to the Brentelle, where Carrara's troops were waiting for him, surprise, surprise. The battle ended in a very bloody stalemate. Both sides claimed victory, of course, and retreated to count their dead. Rumor holds Padua the victor, but it's a Pyrrhic victory at best. Raniero argued to press on and besiege Padua, but his civilian supervisors said no way in hell. I hear it got heated. Raniero accused the supervisors of taking bribes from Carrara and withdrew his army to Abano, where word reached him that the Hungarians are approaching the Piave. The Senate summoned him to Venice to discuss strategy, which he was not happy to hear."

"What do you make of it?"

"If we fuck Raniero around, he will quit. But *if* Giustinian can block the Hungarian advance at Nervesa, Raniero *could* take Padua and end the war."

"Serenissimo hates that word, *if*. He says it's the most

dangerous word in the language, giving scoundrels refuge and madmen wings."

Still preoccupied, Donato can't conceal his turmoil, and I can't stand it.

"What's the matter? I've never seen you like this."

He clenches and unclenches his fists, averts his eyes, and says, "I have a confession to make, which is never easy."

All manner of things cross my mind, but I hold my tongue.

"You are exactly who I think you are," he says, "but I'm not exactly who you think I am."

"You're Donato Venturi, captain of the Treviso cavalry and of my heart."

"But I am more than my love for you, just like you are more than your love for me."

His evasions infuriate me. "You're scaring me. Say what you came to say or get naked and fuck me."

"I wish it was that easy." He sits, interlaces his fingers, and flexes them, staring at the floor. He bears no wounds, but his eyes look wounded.

"Let me tell you a story," he says. "This was long ago, when I was eight. My mother died only months earlier. Palazzo Venturi was dark, the walls damp as always, with salt leaching up through the bricks furry with mold. The larder and my father's purse were empty. We had one candle he used sparingly. I was so hungry that my father banished me to my room so he wouldn't have to see my misery. He paced, back and forth, back and forth, waiting for an important visitor. I hid so I could listen without being seen."

Donato pauses and takes my hand in his. "No matter what I say, don't interrupt me. Do not interrupt me. You can say anything you need when I'm done."

I nod silently, having no idea what I'm agreeing to.

"The first knock on the door that night was Ruggiero Gradenigo. He was fourteen, as mean and shitty as ever, treating my father like a slave. The next knock was your father, who treated both my father and Ruggiero like slaves. I couldn't follow most of what they were saying at first, but names and places stuck in my mind, like fantastic pennants of distant glory. Your father announced he had met with the count of Savoy and the king of Cyprus at the Grimaldi castle in Monaco, and that all they cared about was mustering another crusade. Marcantonio told them Venice could be their greatest ally if the old regime was smashed and Ruggiero, a prince of the blood, sat on the throne of Venice. He pointed out that the count of Savoy and Ruggiero were cousins by marriage through Ruggiero's mother. That scared my hunger pangs away. My father, Jacopo Venturi, lowest of nobles, cautioned your father that one insurrection had already failed and another failure would cost them their heads. Things like that stick in an eight-year-old's mind.

"Another thing stuck in my mind. Ruggiero said the old doge would soon be dead." Donato imitates Ruggiero's greedy whine. "'Then will I be prince, Father?' And Marcantonio said, 'Soon enough.' But the words sounded like a reproof to me.

"I'm not like you, as you know. I remember little of everything that happens, but I remember this night as precisely as you remember everything. Marcantonio said,

'One day soon, Marino Faliero will be elected doge. He will slaughter every last Celsi, Contarini, Morosini, Dandolo, Giustinian, Priuli, Cornaro, and Ziani, the whole traitorous cabal. But Faliero is old and won't last long. Once his job is done, we need only mobilize the people around a handsome young hero and seize the palace.'

"Ruggiero fell to his knees to kiss his father's hand, but Marcantonio pulled his hand away. He looked disgusted. He said, 'You must learn to be better than yourself, boy, or you will be eaten by the lion you dream of riding.'

"My father, still pacing and wringing his hands, also thirsted for vengeance against the other nobles as much as your father. But unlike your father, he feared danger and discomfort. He said, 'That's months or years away. What will we eat in the meantime? The butcher, the baker, and half the Rialto are taking me to court for nonpayment.'

"'Ruggiero must marry a rich commoner,' Marcantonio said. 'One with a huge dowry and her heart set on marrying a noble. That will take care of all our needs. When he sits on the throne, you need never worry about money again. Leaf by leaf, twig by twig, branch by branch, we are building the Republic's funeral pyre. We will burn it to ash and sow the ground with salt.'"

After a long pause, Donato says, "That's what I know. What I've known all along."

"That our fathers are traitors and murderers? I knew that. It damns them, not you."

"You're missing the point. I played dumb when we met. I misrepresented myself. I knew all about you before

I ever saw you. Believe me, falling in love with you was the farthest thing from my mind. We had an assignment together, and I vowed to hold my tongue rather than burden you with a toxic knowledge that maybe you knew and maybe you didn't. Fortunately for us and for Venice, Faliero's coup failed. But your father is sticking to his plan."

"Only, with me as prince instead of Ruggiero," I say.

Donato grabs my hands, his voice hoarse with emotion. "But the instant I saw you, I was lost. Lost and found. You resonated down my spine like a siren's song. The next thing I knew, I was doing things to please you, to intrigue you, to attract you to me as I was attracted to you. I lied. I played dumb. When my conscience ached to bursting, I accused you of withholding from me. Because if you were withholding from me, then we could forgive each other and move on. But the only thing you withheld, until the Priory of Brotherly Love, was your love for me. I lived in dread of the day you would discover my dishonesty and turn away from me, completely, forever. Then I feared, yes, I fear, even though you think me fearless, that you could never forgive me, that I had turned from a swan back into a dog. You never found out, but the weight of the deception crushes me. Can you forgive me?"

"I was afraid too," I say. "Afraid you couldn't love me or wouldn't love me. Afraid that I couldn't live up to you. Your love makes me a man entire, no longer a man incomplete. I told you even death couldn't put an end to it. There are things in this world I can't forgive, but you aren't guilty of those."

I bar the door to my room and undress Donato as I

undress. Unlike the palace, the arsenal does not spy on me. We stand naked, face-to-face, Donato oddly hesitant and submissive.

"If you want me to forgive you," I say, "throw my legs over your shoulders and fuck me. I want to feel your sweaty body. I want to watch your face when you fuck me. I want to see you come inside me. I promise I will forgive everything."

Charged by his mission, Donato becomes the Donato I know and dream about. His passion verges on upheaval, as if he were purging our sins and transgressions with love. He brings me to tears, so satisfied and devoutly loved. Our opposed currents collide in lightning and thunder, reaching an ethereal calm filled with wonder.

Forgiven, Donato sleeps on his back, as always, his hands across his chest, as if carved atop a marble sarcophagus. He is motionless until he leaps out of bed the instant morning light strikes his eye, alert and battle-ready, scrambling for his clothes.

"Must you leave so soon?"

He pauses, caught in the middle of an action so habitual he never questions it, and he laughs at himself. "Soon," he says, "but not that soon..."

"Then leave your clothes off so I can enjoy you in the morning light."

"How would you like me?"

"Erect."

"As you command..."

Chapter Thirty-Four

Bad News and Worse

AFTER THE DOGE'S morning Mass, Donato reports the news from Treviso to the Doge's Council. The Lovo brothers, Simone and Antonio, two of Carrara's top generals, jointly laid waste to the Trevisan countryside and again stormed Treviso. To aid our garrison, the valiant townspeople took up hoes and axes against the enemy. The Paduans pulled back at the sight of two thousand angry townsfolk with pitchforks and shovels. We slaughtered many of them as they ran until a Polish knight with a spear in each hand galloped forward, killed two of our townspeople, dashed back, grabbed two more spears, and did it again. The Paduans took heart, regrouped, and charged. By afternoon, they claimed the field, leaving hundreds of dead and dying townspeople in their wake. They marched a thousand of ours to Padua as spoils, but they never breached the fortress. We retain the fort at Solagna, and twice they have failed to capture Treviso.

As Donato finishes his report, a startling thunder rolls through the palace, silencing the debate. Guards open the chamber doors as six mounted Hungarians, all in full armor, rein in their steeds at the threshold of the council chamber. We watch, stupefied, as they dismount and raise their visors with utter contempt. Papal Legate Uguccione da Thiene and his retinue follow on foot behind them.

The Hungarian ambassador spews indignation. "You seized Lord Carrara's tower at Solagna."

"That's right," Bruno Badoer says.

"That is an act of war, forbidden by the treaty of 1358."

Pantaleone Barbo squares off against the Hungarian. "Lord Carrara recalled all Paduans banished for debt, murder, or any other crime, offering them amnesty for serving six months in the field against us. Lord Carrara also posted Antonio Lovo with one hundred cavalry and two hundred infantry to the fortress at Sant'Ilario, which is ours by right and custom since 819. He dispatched Giovanni da Peraga to Mirano Castle with two hundred cavalry and two hundred foot soldiers, and Simone Lovo, with an equal number, to Camposampiero. Paduan militias rampage freely across our border, pillaging and raping our villages. Who is provoking whom?"

The Hungarian ambassador sneers. "You leave Lord Carrara no choice. You burned the entire Padovano."

"This is not a question of the chicken or the egg," Barbo says. "Carrara began this, and we intend to finish it."

Uguccione da Thiene raises his hand for silence. "You both know very well what is at stake. The March of Treviso, possibly the whole region, now risks famine. Were it not for the fodder generously provided by your fellow princes, your flocks would starve entirely because everything has been burned to the ground. Signor Della Scala of Verona distinguished himself more than most in such blessed acts of generosity. Misery will increase tenfold when the rivers flood the farms and vineyards in Vicenza, Verona, and Padova, destroying crops and damaging herds and homes. It appears the Lord God is trying to tell you something. Beat your swords into plowshares and save these provinces from perdition."

The Hungarian ambassadors bow curtly to the papal legate, storm from the hall, and their horses' hooves beat a bellicose tattoo on the marble floors.

"We shall see," Serenissimo says in the resounding silence after their exit. The legate departs, and our council adjourns to consult their various committees of experts and advisors. Serenissimo invites me to join him in the Evangelist's crypt.

"First things first. Brother Bernardo only got as far as Mestre. He begged accommodations at a whorehouse in Mestre and, luckily for us, one of Carrara's assassins pointed him out to the peacekeepers, knowing there's a sizeable reward on Bernardo's head. We'll hold him until we have some leverage with the Holy Father; then we'll hang him."

"Where is he?"

"In the cell Marino Faliero spent his last hours in, where we swore our fealty, you and I."

When the last night bell sounds, I climb the secret stairway the doge opened to me in return for my pledge to use the privilege wisely. I no longer have to climb walls or sneak past guards to go out. The outside key is where I left it two years ago, when the ruse became unnecessary, but no torch awaits inside. I feel my way along the wall, climbing the treacherously tall stairs in darkness. I pause at the top and crack the door to the cell block.

Silent, lit by a single torch, the deserted labyrinth of barred doors offers no clues, but I need none. I could find the door blindfolded. No light creeps out through the cracks in the crude oak, no sound within but the labored breath of a sleeping man. I debate whether to knock. Any sound could draw an unseen guard's attention. The penalties for being found here, unauthorized, can be extreme depending upon how my presence is twisted by the Ten. I clear my throat, not loudly but distinctly, and listen for acknowledgement.

I clear my throat again. I put my ear to the door and whisper through the cracks. "Father, is that you?"

An agonizingly long silence.

"Father, if you're there, speak to me."

Footsteps within. With one slab of oak between us, he whispers back.

"I have many sons. Which are you?"

"Niccolò."

"Ah. What a surprise. I never dreamed you'd come to gloat."

"I'm not gloating. I'm mourning."

"I'm not dead yet."

"I mourn the father I never had. Good riddance to the one I've got."

"You haven't come like a good, faithful son to spring me from this cage?"

"You deserve this and more, for being stupid if for nothing else. Why do you trust idiots with your life?"

"I have no choice. Ruggiero lost his mind, and you aren't available. I'm forced to rely on whomever Fortune provides... With you on my side, I could accomplish miracles. Forced to rely on fools, I stumble and fall."

"Why did you try to kill me before my first birthday?"

"I believed I didn't need you. I had Ruggiero. You only complicated things."

"And now?"

"Now, alas, I know I was wrong. You're the prince awaiting his proper throne, and I bet on Ruggiero. You see how that turned out. I was blind. Ruggiero's mother was a blood princess and yours a ten-year-old whore. Unfortunately, the obvious choice was the wrong choice. But trust me, in my shoes, you would have done the same thing."

"I'd never be in your shoes. I'll die first."

The smart slap of boots on stone alerts me to an approaching guard, heavily armed from the sound of him, and they brook no mischief.

"Goodbye, Father," I say. "For the last time."

"Don't be so sure. Fate is fickle."

*

IN THE MORNING, the Lord of the Night interrupts the Doge's Council meeting.

"Brother Bernardo of the Hermits," he says, "is gone."

"Gone? What do you mean, gone?"

The Lord of the Night shrugs, bows, sweeps the floor with his cap. "He was not in his cell this morning."

Serenissimo leans forward, jaw clenched, his eyebrows furrowing his brow. "He just walked out?"

The Lord of the Night sweeps the floor with his cap again and speaks with an obsequious smile. "It's not quite that simple, Exalted Serenity. If I may explain."

"This better be good."

"It's better than good, sire." More floor sweeping. "When the morning guard arrived, they found the night guard unconscious, drugged. Inside the empty cell they found this."

He pulls a piece of paper from his sleeve and hands it to me to read aloud for all to hear.

"Great gentlemen of the Republic, forgive me for refusing your hospitality, but I have desperate work to do among the poor and needy. We all know Lorenzo Morosini should be in this cell, not me. He is a senator. I am a humble friar. I simply passed along what he gave me. Yet here I am in the cell of a fallen doge while Morosini sips wine from Crete in a marble palace. Right this wrong, and don't bother looking for me. Clean your own house rather than persecuting a man of God beyond your jurisdiction. Signed Brother Bernardo of the Hermits."

"He's given us Morosini." Vendramin's face registers shock and delight. "In writing."

Pantaleone Barbo's face screws up tight, his eyes wide

with puzzlement. "Why would he do that?"

"Morosini is no longer of any use to him," Serenissimo says, "or anyone else, for that matter. It's also a warning not to tangle with the pope over a humble friar."

"A battle we could easily lose," Barbo says.

Serenissimo nods solemnly. "Or win at far too great a cost. Jail Morosini immediately, and we'll try him for high crimes, but let's button our lips about Bernardo until we find him and draw and quarter him. We can sort the pope out later. Find out who abetted Brother Bernardo. And you..." Serenissimo glares with icy fury at the Lord of the Night, a man of previously impeccable record and reputation. "You have a lot to answer for."

The guard at the door announces the arrival of a courier from Solagna. Before backing away, pale and shaken, the Lord of the Night stands aside to let him enter. The courier cringes and shuffles, the bearer of bad news. "Five thousand Hungarians are camped at Collalto Castle, preparing to cross the Piave River near the Abbey of Sant'Eustachio."

"I assume General Giustinian knows the Hungarians are knocking on our door?" Serenissimo asks.

"The general rode out at dawn with the entire Treviso garrison in arms. He plans to cut the Hungarians off at the Piave before they can join up with Carrara's army. He plans to slaughter them separately rather than take them on en masse."

Chapter Thirty-Five

The Battle at Nervesa

Testimony of Donato Venturi before the Doge's Council and the Council of Ten:

In the name of God and our Savior Jesus Christ, in the year of our Lord 1372, on the tenth day at the beginning of the month of December, indiction fifth, in Rialto, the following is the true testimony of Captain Donato Venturi concerning the events of the ninth day of December at Nervesa on the Piave:

OUR FORCES CONSISTED of 1,000 cavalry, 1,000 seasoned battlers, 1,000 armed infantry, 500 experienced skirmishers and pickets, and 500 recruits who had never seen battle. Our pickets reported that the Hungarians were camping at Castle Collalto and would cross the Piave River at dawn near the site of the bridge Lord Carrara burned in retaliation for our attack on Solagna.

We expected their vanguard to reach the river by the first hour of day, their infantry after, their supply train last. They descended a gentle plain toward the bridge site, the river at that point a quarter mile wide, mostly shallow channels separated by aits, sandbars, and a single swift-flowing channel. We deployed our main body in a phalanx on our side of the river, flanked by two wings of cavalry. In our favor, the sun was in their eyes, the prevailing wind favored our missiles, and the enemy had a tricky river to cross. The shortness of December daylight required a quick, decisive victory before the sun inclined against us, and an indecisive outcome carried the battle over to the next day.

General Giustinian led the central phalanx, 400 shield bearers, 400 mounted men-at-arms, 1,000 spears and swords—many of our nobles along with most of our finest warriors—as well as 200 skirmishers also inside the shields. I led the right cavalry, 500 of our best horsemen, with Gerardo da Camino on the left. Each wing had 300 shield bearers, mobile and skilled, to protect our horsemen. I suggested to General Giustinian that we position ourselves farther uphill to secure the advantage of high ground. He said we had no way to compel the Hungarians to attack us if we were uphill, that they might just as easily pin us until we starve. He pointed out that they had to ford the rocky, twisted Piave, and that was advantage enough.

To our surprise, the Hungarians halted just out of our range while their infantry marched in and formed ranks behind them and waited, and waited, forcing us to wait while the sun slowly approached its apex, giving our advantage to the enemy. Impatient to engage, Giustinian signaled the skirmishers to break ranks and, under cover of shields, dart forward into range, unleash a storm of arrows and bolts, and retreat while others did the same from the opposite side, the enemy never knowing where the next storm would come from. Instead of attacking, the enemy retreated up the bank, out of range.

They must have expected the bridge to be there, and not knowing Lord Carrara had burned it, they were reluctant to ford the river, or so it seemed. Shortly after midday, they finally began their advance. Heavy armor weighed down the men and horses struggling across the rocky riverbed. A knight fell from his horse as it stumbled on submerged rocks and both nearly drowned before infantrymen lifted them out. They were distressed but too proud to retreat. But the sun was now in our eyes, and we had lost our advantage.

Count Lodovico of Hungary, a valiant knight, charged through his stumbling army with three knights fast behind him, and our cavalry met them. Lodovico bore down on Ferruccio of Mestre, one of our best riders, who tried to slash the throat of Lodovico's horse, but Lodovico managed to drive his spear between Ferruccio's shoulders and out his chest. Ferruccio fell and Lodovico trampled him, then hacked the throat of Tomaso da Murano, the glassmaker's son, and impaled Eros, son of a Rialto fruit vendor. Men I knew by name. Men I had trained.

Once across the river, the Hungarian cavalry collided with our phalanx. They could not retreat, so they circled wide and deep along our flanks, unprotected. We struggled to hold our phalanx against their charges. Dead Hungarians piled up along the riverbank.

Few of you gentlemen have done battle, but those who have know whereof I speak. Suffice it to say that each instant is a fight to the death. Spears, swords, and bolts come from every direction. Often you can't tell if a blade is friend or foe. The rolling thunder of death, muffled by your helmet, and the heat, the sweat, make your brain throb as if a strap of water-soaked leather tied around it is drying in the sun, slowly crushing your skull.

Benedict Ongero, a Hungarian knight of skull-crushing renown, was general of the field. He wanted an immediate trophy, a Venetian noble, and recognized Arrigo Dandolo, grandson of our illustrious doge. Benedict charged, unhorsing Arrigo with a spear through his right buttock. Arrigo hit the ground and was crushed under the hooves of Benedict's charger. Another of Benedict's knights hacked Antonio Moretti's head off. Giacomo Benedetti, the much-admired son of one of our most ancient noble houses, caught a spear in the base of his neck that smashed through his teeth. Domenico Carducci, a noble of Castelfranco, chased the Hungarian knight and speared him, but the blood sprayed in Domenico's eyes, blinding him for an instant as he was unhorsed by Magyar scimitars. Those, gracious sirs, were only the men I knew by name.

Captain Gerardo da Camino spotted a squad of Hungarians converging on General Giustinian and hacked a path through the gore to aid him. Our men took heart from the damage inflicted on the enemy, but some, less skilled in battle, broke ranks and rallied behind our general instead of holding their position.

At that point, I noticed a dust cloud coming from the hill behind us. Carrara's cavalry. Everything became instantly clear. The enemy had prearranged the ambush. The Hungarians stalled along the river until they knew that Carrara's cavalry was almost upon us, trapping us between their two armies.

Trumpets announced the Carrarese cavalry as our own trumpets roused our forces from their disarray to attack. Benedict Ongero of the lightning sword, favorite of King Louis, shouted, "Kill now or be killed later." Magyars charged our generals. Ongero reached Gerardo da Camino with his longsword raised and sliced Gerardo's horse through the neck. The horse buckled and Gerardo hit the ground. He leapt to his feet, enraged that Ongero had killed his best horse. He ripped the spear from the enemy's hand and plunged it through Ongero's shield before being struck from behind by a hammer that crushed his skull.

Our recruits started bolting, and Giustinian rode after them to rally them, leaving his standard behind. A Hungarian, mad for glory, slashed our standard-bearer through the collarbone. He then grabbed the lion of St. Mark, raised it high, and shouted, "Victory," from the middle of the chaos. Many of our men, uncertain what was happening, fought to the death while others, including the new recruits, bolted. The Hungarian Ongero and his cohort surrounded Giustinian and took him prisoner, claiming the day. The rest of our army retreated. Our standard hangs in shame from the church of San Antonio in Padua.

*

LEONARDO BEMBO, HEAD of the Ten: How did you manage to escape?

Donato Venturi: Many of us were able to retreat. The rest were slaughtered.

Leonardo Bembo: It is your testimony that General Taddeo Giustinian did not flee the field of battle, losing the day, the standard of the Republic, and thousands of lives?

Donato Venturi: It is my testimony, sir, that General Giustinian was captured by Magyar knights while attempting to rally a bunch of deserters to face the enemy with courage, discipline, and honor.

Leonardo Bembo: If Giustinian had deployed as you suggested, taking the high ground, would the outcome have been different?

Donato Venturi: If the wind had been blowing in a different direction, would Enrico Dandolo have breached the walls of Constantinople? There's no right answer. We don't know. Had we taken the high ground and deployed uphill, the Paduans could not have attacked our rear. But the Hungarians had already beaten us. We were outnumbered three to one. The Paduans arrived at a field already piled high with bodies, ours and theirs. I can only say that it would have gone differently. God alone knows more.

*

AT THE CONCLUSION of the hearing, I manage to catch Donato before he rides back to Treviso to resurrect the vanquished garrison. I have a thousand questions. Donato has little time.

"Are you certain Giustinian wasn't deserting a humiliating defeat?"

"Let's just say that if he was, it's completely understandable," Donato says. "Losing the battle was no reason to lose his life. The enemy carried the day but not the war. Their losses were huge, forcing them to retreat under cover of protecting Padua from Raniero."

"What's going to happen to Giustinian?"

"Carrara will house him and feed him and hold him as a high-level hostage. He's a noble and a general, not a butcher's son to throw in Ezzelino's tower."

"He's a noble, but he's not like the rest of them."

"Don't bet your balls on it."

Donato rides to Treviso. Serenissimo paces in his study, stung by the magnitude of our defeat and the Hungarian advance, carrying on a conversation with shadows.

"This cannot stand," he says when he sees me. "It should never have happened."

"But it did."

"Yes, but how? Giustinian has been known to falter under pressure, but that's why I put Donato there. I blame Donato. He's been distracted lately. He should never have allowed such an ignominious defeat."

"What could he have done?"

"I don't know. That's his job. Losing stupidly proves he's distracted."

"Distracted by what?"

"Not what. Who. You, of course, and I don't know what to do about it."

"Then you know about us?"

"I'm not blind."

"Who else knows?"

"Giustinian, I imagine."

"But that's all?"

"Isn't that enough? Here I was praying to heavenly apostles and all the angels on high that you'd deny it. What a ridiculous old man I've become."

"What are you going to do?"

"The question isn't what am I going to do; the question is, what are *you* going to do?"

"I beg you again. Post me to Treviso. Donato will be less distracted."

"Or more so."

"What distracts Donato is my absence. Put us together, and my influence will change Donato for the good."

"You honestly think you can change Donato? I'd love to see that. But that's not our most pressing problem. We must retaliate immediately. We look broken. Our people are more demoralized than before. We must strike another blow like Solagna, something to turn the tide of this accursed war. We must attack. Attack. Attack."

"I have an idea, sire, a good one. All I beg in return for victory is that you assign me to the army as Captain Venturi's lieutenant."

"One thing at a time. What's your idea?"

Chapter Thirty-Six

The Tower of Curano

I HAVE A big idea and very little time. During my map-making expedition, the tower at Curano stood out from the surrounding eaves by virtue of its location at the confluence of key waterways commanding the routes in and out of Padua and beyond. Until Nervesa, the main theater of war lay between Padua and Treviso, with all eyes jealously watching the Alpine passes for Hungarians. With land warfare our crushing disadvantage, I puzzled how to leverage our maritime supremacy. Seizing the tower and invading the water routes to Padua would shift the theater of war to our favor.

Before anything else, I send for Girolamo da Burano because he alone can ensure this victory. Lead oar and carpenter on Giustinian's galley *Lion of Venice* during the war in Trieste, Girolamo made our victory possible. At the time, I was fifteen, had never been at sea, never been outside Venice, never been at war, and knew nothing. But faced with certain defeat, I had a strategy Giustinian was desperate enough to try. When I told Girolamo what I needed, he laughed at me, but under Giustinian's orders, he obeyed. Girolamo proved to be an Alexandrian library of wisdom concerning vessels, rivers, the lagoon, the sea, the winds, the stars, carpentry, architecture, and human nature. Ferociously strong and fearless, he would never willingly tell a lie. This makes him a perfect ally, no matter how difficult or seemingly impossible the plan.

In his late fifties now, he lifts me, a head taller than him, like a child before setting me down and throwing his arms around me. "Why have you hunted me down, maestro?"

"Do you know the tower of Curano?"

"Is that thing still standing?"

"Carrara refortified it. He knows how important it is, and we've overlooked it, campaigning in the north instead. We need to use our new riverboats to capture Curano and make it a stronghold to advance our fleet upriver. That's how we win this war."

"I've seen that look in your eye before," Girolamo says.

"Can we do it?"

He shuffles his feet and clenches his fists so tightly the veins pop up along his bare arms. "We built those boats to patrol the rivers, but Curano is a forty-foot tower surrounded by quicksand."

"Not exactly quicksand."

"Show me what you mean."

I quickly sketch that area, marking the channel to Curano, the moat Carrara created around the tower, and the strategic waterways the tower commands.

"A map is only as good as the next tide," Girolamo says, still unconvinced.

He's not wrong. A high tide or a raging storm turns orchards into salt marshes and submerged sandbars into islands overnight. Landmarks come and go. Waterways, flooded by natural causes or human intervention, destroy roads, villages, farms, churches, salt pans, monasteries, and fish farms—all innocent pawns sacrificed by princes diverting rivers with an eye on the endgame.

"I was there recently," I say. "I know what I'm talking about."

"That's what I'm afraid of."

"Getting there is easy. How do we capture the tower?"

Girolamo stares off over my shoulder, chasing a thought. His eyes close, and when they open, he says without hesitation, "We build tall siege towers and mount them on barges."

"We have two barges, but we have barely eight hours if we want to leave under cover of night. Serenissimo wants his victory tomorrow."

Girolamo shakes his head, frowning at my stupidity. "You think this is the first siege tower I've ever built? Back in Trieste, when you asked me to collapse half a mountainside in six hours, I didn't know if you were stupid or crazy. When it all worked out like you said, I thought, this lad must be listened to—because you were still a lad then, no offense. Which is to say, I'm glad to see you're still crazy as ever. So trust me; if we need two siege towers mounted on barges by Compline, two we shall have."

Girolamo divides everyone we can muster into two teams, each building a tower. He issues precise orders, step by step, running from team to team, jumping in where he sees something going wrong. Shouting, hammering, harrying, cajoling, he never stops and never lets anyone else stop for more than a minute to scratch their heads or guzzle water. I try to be as much help as I can, hammering and sawing, while Girolamo grabs a crossbeam overhead, hoists himself onto the scaffolding, and climbs to the top.

Cupping his hands, he shouts, "Work, you miserable beasts of burden. Work like you never worked before, or Lord Carrara will make you wish you had."

When Compline rings, Girolamo slaps one of the rough pine towers. "No upending these. They lock into the deck. The walls of the moat will keep us from tipping too far. We'll be as sturdy and dangerous as their stone tower."

*

WITH THE MOON hardly a crescent, and the sky clear, the stars spread like a map, our fleet pulls out of the arsenal into the lagoon. Girolamo knows the route from days past and doesn't need my map. We pass St. George in the Seaweed and row until Sant'Ilario looms ahead, a squat snuffed candle in the darkness. Without a full moon, we move slowly but steadily, twenty eight-oared vessels ferrying bowmen and sappers to man the siege towers. Another sixteen boats bring up the rear ferrying infantry and supplies.

Venus flirts with the horizon as we enter the channel to Curano, a scant twenty feet wide. Six boats take the lead, each equipped with a powerful winch. The barges trail them, followed by the rest of the fleet. The high banks hide everything but our towers from the surrounding countryside.

A low mist obscures the tower of Curano, forty feet tall, thirty feet square, raised from the mud on an ashlar pedestal. A fortress lurks behind the tower, but we can barely see it in the dark.

Standing in the lead boat, Girolamo relays a signal to the general of the fleet to halt while we ease forward, barely dipping our oars. As Curano emerges from the mist, Girolamo spits. "Call that a tower? It doesn't stand up to our campanile's knees."

"Our campanile isn't in a bog swallowed by marshes."

"But looky there!" Girolamo grimaces, squinting into the fading darkness. "There's no gate," he says. "At least not where it's supposed to be. They must get in and out on the opposite side."

We anticipated a gate at the base of the tower facing us, but Girolamo speaks true. There is no gate. He orders two men to climb the banks. "Find the frigging gate, and don't get killed while you're at it."

We ease up the channel toward the moat until Girolamo raises his oar, a signal to halt.

"See the palisades?" He leans over the gunwale and points with his oar.

In the near beyond, I can see the sharpened ends of stakes poking above the water, pointing directly at our hull.

"Nasty pieces of work," I say. "They'd certainly turn back the faint of heart."

"Those are the ones you can see," Girolamo says. "It's the ones we can't see we need to worry about." Poking the bank with his oar, he propels us ever so gently forward until we bump against something. "That. Underwater. If we'd been in a hurry, they'd have sunk us sure as shit. The ones you can see make it harder if we get past the sunken bastards. No offense…"

Girolamo strips off his tunic and shirt, his trousers and leggings and linen, and stands naked in the prow.

"What are you doing? You'll freeze your nuts off."

"Somebody has to go down there and secure the hooks. Any volunteers?"

For a moment, Girolamo hesitates, his eyes wandering. "Bear grease," he growls. Shivering on this icy December morning, he rifles around in his gearbox and pulls out a heavy jar. He opens it, and we gag on the stench. He smears the grease over every inch of his body. "Won't feel a thing now. Stand back."

He climbs over the prow and eases into water covered with a thin membrane of ice. He disappears long enough for me to start worrying, and then his head pops up on the other side of the boat. He motions for a grappling hook and submerges with it. When his head pops up again, he signals the oarsmen to crank the winch greased to silence. Girolamo guides the rope out of the water while the oarsmen crank slowly. The rope groans, growing tauter as four men crank, then five, the rope threatening to snap just as the submerged stake breaches the surface. We haul it in, strip off the grappling hook, and dump the stake onto the bank. Girolamo dives back into the water to secure the next hook.

When the sixteen submerged stakes have been cleared, all six winches, one on each boat, crank in unison to pull up the exposed stakes. Girolamo shakes violently. We wrap him in a horse blanket and chafe him. The instant he's warmed, he jumps into his clothes and resumes giving orders as if nothing happened. Once the palisades are cleared, Girolamo sends word to the general. The two scouts report that the gate and drawbridge are, in fact, on the opposite side of the fort from the tower.

Girolamo's glower couldn't be darker, but only for an instant. Neither death nor danger cross his mind once it's made up. "Don't make a difference now," he says. "Let's storm this pile of shit once and for all."

The waxing sunlight dissolves the last of the mist, exposing us to broad daylight. At any moment, the men in the stone tower, dozing overconfidently, unaware, expecting nothing, will notice us. With the palisades cleared, we back out of the channel to make way for the first barge with General Delfino in charge, Girolamo at his side. The second barge follows close behind until they split up at the moat, one flanking each side of the tower. The general and Girolamo armor up as the crew attaches tall shields to the siege towers, fitting them together like puzzle pieces from top to bottom, leaving space to hurl spears and javelins and shoot arrows and bolts. The battlers take their stations on the towers. I push forward, but Girolamo's viselike fingers clamp around my neck, pinning me to the spot.

"Stand back," he says. "We can't afford to lose one such as you."

"Hands off, Girolamo. You're not my commander."

"I am," Delfino says. He steps in front of Girolamo. "And you're staying here."

"How can you waste the best bowman you've got?"

"Orders from the boss. His exact words were 'If anything happens to him, I'll cut your balls off.' Take your place with the other auxiliaries in the rear and relish our victory."

"Bullshit. I refuse." A screaming rage consumes me. I grapple with three sappers trying to subdue me until Girolamo pulls them off and stares me to silence with the majesty of his moral authority and the might of our general to back him up.

"You can't do this, Girolamo."

He says nothing. Another furious squall blows apart my military discipline.

Girolamo grabs a rope and binds me with his fiercest knots, saying as he does so, "Remember old Odysseus and the Siren. A sorceress warned him to have his crew lash him to the mast, with orders not to free him, no matter what he said, until they were well past the Sirens and he could no longer hear their irresistible song. I'm doing just that, maestro. We'll set you free when the siren song of battle has passed, and we are victorious and safe. You've done your best. Now let us do ours."

Two men drag me from the barge to a nearby boat, where a nervous lieutenant takes charge, his attention distracted by the flaming arrows raining down from the tower. We meet the barrage from Curano with volleys from both our twin towers. We outnumber them, but they are encased in stone.

"There's a cavalry unit inside the fort," I shout to the lieutenant as black smoke smudges the sky and battle batters our ears.

He sees my mouth moving and draws closer.

"Cavalry inside," I shout. "We don't know how many. If they ride out, they can attack our barges on both flanks. Who's guarding the drawbridge?" Harnessing my outrage, I manage to hook the lieutenant's attention. "Every man who isn't on a barge or boat should be guarding the gate and drawbridge. They can't attack our boats if they can't get out."

"My orders are to stand firm until called forward."

"That drawbridge can drop any instant, and then the cavalry rides out. It flanks us, tightens the noose, and kills our men storming the tower one by one. If we don't stop it, we are traitors."

The lieutenant looks to his lead bowmen, who shout, "Hell yes."

Two explosions, and then screams and shouts rattle Curano as bombards on our barges fire stone balls through heavy iron tubes, smashing the corner of the tower in a shower of shards. These new weapons frighten the enemy more than our siege towers and rouse the men around me, even the captain.

"Let's go," I shout over the chaos. "Before the drawbridge goes down."

The captain slashes Girolamo's knots and frees me. I

grab a crossbow and shield, rally the men behind me, and charge across the mud flat as two more bombards shake the tower.

"Phalanx," I shout at the captain. We herd the men into a rhombus, shield to shield, protecting the bowmen, lances, and sappers inside, firing over and between the shields. With a squeal of chain, the drawbridge thuds to ground.

The advancing phalanx blocks the drawbridge. Our bolts and arrows pierce the shields and visors of their cavalry and set them on fire. Armored riders attempting to escape crash into the moat. Behind them, our sappers and swordsmen fight their way across retractable bridges, storming the stone tower. A catapult rumbles to the drawbridge to hurl boulders and burning debris at our phalanx. We stagger backward under the barrage, and as soon as a gap opens between the bridge and our shields, the Paduan cavalry charges out, swerving around us, not engaging us, but galloping toward Padua with word the Venetians have taken the tower of Curano.

Chapter Thirty-Seven

Fool's Mate

WHEN VENICE GETS word of our victory at Curano, the people take to the streets in a paroxysm of relief like a condemned prisoner granted a last-minute pardon. A ray of hope pierces the doomsday dread gripping the city since the disaster at Nervesa. Nothing constrains the mania.

Inside the palace, different weather prevails. The attack and victory at Curano surprises the Senate as much as the people in the square, but the nobles' response splits along party lines between the warriors and merchant princes.

"Who authorized the attack?" Federico Cornaro of the Ten asks on behalf of the merchant princes. Like everyone else, they had no voice in the decision to seize

Curano but dare not show their pique while joyous celebrations rattle the windows and walls of the palace.

"I did," Serenissimo says, "upon the advice of my general."

"The captain general of our army?"

Gilberto da Coreggio steps forward. "In the captain general's absence, I advised His Exalted Serenity."

Both Coreggio and Serenissimo are lying, but the secret is safe between them. Once again, Serenissimo has tempted the executioner's ax. His debits still outweigh his credits in the Ten's ledger, and they specifically advised him to leave war to the generals and keep his mouth shut. He took a huge risk on my plan for Curano. The victory emboldens him. Now, even the Ten cede to his leadership, if not his authority.

"The question is not who authorized it," Serenissimo says, "but how we follow it up."

Bruno Badoer pounds the table with his fist. "Where the hell is Raniero?"

"On his way to Mestre," Marino says. "At our request, although he's taking his time to demonstrate his disgust that we vetoed his siege. He is reported to have said we could have taken Padua by now, slit Carrara's throat, and sent the Magyars home with nobody left here for them to protect."

Badoer ignores Marino. "He bloody well better have an excuse for why our only victory since he got here was led by the ballot boy."

Badoer creates a furor among those who didn't know, and disapproving scowls from those who did. They don't object to the victory; they object to the glory it reflects on me. More than anything else, the nobles of Venice fear the rise of a popular commoner who eclipses their collective glory. It's why they fear Admiral Pisani and why our military leaders are all nobles. We have no statues of great men in public places, neither in the palace nor the squares of Venice, except for their likenesses on their tombs. I'm not happy about my renewed notoriety either, which is another target on my back.

"We are back where we began," Serenissimo says. "What next?"

"Do you have a suggestion?" Marino asks the question on everyone's mind.

"I'll leave that to the generals."

From my seat behind Serenissimo, I lean forward. "May I speak, Exalted Serenity?"

"By all means, speak. You have better instincts than our so-called wise men."

In stark contrast to the raucous celebration outside, the senators glare at me in silence, some with undisguised anger, some with hatred, some with envy, all loath to admit they need me.

"Lord Carrara certainly understands the strategic importance of Lova," I say. "To his mortal peril, he ordered Hungarian troops to dig ditches and build forts, while the Hungarian princes on whom his fate depends chew their nails, ravening to do battle, then grab their loot and go home."

"We all know that," Federico Cornaro says with a sneer. "Say something we don't know or hold your silence."

"I beg your indulgence, sir..."

Cornaro nods reluctantly as if being forced to listen to the ravings of an idiot.

"Pliny the Elder in his *Natural History* refers to the crocodile as a four-legged curse…"

"No Latin lessons," shouts Badoer. "Get to the point."

"Let him finish." Serenissimo momentarily quells my hecklers.

"…a four-legged curse on land and water. Pliny reports the dolphin, a peaceful trickster, is the mortal enemy of the dreaded crocodile, killing them neither with greater strength nor sharper teeth, but with guile. The dolphin's dorsal fin is pointed and sharp as a knife. The crocodile's leathery skin turns thin and soft across its belly. When confronted with a crocodile's lethal jaws, the dolphin feigns fear, dives beneath the crocodile, and rips open the vulnerable belly with its dorsal fin."

Badoer's face grows redder. "What in hell do dolphins and crocodiles have to do with the Hungarians in Padua?"

"Lova is the crocodile's belly, sir. Carrara's carapace, strong elsewhere, is thin and vulnerable at Lova, where his territory meets the eaves. If we smash him at Lova, all lower Padua is vulnerable to our river fleet. With a channel from Curano to Lova, we can push our boats to the triple walls of Padua. We can fight how we fight best, not with a mounted army but with a mobile fleet ferrying thousands of skilled fighters armed with swords, bows, and spears."

"I heard an 'if,'" Cornaro replies.

"The only 'if' is our commitment, sir."

Silence greets me. Even Badoer pauses to think, an unusual and disorienting process for him. Puzzled, he blurts out, "That's idiotic. You can't fight a naval war on land."

"We just did. At Curano." Serenissimo verges on boiling over. I'm sure others see it, Marino Vendramin certainly, Pantaleone Barbo without doubt. But Badoer, blind to everything the least bit human, does not. Serenissimo shouts directly at him, "Do you have a better idea?"

Flustered, unable to offer an alternative, Badoer diverts, blurting out, "Have we approved replacements for those loose-lipped money-grubbing traitors who sabotaged Raniero's siege of Padua?"

"The replacements were approved unanimously, sir," I reply.

"Then what are we waiting for?" Badoer looks genuinely puzzled. "Get them into the goddamn field and make war. If you say Lova, let's smash Lova."

Federico Cornaro interrupts again. "Need I point out we are at our old stalemate?"

"Which stalemate is that?" Serenissimo fixes his outrage on Cornaro.

"Allow me to refresh your memory, Exalted Serenity. We botched the battle at Brentelle and failed to besiege Padua. We got slaughtered at Nervesa where our ablest general was captured and spirited off to Hungary. And now we face the combined armies of Padua, Hungary, and Austria, outnumbering us two to one. But on the basis of a single victory at Curano, stunning as it was, you want to attack again. Your enthusiasm for attack is admirable but misguided."

"And you'd rather fiddle while Rome burns, you idiot." Badoer spits his words like darts.

"Even as we speak," Pantaleone Barbo says, "a hundred young nobles are ready to take command as soon as the Turk archers arrive."

His middle ground of measured caution clearly disappoints Serenissimo. "Soon isn't soon enough," Serenissimo says. "You heard what the man said. Neither side has staked the high ground yet. Instead, we're building like beavers in places we never gave a thought to, probably the wrong places, while we neglect Lova, which is undermanned and poorly guarded by both sides in this godforsaken war. Why shouldn't we bring in our boats and rip the belly open right now? Let's win this war."

"That's what you say, but fortunately it's not your decision to make, is it?" Cornaro says and invokes the Ten and the Doge's Council. The Senate adjourns in disorder, the factions arguing among themselves. General Coreggio, Marino Vendramin, Serenissimo, and I adjourn to Serenissimo's chambers.

"Let's do what we did at Curano," Coreggio says. "Attack and ask later. If we win, they will have to cheer."

"I'm rather attached to this battered old head," Serenissimo says, "and those old boys mean business. Maybe if we give them a little time, they will put their heads together and come up with our idea as if it were their own."

Much verbal grappling occurs over the next two days until the Ten agrees to muster our river fleet, complete the dig from Curano to Lova, and press our naval advantage. But when I again ask Serenissimo to assign me to the field, he laughs.

"I'm not wasting you as a digger, knee deep in mud."

His fingers hover over the chessboard on his desk. He moves a white pawn to the king four square and looks at me expectantly. As soon as I move the black pawn to king five, he moves his knight to king's bishop three, a common opening and standard reply.

"Opening moves and midgames," he says, "generally amount to waiting for the enemy to make a mistake with no clear endgame in sight. I build a fort. You build two forts. I dig a canal; you block it and build your own. We need strategy."

He returns the pieces to their original places and rotates the board so I'm white and he's black. I move my king bishop's pawn to bishop four. Serenissimo advances his king's pawn, setting up a fool's mate. "I see your point, sire." I move my king's knight pawn forward two spaces, and Serenissimo slides his queen to king's rook four.

"Checkmate," he says. "In three moves. That's what we need."

"There's still time."

"Easier said than done. We need Carrara to make the right mistake in order to checkmate him in three. Give it some thought."

I retreat to my room and climb onto the high window-sill overlooking the roof of St. Mark's, watching and listening for Donato, until his feet land on the roof with a muffled thud and he disappears between the domes, emerging below me where the palace wall abuts St. Mark's. He stares up, a shadow among shadows, only his eyes glittering in the moonlight. He scales the decorative raised bricks crisscrossing the palace wall like intersecting steps. I drop back into my room as Donato reaches the windowsill and swoops down, a raven, his black cloak spread like wings in which he enfolds me.

"I've come to celebrate your latest victory. Sorry it took so long."

"Girolamo's victory."

He grabs me by the ears and shakes my head. "Stop that. Take the credit you deserve. Soldiers talk. I know what happened."

Donato drops his cloak, and our dance begins. I unbuckle his sword belt and set it aside. Next, I unbuckle and remove his leather breastplate. He plants his palms on his head, giving me access to his fastenings, the muscles in his upper arms swelling. I inhale the familiar musk of his armpits, the left more acrid than the right, mysterious and enticing. After removing his breastplate, I kneel to unbuckle his greaves, set them aside, and remove his boots and leggings, leaving only a sheathe of chain mail from his neck to his thighs, his loins wrapped in linen. I stand and Donato extends his arms so I can lift the mail over his head, and when I drop it, it jingles like coins on the terrazzo. His broad chest and shoulders gleam, lustrous as highly polished ebony in the light of the fat white candle Serenissimo supplies me because he knows I like to read in bed.

I drop to my knees, my hands at my sides, admiring this magnificent man. Donato pushes his hips forward for me to unbind his loins. "What are you waiting for?"

"I'm not waiting for anything. We're always in such a rush I don't have time to look at you."

He looks down at himself, running his fingers over his scars. "Looks pretty beat up if you ask me."

"The scars make you more precious. Like Serenissimo's jade vase from Cathay, perfect except for cracks repaired with delicate seams of gold, no longer perfect, but better than perfect, perfected with loving care. Your body reveals deep vulnerability beneath your awesome power. How did you get so strong?"

"Working in the arsenal from the time I was eight," he says. "For the first few years I was the outsider, the Black boy. I never told a soul my father was a noble of Venice. I hid myself in their version of me. Only Orsino Bellarosa and Serenissimo knew my true origin, and neither revealed my secret. They wanted me to learn the tough lessons, so they left my survival to me. No matter where I worked, I did the heavy lifting—oars, beams, frames, oak, ash, maple, mallets, hammers, pitch cauldrons—moving, lifting, mounting, removing. When my weapons training began, I quickly learned different weapons require different strengths, and I focused on reshaping my body while developing stamina. I had no friends and nothing to do but work and sleep, so I concentrated on perfecting myself until my sword felt as light as a reed and a great lance was a willow branch in my hands. Eventually, I could wield them for hours without tiring, hurling them higher and farther than any man in the arsenal, where there are some real beasts. Have you looked at me enough?"

"I'm not *looking at you*. I'm basking in your glory."

"It's time for me to bask in yours."

"I'm hardly worth basking in."

He laughs at me. "You're perfect. My very own Adonis. Your body has changed under my tutelage. You're thicker and stronger. From the back, I hardly recognize you."

We stand perfectly still, savoring each other with our eyes. When he reaches for me, I pull back.

"Let's just look a while longer."

"Come closer."

"No touching."

"You don't want to grapple, just a little?"

"Not yet."

We circle each other, almost touching but not quite, watching our bodies move, dancing without music, until Donato runs out of patience and pulls me toward the bed. He touches me, exploring what he sees, caressing each surface and probing each recess. His cock stands at high alert. Our swords cross as we drift in each other's eyes, inebriated.

"I want to fuck you more than anything in the world," he says. "But I'm not going to. I am going to stand here like a good soldier, awaiting orders. Tonight, we march to your orders, not mine, sir. Whatever you've been really wanting and holding back, let go."

I close my eyes and explore his body with my hands, a blind man reading features with his fingertips. My hands barely encircle his neck, a massive plinth supporting his noble head. The angular muscles at the base of his neck slope outward, yoking the dense globes of his shoulders. His wide chest, deeply cleft in the center, consists of two symmetrical plates of muscle articulated like Roman armor, tipped on each side with a thick black nipple growing erect at my touch. I continue reading his body with my fingertips, following the veins running like cords under the skin. He claps his hands behind his head, opening his armpits, no simple declivity but a complex intersection of muscles from his arms, his chest, and his back flared like wings for my enjoyment. His torso tapers from the wide yoke of his shoulders to his narrow loins, and then his thighs burst, each as stout as both of mine together and finely etched with plaited straps of sinew. His immense erection brushes my face as my fingers descend his thighs, tapering dramatically to his knees. I embrace his calves which swell the narrow pillars planted in his brute feet, marched-out, massive, manly feet carved from onyx and gilded with candlelight.

I bend to kiss his feet and run my tongue up his leg, kissing his knees, his thighs, his bush and belly, taut as a drum beneath my tongue. Donato cedes his body and moans his appreciation for the lightness and intimacy of my touch. His cock, which has often penetrated me and no longer intimidates me, hangs engorged, covered with a thin caul of skin stretched smooth, pendulous and awe-inspiring. Seeing him in dreams arouses me; seeing him thus overwhelms me. I lean closer, and his cock rises to meet my lips, the unsheathed head lighter in color than the rest of his skin, while the shaft is darker, a lustrous black with a liquid pearl leaking from the tip. I catch it on my tongue.

"Is that what you want?"

"It's what I've always wanted."

I nuzzle the underside of his cock with my lips, and the head swells further. Below the furled cap, the triangle of his most sensitive skin exposes itself. He pants as I tease it gently with my tongue, down the shaft to the base, where his balls hang, heavy walnuts in a velvet sack. He bends his knees so I can admire how his cock continues behind the sack all the way to his anus. I trace the ridge with my finger and slide it inside him. His cock pulses, dropping more pearls. The head alone fills my mouth, and I quickly reach a limit, thinking I might faint, devoid of breath, but I yield to the urgent pressure of his cock massaging the spasms of my throat.

"Oh, God, just like that." He groans, tenses, but falls short of spiraling over the precipice. Tears sting my eyes as I look up at him, smiling ruefully.

"I'm sorry," I say, thinking his failure to climax somehow my fault.

"You don't have to do this..." he says.

"Yes. I do. This is what I want."

He tousles my hair. "Then let me help you." He lifts me and arranges me on the bed so that my head tilts back over the edge. Standing over me, smiling, he straddles my face and eases into my open mouth. This angle of approach makes the curve of his cock congruent with the curve of my throat. He sighs, rocking his hips, moaning as he goes deeper, his inner thighs pressing against my cheeks. His movement grows more fluid, and although I do my best to relax and accept, the fever pitch of his ardor still doesn't reach climax.

"Breathe through your nose." He eases back. I am dizzy, insanely aroused, and starved for air, wanting his climax more than my own. He adjusts his body, bends forward, and plants his palms on either side of me. Sweat bathes his chest, his belly, his groin. His nipples draw near as he rocks his hips, shoulders bent forward, and buries himself to the hilt as both of us strain for release. He bends closer, drops his head, and swallows my cock whole, shocking me into a new realm of ecstasy. I fumble for his nipples and twist them, hard, then harder, until he bellows at the precipice, triggering me, and we come together, gasping, choking, laughing, crying.

"You can spit," Donato says. "I won't be offended. That's what horny soldiers do when they suck each other in the field."

I shake my head and swallow. This is my wine and wafer, his essence mingling with mine, enclosing us in a loop, our life streams merged. This kiss means many things, but most of all, it means we are forever one.

"You're a fast learner," Donato says when we catch our breath. "I've never had it quite that good."

"Neither have I. I couldn't have imagined it before this hour."

We lie in a daze until the bells of St. Mark's sound first light, and day begins. Donato dresses to leave, and in the ebb of our lovemaking, I return to the problem Serenissimo posed: checkmate in three. I summarize the discussion for Donato, who listens intently as he fastens his boots and straps on his greaves.

"I don't know much chess," he says. "But I see the problem. Let me think about it."

Chapter Thirty-Eight

St. Mark's Day

"YOU'RE LATE," THE doge says.

"Actually, I'm early, Exalted Serenity. The celebrations don't begin until the sixth hour."

"Something fishy is afoot."

"Fish don't have feet, sire."

"Come along. You'll see what I mean."

We go to the Senate chamber, where his advisers and the Ten sit in stony silence on the dais. I did not expect to see Raniero of Siena biting his fingernails, eyes lowered, knee jiggling. An angry frown twists his brow under ill-kempt golden curls. As soon as we are seated, all eyes turn to Raniero, who stands abruptly and speaks.

"I come to tell you gentlemen that I quit."

Thunderous silence. He reaches behind him for the standard of St. Mark and thrusts it at Marino Vendramin, the man closest to him. The chamber remains ferociously aghast.

"Would you care to explain?" Pantaleone Barbo asks.

"Those supervisors, lousy civilians, are stupid and ridiculous. They blocked my siege of Padua when I could have won. Now look at the mess. They insulted and disrespected me. I suspect they take gold from the Carrara. There is no other excuse for what they did. Watch out for them."

"We needed you at Nervesa, not tied down in a siege of Padua," Barbo says.

Raniero shrugs his shoulders. "I had a chance to win this war for you, and you got in my way. I'm through here."

Bruno Badoer's Olympian scowl should wither Raniero, but he is too proud to notice. "We told you the Hungarians were in Gorizia. Did their arrival dampen your ardor for battle?"

"I answer to you no more. I was trying to do what I was hired to do, but your idiots prevented me. Our business is finished."

The eyes of the Ten turn to Domenico Michiel, the civilian supervisor with whom Raniero came to blows over besieging Padua.

"The siege was ill-advised," Michiel says. "We could not allow it. With the Hungarian army marching south, we would have been encircled."

"It's all water under the bridge," the doge says. "Our victory at Curano has shifted the center of the war where it belongs."

"I congratulate you on your victory," Raniero says. "And now I take my leave."

He arrived amid bells and rejoicing. He leaves under a dark shadow. Fortunately, Curano gives us hope.

"Gentlemen," Pantaleone Barbo tells the senators, "we must confer now. We will advise you as soon as we have something to report."

Raniero and the senators depart, leaving only the Doge's Council, who adjourn to a private council chamber.

"Good riddance to bad rubbish," Badoer says as the door closes. He turns to the doge. "Now what?"

"Find out if our idiot supervisors have taken gold from Carrara. If that's true, throw them in prison. We can't do anything else about that."

"And who shall lead us?" Pantaleone Barbo arches his brows and waits.

"Gilberto da Coreggio," the doge says. "He's the best general on hand. I refuse to throw more money away on mercenaries."

"Good," Badoer says. "A Venetian, noble and true."

The decision is unanimous.

"Now it's time to celebrate," Serenissimo says, his tone sour with irony.

Of all Venetian holidays, St. Mark's Day takes pride of place. By venerating our patron saint, we also venerate the Republic represented by our doge. As a political fact as well as an article of faith, Venetians consider our doge the pope's equal, not his vassal. The doge derives his moral authority directly from St. Mark, just as the pope derives his from St. Peter. Prior to the ceremonial Mass celebrating St. Mark, the papal legate and the doge confess simultaneously to the same priest, demonstrating their equivalence. Thus, the believers believe.

The doge's procession swells to over 150 senators, committee heads, musicians, generals, and foreign ambassadors. The Knights of St. Mark carry the sacred sword of justice, the golden umbrella under which the doge walks, and the purest white candle, gifts from a pope to a doge centuries ago. From the palace, we march around St. Mark's Square, already thronged with cheering masses, into St. Mark's Basilica, where the bones of the Evangelist sleep in the crypt below the high altar. The magnificence of this greatest of churches echoes more powerfully than the drumbeats of war, at least in this glorious moment. Brass choirs fill the domes with brazen fanfare, followed by a Magnificat sung by voices in the choir and on the women's balconies amid the high arches. During the Magnificat, the doge places a white candle on the high altar and lights it, an act he performs only on St. Mark's birthday.

After Mass, the doge greets the procession of guilds and lay confraternities, each bearing their most precious relics: a bone from St. Roch's finger; St. Mark's episcopal ring; a single thorn from Christ's crown of thorns, displayed in gold and silver reliquaries studded with jewels. They also bring golden bowls embroidered with silver filigree and filled with white candles.

The head of the Confraternity of St. Mark, the most exalted position for a commoner, presents Serenissimo with a fragrant candle tattooed with brilliant pictures of

St. Mark visiting the lagoon, the Contarini coat of arms artfully embroidered into the filigree framing the pictures. The representatives of lesser, more plebian guilds distribute simple white candles to the assembled clergy, the ambassadors, the papal legate, and the other members of the doge's retinue. The procession of the guilds winds around the square to celebrate the close and personal connection of our doge to every class of Venetian society. To enhance the general merriment, each guild and confraternity brings musicians with them, playing in turn, vying to outdo one another in skill and inventiveness as they march before the doge's dais.

Serenissimo sits on the throne nodding recognition to all of these men, the bedrock of Venetian supremacy. The repetitive nodding pains him greatly because on this day, only he wears a tall, pyramid-shaped miter resembling the pope's. Serenissimo taps his toe to the rhythm of the music, but I hear only the relentless drumbeat of time—the call to arms, my twentieth birthday, the Evangelist's birthday, spring's awakening, and the steady advance of war. Beyond St. Mark's Square, the basin and the lagoon sparkle in the sun, liquid jade as crowded with boats as the square is with people.

But the festivity plunges me into despair—the silken standards, the mighty generals, renowned ambassadors and nobles, the drums and trumpets, even the shower of gold coins imprinted with the doge's likeness scattered to the multitude, which never fails to raise the hopes and spirits of the people. *Vanitas, vanitatem.* Our splendor cannot save us. To my ears, the trumpets ring hollow, tarnished, and fragile—the splendor only an elaborate mask over the abyss at whose precipice we dangle so precariously. In the endgame, gold and jewels are only spoils of war.

Following the festivities, Serenissimo, Admiral Pisani, who is visiting from the east, and I slip into the deserted chapel of St. Nicholas in the palace. Marino joins us lest Serenissimo be accused of holding a private meeting. Serenissimo fears neither Marino's ear nor his discretion. Guariento the Paduan painted the walls of the chapel, depicting the triumph of Doge Ziani and Pope Alexander III over Frederick Barbarossa, the Holy Roman Emperor. Barbarossa prostrates himself in front of St. Mark's Basilica in an act of submission. The pope places his gold-and-pearl-embroidered slipper on Frederick Barbarossa's head. Serenissimo sees what I'm staring at.

"That's where we'll end up if we lose this war," he says. "May we never live to see it."

"I hate to be the bearer of bad news..." Pisani does not fear Serenissimo will kill the messenger as much as he fears breaking a great man's heart. I see it in his eyes. He loves Serenissimo as much as I do, and it pains him to deliver a heavy blow.

"You never beat around the bush," Serenissimo says. "Tell me what you know."

"A Castilian fleet passed through Corone on their return from Constantinople, and I spoke with their admiral."

"Is he reliable?"

"He had no reason to lie."

"What did he say?"

"He told me that Genoa offered King Louis a fleet of

galleys against us in return for sovereignty over Tenedos."

Serenissimo's eyebrows slump downward, nearly covering his eyes, and he twiddles the gold buttons on his robe of state. "I told them," he says. "Over and over again. I told them in no uncertain terms, but no one listened. The rest of this menagerie, Carrara, the idiot legate, the Austrian clowns, even the French pope, are nothing compared to bloodthirsty Genoa."

"There's more," Pisani says, shoulders drooping. "We currently govern Tenedos by decree of John V, emperor of the east. The Castilian admiral also told me that Genoa has promised to overthrow the emperor and set his son Andronikos on the throne if Andronikos guarantees to grant them perpetual lordship of Tenedos. That news is months old; the coup may already be underway."

Serenissimo's worst fear comes true, Genoa controlling the sea-lanes and the riches of the east. We barely managed to wrest Tenedos from the emperor's hand. The golden bull in our archives granting us sovereignty over the island means nothing if Andronikos usurps the throne.

"And if we lose Tenedos," Pisani says, "we lose the game."

"You don't need to remind me," Serenissimo says, not sharply but sadly. "Soon, we'll have nothing left but salt to sell, back to the way it was a thousand years ago."

Pisani kneels and kisses Serenissimo's hand. "I have seen what these hands can do in peace and in war. You can still save our Republic, Exalted Serenity."

"You are a far more likely candidate for that job," Serenissimo says, and without further ado, he retires, exhausted, leaving me alone with Pisani. My old friend looks at me admiringly.

"You've put on six inches and forty pounds since I taught you to ride. I'd say you're doing well."

"I do my best. But Serenissimo is an overzealous nursemaid and won't let me fight in this war, despite the fact that I'm most valuable on the field."

"Somebody has to look out for the old man." Pisani doesn't smile, and his serious eyes sober me. "If we lose a good soldier, we lose a good soldier. We weep, our hearts mourn, but there are other good soldiers. If we lose you, we lose a unique and indispensable asset helping Serenissimo stay the course. Don't underestimate that. Now, forgive me. I have more business to attend to, nowhere near as pleasurable as your company." He shakes my hand, thinks better of it, and embraces me like a beloved cousin.

Chapter Thirty-Nine

Pawn to King Four

IN THE SILENT hours between Matins and Lauds, while Marino Vendramin dozes outside the half-closed door of Serenissimo's study, Serenissimo summons me. He stands in front of the fireplace where no fire burns, jabbing the air with an iron poker. I shift from foot to foot uneasily, not knowing why he has called me.

Without turning around, he says, "You might want to sit down for this."

I sit, take a deep breath through my nose, set my hands on my knees, and breathe out slowly through my mouth, curious and terrified.

Serenissimo turns toward me without looking at me. "I know what I've said in the past, so I apologize for contradicting myself, but things have changed and not in a good way for us. I don't have to explain that to you." He sets the poker down. His gold robe sweeps the cold ashes across the marble floor. "Believe me when I say I have wrestled with this all night, like Jacob with the angel."

I flip through the many transgressions I have committed despite my best efforts to live up to his expectations, and none seems equal to this moment.

"I just don't see any way around it," he says. "My mind is made up."

Words clearly intended to convince himself, not me.

"Pardon, sire. Please tell me what you're talking about?"

He hunches over his desk, silent, looking deep into my eyes.

"I'm sending you into the field as a special attaché to General Coreggio."

All my anxiety, months' worth, years' worth, explodes in fireworks and confetti.

"It wasn't an easy decision to make." Serenissimo relaxes as he stands behind me, resting his hands on my shoulders. "But I keep running up against the simple fact that we need every possible advantage we can muster, and I can't justify holding you here when you are so incomparably valuable in the field. If we win Lova, Louis must withdraw his army."

Marino speaks up. "You truly think King Louis will give up that easily?"

"He has sacrificed all the men he can afford, and it has gotten him nowhere."

"He has allies, and he has plans. He might not give up

so easily."

Serenissimo rises to his full height, glaring at Marino. "I swear by all that is right and holy that when Carrara loses the next battle, Louis will cut his losses and drag the Voivode of Transylvania back to Hungary, trailing his army behind him. Louis has no use for Carrara if the lord of Padua can't hold his own. The Turks are storming the Istrian gate, Serbia has fallen, and the pope won't muster a crusade. Louis's hands are full."

"Of course, Exalted Serenity," Marino says. "But *if* they win?"

"Sometimes you say the stupidest things." Serenissimo slams the door in Marino's face and takes my hand. "Marino is ridiculous. Failure is unthinkable. We will win. You are a peerless marksman, a brilliant tactician, a walking encyclopedia. Put your head together with Donato and Coreggio. Do something brilliant. Win this infernal war."

"I'm honored, sire." I kneel and kiss his hand. "I can always count on you to do the right thing, just as you can always count on me. I can't promise victory, but I can vow to make every effort humanly possible to win."

"Report to General Coreggio at field headquarters in Gorgo di Onaro. Donato is already there. Keep an eye on him. It appears you are the only one he still listens to, and you well know he can be fatally impetuous." Serenissimo holds up his hand to silence me before I can speak. "I know. Caesar was also impetuous, but Donato is only Caesar in your mind, despite the many traits they share."

"When do I leave, sire?"

"What are you waiting for?"

*

I LEAVE DELFÍN behind. She was not bred for battle. I row alone across the lagoon to Curano. Captain Orso, the day officer in charge, remembers the stink I made when Girolamo hog-tied me during the battle for the tower. He also remembers my gambit to divert Carrara's cavalry from our boats, ensuring we won day. He treats me with exaggerated respect and takes me to his quarters to debrief me, spreading a hastily drawn map on his table.

"Here we are." He points to Curano, marked with a crude sketch of a tower resembling the rook on a chessboard. He traces a line with his finger. "Here's the channel dug. We reached Lova and have to connect the dig to the Fiumicello River, here, this way to the Brenta, this way to the Bacchiglione, which encircles Padua proper. All lower Padua is at risk once we finish. That's why they're desperate to stop us."

"How secure is the garrison at Lova?"

"Our fort is on this side the river, facing that crude bastion they threw together on the opposite side. We established our field headquarters at Gorgo di Onaro, three miles east of Lova just in case. As soon as we built Gorgo, Carrara moved his field headquarters to a new fort at Campagna a couple miles away. Carrara is at Campagna, along with Novello, two top Hungarian generals, the voivode himself and all his men, and a thousand Paduan cavalry and infantry. Donato believes their main objective is to block us from the Fiumicello and wreck our dig."

With thumb and index finger, I trace arcs on the map. "Gorgo is equidistant from Lova and Campagna.

Campagna is equidistant from Lova and Gorgo. The pieces are all in position, carefully covered. The only thing we don't know is who will make the first move."

"Don't get me started on that," Orso says. "I would if I could, but I'm under orders to protect the dig until further notice, so that's what I'm doing."

I yawn, and Orso puts his map aside. "You look weary. Would you like to sack out for a while?"

"No. I'm fine. I'll be even better when I get to Gorgo."

"Then you better get going."

He provides me with a fine horse and offers me an armed escort to field headquarters. I'm inclined to refuse the escort until I notice, among their number, my old friend Matteo, whom I last saw in Cavarzere when Alex departed with the pilgrims. I sneak up behind Matteo's horse and flick its haunches. The horse stamps and nickers, and Matteo glares back, annoyed, until he sees me and vaults from his saddle. He grips me in a bear hug, beaming his irresistible smile, and slaps my back.

"Damn, old friend," he says, "I hear you did it again."

"Me and a legion of fearless Venetians."

"I see you know each other," Captain Orso says. "Matteo's a good man. Best master of horse in the army."

"I met Matteo in the palace stables," I say. "He took care of my horse."

"The horse the doge himself gave him," Matteo says. "Delfín. She's a beauty."

"We'd best leave," I say. "The general expects me."

Matteo and three men-at-arms accompany me as we cross the strange countryside, where bogs, lakes, and fields scramble together like eggs. Matteo and I ride side by side, allowing the others to pass far enough ahead that they can't hear us.

"Oh, brother," he says. "What a blessed relief to see you. I've been dying to talk to you. That was some stunt you pulled at Curano."

"I'll wager that's not what you've been dying to talk to me about."

"You haven't changed a bit." He speaks with an indulgent smile. A loving smile. "Business first, always. Or are you worried I'll start telling you I love you again, or something? Because if you are, I want you to know I've moved on, found greener pastures. Well, not greener. There's nobody better than you. But believe it or not, there are others out there who think I'm the peaches' fuzz."

"You are, and I'll love you always."

"I know. *Just not in that way.* But it doesn't matter now. I'm getting married. Nice girl from the parish. She thinks I'm the second coming of Our Lord and Savior, and she's not squeamish about sucking my cock."

"I'm happy for you."

"No, you're not. You think I'm a hypocrite as well as a sinner. But you know what? I figured if I couldn't have you, what the hell, right? Anyone else will always be second best."

"No, I envy you," I say. "At least the monks aren't itching to burn you."

"You don't seriously still worry about that, do you? I mean, how could you, with the doge to defend you and Black Hercules as your captain."

"I worry about everything; you know that."

"Does everything include Donato?"

"I worry that he'll be killed, that I'll lose him, that I won't be able to spend the rest of my life with him. Why did you ask?"

"Forts are funny places," Matteo says. "Soldiers from all over. They've seen different things. Talked to different people. All manner of bullshit abounds, of course, but under some piles of bullshit, there's often a kernel of truth."

"Are you saying you've heard things about Donato?"

"Don't be like that. I'm your friend. I worry about you. No matter how far apart we may be, you're always in my heart, and I want you to be happy. I worry about you being hurt again, like with Astolfo, the asshole of Castle Moccò. Don't think I'm jealous, because I'm not. I know that even if Donato vanished into thin air like the pea under a mountebank's shell, I still wouldn't stand a chance with you. I know that. But I still care."

"Tell me what you heard."

"Well, I heard that something may have happened while you were visiting King Louis. A Hungarian prisoner was shooting his mouth off because he had nothing better to do, rotting in prison and all."

"What was his name?"

"Doesn't matter. They all sound alike. He was definitely one of the king's men, had that fleury French thing on his shield. A real warrior we managed to capture. But he said he was there when you were, and that's where he heard it."

"Is he reliable?"

"I don't think anyone is reliable. But if it matches what you know, then maybe there's something in it. If not, it's plain old-fashioned bullshit. He said a soldier in his outfit was on guard duty at the palace. His boss sent him to fetch Donato and take him to the king. Apparently, good King Louis wanted to see if it's true that Africans have exceptional equipment. He brought Donato to the king, waited outside, and escorted Donato back to your room."

I did wake up in Visegrád and Donato wasn't there, but if he'd had a secret meeting with the king, he would have told me.

"That's a disgusting lie," I say. "Why would you repeat such obvious filth?"

"I didn't say I believe it. I said that's what I was told by a man who heard it firsthand from his partner who thinks the king is a piece of shit anyway. He's a soldier, in it for the money. It's what he does. But he's got no reason to lie. He thought it was hilarious. He was laughing his ass off making the noises King Louis made when Donato took him for a ride."

"What's wrong with you? Jesus, Matteo. Are you ten years old?"

"Don't shoot the messenger." Matteo backs out of my measure. "I'm telling you what the man said. If it fits, wear it. If not, throw it away. But don't be mad at me. If it was me, you'd say something, wouldn't you?"

He knows I would, but that doesn't dull my outrage at hearing him repeat vulgar rumors. We rejoin the others and continue in silence. We twist through ditches, fording rivulets and streams diverted at one time or another. The landscape alternates between boggy and solid, with reed-clogged lakes of brackish water, sweet stream-fed ponds, and stands of oak, ash, and willow in meadows hemmed with sea grass and wild orchids. Ducks quack, geese honk, coots cluck, seagulls screech, and ominous buzzards circle overhead.

Chapter Forty

Greek Fire

AS WE ENTER the fort at Gorgo, General Coreggio waves and circles to meet us as we dismount. "Welcome," he says. "You're a sight for sore eyes."

"It's that bad?"

"It's not. Donato is. He's got a bug up his ass, and you know how that goes. Come inside, and we can talk in private."

He dismisses my escort, who immediately returns to Curano. We repair to his quarters, spotless, over-cared for by men with time on their hands who are filled with anxious energy and condemned to wait.

"What's the bug up Donato's ass?"

"He'll tell you first thing he sees you, no doubt. In the

meantime, here's what we know for certain. At Campagna, we've got Carrara, Forzatè, a herd of Paduan nobles, and one thousand six hundred country boys on foot. Plus the Voivode of Transylvania, with two thousand Hungarians. Carrara put the voivode in charge, and he turned around and hired every scrapper and thug capable of walking or throwing a stone. Maybe six thousand men total, split into four groups. Carrara himself heads one group, his boy Novello another. They're hiding behind the voivode's skirts at Campagna. One of the king's cousins oversees their sorry excuse for a garrison at Lova."

"But nobody has attacked?"

"The voivode talks a good game, but so far, it's all talk."

"What are they waiting for?"

"Venus to trine Neptune."

"Seriously?"

"King's orders."

"Then what are *we* waiting for?"

"For Venus to trine Neptune, I guess."

We both laugh over that.

"No, really, what are we waiting for?"

"You."

"That's ridiculous."

"That's what Donato says. Wait until you've heard him out. Then we can talk more. In the meantime, get some rest after your travels. Eat, nap, take a nice leisurely shit. It may be the last opportunity you get for a long time."

He shows me where to throw my gear and where I'll sleep. "Heads up," he says with a sly wink. "Serenissimo cautioned me to heed your advice."

"He's like a grandfather bragging on his grandson. I apologize for his zeal. Listen to me at your own peril. Where is Donato? I have messages for him."

"He's reconnoitering. He could be back at any time. Or not. You know him."

"Where is he reconnoitering? I might look myself."

"Yonder, across the lake, toward Lova, I suspect, but I strongly advise against going alone. There are more enemy pickets and spies in those swamps than mosquitoes, and if anything happens to you, I'll spend the rest of my life digging ditches."

I accommodate him by eating, but I slip away as soon as I can, heading west toward Lova.

I am a son of Venice, a city poised at the apex of splendor and squalor, afloat in the chimerical lagoon where roads are canals. Churches and wells cram our squares, unparalleled palaces stand cheek by jowl with overcrowded hovels a breath away from a random spark that may burn them to ashes. Having known only this for most of my life, other cities pale in comparison. On the mainland, the light is less luminous, the colors less vibrant, the buildings less exuberant, life less varied and fascinating. Everything on terrafirma pales in comparison except for the one thing we lack—the vast rush and tumble of unconstrained nature. I find hillsides thick with vines of fragrant trumpets, quicksilver streams leaping over mossy stones, green canopies of leaves bathed in sunlight and dappled with shade, and grapevines heavy with dusty purple grapes. All of this under a menagerie of clouds overhead like a whimsical zodiac of rabbits, egrets, and dolphins.

Despite the ravishing surrounds, Matteo's gossip agitates me. I cannot forget waking up that night in Visegrád. Donato wasn't in his bed. I waited for him to return, and when I questioned him, he said he was restless and thought he'd chat up the guard, ask him who else had been visiting the king lately, sifting through gossip for gold. I quiet my anxiety by listening and observing, trying to suss where Donato may have gone and why.

I follow the stream running west toward Lova and wonder why Donato would waste his time studying the precincts of Lova. Our soldiers know every nook and cranny. Donato would more likely want to study Carrara's field headquarters at Campagna where the vaunted voivode plots to slaughter us. The voivode with both Carraras, father and son, in the same place at the same time, must be catnip to Donato.

I consult my compass, the mostly faded insignia of three dolphins stamped on its hinged lid. Lova lies almost due west; Campagna, northeast. Across a shallow valley, a hill rises opposite Gorgo by two miles. Campagna crowns the hilltop. On the valley floor, the ground turns to sand and clay. My horse's hooves sink deep, making progress slow until I start up the opposite side, where wide swaths of trees have been hewn to build the fort. Donato would never leave himself this exposed. I veer right, holding to the same general direction but angling toward the remaining trees flowering in the sun. A cloud of fragrant pink blossoms conceals me as I climb higher until I can see the fort of Campagna. A hastily dug moat encircles the perimeter wall and rude drawbridge.

I tie my horse deep in the trees. From this vantage, I

can easily discern the contours of the buildings but no details, only thatched rooftops poking over the walls. Soldiers lounge outside the closed gates. I inhale the perfume of the trees, wondering if it wouldn't be better to live amid the hills and fields and purling rivers of terrafirma, when something sharp jabs my back. When I try to turn my head, I'm stopped with cold steel.

"Don't move." A closed visor muffles the voice, with only the narrowest eye slit to see through, making it impossible for him to see sideways, only dead forward.

I don't move, compliant, until the spear in my back eases, and I tumble forward, rolling left, out of his field of vision. Carrara's red chariots emblazon his white surcoat.

"I said don't move." He dives on top of me and pinions me. When his visor flips up, I see brown skin and blue eyes. Donato laughs merrily. "You fall for it every time. Now kiss me." He lifts off his helmet and throws it to the ground.

"You're such a dick." Annoyed and overjoyed at the same time, I embrace him, and my annoyance turns to apprehension. "Why are you dressed like the enemy?"

"To stay alive."

"What are you doing with a spear?"

"When in Rome..." He pulls off his surcoat. "There. Recognize me now?"

"I wonder, sometimes, if I know you at all."

"What does that mean?" He seems uncertain whether to laugh. Had it not been for Matteo, suspicion would never have poisoned my mind, but I heard what I heard.

"We're so rarely together," I say. "I have no idea what you do when I'm not around."

"I feel there's a question in there somewhere." He holds my face steady and studies my eyes.

"Have you been entirely faithful?" I ask.

He pulls back and folds his arms across his chest, scowling. "You tracked me down to ask me that?"

"Among other things. Have you? Been faithful?"

Anger erupts. "Of course I have. I told you I love you. Only you."

"You haven't fucked anyone else?"

"Who else would I have fucked?"

"King Louis."

He grips the trunk of a crabapple tree and shakes it furiously, creating a snowstorm of blossoms as he groans with annoyance and disbelief. "What in God's name are you talking about?"

"Something I heard."

"Who would tell you shit like that?"

"That doesn't matter. Is it true?"

"Do you suspect me of donning the enemy uniform so I can climb into bed with the Voivode of Transylvania or maybe Novello Carrara?"

I have never seen Donato this cross. "That hadn't crossed my mind."

"*Yet*. Watch out, my love, suspicion is quicksand. Soon you'll be in over your head."

"The person who told me interrogated a Hungarian prisoner..."

"And you believe the secondhand ravings of a prisoner-of-war over me, the man you swore to love as much as I love you?"

My heart sinks. From every angle, I lose. I have

exposed and humiliated myself for the idiot I am to the man I love most in the world, whom I should never doubt for an instant. Like a child who accidentally breaks his mother's favorite dish, the one she keeps high on a shelf, never eats from, and only admires for its beauty, I crumble, unable to deny what I've done and ferociously ashamed of my idiocy. I bury my face in my hands and sob. He waits a long minute, pulls my hands from my face, and licks my tears. We sit on the ground, his arms around me.

"I'm sorry for being such an idiot," I say.

"Such an *earnest* idiot."

"Can you forgive me?"

"We do stupid things under great pressure. I couldn't wait to see you because I thought long and hard about the problem you posed, and I think I found a solution."

He bounds into the trees and returns with Mercury laden with two satchels. He unties the first and sets it down gingerly. He opens it and spreads the contents on the ground, handling everything with the same deftness I saw in Treviso when he handled the quicklime.

"Are you going to tell me what your solution is?"

"Greek fire."

His eyebrows mock my disbelief.

"Bullshit, Donato. The recipe for Greek fire is an imperial secret."

"Any secret worth keeping rarely stays secret for long."

"Where did all this gear come from?"

"You have Abdul. I have Kemal. Be careful with these jars; they can explode."

He arranges the sealed jars in front of him, along with a funnel and long-handled wooden spoon, several stoppered bottles filled with powders, and the fine twig brushes grandmothers use to sweep their stoops. "It's not *exactly* Greek fire but behaves like it in all the important ways. It burns fiercely, the smoke is toxic, it sticks to everything, and keeps burning. If you try to douse it with water, it burns hotter."

"What are you planning to burn?"

"Yonder fortress, shitty wooden walls, thatched roofs, and all—up in flame no matter how they try to stop it. You're welcome to join me. We will force them to flee in complete disarray. Every last one of them will bolt across that drawbridge to save their skins, including Lord Francesco Carrara the Elder, the brat Novello, and the Voivode of Transylvania. That's our first move. Pawn to king four."

"So your plan is to burn Campagna and drive the enemy into the field."

"My plan is to surprise them and scare the shit out of them and then drive them into the field in utter disarray. They will run for Lova, their closest fort, where our troops already hold the high ground, poised to slaughter them."

"What makes you so certain they'll head for Lova and not Serraporci or Medicina?"

"You said it yourself. They have to wreck our dig from Curano at all costs."

"We burn Campagna, they flee. We hold Lova. They regroup. I don't see a checkmate."

He reaches behind him and hefts his spear. "This is for Francesco Carrara. Straight through his twisted heart. Checkmate. That's why I am wearing his surcoat."

I don't believe my ears. I yank the spear from his hand. "Have you lost your mind?"

"Checkmate in three. Burn the fort, rout the enemy, kill the king. When Carrara goes down, his army will collapse, and the war will be over."

"Go ahead," I shout. "Burn down the fort, spook them before the battle, drive them out in disarray. But before you can kill Carrara, even if you are wearing their little red carts, they will kill you. Without question. You can't possibly get away with it unless you make yourself invisible. Which is stupid."

"You're such a pessimist. This is exactly what you wanted, checkmate in three."

"What does it matter if you're dead?"

"Sometimes I wonder what matters most to you. I can do this, whether you help or hinder me."

"I need you, Donato. Serenissimo needs you. The Republic needs you. You can't get killed on a fool's errand. I will help you burn the fort, no question. But I can't let you commit suicide."

"How is it you still don't understand? This is war, my love."

"I won't let you. I can't. It's impossible."

"It's not impossible. It's difficult; I'll grant you that. It takes guts, some craziness, and massive hand-eye coordination to hurl a spear dead center into a fast-moving target. But the rest is child's play. In the chaos of battle, they won't know who did it."

"Somebody will."

"That's what my sword is for, and yours, if you're with me."

He isn't listening. My words aren't registering. He won't be deterred from his mission.

Donato unties the second sack and throws me a black friar's robe, shouting, "Put this on."

I cross my arms over my chest, refusing, and he grabs me by the shoulders.

"Whether we do this or not," he says, "one of us may die tomorrow, neither of us if we're lucky, both of us if we're not. Let's be optimists and take joy in murdering the monster single-handedly responsible for this whole bloody mess."

"Fire, yes. Suicide, no. I will stop you, Donato."

"You would kill me to stop me. That's why I love you. But you won't because you know I'm right. Now put on the robe."

The capacious robes hide us like enveloping shadows, showing only four blue eyes. He carefully repacks the cargo of Greek fire and eases the satchel over his shoulder. Staying within the sheltering trees, we creep slowly toward Carrara's fort. As darkness descends, we become creatures of the netherworld like Brother Bernardo.

When the darkness is complete, we dart between shadows the half-moon casts through scattered clouds. Cautiously, we approach the moat, broad but not deep, an obstacle for a charging army but no challenge for shadows. Donato hefts the satchel over his head, and we slog through the brackish murk, which leaks into our ears but never rises above our heads. Invisible in the dark, we climb the opposite bank to the wall girding the fort. Guards in the towers flanking the drawbridge fail to notice us. At the base of the wall, Donato crouches, unpacks silently, and counts out the stoppered jars. He hands me a brush and several jars in a cloth sling to hang over my chest.

"Watch me," he says. "Then do what I do, carefully, very, very carefully. Work to the left and stay close to the wall. Don't make a sound, and you won't be seen. I'll work around to the right. We'll meet on the far side. You don't need to be thorough, just quick. Spread the mixture broadly with the brush. It doesn't take much."

I dip the brush into the stinking concoction and slather the rough-hewn wood, hoping no one inside catches a whiff of the quicklime, saltpeter, bitumen, pitch, and naphtha worked into a noxious glue that makes me gag. We meet on the far side of the fort and race back to our hillside.

Chapter Forty-One

The Battle of Lova

"HOW WILL WE light the fire?"

"That's the beauty of it," Donato says. "We don't have to. The sun will. By the second hour of morning, Campagna will be in flames."

"I take it the general knew where you were and what you were doing and lied to me."

"Trust is something you build, not something simply handed to you."

"You're still wearing the red carts and carrying a spear."

"You are an observant fellow."

"You're still intent on committing suicide..."

"I'm intent on ending this war as quickly and

decisively as possible."

"And you truly believe killing Carrara will do that?"

"As a matter of fact, no, I no longer do. It occurred to me as we worked that as satisfying as killing Carrara would be, it won't stop Louis."

"Thank God."

"Killing Carrara is like capturing their queen. The king still stands. Killing the voivode—that's checkmate. Carrara will crumble; we will win the battle and end the war."

"Holy Mother of God. You're completely mad."

"Maybe I am, but don't try to stop me. If you're with me, ditch your surcoat. It will only get you killed where we're going. No need to advertise which side you're on. Your mail protects you. Grab some ivy to wrap around your helmet when we reach the enemy. The voivode ordered all his men to wear ivy on their helmets so they can distinguish themselves from us. Now sleep if you can. We have a big day tomorrow."

I lie in angry silence until night fades and first light brightens the eastern sky. I have yet to figure out how to stop Donato, knowing well that no appeal I make will deter him.

The sun warms as it rises. The fire doesn't spark to life and slowly spread. When the sunlight reaches a certain intensity, the Greek fire explodes all at once, instantly engulfing Campagna in sticky flames that every effort to douse only feeds. Smoke chokes their lungs. Ashes sear their flesh. The firestorm whips the enemy into chaos. Nobles and knights flee on horseback, the cavalry behind them, while the rest stagger out on foot. Some are in flames, running as best they can to get clear of the conflagration. Others jump into the moat or roll in the dirt, desperate to douse flames that cannot be doused.

Donato gathers his reins to ride after them, but I grab them out of his hands.

"I told you I won't let you."

"What comes first, you or the Republic?"

"The Republic."

"Then let me go. I must kill the voivode before he reaches Lova. One moment of shock and confusion is all I need."

Donato yanks his reins back and chases after the enemy. I follow, angry enough to kill him myself. Carrara, his son Novello, and the voivode lead the fleeing cavalry. Their infantry falls farther and farther behind, scattering us like lost sheep in confusion, their surcoats smoking and shields charred, some blistered, others blinded, uncertain when or where our cavalry may cut them down, knowing only that we will.

Donato pursues the voivode, and I pursue Donato. When he suddenly reins in his steed, I stop alongside. He points with his spear. "There, the cross and eagle, that's the voivode's standard. He's under it as sure as the sun sets, looking as mean as Carrara looks scared. It's too dangerous for you to follow me."

Thunder shakes the ground beneath us, our second cavalry detachment pursuing the fleeing enemy.

"Ride with them," Donato says. "When you reach the enemy, wrap your helmet with ivy and find the voivode's standard. I'll be there."

Donato races away. Once spurred to action, he has no

capacity for doubt; he focuses his passionate intent into a single white-hot flame and disappears into the dust of desperate men as our second cavalry unit sweeps me up in their momentum. I search for the voivode's standard, trampling the fallen underfoot. In the middle of this juggernaut, I can neither gauge distance nor see clearly in any direction, blinded by horses, dust, and rampaging men.

"Up shields!"

The shout ricochets through our cavalry. We cover our heads with our shields against a hail of flaming missiles from the voivode's bowmen. Manes burn on lathered flanks, and men's haunches smoke in the rain of fire. When a gap opens between rampaging horses, I fight through to escape the chaos, seeking only to reach the voivode's standard.

No man stays alive in battle without knowing what is happening around him. With a closed visor, a combatant only sees through its narrow eye slit. An open visor permits a full field of vision, but is vulnerable to spears and axes. In close fighting, visors go down; outside the red-hot center, visors go up for air and vision. Now that I'm outside the cavalry stampede, I take half an instant to find my bearings, visor up. Three horsemen in white surcoats splattered with red carts and blood, visors down, break free from the riotous combat, almost trampling me. My horse screams and rears, knocking my visor down with a violent clank. Their visors raised, I clearly see their leader's face: my brother, Ruggiero Gradenigo, slaughtering Venetians on behalf of Francesco Carrara. He spurs his mount and raises dust around the edge of battle toward the voivode's standard, fluttering above the carnage.

Between me and the voivode, a thousand men in white surcoats with red carts, visors down, unleash a torrent of spears and a firestorm of bolts and arrows at my countrymen. I snatch the ivy from my belt, fasten it tight around my helmet, and skirt the battle to the voivode on the opposite side. I don't know how to find Donato, only that he will be there.

Our last wave of cavalry tears into the enemy's rear. Red surcoats with gold lions fill the narrow slit of my vision, charging, thrusting, hacking with bloody sword and spear in perpetual motion. The low winter sun blinds me. I squint tightly but still can't see until I lift my visor, knowing full well I shouldn't. I notice, first off, that the voivode's visor is up, that he too squints, his face calculating, stony, infuriated, while the Carraras, father and son, hide under a canopy of shields. I veer and weave and wheel around the helmets, breastplates, swords, gauntlets, and greaves, searching frantically for Donato's white destrier, Mercury, or a glimpse of brown skin disguised under red carts. Battlers slam into me as I duck and dodge to the forward edge of the tumult, 180 degrees from where I started. I am almost behind the voivode, with still no sign of Donato, until a familiar glint catches my eye. The sun ignites an incandescent ruby scintillating like a miracle from God—Alex's gold dolphin, which I gave Donato as my pledge.

The tumult cracks enough for me to clearly see Mercury. I dig my stirrups into my horse's flanks to reach him, meeting resistance every inch until Donato sees me. He

speaks with his body, his hands, his eyes, sending semaphores of danger and direction. He is about to raise his
spear for a lethal blow through the voivode's open visor
when a bombard explodes nearby, hurling the battlers
into anarchy. Lieutenants close ranks and circle the voivode, but he forces them back, brandishing his infamous
spear, ravening for the kill and shouting into the abyss.

"Death to Venice! They are meat. We are butchers.
Kill! Kill! Kill! Kill! Kill!"

And his men chant, "Kill! Kill! Kill! Kill! Kill!"

Donato maneuvers Mercury until he faces the voivode, visor up, spear raised. But before he can hurl it, an
enemy horseman, visor up, charges him, driving his spear
through Donato's forehead. Ruggiero Gradenigo, transfixed for an instant by the gold dolphin with ruby eyes he
last saw around my neck, violently yanks on his spear,
topples Donato from Mercury, and tramples him.

A riderless horse, mad for flight, knocks me off my
steed. I am crushed too tightly by embattled bodies to
draw my sword. Ruggiero jumps from his horse, plants his
feet on Donato's chest, pulls his spear from Donato's
brain, and plunges it into his heart. A rictus of hideous triumph disfigures his face. Fumbling for the gold dolphin
with ruby eyes, he doesn't see me charging until I stand
over him, visor raised, gripping my sword with both hands
over his chest. Underestimating me as he always does, ignorant of my newly acquired swordsmanship, he forgets
the dolphin, leaps back, and draws his sword to dispatch
me, but not quickly enough. I plunge my blade into his
exposed flank, twisting to force him to his knees, raging
and helpless as I stomp him flat, pinion him with my

boots, and with every ounce of strength in my being, plunge my sword into his heart again and again. His eyes register a stark, sorry disbelief, open but unseeing as I wield my sword to hack unmercifully, severing his head from his shoulders.

A tidal wave of battle swamps me, led by the voivode who, with spear and sword, kills Venetians right and left, rallying his army to slaughter. Tangled in a forest of legs, kicked and twisted and trampled, I dodge blades and axes and bodies. Losing my bearings, I see no way out. Donato's body disappears amid the butchery. I claw back to where I think he was, but two pairs of hands drag me away. Venetian foot soldiers, seeing my face, recognizing me, pull me along, beating a horrified retreat in the face of the unthinkable.

The voivode, a prodigy of bloodlust, tramples our line, thrusting his spear over and over into Venetian chests and backs and loins, implacable and unstoppable, slaying everything in his path. Spurring his warriors into our collapsing infantry and fallen cavalry, the battle turns against us, and they murder us in an utter rout as we abandon the blood-drenched field.

Chapter Forty-Two

St. Martial's Day

THE VOIVODE BEARS our standard to Padua, carrying the day for Lord Carrara, but the mounds of bodies stand as mute testimony to another victory won at too great a cost. Shocked but not ended, the battle lurches like the boar, fatally wounded but not yet realizing it is dead until it drops. Both armies withdraw from the field to lick their wounds and plot their revenge. The setting sun casts a lurid shroud over the silenced battlefield.

I dig among fractured bodies, shattered shields, broken lances, dismembered corpses. The earth oozes blood, blackening my fingers as I search for Donato in the failing light. A will-o'-the-wisp flickers across the field, then another, and another, bobbing over the dead like fireflies.

The light draws me like a moth. Spread in a loose web, black-robed friars, lanterns aloft, pick through the remains as their brothers light bonfires around the field of the dead.

"What are you looking for?" I ask an old and weary-looking friar. His lips move, but his expression doesn't change.

"We separate the living from the dead."

"Are you Paduan or Venetian?"

"We are humble servants of the Lord, come from Our Father's house, which knows no nation. If they breathe, we succor them, and if not, we bless them."

"What becomes of the dead?"

"*Follow me*, Jesus said, *and let the dead bury their dead.*"

"But the bodies..."

"Have you never been to war?"

"I have, but not like this."

"We leave them for the good people who come to bury or burn them, just as we did during the great plague when so many died we ran out of places to put them."

"I am looking for a certain soldier. Perhaps you saw him?"

He shakes his head, hapless sorrow engraved in the coarse wrinkles of his face. "After so many, they are all the same."

"Except for the man I speak of, with black skin and sapphire eyes."

He stops shaking his head. His brow unfurls. "An African, you say?"

"Black, yes, but Venetian. A compact and muscular

man with a handsome face."

"Follow me."

He takes my hand, Virgil guiding Dante through hell. We approach a bonfire where several of his brethren cluck, mournful hens unraveling corpses stacked in heaps.

"Brother Antoninus," the old friar says, "did you not speak of seeing an African?"

A surprisingly young and fresh-faced novice answers, "I did, brother."

For an instant, my hope knows no bounds. "Was he alive?" I ask.

"Sadly, he has joined the angelic choir, my brother."

"You're certain of that?"

"I have seen too many corpses not to know the living from the dead, but only one with black skin."

"Where is he?"

Brother Antoninus weaves a path through the piled bodies. I stay close behind, following his lantern through the darkness.

"Paduans on this side," he says. "Venetians over there. That makes them easier to find when someone comes looking." He steps gingerly between the bodies. "Is it not unusual that he is Paduan?"

"His father was," I say. "His mother was an African princess."

The sight of Donato's leg stops me in my tracks. My jaw quivers, my hands shake, and unfallen tears steal my breath. As I hide my face in my hands, my struggle to control myself unnerves the young friar.

"It's unusual for a Venetian to weep over a Paduan,"

he says.

"We were like brothers until the war separated us."

Stiff, awkward, and gray, Donato's limbs seem rimed by the icy breath of winter. I cannot see his eyes, rolled back in his head. I will never see them again. They are locked in the labyrinth of memory.

Brother Antoninus lowers his lamp closer to the body. "Have you come to claim him?"

"My horse was killed. I have no way…" Dry sobs wrack my shoulders. I am useless. I should be dead.

"He rests in peace," Antoninus says. "We'll take care."

"Can I be with him a moment, alone…"

Antoninus leaves the lantern with me and disappears into the darkness on silent feet. I find the gold dolphin with ruby eyes against Donato's chest, but I also feel something else. I extract a small square of tightly folded paper. I pull the necklace off him, kissing the dolphin before placing it around my neck and tucking it against my heart, for all the good it does. It couldn't save Donato.

I break the wax seal on the meticulously folded paper, which opens like a fan, covered with Donato's fine labored hand.

> *Niccolò my soul. If you are reading this, I am likely dead.*

> *A coward to the end, I never truly confessed, and I beg your forgiveness with all the love in my heart for never saying these things to you when I could.*

But I couldn't. Maybe now you can understand and forgive. Maybe not. Either way, I owe you this much at least.

Yes, I fucked King Louis. Not from desire, from diplomacy. Always hoping to learn something valuable to our victory, which I did not. He was a pig in bed and dismissed me as soon as he was satisfied. I dirtied myself for no good reason and perjured myself to spare your tender heart. Mea culpa.

I told you that your father killed my mother when he tired of her, as was his wont, but I withheld the most important detail of all. I have never known such love as I shared with you and didn't know that I was even capable of it. I feared if you knew the truth, you might reject my love entirely, and I couldn't bear that.

I am the greatest coward of all, but you are the bravest soul I know, so know this. Your father is my father. Like Ruggiero, I am your brother, darling Nico. I could not resist my love for you and allowed it to silence me. Free of me, you can love an honest man who will not mislead you to keep you.

Yes, I chose this mission, knowing I would likely be killed. If I die honorably, maybe my treachery won't weigh as heavy on your heart. I will never know if my plan succeeded, but I hope, for your sake, that it did. That the war is over, and that you are free to find the love you deserve, quit of me, who loved you more than life itself.

I only wish that you can forgive me because if you can forgive me, you will have forgiven yourself. You are your own harshest judge, but this time, the fault is all mine. Release yourself from guilt and sorrow. Move on gloriously. Live well, beloved. Make your mark upon this world, and believe me when I say you are better off without me.

Donato Venturi.

*

UPON MY RETURN to the palace, Serenissimo weeps for Donato.

"He died a hero," I say, "murdered by a villainous traitor."

"He died a fool." Serenissimo scowls, not angry, but bereft. "He shouldn't have tried it in the first place. We sorely need his leadership. Like Pisani and Zeno, he was one of the few with the spirit to inspire men to victory against overwhelming odds."

"He knew if he killed the voivode, the war would be over. And it would have, had Ruggiero not struck him down."

"That word again, *if...*" Serenissimo shakes his head, slow and implacable, fatherly sorrow mingling with abject desolation. "I know, I know, I know... Trying to change his mind was like trying to change yours. The two of you, peas in a pod..."

"He was my brother, Exalted Serenity, like Ruggiero."

As I say the words, I watch to see if he already knows, but I cannot tell. He pulls me to his chest, hugs me tightly, and gently kisses my head.

"I'm sorry," he says. "So, so sorry. For everything. I know your grief outweighs mine, being of a different order, a matter of quality, not degree...and all the harder to bear."

"At least Ruggiero is dead."

"I'd rather we had quartered him between the Columns of Doom. You're absolutely certain he's dead?"

"I cut off his head to be absolutely certain."

"We sound like two ghouls." Serenissimo shivers, pulling his gold robe tighter around him. "Brother Bernardo is next. As soon as we get our hands on him."

"Do we know where he is?"

"Hiding in a church I presume, probably in Padua. Out of our reach. But he never stays put for long."

"I still worry about Mama."

"Lay those fears to rest. I housed her and Giasone in a cottage inside the arsenal, where no harm will come to them, at least not from him. And we will get him. Now, rest. Sleep. Read. Dream."

"I can't rest, or sleep, or read, and I have nightmares instead of dreams. Work is the only thing that keeps me from going mad. If you pity me, if you want to help me, give me work, endless work, oceans of work, work everlasting, each bit desperately important, more than I can ever hope to accomplish. Pile it on, sire, give me no quarter, punish me with work for failing to protect Donato."

"Alas, there is plenty of work to be done," Serenissimo says. "We still have a war to win. Report back to General Coreggio. The Turkish archers arrive within the week."

"So much for swearing off mercenaries."

"Punish you, I will, young man. Don't think I won't—unless you learn to hold your tongue. I said archers; did you not hear? Not sulky, spoiled, aristocratic generals and their legions of looters and rapists. Five thousand archers to slay the voivode and his Hungarians and their boss and their boss's snotty son and the whole damn clan until Padua is cleansed and Venice is secure. Mark my words."

*

UPON MY RETURN to Gorgo, General Coreggio flinches upon hearing the details of Donato's murder. "He deserved better. He was the best of the best that our Republic has produced. His loss will be felt long after he is forgotten. A great future awaited him."

"Alas, dead men have no future."

Coreggio and I pore over maps and sketches I've drawn, searching for a strategic advantage. Carrara's victory at Lova was indecisive, and both armies retreated. Another battle looms, one in which we must be decisive. We rally the remains of our army, welcome the Turkish bowmen, and search for answers. We have studied the same books and learned from the same masters. We must devise a stratagem to lure the voivode and all his armies into an inescapable ambush.

"Carrara knows we have five thousand Turkish archers," Coreggio says.

"Five thousand Turks who hate King Louis more than we do. That should flay the voivode's nerves and weigh heavy on his plans."

"He didn't press their victory and attack," Coreggio says. "Instead, they retreated to retrench and celebrate our humiliation. We must secure the fort at Buonconforte to make way for our boats to reach Padua."

Coreggio, a tireless fighter and indefatigable patriot, lacks the originality of thought that distinguished Donato. Nor can I match Donato. But with Giustinian still imprisoned in Hungary and the absence of minds such as Admiral Pisani or Carlo Zeno, Coreggio and I are the best we've got.

"Even five thousand archers can't ensure us victory if Padua outsmarts us," I say. "We must lure them into a trap they don't see coming until it snaps shut. These maps aren't good enough. They only show waterways and distances, not the ravines, the hillsides and gullies, the bogs, the fields and ditches and hillocks—everything we gallop past, racing from fortress to fortress, which are the very things victory depends upon. We must analyze the lay of the land."

*

WE RIDE TOWARD Lova, recently the red-hot center of the war, now a barely glowing ember. The enemy army retreated southwest to Piove di Sacco, safe from surprise attack.

"The voivode believes we are fatally weakened," I say, "needing only one final blow to collapse. Carrara knows us better. He's not celebrating. He's pulling out his hair. Our opportunity lies between Piove di Sacco and Lova."

May turns into June. Blossoms fall from the trees, and fruit ripens in the sun as we hide from prying eyes to scour the terrain for the winning high ground. When Coreggio tires, I beg him to send a replacement to join me because I cannot stop. I must keep moving, memorizing landscapes, making assessments, planning, comparing, compiling lists, places, men, weapons, and history, always history. I try to banish Donato from my waking mind, though I can do nothing to keep him out of my nightmares. I cease to feel hunger, longing, desire, even loneliness. Guilt and despair consume me outside my desperate need to win this war in Donato's honor, the least and last thing I can do for him.

The stars on the eve of St. Martial's Day look strangely familiar. They unlock a chamber in the labyrinth of memory where King Louis's astrological maps lurk. The same sky. Venus trines Neptune.

Aware that Carrara knows the exact number of our Turkish archers, we flagrantly display a number of them at Lova, atop the wall and around the dig. At the same time, we flagrantly ignore our fort at Buonconforte, the gateway to Piove di Sacco, where the enemy prepares their final blow. Buonconforte has changed hands so often that we sometimes sleep in beds warmed by our enemy and wash one another's dishes. The voivode can only assume we expect him to attack Lova where, to all appearances, we have mustered for the decisive battle. That makes Buonconforte an irresistible, low-hanging fruit ripe for plucking. If I have learned nothing else, I know men believe what they see.

Three thousand archers hide in and around Buonconforte with thousands of cavalry concealed behind trees laden with green apricots lining the approach. Only a fraction of our army remains at Lova in case the enemy fails to meet our expectations.

The Hungarians and Paduans number eight thousand, making us evenly matched, our side heavy on Turkish archers. The Hungarian knights in heavy armor hamper the march of Paduan nobles, prisoners sprung from jails for the fight, farm boys with goat shit under their fingernails, and English mercenaries as likely to turn tail in tight spots as not, led by Voivode Steven of Transylvania.

To reach Buonconforte, the enemy must cross miles of lowland through the bed of a vanished river hemmed in on both sides by vast thickets of purple verbena, the air as sweet as the going is rough. Two miles short of Buonconforte, the banks on either side of the dry riverbed climb the shoulders of low hills. Therein hides every foot soldier under our flag, deep amid the mad purple bushes and ancient tangled trees, with thousands of Turkish archers, armed with bows and scimitars, ready to charge as soon as the enemy appears.

The heavily armored knights on horseback lead the enemy advance, followed by regular cavalry, then infantry, with their supply train bringing up the rear. Banners waving, standards flying, armor and weapons shining, they march slowly along the dry bed of the diverted river.

Unseen in the purple-flowering hillsides, our troops stand ready, armed not with spears and swords but with pikes, spiked clubs, and long poles barbed with steel.

As the enemy approaches, our mounted Turkish archers fan out, unseen but near enough to strike panic in the enemy when they launch their arrows. As the enemy van reaches the tightest stretch of riverbed, squeezed between the encroaching banks, I fire a single flaming bolt into the air, signaling our charge, and race toward the enemy van, where I hope to see the voivode's face when he realizes his goose is cooked.

Our troops charge out of the purple bushes attacking the enemy line. Brandishing their weapons, bellowing with a deafening roar, they attack the horses, not the riders. The voivode pushes up his visor, stunned and dismayed by the ragtag army of a thousand pole-bearing, club-wielding, cursing savages slaughtering his cavalry, horses first. The knights can't get close enough to strike us with sword, club, or spear, before their horses collapse beneath them, crash to their knees, thrash and roll, crushing their riders. We target the unprotected undersides of even the most heavily armored steeds, ripping their bellies open like dolphins to crocodiles. The horses scream, panic, stampede, and crash to the stony riverbed overflowing with carnage.

Enemy archers and infantry try to protect their cavalry as our Turkish archers unleash storm after storm of bolts and arrows. The voivode, Carrara the elder, his son Novello, and the other nobles of Padua beat a retreat under raised shields, but our cavalry cuts them off.

The battle takes less than an hour. The Carraras

escape, but the voivode, the mad but valiant nephew of King Louis of Hungary, insists on fighting to the end. As soon as we capture him, his army collapses, scattering under a rain of fire. Our victory is undisputed and complete. We have captured the voivode and take him to Venice with a hundred other enemy nobles, ours to keep until Louis offers up Carrara and returns Giustinian to ransom his nephew.

The war is over.

Chapter Forty-Three

Jubilation

EVERY BELL RINGS, not alarms but joyous peals of victory, celebrating the peace between Padua and Venice. Peace at last. Peace too late. Peace again, but what did Donato say? A brief respite between wars. Best left forgotten.

Drunken crowds dance in the streets, around bonfires in the squares, amid jugglers, tumblers, musicians, confetti, and kissing. I cannot join. My heavy heart refuses. Everywhere I go, I am reminded of Donato. Seeing myself reflected in the surface of the guard's shiny shield outside the Great Council chamber reminds me of the joy Donato took in shaving, regarding himself admiringly, opening his eyes wide, checking the brightness of his smile. My heart crumples. Things people say casually sound inadvertently cruel. Certain words make Donato reverberate in labyrinthine memory. I expect to see him around every corner, throwing his arms around me, laughing, shouting, "You didn't really think I died, did you?"

Near the ceiling of the Great Council chamber hangs the black veil painted over the portrait of Doge Faliero, beheaded for treason. That veil reminds me of the painting on my bedroom wall, the valiant seaman delivering his majestic votive galley to the Virgin. Donato teased me, saying I thought that sailor more beautiful than him, which I didn't. My second night home from the battlefield, I pilfered a shroud from the sacristy of St. Mark's to hide the painting, to no effect. Like Faliero's black shroud, it only calls attention to itself.

Every member of the Great Council shows up, filling their newly completed chamber. The fresh pigments of the painting above the dais sparkle jewellike in the reflections bouncing through the windows off the water below, scattering rainbows across the fields of the blessed. My eyes drop to the fields of perdition below, where the demons tormenting the sinners grimace hideously, their skin black. Please, God, if you can hear my plea, grant Donato peace.

Today's particular excitement owes to the fact that the treaty ending the war between Padua and Venice requires that either Lord Carrara or his son Novello appear before the doge, publicly apologize for their crimes, and swear fealty to our Republic. No one expected Carrara to show up; Novello comes in his stead. And after much tearful pleading, the elder Carrara prevailed upon Italy's poet laureate and close personal friend, Francesco Petrarch, to accompany Novello. Rumor has it that Petrarch has written an oration for this unique occasion. Anticipation, curiosity, and cynicism run high.

How Donato would have laughed.

The Doge's Council and the Ten attend a special Mass before the ceremony, which I skip. Serenissimo delivers a simple opening address to the assembled Great Council about how glad everybody is that the war is over, especially King Louis of Hungary. His royal relatives forced him to pull his army out and abandon Carrara's adventure in order to ransom the voivode and the other captured Hungarian, Polish, and Transylvanian nobles. Serenissimo doesn't mention that. He treads lightly, praising our military, claiming victory not only in the field but in the hearts of the people.

Trumpets announce the approach of Novello Carrara and his escort, Petrarch. A knock on the door signals their arrival. Every eye turns to watch the mighty brought low. Petrarch looks older than his years, his health failing in his sixth decade. The wreath of poet laureate crowns his simple monk's hood. He walks with difficulty, leaning on Novello's shoulder. Novello summons more dignity than I thought possible wearing a robe embroidered with more jewels than I thought possible. His expression, stamped from his father's mold, appears driven, haunted, yet defiant, even amused. The old poet and the young tyrant do what they must. Novello kneels before the doge to make his apology. He admits no specific crimes, only alluding to those well-known or enumerated in the treaty. When he finishes, the doge bids him rise, saying, "Go and sin no more, neither you nor your father."

The snickers and murmurs accompanying Novello's apology cease the instant Petrarch stands forward. Many a wager rides on what he might say. A well-known intimate and supporter of Lord Carrara, dare Petrarch offer an apologia for our rapacious enemy, or will he disavow the tyrant? An anxious silence hangs in the air as the poet mops his brow, looking slightly perplexed. His mouth gapes, empty and embarrassed. His eyes reveal his consternation.

"Forgive me, great nobles," he finally says, "but my words have flown like doves startled from the cote. Forgive an old man, weary from travel, and allow me to beg your indulgence, that I might rest and recover my scattered wits."

The Great Council, disappointed and more curious than ever, agrees to reconvene next morning to hear Petrarch's oration. The nobles race off to gossip and speculate. I accompany the doge to his apartment.

"You've got to hand it to old Louis," Serenissimo says. "He managed to screw Carrara without soiling his own linen. He is a hero at home for returning the voivode and the other hostages. Louis most certainly picked Giustinian's brain clean before sending him back to us.

"Louis is bruised but still sits on his throne. He lost men, only men, no territory, no power. Carrara, on the other hand, is a complete disaster. His brother Marsilio offered to kill him if we promised to make him ruler of Padua in return. Everyone but Novello hates old Francesco."

"Novello hates him," I say. "Like Catullus said, '*Odi et*

amo.' He loves him, and he hates him. In time, he will only hate him. If he can, he will dethrone him or murder him."

"I can always count on you for thoughts darker than mine."

"I'm sorry, sire. My heart aches."

"Here's something to ease it. Carlo Zeno is here from Constantinople and has asked to speak with me, and Marino, of course, so I don't get in trouble. Everyone else is too entangled in this Petrarch bullshit to care."

We meet in the doge's study. Carlo Zeno, one of our most illustrious admirals and generals, stands barely as tall as me, his skin tanned by the Aegean sun, his features undistinguished but for his eyes which miss nothing. Neither as tall, nor as handsome, nor as elegant as Vettor Pisani, Zeno comes from an even older and more illustrious family that has given us more doges and has grown far richer than the Pisanis, who, except for Vettor, languish in disgrace. The rapport between Serenissimo and Zeno, forty years his junior, reminds me of his rapport with Pisani, that of a proud father alert to every nuance of the younger men's brilliance and talents.

"You look hale and happy," Serenissimo says to Zeno. "Do you owe it to anything or, should I say, *anyone* in particular?"

"I lost my Greek wife, as you know, and my Venetian wife, though far away, is as loving as ever. You can't blame new love for my happiness. Blame good fortune. In Constantinople, I met, purely by chance, a bright young man in search of a clerk's position on one of my galleys. He is Venetian by birth, although he won't much talk about it. His family is common, dirt poor, and he ran away at fourteen to seek his fortune. He learned reading and writing at a monastery, and everything else he knows he taught himself. He's a lovely lad with fair skin and hair, well-spoken, a prodigy at bookkeeping, runs an abacus with the best of them, and is a bowman to beat the devil. He even taught himself celestial navigation. He has improved my affairs beyond words, saving me money, catching cheats, straightening out my books, and shooting pirates to boot. How often does that happen?"

"Does this prodigy have a name?"

"Alessandro Bentornato. No older than our ballot boy and every bit as bright and gifted."

"Did you bring him with you?"

"No, he's minding the store while I'm away."

"Indulge me," Serenissimo says. "I'm anxious to hear the situation in the east."

Carlo Zeno frowns, shifting uneasily, uncomfortable, like Pisani, bearing bad news. "The eastern empire, which is to say the city of Constantinople, verges on total collapse, and I don't have to tell you what that means. The emperor, despairing of any help from the pope or any other Latin, and almost toppled in a palace coup, sealed a mutual protection pact with Sultan Murad."

"Murad protecting the emperor from Murad? What idiocy."

"He's desperate, Exalted Serenity. He caught his son Andronikos red-handed, hatching a plot with Murad's son to overthrow their fathers and seize control. Murad blinded his son. The emperor botched even that. But Genoa is taking full advantage of their chaos, acting like Tenedos is theirs."

"Make sure Genoa doesn't claw it from our grasp."

"We do what we can, sir, but without the support of a fleet, we're crippled."

"The fleet will soon be back to support you. Give me the name of anyone who says otherwise."

Serenissimo's joy at seeing Carlo Zeno fades under the weight of the news. "I've been afraid of war with Genoa since my coronation," he says. "If Genoa allies with King Louis, Padua, and the Austrians, Venice may no longer reign as mistress of the seas. We'll all be oarsmen on their galleys."

"That will never happen," Zeno says, "not so long as I have breath in my body."

"Petrarch can be a fatuous ass, but he has—had—a brilliant and facile mind. During our last war with Genoa, he cautioned us to beware our fratricidal strife lest one of Italy's two eyes be put out and the other dimmed."

I hear them, I register their words, but my mind lingers on Zeno's remarkable Alessandro Bentornato, marksman, sailor, and clerk. Can he be our Alex? The place, the time, his age, appearance, intelligence, and skills, are all congruent. Is that too much to hope for?

The Great Council reconvenes next day at the third hour. Novello Carrara once again leads the aged poet laureate to the rostrum.

"Illustrious senators," Petrarch begins, "Most Exalted Serenity, distinguished nobles of Venice, it is a momentous honor and the fulfillment of a life-long dream to stand here addressing you. I promise to neither insult you with empty flattery, nor criticize you without warrant. I have enough to criticize in myself."

Serenissimo nudges me. "Amen to that."

"As a result," Petrarch says, "I have always eschewed the duties of critic or adviser."

"Liar," Serenissimo hisses under his breath.

"But at this splendid dawn of peace, love and fear compel me to speak—love of peace and fear of strife, which I pray you hold as dear to your hearts."

"Where were you eight months ago?" Serenissimo mutters behind a smile.

"Eating sweetmeats," I whisper, "with Francesco Carrara."

Petrarch recites long quotes from Cicero before concluding, "Jealousy between states is a disgrace. Hunger for another's wealth, land, and people only feeds on your success, making you hungrier. If you are waiting until your hunger is satisfied to stop coveting, know this, that time never comes. I have never ceased to pray for earthly affairs to proceed harmoniously, but at times, I grow anxious and afraid because of what I see around me. You, the princes, rulers of our Italy, must learn to be content with what is yours, to abjure wars, armies, and destruction. Good rulers are friendly, not frightening. It is as wrong to be feared by your subjects and your enemies as it is blessed to be loved by your people and your neighbors, as you and Lord Carrara so manifestly are."

Serenissimo grips his knees with his fingers and can't suppress the words only I can hear. "No one fears Lord Carrara more than his own people, nor loves him less."

"Beware," Petrarch says. "He who is feared by many must fear many. But love reaps love in return. The good ruler is not protected by arms but by the love of his people.

Love and beneficence are ladders not only to glory but to Our Father's house. Cherish justice and loyalty, love your subjects, honor and defend your homeland, but know that peace alone is the way to heaven, and who does not seek that road?"

Petrarch disappoints all, neither addressing his support of Lord Carrara, nor denouncing him, mouthing platitudes instead. The oration cannot end soon enough, and at its finish, Serenissimo and I repair to the Evangelist's crypt.

Serenissimo says, "I can assure that fatuous windbag that peace is the farthest thing from Carrara's mind. He hasn't given up trying to destroy us. He awaits new allies."

"Liars, cutthroats, thieves," I murmur.

"What's that?"

"Something Donato said."

Serenissimo's expression softens from scorn for Petrarch to compassion for me. "That nerve is still raw. Give it time."

"Time weighs heavy when filled by loss. I loved Donato as I will never love again. I don't know how to face the rest of my life."

"I'm going to tell you something," Serenissimo says. "And I don't want you to take it wrong, but like it or not, it must be said. No one will ever take Donato's place in your heart. Nor should they. But sooner or later, someone else will carve his own niche. A new and different love will thrive, maybe greater or sweeter or easier, maybe not, but you can bet your last ducat that it will be unique and fulfilling."

"I can never forget Donato."

"You mustn't forget Donato. He will always be the standard against which you measure, but you never know when someone will exceed that measure and set a new standard. Don't forget I, too, was once young, loved madly, sometimes unwisely, and made mistakes painful to myself and others. You're still so young, with so much before you, things that now you can't possibly imagine..."

"I hear you; I can parse your words. My mind comprehends that what you are saying is true and correct, but right now, it doesn't feel like it."

I try not to weep, yet fail.

Serenissimo lays his hands on mine and speaks in a voice filled with tenderest concern and deep understanding. "All I'm saying is, keep the door to your heart open. Never shut it. Never lock it. With a closed heart, nothing is possible. With an open heart, anything is possible."

Acknowledgements

To my editor, Elizabetta McKay, I love you. A heartfelt thank you to Raevyn, my publisher, for taking these books from my head into the real world. My deepest gratitude to my soulmates—Steven, Phyllis, Luke, Laura—for their unfailing love and support during the long gestation of these books. Thank you, Amy Worthen, for your openness and expertise making these books better. Boundless gratitude, Vincent Virga, your enthusiasm inspired me. Thank you, John Pull, for your passionate advocacy. Michael Warr and Ashley Bullitt, a long road traveled; thank you for still being present. And Arf arf to Zelda, Mona, and Buddy for keeping me sane.

About Larry Mellman

Larry was born in Los Angeles and educated in literature, political science, and life at the University of California, Berkeley. He has worked as a printer and journalist in Los Angeles, San Francisco, Chicago, and St. Paul, Minnesota. Larry also worked with Andy Warhol and the Velvet Underground on the *Exploding Plastic Inevitable* in NY, Provincetown, Los Angeles, and San Francisco, was mentored by Dean Koontz, and shared a palazzo in Venice with international opera singers Erika Sunnegårdh and Mark Doss."

Following a stint as a newspaper executive, Larry lived in Venice for many years, where he taught English, led tours, and immersed himself in the history and art of the Venetian Republic. *The Ballot Boy* was born in Venice and completed in St. Paul.

Larry is a lifelong social activist and writer, a voracious reader and researcher, an opera fanatic, and devoted walker. He currently lives in St. Paul with his partner of twenty-one years and his ex-wife of twenty-five years. His son is a pianist devoted to blues and jazz.

Email
larry_mellman@hotmail.com

Facebook
www.facebook.com/Larry.Mellman

Twitter
@LarryMellman

Websites
www.larrymellman.com
www.theballotboy.com

Other NineStar books by this author

The Ballot Boy Series

The Ballot Boy

Coming soon from Larry Mellman

Queen of the Sea

The Ballot Boy, Book Three

I KNOW WHEN I'm being followed because I have been followed all my life—by my father, Marcantonio Gradenigo, a demon from hell, and by my stepbrother, Ruggiero Gradenigo, stamped from the same mold. The second time I killed Ruggiero, I cut his head off to make sure he was dead and would never show up again. Ergo, the black shadow dogging every turn I take belongs to my father. No one else has reason to follow me, an inconsequential cog in a vast machine. My father alone could cast the shadow lengthened by the low angle of the sun. He calls himself Brother Bernardo now. I am as certain it is him as I am that this is the year of our lord 1376, my name is Niccolò Saltano, and I am ballot boy to the sixtieth doge of Venice, Andrea Contarini.

Risking death, with a huge price on his head, Brother Bernardo slips into and out of Venice, trying to recruit me to his insurrection and other nefarious business. He hides under the cowl of a hermit brother of St. Augustine; only his abbot holds jurisdiction over him. Brother Bernardo refuses to accept that I will never join his cause. We captured him twice before, and he escaped both times. Serenissimo, my doge, wants my father's head on a pike. The murder of his former abbot complicates matters. With few questions asked, Francesco Carrara, lord of

Padua, our intractable enemy, handed Brother Bernardo the job, making him his own abbot, untouchable by all but the pope, and the pope is no friend of ours.

Brother Bernardo knows Venice better than I do, but he doesn't remember detail the way I can. I never forget anything I've seen, anywhere I've ever been, everything I've read or heard. It's an onerous advantage, but at times like these, an advantage nonetheless. Rather than trying to outfox Bernardo in the brackish mud of our backwater parish, I head straight for the square to denounce him to the peacekeepers and angry parishioners. Discerning my intent, he hangs back, watching to see what I'll do next.

He's sixty years old, and I'm twenty-three. I tell myself he can't give much of a chase, and I'm ferociously fit, so I take off. I've outrun him before, but this time, I want to trap him and kill him, ending our nightmare once and for all. I run toward the bridge linking St. Nick's to Angelo Raffaele, taking the stairs three at a time and vaulting off the far side, but he's right with me, as if he knows where I am going. And I, who should know better, underestimated his stamina.

Memory maps unfurl behind my eyes—Venice, our infernally twisted archipelago of islets stitched up with bridges. Every street ends at the lagoon, offering no easy out. I need the right place and enough time to hide myself and lay ambush, so I plunge into back alleys toward St. Nick's. As a kid, routinely chased and bullied by neighborhood thugs, this was my escape route. I can navigate it with eyes closed. Brother Bernardo can't. I whip around one corner and another in a frantic zigzag between close walls at sharp angles until I emerge behind the church and duck into the bell tower before he sees where I've gone.

The only light in the tower falls from the mullioned windows eighty feet above in the belfry, where three bells ring to awaken the parish and put it to sleep. A wooden stairway clings to the brick walls of the central shaft, twenty feet on each side, four hundred feet square. A lancet window slender as a sapling lights the second landing. I climb to the belfry and look out the window.

At the edge of the canal beyond the tower, Brother Bernardo sniffs the air for me like a ravenous boar. He swivels toward the base of the tower, and his eyes follow the masonry to the belfry, to the window where I watch him. As he approaches the tower door, I lose sight of him, but I can hear him. He steps inside, bars the door behind him, and pauses while his eyes adjust to the dense darkness slashed with sharp shafts of bright sun. He tilts his head upward, following the line of the stairs to the belfry where he sees me step out of the shadow. A twisted smile disfigures his face. He lusts after me the way a starving hunter lusts after a twelve-point stag. If he ever accepts my refusal, he will have no choice but to kill me. Tempting fate again, he's back for one last try.

"What is it this time, old man?"

"That's no way to greet your loving father."

"You weren't so loving when you tried to kill me as a babe in arms."

"A fantasy your mother dreamed up to make you hate me. No, my son, the worst I did to you was bet on the wrong son, and I've already apologized profusely for that. I was wrong. And I'm tired of apologizing."

He climbs toward me as I descend, eight flights of stairs separating us.

"You'll never have to apologize again," I say, "and we will never again share this earth. There's not room enough for both of us."

"Isn't that what Pompey told Caesar?"

"It's what I'm telling you."

"Music to my ears because I am sick of your stubbornness and stupidity. That's why I came. Cast aside your blind allegiance to that played-out old fakir, whose ass you wipe, and step up to fate as a man, a hero, a conqueror, under my aegis. Or die like a dog, here, now. Join me and take everything you want. Say no and join your beloved Donato in hell."

He pauses on the second landing as I reach the seventh. "My heart breaks," he says, "that you would give up such a brilliant future. Donato would be appalled. He valued valor and ambition above all, and if not for the color of his skin, he would have made a far better prince than you. He had no more loyalty to the doge or the republic than I do, but he stupidly thought they would prevail and chose them in the same ignorant way I chose Ruggiero over you, both sorry mistakes. Did you know Donato was your brother when he fucked you?"

"I found out after he died."

"And you never suspected?"

"He came with the doge's imprimatur. I suspected nothing."

"As the ancients said, when the cock gets hard, the mind gets soft."

"Donato was a great man, and I loved him."

"What did you love about him besides his magnificent body?"

"Everything."

"Then you must love me, because I am as much him as I am you."

He reaches the third landing as I reach the fifth. His sword drawn, pointed at me, he lunges up as I leap down, meeting on the fourth landing. I dance cagily as he slashes the air between us to intimidate me, talking all the while. "I'm not being vindictive, but unless you join me, you are too dangerous a piece to leave on the board. Stop being a fool. Cast your lot with me and reach heights of greatness your pitiful doge can't even imagine."

"You destroyed my mother. You tried to destroy me. You destroyed my friends and countrymen, and you want to kill my doge, who is a million times better than you." I slash upward, smashing his sword from underneath, and he staggers back against the wall, having underestimated me.

"Better doesn't matter," he says, recovering his balance. "Winning matters. Louis of Hungary, Carrara of Padua, Leopold of Austria, and the idiot emperor of the east will kneel at your feet when we're done. How can you refuse the one great man in this world who loves you for exactly what you are?"

Our swords tangle, not lethally at first, as we take each other's measure in this cramped space. He smashes my clumsy lunge aside, grabs me by the throat, and pulls me toward him until our foreheads touch.

"Why must you refuse me?"

"When you fail, you and yours will be drawn and

quartered, hung between the Columns of Doom for beggars to spit on. Bajamonte Tiepolo, a greater man than you, failed to his eternal shame, and they drove him out, razed his palace, and sowed the earth with salt. Marino Faliero, a doge, failed, and the Ten chopped off his head. No coup has ever succeeded in overturning our republic. What makes yours different?"

"*You.* The hero of Trieste, of Curano, and Borgoforte. The little people adore you, the warrior ballot boy, and you betray them with your blind obedience to the wreck of a mediocre merchant who rose far above his station. When your doge was forced to accept the crown, he bemoaned he was not man enough for the job. He spoke truth for once. Ruggiero should have taken the throne of Venice after our coup, but he proved inadequate to the task and deserved the death you dealt him. Donato, by virtue of his color alone, could never have succeeded. But you will be invincible, beautiful, brave, a true hero seated on the throne with me standing behind you."

"Byzantine style, your dagger in my back."

"You will learn to trust me."

"I'd rather kill you."

He pins my sword to the floor and claws off his hermit robe, revealing mail underneath. Something else I didn't expect. But it doesn't matter. Fate directs the clash of our swords. He's stronger than I remembered. Not a precision instrument, like Donato, but a practitioner of relentless brute force, making him fearsome but unsustainable, little consolation as he lunges and thrusts, shivering my sword like lightning. He advances no matter what I do. His sword presses against my heart.

"Last chance." His eyes lock on mine, begging, and for that instant, he is entirely in my power. I kick him where no man can withstand, and as he crumples, I leap into the void and grab the ropes that toll the bells, twelve hundred pounds of bronze. The rope rips my hands and burns my arms, but I hold fast, plummeting downward, the headstock swinging in the belfry, the clappers slamming the bells like bombards. I fall until my toes almost touch the floor. For an instant, I tender jumping down and bolting, but then just as suddenly, the headstock in the belfry tips over into its heavy backswing, pulling me up, while the clanging bells summon the parish to the tower, snaring Brother Bernardo in fortune's net. As the weight of the bells pulls me up, past him, Brother Bernardo hurls his sword like a spear. I swing wide, rising higher until my weight triggers the headstock, and I plunge downward, down and up, the brazen clangor of the bells battering our skulls like Vulcan's hammer.

There's a muffled banging on the door. As I'm pulled up toward the belfry, too high to jump down, Brother Bernardo unbars the tower door and bolts past the priest and the gaping onlookers. With the bells ringing out his infamy, he vanishes.

Connect with NineStar Press

www.ninestarpress.com

www.facebook.com/ninestarpress

www.facebook.com/groups/NineStarNiche

www.twitter.com/ninestarpress

www.instagram.com/ninestarpress

Made in United States
Orlando, FL
24 July 2023

35421333R00241